DEAD OF WYNTER

FROST INDUSTRIES - BOOK TWO

MONTANA FYRE

DEAD OF WYNTER

A DARK MAFIA ROMANCE

FROST INDUSTRIES
BOOK TWO

MONTANA FYRE

ISBN (Paperback) : 978-0-6454851-4-1

First edition, 2022.

Front cover and book design by Montana Fyre.

Edited by My Brother's Editor.

www.montanafyre.com

Acknowledgments

Frost Industries came to me years ago. It was four stories that seemed to work together, and a few names that I loved, but would never be able to pepper into any other series. And Wynter was the first name that came.

Over the last few years, I've plotted here and there. I've made notes in a thousand different note books (most of which I've lost), I've written quotes that found their way into the book, and I've fallen in love with the characters you'll meet in this book.

I've loved every second of writing this series so far, and I truly feel like I've found my author groove writing dark romance.

As always, I would first and foremost like to thank my wonderful husband. He supports me with every decision I make, he talks me down when I'm ready to throw in the towel, and he loves me even when I don't love myself.

My friends and family who support me endlessly and have

been my cheerleaders since the beginning of this journey.

Ellie, my wonderful editor, who picks up all my Australianisms and fixes the same mistakes in every book I write (will I ever learn? Clearly not).

And to all the readers who have been on this journey with me. It's an incredible adventure and I couldn't do it without you. Thank you for taking a chance on me. Thank you for reading the words I write. And thank you for taking the time to review my books. It honestly means the world to me.

So without further ado, I hope you enjoy Wynter and Everett's story as much as I loved writing it.

Trigger Warning

This book contains dark themes, violence, elements of BDSM, sexual assault and other subjects that some readers may find distressing.

To all the dark romance readers who love an over the top jealous possessive anti hero on paper, but would throat punch a guy who pulled the same shit in real life.

I'm right there with you.

Be with me always - take any form - drive me mad!
Only do not leave me in this abyss, where I cannot
find you! Oh, God! It is unutterable! I can not live
without my life! I can not live without my soul!

- EMILY BRONTË, WUTHERING HEIGHTS

PROLOGUE
EVERETT

F or me, love is not patient, nor is it kind.

From the moment I fell in love when I was fifteen, it had been hard and painful. Full of loss and frustration. Because I'll never be good enough for the woman I love. That's the hard reality I've lived with every single day for the last twelve years.

There was a time when I allowed myself to have her. Just a taste. Stolen moments I'll always remember. But even then, I knew someone like me could never be with someone like her.

And so I watch from the shadows, looking over her life, protecting her from a distance, and seeing her live without me. Seeing her happy is bittersweet because I remember a time when I was the one that put the smile on her face, when I was her whole world, when she looked at me like I hung the moon just for her. She looked at me like I was the creator of worlds, and there's only one thing that has stopped me from seeing it again.

Her life. Her safety.

The reason I left all those years ago to live a life in the shadows was to keep her safe. A man like me has enemies, more than I can count, and it was safer for me to let her go than to stay and put her in danger. Every moment we spent together was a risk I shouldn't have taken, but I will never regret my selfishness. Those memories are the ones that keep me from the darkness that beckons me.

I come from a long line of bad people. People who have no right to walk the earth with people like Wynter. Their legacy taints me, making me wrong for her in so many ways, but the only time my world has ever felt whole was in the moments when she was in my arms.

I stare at my computer, trying to find it in me to finish the design for the prototype missile Storm wants to start production on next year. I used to love doing shit like this. I've loved tinkering with things since I was a kid, even if I rarely had the opportunity. But things have changed. I've changed. The moment I graduated college, Ron Saint James hired me as head of product design. A fancy title that basically just means I design and build weapons, security systems, and anything else that's asked of me.

I think about putting the cameras I have scattered around Wynter's apartment on. When I put them there, I told myself it was for her safety, but if that were the case, I wouldn't watch them as often as I do. I would have one of our security guys watch them to make sure she's safe.

But she's mine. Even if I can't have her physically, she will always belong to me.

Instead, I scroll through the file on Angelo Russo for what feels like the millionth time. There's nothing new. No new investments. No new property. No new transactions. He's gotten smarter over the years, but to me, he'll always be a fucking moron. To trade in skin in a city owned by the Saint James family only proves how dumb he is, and if that doesn't, threatening one of their women does.

Letting him walk away after taking Emerson is one of the hardest things Storm has ever ordered me to do.

My phone buzzes on the mahogany desk, and I reach for it without checking the caller ID. "Hello?"

"There's been an accident." Storm's voice is cold and distant. The distinct sound of ice against a glass tips me off to his drinking.

"Is everyone okay?" I sit up straight in my chair, quickly pulling up the feed for Wynter's apartment, the need to check she's okay overwhelming me. My heart beats in my chest painfully when I see the lights are out. She's not home. She should be home from Rayne and Emerson's wedding by now.

"No," Storm croaks.

"Storm, what the fuck happened?" I snap. The idea Wynter could be injured, that someone could have hurt her, makes me both violent and sick to my stomach. I can't handle the thought.

"One of Russo's men ran my parents off the road," he tells me. "They're dead."

The words hang between us long after he says them, but I don't have a response. The Saint James family were my

3

second home, the safe place where no one hurt me, no one made me do unthinkable things against my will. They were warm and loving, and even if they had their own darkness, they were more welcoming than anyone had ever been in my life.

"I'm so sorry," I whisper. The words seem like so little considering the circumstances, but I have to say something.

"They were your parents too, brother," Storm says quietly. "Everyone is on their way to the estate. Wynter and I just got here."

"I'm on my way." Standing from the desk, I barely stop to pick up my wallet and keys before I'm out the front door.

I expect for Storm to argue, for him to tell me it's best I not see her, but he doesn't. "Good. She's going to need you."

We're going to need each other.

DEAD OF WYNTER

ONE
WYNTER

I've never felt pain like this. Never felt grief so excruciating I can barely breathe through the agony. But then, I've never lost my parents before either. From the moment the police arrived at my front door until now, all I've felt is a pain so deep I can barely breathe. It steals the air from my lungs, the tears from my eyes, and the hope from my heart.

A life without them seems so bleak, like a life I don't want to live at all.

But there's something that cuts even deeper than my pain, and that's the pain of my siblings. Snow hasn't stopped crying. Her hysterical sobs almost break me. Storm is stoic as always, the true head of the family he's been since Dad retired a few years ago. But underneath the mask he wears when he faces the world is a man facing the reality of life without the people who raised him. Rayne and Emerson are curled up on the lounge together. His head resting in her lap as she strokes his dark, messy hair carefully. It's their wedding day. The happiest day of their lives. But it's tainted now. Tainted with death, and pain, and darkness, like so many other parts of their life.

I find myself hoping to wake up from this nightmare, from the dream that just won't end. But eventually I'll have to face the harsh reality that this is our life now. Our family losing its monarchs too soon.

I squeeze my eyes shut to ward off the tears that threaten. We were meant to have more time. They were meant to see the rest of us get married. They should have held our children and spoiled them rotten. They should have died when they were old and gray, not the young and vibrant couple that had taken over the dance floor just a few hours ago.

But there's no more time. No more weddings. No grandparents for our children. Nothing. Our family will never be whole again.

A knock at the door startles me as I look at my siblings, expecting one of them to head for the door to let someone they invited in. But when none of them make a move and Storm looks at me meaningfully, my legs move of their own accord. The family estate is expansive, much bigger than the six of us ever needed, but it holds a homely feel I'll never be able to give up. It's why we fled here after I gave my siblings the news, because this is where our family became whole. It's where we lived when my father rose to power, when he took his life back from people who wanted to destroy him.

I walk down the long hallway, the movement so like the one that led me to being told my parents were dead just a few hours ago, and yet, somehow, this seems more ominous. Something about the way Storm looked at me as I left the room makes me unsteady on my feet, or maybe it's just the exhaustion of the day and the rollercoaster of emotions we've all been through.

Either way, by the time I reach the heavy wooden door, my hands are shaking.

The porch light illuminates a figure on the other side of the stained glass, and given the hour, normally I would have at least picked up mace on my way. But alas, if anyone is brave enough to attack the estate, they probably deserve whatever reward comes with me answering the door.

All the air leaves my lungs when I swing the door open. My mouth drops open, and fresh tears for a different loss fill my eyes as I stare at my past. His body is covered by a suit so similar to the ones my brothers wore, the muscles underneath the expensive fabric barely contained, the dirty brown locks of hair I've run my fingers through more times than I care to think about is wild and untamed, but it's his eyes that capture mine and holds me prisoner. A blue so deep the depths of the ocean couldn't compete. The fleck of gold you would miss if you weren't staring in the right light glints at me, and my hold on the door tightens as my body threatens to crumple.

Everett Masters is the last person I ever expected to see again. The man who broke me, who disappeared, never to be heard from again, the man my brothers don't think I know works for Frost Industries.

"Wynter," he whispers, my name sounding like a prayer on his lips.

As if out of instinct, my hand holding the door swings forward, and a moment later, the heavy wood slams in his face. The sound echoes throughout the house, the space too large to handle such a large bang.

I stumble down the hallway, holding on to the wall for support as my insides war against themselves. The hatred I have for the man standing at the door is almost overwhelmed by the love still lurking under the surface. I've loved him since before I even knew what love was, and before I knew how much it could hurt.

"It's for you." I glare pointedly at Storm, and the ghost of a smirk tugs at his lips, as if he saw my reaction coming from a mile away and relished in how uncomfortable it would be for me to be in the room with the only man I have ever allowed close enough to break my heart. The only man I have ever accepted into my body. Not that my brother needs to know I lost my virginity to his best friend.

I throw myself into the seat between Rayne and Emerson, and Snow, who immediately curls into me, her tears soaking through the fabric of my sweater. None of us were ready to lose our parents, but she's still so young. The baby of the family. She should have had more time. We all should have.

Storm leaves the room, his grey eyes meeting mine once more over his shoulder as he takes the final sip of the scotch he's been nursing since we got here and places the glass on the small bar by the lounge's entry.

"Who was at the door?" Snow asks between gentle sobs.

I worry my bottom lip between my teeth as I consider my answer. She knows about Everett. She held me as I cried after he left. She saw the broken, jagged pieces he left behind and helped me glue the unmatching pieces back together even though they didn't fit. "Everett," I say quietly, meeting Rayne's stormy eyes as his name slips between my lips.

"About time," he murmurs, looking up at Emerson with a

gentle smile. I've never seen my brother look at anyone, or anything for that matter, as he looks at her. The love between them is obvious, so clear behind eyes so dark they're almost black. It makes my heart ache for that kind of connection. The kind of connection I thought I shared with Everett.

"What's that supposed to mean?" I hiss.

He smirks. "You'll see."

But as I watch Everett walk into the room beside my brother as they had so many times during our childhood, I can't help but see the boy I fell in love with in the dangerous man he's become. His eyes meet mine again and I barely draw in a breath, his gaze suffocating in its intensity.

Everett is everything I ever wanted, until he broke my heart. Now he's everything I can never allow myself to long for again. Because my heart can't handle a break like that again, the jagged pieces from the last time are barely mended.

TWO

EVERETT

Breathing the same air as Wynter settles something that's been wild since the day I crept out of her bedroom all those years ago, never to see her again. Or so I thought at the time. I guess back then I underestimated my need to be near her, to watch every move she makes. I gave myself too much credit in those early days when I thought I could walk away and just be okay without my heart, but I quickly realized I couldn't live without her.

Slowly, I became more and more obsessed with her. Watching her, following her, protecting her from a distance. It was the way things had to be at the time, the way things should still be. But staying away from her has been like breathing underwater. Impossible. Eventually I had to come up for air.

Our eyes meet across the room where she's curled up with Snow. Her blonde hair is piled on top of her head, the curls from the wedding thrown haphazardly out of her face as she comforts her baby sister.

I can't imagine the loss they're feeling, the emptiness they must have in their hearts, because I feel it too, and they weren't my parents. Not biologically, at least. But they were in the ways that mattered. They came to my sports games even if Rayne or Storm weren't playing. They helped me with my homework when I got stuck. They wrote letters of recommendation to all the best colleges. They did all the things my family would have done if they weren't the scum of the earth.

There was a time toward the end of school when I lived here that I didn't have to face my nightmare home life, or the danger my family forced upon me every day just by breathing.

"Why is he here?" Snow's glare is almost as deadly as her sister's, the fire behind the youngest, most naive Saint James's eyes almost burning my skin with its intensity.

"Because he's as much a part of this family as the rest of us." Storm shrugs as he pours another whiskey and hands it to me.

I don't drink often. I hate being out of control, and more than that, I can't protect Wynter if I'm drunk. My sole purpose on this earth is keeping her safe, and I won't risk that for a few hours of drunken fun. But considering I had to watch a man I considered a brother get married today from afar, and the people who were more my parents than the ones responsible for my birth were dead, I think I deserve a drink just as much as anyone else in the room.

"He stopped being a part of this family when he broke Wynter," she snaps, pushing up from her seat and walking toward me in quick, clumsy steps.

Everyone underestimates the youngest Saint James, but I know better than that. She has a fire that I don't think anyone

14

will ever be able to tame. And more for them if they try.

"How dare you walk into this house after everything you did to Wynter. You have no idea what you did to her when you left."

Her words are harsh, but she's wrong. I know exactly what I did to her when I left. Wynter and I are two parts of the same whole, and when I left, I tore us both in half. I've been walking around for the last eight years without half of my heart, half of my soul, half of my very being, just the same as she has.

"Snow," Storm warns. "You don't have all the facts."

She turns to her brother, staring at him incredulously as I glance at Wynter, staring at me with confusion. After all these years, she doesn't know why I left her asleep in her bed one morning and never came back, but she'll know soon enough. Once she's past her grief, past the pain of losing her parents, she'll know exactly why I couldn't stay.

"He broke your sister's heart!" Snow yells. "What other facts matter?"

"We're not doing this right now, Snow. Everett has every right to be here. Mom and Dad always saw him as a son, even after what happened between him and Wynter. Just know that he didn't leave because he wanted to or because he didn't love Wynter. Let's just leave it at that for tonight. It's been an emotional day, and it's late. Let's go to bed, and we can start looking at funeral arrangements in the morning."

As if my presence had made them forget what the next few days would look like for the family, Snow and Wynter both

15

choke back a sob, and it takes everything in me not to reach for her, not to hold her through her pain. But I suspect if I reach for her, I might lose an arm.

My little dove is a spitfire. She doesn't admit her pain easily, not since I broke her. She's a queen in every way and accepting comfort from me is against her nature.

If nothing else, when I left, I made her stronger. A phoenix rising from the ashes of her broken heart.

Rayne helps Emerson from where she's perched on the edge of the lounge, her movements still stiff from her healing injuries from when the Russos took her. She looks at me nervously before stepping forward and wrapping her arms around my body carefully. "I'm sorry for your loss. And thank you for all you did to save me. I didn't get a chance to say it at the time," she whispers, but I know the others can hear.

When shock crosses the girls' faces, I realize they likely didn't know I had any part in Emerson's rescue, and a little bit of the ice they both feel toward me melts.

"You're welcome. I never want them to know what it feels like to live without their heart as I have." I don't bother to whisper. What's the point? Wynter will soon know everything that we've hidden from her over the years for her own safety. She'll soon know that leaving her went against everything in my blood.

Rayne gives me a weak smile over her shoulder before tugging his new wife against him and disappearing up the stairs.

"Take your old room," Storm says as I finally tear my attention from Wynter.

I want to talk to her, to pour all the broken pieces of my heart out and tell her exactly why I had to break us all those years ago. But there's a lifetime ahead of us for that conversation, because I'll never let her go again.

I stayed away. I did what was right. But I can't do it anymore. Wynter is the other part of me, and I want to feel whole again, even if it means I have to spend the rest of my life protecting her.

I nod and head up the stairs, somehow dragging my gaze away from hers as I slip into the room I slept in more often than my own in my last years of high school. My eyes dart around the space that feels like I used a lifetime ago. Realistically, eight years isn't that long, but I'm a completely different person than I was then.

I close the door behind me and wait for the click of doors and the house to go dark before finally laying my head on the pillow. Storm and Rayne aren't ready to start thinking about this yet, but Russo started a war tonight. He hit the family where it hurt, and while we can take tonight to lick our wounds and mourn the only parents we had, tomorrow is a new day and as the sun rises, vengeance will come right along with the light it provides.

THREE

WYNTER

Awareness comes to me slowly. The edge of consciousness beckoning me from my dreamless state and back into my sordid reality.

Somewhere in the back of my mind, I hoped it was all a dream, that I would wake up this morning and my mom would be in the kitchen with a cup of coffee in hand as she read the paper to Dad, which had been their morning ritual our whole lives. Long before we got out of bed in the morning, they coveted that time for themselves, and when we all moved out and started our own lives, they never stopped.

I reach to my bedside table, fumbling around for my phone until my fingers brush along the cool metal. The time flashes onto the screen and I groan. It isn't morning. Not really at least. It's five o'clock, and now the harsh reality of my day has settled on my chest. There's no way I'm going to be able to go back to sleep.

I swing my legs out of bed and wrap myself in a robe I keep

here. It's not uncommon for me to spend the night here, not wanting to drive home in the dark after visiting my parents, so at least I have something to wear. Packing a bag was the last thing on my mind as I barreled out of my apartment after receiving the news that my parents were gone. All I could think about was telling my siblings. That was the hardest part, being the one to break their hearts, the one to tell them that our parents were dead.

I pad across the wooden floorboards, the old estate we moved into when I was too young to remember still has most of its original features. Fireplaces, crown moldings, a spiral staircase that leads to the attic. I spent some of my happiest memories in these halls, and now I'll have to plan to lay the two people I loved more than anything to rest.

The stairs are cold under my bare feet as I make my way down to the kitchen. If I can't sleep, I may as well make some breakfast for everyone for when they wake up.

A figure sitting at the dining table elicits a squeal from my chest as I slap my hand over my mouth. The last thing I expected at this time of the morning was for anyone to be awake, but as I stare into the darkness, the only light coming in is the cloud-covered moon, I know it's Everett. I would know his presence anywhere.

Even through the wall our bedrooms share, I could feel him as I fell asleep last night. It was oddly comforting, considering he tore my heart out and stomped on it. But having him around feels right, even if I'm too stubborn to admit that out loud. Storm was right, Everett has always been a part of this family, and there's no reason he shouldn't be a part of it as we mourn the people who raised us.

"Sorry," I mumble, stumbling toward the fridge. I'm not particularly hungry, or thirsty, for that matter, but I'll do just about anything to avoid any contact with him. I know the risk of letting myself get close to Everett, and I'm not willing to put myself through that again. I stare into the fridge, my eyes running over the contents three times before I tug the orange juice out and turn toward the counter, only to collide with a wall of bare muscle.

His scent immediately overwhelms me, the same as it had been all those years ago. His proximity knocks me off kilter. The electricity buzzes between us the moment our bodies collide, making it hard to breathe, even if it's one sided. Everett doesn't care about me or my heart. He made that clear when he left, never to be heard from again.

"Are you okay?" he asks on a whisper, his hands grasping my forearms to stop me from losing my balance.

I nod, trying to brush his hands from my body. I can't think when he touches me, and the last thing I need when he's near is to not be able to use my brain. "Yeah, fine."

His grip on me doesn't let up though, in fact, if I'm not mistaken, it only tightens. But surely that's my imagination, wishful thinking that Everett could still feel something, anything, toward me.

I meet his eyes in a moment of weakness and my stomach drops at the look in the deep blue pools. Full of fire and regret, pain and longing. The things I've felt every time he's crossed my mind over the last eight years.

Slowly, as if not to spook me, one of his hands moves from where it's holding me up to cup my cheek, the movement too intimate, and yet it feels like coming home. "I never thought I'd get to touch you again," Everett whispers as his thumb brushes along my bottom lip. "I should have known I could never stay away from you, no matter how much I should."

My mouth drops open. So many questions, and yet I can't voice any of them. All I can do is lean into his touch, relish in the warmth in places that have been ice cold since he left. The void he left in my life suddenly feels full, even if it is temporary.

A small smile tugs at his lips. "I always was the only one that could render you speechless, dove."

"Don't call me that," I snap, tearing myself out of his hold. The sound of my nickname on his lips pulls me back to reality, reminding me of why I can never let him touch me.

"Wynter." He reaches for me, pain etched into his brow, but for once, I'm faster than him.

"No, Everett. Listen to me, I understand why you're here. They were your family as well, and honestly, Storm and Rayne need you here, but we are done. You made your feelings for me very fucking clear the morning after you took my virginity and left without a fucking trace," I hiss, the venom in my words sounds like someone else is speaking, and yet it's my mouth that moves.

"You have to know it wasn't like that, Wynter. You have to realize I didn't leave because I wanted to, that I didn't stay away from you for eight years just because I wasn't feeling it or because I wanted to steal your virtue and then run for the hills."

He stalks toward me, and I can't help but back away until my back hits the wall. A moment later, his arms cage me in, his heavy body only a breath from mine.

"I'm not going to push you today, or tomorrow, and maybe not even next week. But I promise that we will be talking about this, and you will hear me out. I've spent the last eight years forcing myself to stay away, and I don't have the strength to do that anymore."

"Even if I want you to leave me alone?" I ask.

"Even then, dove. Even then."

Our eyes lock in a battle of the wills, neither of us willing to pull away first. My body screams at me to move, to get as far away from the man that broke me as I can, and yet I just keep looking into the deepest blue I've ever known. Questions hover at the edge of my mind, but I can't grasp on to any of them for long enough to speak the words, until the one that make the most sense to ask, the one I should have asked the moment I opened the door last night.

"Why did you leave me?" The words are barely audible, barely loud enough for my own ears, but he hears them.

FOUR
EVERETT

"Why did you leave me?"

Her words hang between us, so gentle I'm reminded of the girl I first fell in love with all those years ago. She's not that girl anymore. The years have hardened her, and I was a part of that.

But I don't have an answer for her. Not one that doesn't have a long, sordid story to go along with it, and not without shifting her focus away from her grief. I close my eyes briefly, tamping down the need to claim her again, to take her up to my room and fuck her so hard and so deep she forgets I ever left her, that we ever spent any time away from one another.

"Dove," I say softly. "I will tell you everything, but not right now, not after what's just happened. All you need to know right now is that I'm not going anywhere. We will never be apart again."

It's almost impossible to keep myself from pressing into her, from feeling her tight body pressed against me for the first time in almost a decade, but I hold myself back. As much as I would love to push her, I can't. It's not fair to her for me to use her vulnerability against her, even if the darkest parts of my soul scream at me to do just that.

Wynter closes her eyes, breaking our connection, and I almost reach out to open them again. She doesn't get to hide from me, that's not how this is going to work, and she'll learn that soon enough. She'll learn that I am, and have always been, her entire world, and now I'm back to collect on it.

"Fuck you." Her hands push into my chest, the first time she's willingly touched me and I'm so taken off guard by the contact I stumble back slightly, just enough for her to break free. "I'm not that girl anymore, Everett. I'm not the girl you left behind without a second thought, and I won't ever be that girl again. Don't make promises you can't keep. We both know you're going to get bored and leave again, and I wouldn't expect anything else from you."

Before I can reach for her, she's gone, retreating back to the safety of her bedroom, as far away from me as she can get. She's right. She's not the girl I fell in love with, but she doesn't realize I've been watching her grow, watching as she has turned into the queen she was always born to be. I've watched her train with Storm and Rayne so she can protect herself and watched her take over a boardroom. She's wrangled investors better than anyone I've ever met, and last year when some guy tried to mug her, she broke his arm in three places before flicking her hair over her shoulder and walking away with her head held high.

Wynter Saint James isn't the girl she was when I fell in love with her, but she is the woman that was always destined to stand by my side.

"She's not coming around then?" Storm chuckles from the doorway.

"You could say that," I say, my jaw tight set.

"She's not as pliable as she was as a teenager." He shrugs as he crosses to the coffee pot and pours himself one. "Admittedly, that's probably partially my fault. When Dad retired, I had to train my successor, and we both know Rayne doesn't have the temperament."

I laugh, my head dropping back at the thought of one of my oldest friends in a position where he would have to wrangle a team of executives one minute and organize a coup the next. "I know. I've watched." I've never made a secret of my stalking tendencies when it comes to Wynter. It was the only way I could stay away from her. Being able to watch was the only thing that kept me sane without my heart.

Storm shakes his head as he takes a seat at the table, and I move across the room to do the same. The place where Wynter's hands shoved me still tingles, electricity coursing through my entire body. "She'll understand once you lay it out on the table, but she's not ready yet."

"I know. I can wait. I've waited this long."

FIFTEEN YEARS AGO

The girl runs through the hallway, right past the lounge area I'm sitting in with Storm. I've never been to his house before, not since they moved to this big house at least. The girl is beautiful. Her long blonde hair falls against her back in soft waves, her tutu from ballet only serving to make her look like an angel. She's gone so quickly that I almost think she was a figment of my imagination.

We used to hang out at the apartment they lived in all the time. A safe place for me to get away from my parents. Their family is warm, and every time I see Mrs. Saint James, she pulls me into the biggest hug. We don't hug in my family. It's seen as having a weakness, and the Masters family doesn't show weakness, not even to their children.

But every time I've been to their house, I've never met their sisters. They're always off at a dance class or something, and I'm never allowed to stay out that long. The only reason I was allowed to come over at all today was because my parents have gone away, left me to fend for myself for the next few nights, and Mrs. Saint James wouldn't hear of it.

"Who's that?" I whisper to Storm.

"That's my sister, Wynter," he tells me, his pen scrawling across the page as he makes a note from his textbook.

I can't tear my eyes away from the doorway she ran past, the moment replaying in my mind over and over again until she materializes there again. Her shy smile and ice-blue eyes capture me immediately, making it hard to breathe.

How can someone so perfect exist in a world full of darkness?

"Dinner will be ready shortly, kids," Mrs. Saint James yells from the kitchen, her head poking around the corner. "Oh good, Wynter, this is your brother's friend, Everett."

Her eyes widen for a moment, looking impossibly large on

her petite face. "It's nice to meet you," she whispers, taking a tentative step toward me. She's changed out of her tutu now, but the dress she wears still makes her look like a princess. And I guess she is one.

Everyone knows the Saint James family is rising royalty. At least that's what my uncle says. He always talks about them when he's angry, but I never understand why he's so angry. They've never been anything but nice to me, and they may not realize it, but they gave me the greatest gift anyone has ever given me when they killed my father.

Our eyes lock and the air leaves my lungs in a sudden whoosh. I've never had anyone love me before, never had anyone but this family care about my wellbeing, so I don't know a whole lot about love. Only what I've learned in school and seen in the movies.

It seems insane as the thought goes through my mind, but something deep inside me settles as our hands connect in an innocent handshake, the contact only making it more clear to me what I knew the moment she ran past the room, even if I didn't know what the feeling was right away.

From the moment our eyes locked, I knew Wynter Saint James was the love of my life.

FIVE

WYNTER

T he man drones on for what seems like an eternity. His gray hair is receding and the wrinkles on his face are deep as he looks at each of us somberly. But I guess that's what happens when your job is dealing with grieving families. It must take it out of you. And apparently ages you as well.

"Have you given any thought to flowers?" he asks, and the table collectively turns to me as if I have all the answers. I should. I have the funeral plan sitting in front of me, the failsafe our parents prepared for the event of an untimely death such as this one.

They meticulously planned their own farewell, better than I ever could have in their absence, and if that's not the most morbid thing about this entire ordeal, I don't know what is.

I look across the table and my eyes clash with Everett's, a mixture of concern and sadness pooling at the surface. For someone who grew up without being allowed to show emotion, his eyes are the most expressive of anyone I've ever met. From the first moment we met, I saw everything he was thinking long before he said the words.

"Lilies," I reply quietly, tearing my eyes from the ones I once loved staring into, but now all the deep blue pools make me feel is pain.

Mr. Sampson nods and takes a note, his pen scrawling across the paper, the only sound in the huge, ostentatious house. Mom and Dad never liked the estate, but it was expected of them to live somewhere like this. Somewhere with walls around the property to keep us safe, more security than you could count, and so many rooms I still get lost even after living here throughout my teens and visiting at least once a week since I moved out to go to college. But it would be Storm's now. As the head of the family, he already should have been living here, but he was putting it off, just as displeased about the prospect of living in the obscene estate as our parents had been.

"And will there be a color scheme? Some people like to have muted tones, and others prefer to make it more of a celebration," he tells us, and I watch as Rayne's eyes turn murderous.

"What exactly would we be celebrating?" he growls.

"I know this is a difficult time, but a funeral is a celebration of life, and it should be treated as such. People grieve in different ways, as I'm sure you are aware, and some choose to do that with bright colors."

Emerson takes Rayne's hand in her much smaller one, stroking the back of it gently to soothe him. She may never know the man he was before she came along. The cold, harsh man that had grown up too quickly, who only showed kindness to his family, was gone. Now the enforcer of our business had a soft side, he helps people, cares about perfect strangers, all because she does.

I take a deep breath, ready to make excuses for my family's hostility toward him, but then I stop myself. Why should I make excuses for my family's grief? They have every right to be feeling the things they are, just the way he would if he lost someone close to him. Grief isn't linear, and that's something I'm sure he understands. "I'm sure you can understand we are still in shock. Our parents died last night under suspicious circumstances. We are not in a place to think of this as a chance to celebrate their lives because we are still accepting that we have to live the rest of our lives without them." I look to Storm, who gives me a small nod. "I think perhaps this is enough for today. I will send you everything else we want by email over the coming days, and if you have any questions, please reach out to me." I stand from my seat, making it clear that we're done here.

"Oh." He looks around at my siblings as they stand one by one.

I never should have organized this for today, but when I called the funeral home Mom and Dad had listed in their instructions and they said someone could come around this afternoon, I wasn't really in a place to argue the point.

"Okay, that will be fine," he stammers as he gathers his paperwork from the table, taking several attempts to organize them into a neat stack and shove them back into his folder.

"Thank you for taking the time to come see us today." I force a smile to my lips, but they barely twitch in response.

33

We say a swift goodbye at the door before I move back to the living room, where everyone has returned to their seats. I sigh and take my own beside Snow, taking her hand in mine. She's taking it the hardest, and she's never dealt with adversity well. Hell, when she was in high school and wasn't crowned prom queen, she had a three-week meltdown and missed her graduation. I can't see the loss of our parents being any better than that.

"What the fuck did that guy think we have to fucking celebrate?" Rayne slams his hands down on the table, but none of us startle. We've all been around for enough of his outbursts that they don't surprise us, even Emerson. She just takes one of his hands in hers again, squeezing it for support.

"I want to know what is being done about Russo?" I turn to Storm. "We can plan a funeral until our hearts are content, but they won't be at rest until he's six feet under." I can feel Everett's eyes on the side of my face, burning a hole with the intensity of his stare, but I ignore him, too fired up with a new purpose. "I don't know about you, but I'm not going to be able to rest until he's paid for what he's done."

Storm's head drops into his hands and he tugs at the ends of his dark hair. "I've got Tommy on it. He's on Angelo, and he's got all our best guys on Paul and Tony. We're limited on manpower because this place takes so much, but I think we all need to stay together."

"We are not just sitting on our hands, Storm," Rayne growls. "First that fucker kidnaps my woman, and now he's murdered our parents. We have to take the fight to him. We never should have let him live. They would be alive if I'd killed them," he whispers the last few words, the despair in his voice almost enough to break me.

"We're not doing the could-have, would-have game. We need a plan. We need to end this so we can grieve," I tell them, my hands placed flat on the table as I lean toward them. "I want Angelo Russo's head for what he's done to this family."

They all stare at me with varying levels of shock and pride written all over their faces. I'm not a bloodthirsty person. Despite my extensive training with my brothers, I've never pulled the trigger and ended someone's life, but I could if the need ever came up. If I needed to kill someone to protect myself or my family, I wouldn't even blink before squeezing the trigger and walking away guilt free. You don't grow up as the princess of a crime family without knowing how to protect yourself and without the thought that someday that training may be the difference between life and death.

Everett stands from his seat and crosses to where his laptop is charging across the room, immediately coming back with it. "I couldn't sleep last night, so I started tracking Russo's financial activity. There's no way he used one of his own men to take out the founding members of the family. Not even Angelo Russo is dumb enough to think his team is capable of a hit of that scale. There's been a lot of money going in and out of their accounts, both on and offshore, and if I had to hazard a guess, I think they've used the shipment they took to fund the hit."

I nod slowly. It feels good to be using my mind so I can't focus on the grief threatening to overwhelm me every time I think of my mother's smile or my father's wit. It's always hovering at the edge of my consciousness, and somehow I think vengeance might be the only way I can sleep at night.

"Okay, can you track where the money or the shipment are going? Who they might have hired?"

Storm clears his throat. "I have a couple of guesses, but at the moment, that's all we've got. We can't prove that they're using the shipment. We have no idea who drove the car off the road. And I don't think it's a good idea that you girls get involved."

I stand from my seat and glare at my brother, anger simmering deep in my veins. "Do not tell me what I should and shouldn't be doing, Storm. You and I both know I am not someone who can sit on my hands and wait for things to play out. I want Russo to suffer for what he's done to this family. For what he did to Emerson, and for murdering our parents. And I'm going to be just as involved as you on this, whether you like it or not."

DEAD OF WYNTER

SIX

EVERETT

I've loved Wynter for as long as I can remember. From the moment our eyes met for the first time, those icy blue irises so full of innocence, I knew she would be the girl I would marry. But as I stare at her now, the fierce fire burning in those eyes I've lost myself in too many times to count, I've never loved her more.

She stares at Storm with a mixture of anger and fear, knowing she could very well be doing this on her own if he doesn't agree. She's going toe to toe with the man most of the city, if not country, fear, and she's doing it without so much as blinking.

She calls herself a princess, but I've always seen her for what she is. Wynter Saint James is a fucking queen.

"Wynter, you're not built for this. You're great with everything Frost Industries, but I don't want to stain your soul with the other shit our family deals with. I've never wanted that."

"And what happens if something happens to you?" she snaps,

and we all collectively flinch at the harshness of her words. "You trained me to take over both sides of the business, Storm. You don't just get to pick and choose when I do and don't see the bad side of this business. I know how we started. I know Frost was founded with blood money. I know what you and Rayne do when you're out late at night. If there was ever a time to include me, it's right the fuck now."

"She's right," I say. "She can't be your succession plan if you never let her see the dark side of what we all do."

Her head snaps around to me, the glare softening slightly as she considers my words. I have an inkling that she always knew I was still involved in the business, despite Storm and Rayne keeping it on the down low.

"You're just saying that because you want back in her good books," Rayne growls.

"No, I'm saying that because it's the truth. Wynter has always been stronger than any of you have given her credit for. Your dad always sheltered the girls, always kept them away from what he did, and he taught both of you to do the same. But Wynter, and Snow, for that matter, are more capable than anyone has ever allowed them to be. And if you think me defending her is going to do anything other than piss her off more, you don't know your sister very well." I chuckle.

Storm drops back into his seat and sighs. "Fine. You can help. But you will not leave this house without one of us with you. After what happened with Emerson, I don't trust anyone with any of your safety. We are all going to stay here until further notice, so if you need anything from your apartments, I suggest you go and get it now. We will all be working from here, with exception of Rayne, who will only leave to take care of problems if absolutely necessary, and he will have myself, Everett, or Tommy with him."

Snow groans and throws her head back. "This is so unfair."

"Do you want to be dead? Because that's what could happen if you leave this house unescorted and Russo or his men get near you." Storm stares at her pointedly and the blood drains from her cheeks. The baby of the family doesn't love the word no. She didn't when she was a kid, and that hasn't changed as an adult either.

Tears well in her eyes as she looks to Rayne and Wynter for support. "Of course I don't want to die, but I also don't want to be a prisoner." She pushes her chair back and storms from the room before anyone can attempt to stop her.

Emerson looks like she's about to follow, but Rayne places his hand on her arm. "She'll come around. She's just used to getting what she wants and doesn't like it when she doesn't get her way."

She looks to the stairs Snow disappeared up and sighs. "It's hard for her to live in all your shadows. She thinks everyone has a role in the family but her, and every time you lock her up, she doesn't see it as you trying to protect her. She sees it as you taking away all that she has," Emerson tells us.

She hasn't known any of them long, but her honesty will get her far in this family. That and her unwavering strength. She hasn't flinched once while we started talking about Russo, hasn't looked uncomfortable to be a part of a conversation about war and murder. You would never know she hadn't grown up around this shit the way we all did. She fits.

"I understand that, but we've already lost our parents, I'm not risking losing her as well. She's going to have to swallow all that shit for a minute and let us take care of this, and then on the other side, we'll give her something to do within the family," Storm replies.

Emerson chuckles. "That's the point though, she doesn't want you to *give* her something to do. She wants to earn it just like the rest of you did, but she's sheltered. It's no one's fault, it's just the way it is with youngest children sometimes."

"Sweet girl, your counselor is showing." Rayne laughs as he wraps his arms around his wife and tugs her into his side.

Fuck, it's nice to see him happy. He's always lived a tortured existence. He was the first one to kill a man, and he's never recovered from it. Don't get me wrong, the man loves his job, he loves taking care of problems and if a little bit of blood and the occasional torture session is a part of that, you'll never hear him complaining, but sometimes I worried the darkness would take over. Emerson is the bright light someone like him needs, just the way Wynter is mine. Whether she's known it or not, she's always been the light at the end of the tunnel for me, the guiding light in everything I do.

"Sorry, I don't mean to overstep. I just want you all to understand why Snow feels the way she does." Emerson's cheeks turn a bright shade of pink and she looks down at the table.

"You're just as much a part of this family as the rest of us, Emerson. Don't ever hesitate to say your piece," Storm tells her. "But Snow is going to have to live with it for now, just like the rest of us. We're all in lockdown the same way she is, and this is not something I am willing to negotiate. Once

Russo and his organization are six feet under, we can get back to business as usual."

I nod in agreeance. "It's important that we take some time to grieve as well. If we go into a war with hot heads, it's only going to mean more casualties."

"I agree." Emerson smiles shyly. "I know I'm new to all this, and that you've been doing it a really long time, but I have a certain amount of insight into how the human mind works, and Everett is absolutely correct. If you go into this guns blazing and wanting to avenge your parents as soon as possible, you'll do so without clarity, and I imagine in this line of work that is dangerous."

Rayne's face is full of pride and love as he looks down at her, and I can't help the pinch of jealousy that I can't do that with Wynter yet. Or ever really. When we were together before, we were never really together. We were best friends. We were everything to one another. But no one knew we were that. She was scared her brothers would kill me, and honestly, I was a little scared too. But when I had to go to them and tell them I had to leave her, they were never mad, never even blinked an eye. They always saw what we tried to hide.

I feel her eyes on the side of my face long before I turn to look at her. She isn't sure how to take everything I've thrown at her over the last twenty or so hours. Something deep inside me settles at the idea that she can take care of herself. She's not the girl I left all those years ago. The one I was terrified someone would hurt to exploit me. Wynter is a woman now, and I'd like to see anyone try to take her on.

I tear my eyes away from hers and look down at my computer screen, pulling up the financials I had been scouring over late last night. There had to be something here, a loose thread we could pull, a weak link we could use to our advantage, and when I see exactly what that weak link is, I look up at Storm and smile.

Let's do this.

Dead of Wynter

SEVEN

WYNTER

W hen my parents bought a family plot in Chicago's most prestigious cemetery, I laughed at them. I remember the moment so vividly I could swear we had the conversation yesterday, when in reality, it was years ago. I remember laughing so hard at the idea of my young, spritely parents needing to think of something like that, and then I laughed at how morbid it was.

But now it's a reality, one that I'm having trouble accepting. After our family meeting, I threw myself into work and planning. Business didn't allow for me to be away from my role as chief financial officer of Frost Industries for any amount of time, and I could only pawn off so much on my assistant. Clara is great, but I couldn't do that to her. She's shy and the idea of walking into a boardroom on her own in the past has left her having a meltdown. So in between my bouts of depression, planning to take out our enemy, and training with Rayne so my brothers and ex-whatever Everett is, don't worry so much, working, and planning a funeral for our parents, I'm pretty damn exhausted. But the exhaustion is good. It helps. It reminds me I'm alive and that my parents would want me to live despite them being gone.

The cemetery is deathly quiet as mourners arrive. We anticipated a big turnout, but this is beyond what even I could have dreamed of. Hundreds of people surround the two empty graves with the coffins resting at the top. People from all parts of their lives, their childhoods, college, Dad's old job, and then there's Frost Industries. The contrast between the good side and the bad side has never seemed so obvious as it does from my place in the front row. Every time I look around and see a mixture of high-class society, and people who work in the underworld, who make money on other's pain, it's almost enough to make me laugh.

Almost.

Snow holds my hand tightly, her blonde hair curled around her face as she struggles to hold it together. We're trying to show a united front, to prove to the world that this hasn't broken us. But it's come pretty fucking close.

It's the first time we've been seen in public since the accident. We arrived together, and we will leave together. The show of solidarity will hopefully squash any chance of the board thinking they can overthrow Storm and that anyone within the underbelly of Chicago will think they can stake a claim on our territory.

We are showing the world that adversity only ever makes the Saint James family stronger.

"Are you sure you're going to be okay doing the eulogy? I can do it if you want?" Storm asks for the tenth time since we left the house, and probably the three hundredth overall. He thinks the words will break me, but showing emotion isn't a bad thing.

"It's not a bad thing if I cry up there, Storm. We went over this. From a publicity standpoint, if one of us goes up there and doesn't shed a tear, just reads this thing with no emotion, it makes us look cold. Snow won't make it through the whole thing, and you and Rayne will be too strong. It's best it's me." I squeeze his hand and give him a weak smile.

This is the first time I've sat idly for more than a few minutes, and all the things I've been trying to stamp down are rising to the surface, threatening to break through the carefully crafted walls I've put up. Even at night, I'm too exhausted to spend more than a few minutes thinking before I pass out. But if anything is going to break me, it's sitting in the front row of my parents' funeral.

Storm takes his seat beside me, and on the other side of Snow, Rayne and Emerson are wrapped around one another. I'm glad he has someone through this. If this had happened six months ago, I can't imagine how much worse this situation would be. Emerson keeps him grounded and is stopping him from murdering every Russo man he can get his hands on.

But it's the man sitting beside him that I crave. I have to walk away every time Everett gets too close. Having him nearby is a blessing and a curse, because all I want to do is lean on him, and I can't do that without breaking my own heart. When he left, I wish I could say it hurt so much because of our romantic relationship, but that's not what left me crying myself to sleep every night. He was my best friend, my confidant, my everything. Every issue I ever had, I went to him, and suddenly he was gone. I didn't know where he was or what he was doing. I never knew if he was safe or if he was dead in a ditch somewhere. That was what tore my heart out and what I've never been able to recover from. It's the reason I don't let anyone get close, the reason my best friends are my siblings and my assistant. I can't handle the idea of someone I love leaving me again.

The priest clears his throat into the microphone and everyone's attention turns to him as he begins to talk about my parents being called back to heaven.

What a load of bullshit.

We've never been people who go to church every Sunday, only going for special occasions, but having a priest is ridiculous for a number of reasons apart from that one. One, my father was a mafia boss, so even if we were religious in the traditional sense, he was almost definitely going to hell. Two, I would argue that at least thirty percent of the people in attendance are also criminals. And three, who wants to hear that their parents were called to heaven when they were actually driven off the road by our enemy?

And yet the instructions were very clear, to the point they named Father Harvey as the priest they wanted to conduct the service. I'm still curious how they knew a priest by name, but hey, I'm curious about a lot of shit.

"And now, their daughter Wynter is going to share a few words," he says, and it's only the mention of my name that tugs me back to the present.

I stand, carefully straightening my tight, knee-length cotton dress down my thighs. Snow still covers the ground, so I've paired it with stockings and my favorite boots, along with a dark green coat to match my mother's eye color. Carefully I make my way to the front, and it's only when I'm standing beside the coffins that I realize just how many people are here.

Pulling the cue cards from my coat pocket, I take a deep breath to settle my nerves. I've never struggled to speak in public, but right now it seems harder than it ever has before. My heart beats a little too hard, my hands shake to the point I can barely focus on the words I scrawled on the cards, and tears that I've tried to hold at bay gather in my eyes.

My eyes sweep across the crowd again and settle on Everett's. Silently he's telling me I've got this, and it's his strength that allows me to start reading. "I wanted to begin with saying thank you for your attendance today. I always knew my parents were loved, but seeing you all here today really proves that. If you knew them well, you would know that there isn't a thing they wouldn't do for a person in need. When we were children, our home was always open to friends in need, and every single one of our friends gained an extra set of parents."

I'm talking to him now, admitting that everything Storm said that night we found out was true. He was a part of this family, just the same as we were.

"My mother donated to every charity far and wide, never wanting to see anyone go without as she had for many years. My father, regardless of how busy he was, always had time to help others. And that's how I hope the city of Chicago will always remember them."

I read over the next few lines. The ink has run slightly from the tears I shed as I wrote these words. "But what I can tell you about them that you may not already know is that they were the best parents we ever could have hoped for. When we had nothing, we still never wanted for anything. They always made sure we had everything we needed, and on top of that, they gave us love." I choke on the sob clawing up my throat, and panic starts to settle in my stomach. I have to get through this, I can't show too much weakness. "They taught us how to love, and how to be loved. They taught us that no matter your circumstances, no matter how bleak life may seem, if you have love, you have everything you'll ever need." The last words break as they leave my mouth and heavy tears roll down my cheeks. My eyes move from the crowd to the coffins beside me, and my knees weaken.

No, I can't do this. I can't say goodbye to them.

Before I can think to hold on to something, an arm wraps around my waist, holding me steady, and when I look up, I'm met with deep oceans. "You've got this, dove," he whispers. "And I've got you."

I shouldn't lean into his touch, but I do.

I shouldn't allow him to comfort me, but I do.

And I definitely shouldn't enjoy the way his large hand splays across my waist, and yet, I do.

"My family has lost our guiding lights, the people who taught us right from wrong, and how to navigate this crazy world, but we haven't lost our purpose. We will continue their legacy as a family, and make sure the world never forgets the people who always made it brighter."

I had stewed on the final words all night last night. Knowing our enemies were watching only made it more important to make a statement. And the words I chose only served as a message to everyone who thought they could threaten us.

We are coming for you.

EIGHT
EVERETT

The moment her body relaxes into mine feels like a turning point. Since the moment I walked into the house, Wynter has kept me at arm's length. Never sparing me more than a few words, and only when her siblings were nearby. But when her body molds to mine as tears roll down her cheeks, it feels like I'm holding my entire world in my arms.

I guide her back to her seat but rather than sitting her down and moving back to my own, I take the seat and tug her down on my lap. Holding her again is addictive, and I'm not ready to let her go.

I half expect her to pull away from me, to argue that she doesn't need to sit on my lap, but instead she leans her head on my shoulder as we watch the coffins lower into the ground. Wynter and Snow sob quietly, Storm and Rayne as stoic as ever, but knowing them as well as I do, I know they're choked up. Their chests are rising and falling too quickly, their hands poised in fists to hold back the emotion that claws at them.

Even I find myself choking back tears, the idea that the only parents who had ever cared about me rotting in the ground too somber a thought to handle. But holding Wynter keeps me grounded, keeps the demons at bay.

"You did great, dove," I tell her quietly as we make our way to throw roses into the graves. Her hand holds mine tightly, as if she's too afraid to let go, and honestly, the feeling is mutual. The moment I allow her even a second of space will be the moment she runs.

Her eyes meet mine, searching for something I'm not sure she's going to find. "Thank you for being here," she whispers.

"I told you once, and I'll tell you a hundred times, I'm not going anywhere." I pull her into my side and press a kiss to the top of her head. It's something she's going to need to accept, and eventually my patience is going to buckle and I'm going to have to push the point. But today is about our grief.

She looks at me with doubt swirling around in her eyes. She doesn't believe me. Not yet at least. But she will. I'll make her believe me.

Wynter stands at the end of both graves, only a foot between them, and stares at the coffins that have been lowered into them. The roses held tightly in her hands, the thorns digging painfully into her skin.

Storm steps up on the other side of her. "They would be so proud of you, Wynter. I'm so proud of you." Emotion clogs his voice and if I didn't know him better I may think he was about to cry. But Storm repressed his emotions long ago, he wouldn't allow anyone to see his weaknesses, not even his family.

Wynter nods, her body shaking in my hold before she finally drops the roses onto the coffins. "Goodbye Mom, goodbye Dad," she murmurs before turning to her brother. "Is he here?"

Storm nods. "He's in the back. I'm sure he saw your eulogy for exactly what it was, a promise of what is to come."

Wynter looks up at me and I almost expect her to pull away, but instead she leans into my touch. "Let's do this."

Snow, Rayne and Emerson trail behind us. We'd been over the plan over and over again the last few days, making sure we show a united front to the enemy, me included. To begin with, I suggested I continue from the shadows, but I was overwhelmingly outvoted.

It's time to stop living on the sidelines and assume my position with the family, and once some of the dust settles, it'll be time to claim my woman as well.

As we approach the Russo family, Wynter leans into me for support, her face showing none of the tension she holds in her body. The grace she shows as we walk toward our enemy is nothing short of beautiful.

Angelo notices us first, his cold eyes settling on my arm wrapped around Wynter and an evil smile crosses his features. The hair at the sides of his head is graying, and his hairline recedes more and more each time I see him, but if I can avoid it, our visits are few and far between. His attention moves to Emerson and Rayne behind us, a glower crossing his hard features. The trophy he thought he could win for himself on someone else's arm isn't going to do us any favors.

A fake smile appears on his face as we close the gap and I

hold Wynter a little tighter. "I was so sorry to hear about your parents. Such a horrible thing to happen, and they were so young!"

The noise Rayne makes behind us almost isn't human, but he stays put. He won't leave Emerson even for a second with any of the Russo organization around, let alone the man who orchestrated her kidnapping.

"Thank you for coming," Storm says politely. "I'm sure my parents would be very grateful you came to celebrate their lives." To anyone else, his words sound sincere and honest, but it's the venom that seeps into them that tells me he's barely holding on to his temper.

"And Wynter, your words were so beautiful. I'm sure your parents are very proud of you for standing up on behalf of your family." His eyes fall to us, and I can't help the punishing grip on her waist. I can't stand the idea of him looking at her, let alone speaking to her, and my primal need to protect her is almost overwhelming.

"Thank you," she replies, her head held high as she stares at the man who has taken everything from this family.

Paul and Tony, Angelo's cousins, stand behind him, their filthy eyes moving from one person to the other, as if assessing whether we're armed. We'd have to be pretty fucking stupid to bring a gun to a funeral, and that's why there's more security here than at Buckingham Palace. The two sides of Frost Industries colliding like this is already a bad idea. It would only add insult to injury if we were to flaunt that so freely.

Angelo's eyes lock on Emerson and I can't help but look over my shoulder to check on her. She may not realize it yet, but there's not a damn thing anyone in this family wouldn't do for her, regardless how long she has been one of us.

"You lied to me, Emerson."

A smile tugs at her lips, the confidence she exudes is merely a farce, but there's no way he knows that. We checked with her over and over again before we left the house this morning about whether she was okay to be within a few feet of the man who kidnapped her, but she was adamant she be a part of this, and all I see is confidence as I look at her.

"I did. I'm sure you can understand why a mistruth was needed under the circumstances." She flashes the diamond rings on her left hand and shrugs. "It's true now though."

Rayne chuckles and presses a kiss to the top of her head. "A Saint James through and through."

Tony glares at my newest sister and I can't help the impulse to move in front of her, cutting off his line of sight. He hasn't even acknowledged my existence, but then I didn't expect him to. Their denial that I am just as much a part of this family as the rest of them is the reason I've lived in the shadows for so long.

"Nephew," Tony growls.

"Don't call me that." I shake my head slowly. "Calling me that implies I am a part of your family, and I am most certainly not."

"But you are, Everett." Someone steps out from behind Paul and I still. His unmistakable green eyes, the color of moss, have always been haunting, but as he's grown, it's only become amplified. But it's not me his stare is caught on. No, it's the youngest Saint James that seems to have captured his attention.

"No, he's not," Wynter says and my head swings around to face her. "Now, if you don't mind, we have other people to speak to. Again, thank you for coming." Her smile is strained as she looks to Storm to lead us away.

"It's risky being seen with her, cousin. You never know who might want the princess that means so much to two families," Elijah muses.

"Wynter isn't a princess." I shrug. "She's a queen, and you'll do well to remember that."

DEAD OF WYNTER

NINE

WYNTER

Everett's words hang between our families long after he says them, and for some reason I can't help but stand a little straighter at the praise. It's not the first time he's said those words to me but saying them to our enemy makes my heart beat harder. The Russo family underestimates women. It's well known that they think men are the superior sex and women belong barefoot in the kitchen producing as many children as their husband requires of them. But that's not how this family works.

"That may be the case, but you know the risk. Don't say I didn't warn you." Everett's cousin shrugs as if his words weren't an unspoken threat.

I smile and step forward out of Everett's hold. "If you're going to threaten me, Elijah, do it properly. But I guess it's silly of me to expect anything else from a Russo." I've never heard my own voice sound so menacing, but I don't appreciate the way he's speaking about me like I'm not even here.

His head cocks to the side, as if he doesn't know what to make of me. "Didn't your daddy ever teach you that your place is at a man's side, silent?"

Everett growls behind me, but I take another step forward until I'm face to face with four Russo men, their eyes on me curiously. "My daddy taught me not to fear weak men. He taught me that just because I'm a woman, doesn't mean I'm not just as powerful as my brothers. There's a reason Everett chose our family over his own, because we actually know how to treat the people we love. Now, I suggest that you leave, and the next time we see you, I promise it won't be under such pleasant circumstances." I spare each member of their family a glance before turning on my heel and walking away with my head held high.

I hear the whisper of voices behind me, but I don't stop walking until I reach the limo waiting for us. My heart beats painfully in my chest to the point I think it may stop all together, and by the time I'm settled in my seat and the door closes behind us, shielding us from prying eyes, I'm gasping for air. It's been a long time since I've had a panic attack, but the telltale signs are all here. Shortness of breath. The feeling of the world closing in on me. An erratic heartbeat.

Everett reaches for me before gathering me up and placing me in his lap. "You did so good, dove," he whispers to me as tears start rolling down my cheeks. His kindness only makes the panic grow stronger, the thought of leaning on someone other than myself and my immediate family more than my anxiety ridden body can handle. "I've got you, Wynter. I've always got you."

I allow my body to relax into his, needing the warmth and

soothing words he's offering as my entire body shakes on his. He repositions me carefully so I'm straddling his lap, my face pressed against his chest and he's holding me tightly against him.

"Give me your jacket," he says to Storm and a moment later it's wrapped around my shoulders.

Movement on the other side of me makes me startle before a warm hand touches mine. "It's me, Wynter," Emerson whispers. "You're safe now, can you breathe with me?" Her words are soft and carefully spoken, and I can tell this isn't the first time she's helped to calm someone down.

I bury my face into Everett's chest, taking comfort in his familiar scent helping to bring my breathing under control.

"I knew this plan was a bad idea," Storm grumbles from beside us, but I do everything I can to block him out and focus on the steady beat of Everett's heart beneath my cheek, and the calming strokes of his hand down my back as he holds the back of my head in place. Despite what we just did, despite the threats I made to some of the most dangerous men in the country, I've never felt more safe than I do right now.

"It wasn't a bad idea, Storm," Snow says quietly. "It was the right call. Russo underestimates every single member of this family, but more so Wynter, Emerson, and I. They think we're weak just because we're women and showing them how strong she is will make them make mistakes. They'll rush whatever the next phase of their plan is and we'll be waiting."

"She's fucking terrified," Storm hisses and Everett holds me a little tighter, as if trying to shield me from the harsh words.

"You're right, she is," Emerson replies from somewhere in the limo. She's moved away from me again and if I had to hazard a guess without opening my eyes, I imagine Rayne summoned her back to him. "She just stood up to the man who murdered her parents. She's been so busy taking care of everyone else, making sure Frost Industries doesn't crumble while you're all away, and plotting how to take that family down, she hasn't grieved, and then she went toe to toe with someone who wants every single person in this car dead. I think that's a pretty good reason to be terrified."

I raise my head despite Everett's attempts to hold it against his chest, quickly wiping the tears from my cheeks. "Let me up," I whisper. It's not a demand, I'm asking him to let me say my piece and then I'll allow him to coddle me all he likes, even if it is only for today. I will allow myself one day of being held by the man I fell in love with all those years ago, and at the end of today I'll turn my feelings off again and keep him at arm's length. I can't allow myself to fall for him again, not after all he's done.

"Just stay put, dove. We'll be home soon."

"Just for a second," I promise.

Everett sighs and his arms loosen around me as I sit up on his lap. I make no move to sit in my own seat, perfectly comfortable where I'm perched on his knees. "I need you all to stop talking about me like I'm not here. Today has been... overwhelming, and facing Russo was just another part of that. While we stood there, one of those men threatened me, Snow, and Emerson, without ever saying the words. Of course I'm fucking terrified. Of course every single fiber of my being is screaming at me to run. But I won't. Those men killed our parents. They kidnapped and hurt Emerson. They deserve to die, and I'll be damned if I'm not getting my pound of flesh in all this."

The analogy has my own stomach flipping, but it's as true as anything else I could have said. I want to see every member of the Russo family dead, even if it means Everett has no biological family left.

Everett is the product of two families trying to unite in order to restore peace to the city. The man my father over threw married Everett's mother under an arranged agreement between Angelo's father and the Masters family. They thought they could unite and become the largest criminal organization in the country, but the problem with that was that George Masters had no time or patience for a wife, or a child for that matter. The man was cruel, and when he killed her one night after he came home drunk, and forced his son to watch, everything started to unravel.

It was around that time that the Saint James family took over, that we ascended through the Chicago underworld and came out on top, all of Russo's hard work misplaced, and the youngest daughter dead because of their decisions.

Storm stares at me for long moments, assessing me like he does our enemies. He's looking for the weakness in my words, for the hesitation in my eyes, but he's not going to find it. I've never been more sure of anything in my life.

The Russo family needs to be wiped from existence like the scum they are, and I want a front row seat to their demise.

I've been staring at the ceiling for hours. Once I calmed down in the limo, Snow helped me to fix my makeup and we spent three excruciating hours at a wake for our parents. People they hated, people that didn't know them but thought they could capitalize on our loss, people who were looking for our weaknesses. But we showed them nothing.

Everett stayed with me the entire time, his arm wrapped around my waist to give me the strength I needed, and as much as I hate to admit it, I needed him. It wasn't until we got home that I retreated to my room, claiming to have a headache I didn't have. It was the only excuse I could think of to force my family to leave me alone for a little while.

He had hesitantly allowed me out of his sight, and now I wish he hadn't. Every moment I've laid here, all I've been able to think about is Everett's hands on my body, the way he held me so tight it felt like I would die when he let me go. It's not the first time I've laid in bed awake for hours thinking about him, and it probably won't be the last, but it is the first time he's been in the next room.

My body aches for his touch, craves the comfort he can give me, but it's the most basic instincts that need him most. My hand slides down my body, the only thing between it and my bare skin is a short nightgown I threw on to get out of the dress from the funeral. The silk fabric beneath my fingertips only seems to make me ache more.

Images of Everett's fingers trailing over my body, his huge hands brushing along my bare skin until I can't breathe past my need for him. My fingertips brush along my thighs, probing at the edge of my nightgown as I imagine him doing the same, teasing me until I'm panting for him, begging for him to touch me where I need him.

Slowly, I inch my hand up until my fingers touch the wet patch on my panties. A gentle moan slips from my lips as I close my eyes, allowing myself a moment of weakness to imagine how it would feel if it weren't my own hand moving slowly, drawing gentle circles into my clit.

My other hand moves carefully, dragging my nails along my bare skin before circling my silk covered nipple. A gasp escapes my throat and my hips grind into my hand of their own accord. I can barely breathe through how turned on I am, how badly I need the release building under my own touch.

Before long I'm riding the edge of oblivion, teetering on the precipice of an orgasm my body craves almost as much as its next breath, and when I finally allow myself to tip over the edge, a strangled moan tears from my throat and my entire body tightens as waves of pleasure roll over me, taking the breath right from my lungs.

"Was that orgasm for me, dove?"

TEN
EVERETT

The last thing I expect to see when I creep into Wynter's room to check on her is her hand on her pussy and the other on her tits. I should walk out the moment I realize what she's doing, but I can't tear my eyes away from her.

She's right on the edge, I can tell by how tense every muscle is and how she sinks her teeth into her bottom lip to keep quiet. My cock hardens immediately in my sweatpants, and I can't help but reach down and give it a squeeze. He's just as eager to get back inside her tight pussy, but patience is the key. We need to run the long game if I'm going to get her to trust me again, to realize I'm not going anywhere this time.

When she finally allows herself to topple headfirst into her orgasm, it's one of the most erotic things I've ever seen. Her chest rises and falls in sharp pants, the moan that claws its way from her throat makes my balls tighten, and the way her entire body tightens only makes me think about what it will be like for her to come around my cock again.

I lean against the door as I wait for her to come down from her high so as not to startle her. "Was that orgasm for me, dove?" I ask through a smirk.

Wynter's eyes shoot open and meet mine, and the most delightful shade of pink covers her cheeks. Even under the dim moonlight I see the way her milky skin lights up with the color of strawberries, and I long to reach for her.

"What the fuck are you doing in here?" She tugs the sheets up around her neck as she pushes herself to lean against the headboard. Her breaths come in hard and fast, her body still recovering from the bliss she just provided herself.

"I asked you first." I shrug as I take long strides toward the bed.

"No, of course not," she hisses, her body shaking under my gaze.

"Liar." I smirk, taking the final steps until my thighs rest against the edge of the bed.

"Get out," she breathes, and I can tell she doesn't trust her own voice around me, not when I've caught her at such a vulnerable moment.

I shake my head slowly. "Now why would I do that when you're in here coming for me without my permission." I kneel on the edge of the bed and prowl toward her. Part of me expects her to throw herself off the bed to get away from me, but I'm quietly pleased when she doesn't move a muscle, her fingers gripping the edge of the sheet tightly.

"I don't need your permission to come. I don't need your permission for anything." Her voice wavers, the combination of her orgasm and my proximity making it hard for her to speak.

Good. If she can't speak, she can't argue with me about things we both know she wants but won't admit.

I continue my slow crawl across the bed until my body hovers above hers. My bare chest is on fire with the need to press against her, but I hold back. I have to take this slow. I need her to know this isn't just about sex, even if that's definitely a perk.

"Everett," Wynter warns.

"Don't worry, dove. I won't do anything you won't like."

"You don't know what I like," she snaps as she finally tries to roll out from under me, not that I allow her to get very far. My arms act as a cage, holding her exactly where I want her.

"You know that's not true, Wynter," I murmur, bringing my face down until we're eye to eye. "You know I know exactly what you like, and just how to give it to you."

She pushes against my chest. "Get off me. We fucked one time eight years ago, and you disappeared the next morning. It doesn't seem like sex with me was very fucking memorable," she growls.

I love it when she gets feisty. When she gets herself wound up with the things she knows she shouldn't want but desperately does, it only makes for more fun for me.

I chuckle. She doesn't understand, but she will. Soon enough, she'll know just how obsessed I've been since the morning I climbed out of her bed and left for her safety. She'll understand that there wasn't a day over the last eight years that I didn't think about her every single second of the day.

"That's where you're wrong, dove." I brush my lips across her cheek, the whisper of a touch enough for goose bumps to erupt across her skin. "I think about that night every single day, and every single night it's a memory I go to sleep thinking about."

Her mouth drops open, and I'm tempted to take her lips, but not yet.

"Do you know how many times I've jerked myself off at the thought of your pretty lips wrapped around my cock?" I ask. "Or the memory of your pretty pussy taking me so beautifully. Of you begging me to keep going even though I saw the pain in your eyes." I'm taunting her now, bringing the memory of our night together to the surface. Before that, there were stolen kisses and slightly inappropriate touching from the moment she turned eighteen, but never anything more.

"You're lying."

A smirk tugs at my lips as I shake my head. "No, I'm not. There's so much you don't understand, Wynter, so much we had to keep from you for your own safety, but never doubt how much you mean to me. I gave up everything to keep you safe."

She stares at me for long moments, assessing whether she believes the words I'm saying. "Why won't you tell me why you left?"

"Because you're grieving. You just lost your parents, and I don't want to pile on top of that. Just believe me when I say I didn't leave because I wanted to, or because you weren't enough for me, or because I just wanted your virginity and nothing more, because none of that is true. If I could have been here with you every day for the last eight years, we would be married with three kids by now. But those weren't the cards we were dealt back then."

Her eyes widen at my words, and I can't help but smile as I press a gentle kiss to her cheek. "You're the only woman I've ever loved, Wynter. Why would I not want those things with you?"

"I just…" Her tongue darts out to wet her lips as she thinks about what she should say, and it takes every single ounce of strength not to lean forward and nip at it. Her breath on my cheeks is intoxicating and being this close to her while neither of us are fully dressed is dangerous. "I'm so confused," she whispers, her eyes filling with tears. "I don't understand why you would leave me if you loved me, if you wanted to marry me and have kids. It doesn't make any sense. Part of me wants to believe you're lying to me just to get back into my pants, but…"

"But you know me better than that," I offer.

She nods, her eyes falling closed for a moment as she takes deep calming breaths.

"I promise I will tell you everything, dove. I'll lay it all out on the table for you, and you can make your own judgments about me, but I can tell you one thing. I'm not going anywhere ever again. We are going to happen again. I will have you like I should have all those years ago, whether you're willing to admit it or not."

"What if I don't want you anymore?" she challenges.

"But you do. Why would you be rubbing your pretty little pussy for me if you didn't still want me?" I ask, tugging her hand away from where she grips the sheets and bring her fingers to my nose. Her familiar scent only makes me harder, but it feels like coming home. "You smell so sweet, dove," I murmur. "That's the last orgasm you have without my permission."

"Excuse me?" Her brows raise and a look of defiance crosses her face.

"You heard me."

"You wouldn't even know, I don't see how you're going to enforce this rule."

I chuckle. Oh, my little dove, how innocent you are. "I will know, and you will not like the consequences of disobeying me."

Wynter worries her lip between her teeth, and I barely tamp down the groan that claws up my throat. I could be inside her in under thirty seconds, sinking deep into her tight pussy. But not yet. She's not ready, and the next time I take her, she'll know why I left in the first place, she'll know that I never wanted to be away from her, and in a way, I never was.

Because I always knew where she was, what she was doing, and who she was with, and there's a good reason her dating history is so short. Because I made it that way.

DEAD OF WYNTER

ELEVEN

WYNTER

Having Everett so close is like sitting on top of a furnace. The heat his body emits is bordering on painful, and with each moment he hovers over my body, the more overheated I become. I'm trying to process what he's saying, but none of it makes any sense.

Part of me wonders if he's lying to me, and that would make the most sense, because nothing else he's saying makes any, but despite all he's done to me, despite how heartbroken I was when he left, I can't think that he would do that to me.

"You are not controlling my orgasms," I whisper.

I wish I was more sure of my voice, that I could trust it to be as strong as the words felt in my throat, but I know better. When Everett left, he wrecked me for all men. I didn't trust them as far as I could kick them, so I rarely got close to them, rarely allowed them close enough to kiss me, let alone much of anything else, and every single man I did let close, that I liked and thought might like me back, ghosted me after a date or two. For a long time, I've wondered if I'm defective, if there's something wrong with me that makes men run as fast as they can in the opposite direction. And that's why I can't trust Everett, and I certainly can't trust myself around him.

"Oh, but I am, Wynter." He smirks from above me.

"No, you're not," I hiss, bringing both hands to his chest and shoving as hard as I can manage, but he doesn't budge. He just chuckles quietly.

"You will do what you're told when you're told, or you'll be sitting on a very fucking red ass and being denied for weeks at a time."

My mouth drops open as I stare at him incredulously. "You can't do that."

"Oh, but I can, dove. You've been warned, and if you choose to disobey me, you will suffer the consequences."

I half laugh, panic rising in my chest. Logically, I know Everett would never hurt me, that he would never put me in any harm or give me more than I can handle, but there's a voice in the back of my mind telling me to run. Everett doesn't know me anymore, he doesn't know what I've been through since he left, and I don't think he would want to know the woman I've become.

"I can see the wheels turning in your pretty little head, dove. If you're a good girl, all you'll get are rewards." His head dips and he presses a gentle kiss to my cheek, the contact setting a fire in my body I don't know how to tamp down. How is it after all these years, he still has the power to set me alight? "Do you want to be a good girl for me, Wynter?" His voice is deep honey and promises, and I find myself nodding before I can stop myself. He's tempting me like the serpent tempted Eve in the Garden of Eden, and I don't think I'll ever be able to say no to the apple he's offering me.

A grin breaks out across his face, and my core tightens at the sight. Everett's smile has always been my favorite sight, ever since the first time I saw it when I was twelve. "I'm not going to touch you until you know everything. I don't want to take advantage of your grief, and I want to make sure that when I take you, you understand exactly why I had to leave," he tells me and I deflate slightly. His words sounded like a promise of what was to come, and yet he's telling me he's not going to touch me? "Don't look at me like that, dove. You know I'll always take care of you."

His hand moves from where it was planted beside me to my face, his thumb brushing along my bottom lip. His eyes lock on the soft pillow of flesh, and my tongue darts out and brushes against his thumb. Everett groans. The sound rumbles through the room causing my legs to press together in need.

"You're temptation personified, dove."

I almost laugh at his words, because that's simply not true. But I don't want to admit he's the only man I've ever been with. That after he left, I tried to find my way into others' beds, but they always left before that could happen. That the only time I got close enough I was left hurt so badly I spent a week in bed recovering. He can never know how stupid I was.

"I want you to strip for me, I want to see the body that belongs to me." I open my mouth to argue, but he continues. "Save your breath, Wynter. You know just as well as I do that you've always belonged to me, so there's no sense denying it."

"I'm not stripping for you, Everett," I say quietly. There are a hundred reasons he can never see me naked again, but at the very top of that list is that I can't be vulnerable with him like that again, because if he decides to tear the rug out from under me, I have so much farther to fall.

Something primal crosses his face right before the fingers that brushed along my cheeks and lips move to my throat, placing the slightest amount of pressure on where my pulse beats heavily against his hand. "You have two options here, little dove. You can either strip for me, or I will do it myself, and believe me when I say you won't like it when I tear that pretty nightgown from your body," he growls.

My legs clamp together as a rush of need floods my core. His words should scare me, but they don't. I know in my mind, body, and soul that Everett would never hurt me, not physically at least. I take a deep, unsteady breath and lift my body from the bed enough to draw the nightgown over my head before immediately lying back to put some distance between our bare chests.

Everett's eyes hungrily feast on my tits like a starved man staring at the first meal he's eaten in weeks. "Fuck, Wynter. You're perfect," he breathes as his eyes roam over my bare skin. "Your panties too. Let me see my pussy."

I should protest. I shouldn't like his words like I do, but regardless I carefully lift my hips just enough to shove the cotton fabric down my legs without lifting them into his where he's straddling me.

He groans above me as his eyes drag over every inch of exposed skin. "Fuck, Wynter. You're so fucking beautiful."

A heavy blush brushes across my cheeks at his words. He's always had this effect on me, always been able to turn me into a blushing idiot with only a few words, but now it seems so much more significant than it did when we were kids.

A smirk tugs at his lips as his fingers trail across the warmth of my skin. "Watching you from afar was never enough for me," he murmurs.

"What?"

Everett stares into my eyes for a moment, the deep blue pools full of emotion. "It doesn't matter." He shakes his head. "Here's what's going to happen. You're going to follow every single one of my instructions, and I promise you'll get what you need at the end."

I barely stop myself from telling him all I need is him. Barely. The words catch in my throat and burn me from the inside out. No matter how true they are, the words can never be said aloud. I nod once, unable to form words past the ones lodged in my throat.

"Words, little dove."

"I understand," I whisper.

I'm rewarded with one of Everett's blinding smiles, and I find myself wanting to jump at every command just so he'll look at me like that again. "Good girl. Now, I want you to rub your clit for me, nice and slow."

I sink my teeth into my lower lip before trailing my hand down my stomach until my fingers collide with my soaking wet pussy.

"Are you wet for me, Wynter?"

"Yes," I reply quietly, my fingers starting a gentle circle around the bundle of nerves still sensitive from my earlier orgasm.

"Let me taste," he orders, and I find myself obeying immediately.

I drag my fingers through my sensitive folds before bringing my wet fingers to his lips. He sinks them into his mouth, his tongue darting around them as a guttural groan fills the room.

"Fuck, your pussy is just as sweet as I remember." The sight only makes a wave of heat slam through me, and by the time my fingers resume their gentle rhythm, I'm wetter than I can ever remember being.

Everett moves until he's sitting back on his heels, watching every move I make intently. His eyes burn into me with such fervor I'm sure I'm about to self-combust. No one but him has ever looked at me like this, like I'm the most magical creature in the universe to him. It's an intoxicating feeling when a man as powerful as Everett Masters looks at you like you're the entire world, like you hung the moon and all the stars, and it's a feeling I never want to give up again.

DEAD OF WYNTER

TWELVE

EVERETT

The moment I concocted this plan, I knew it was a bad idea. Having Wynter naked beneath me is like putting a prime rib in front of a lion and expecting it not to feast. But I meant it when I said I wasn't going to take her until she was mine again, until she knew exactly why I left all those years ago. The next time I sink inside her tight heat, there will be no doubt about who she belongs to.

I watch through hooded eyes as she presses gentle circles into her clit, her pussy getting wetter by the second as she brings herself closer to the edge. I reach down and squeeze my cock through my sweatpants, needing relief from how fucking hard I am.

"I want to see," Wynter whispers and my eyes shoot up to clash with hers.

I chuckle. "Do you want to see how hard I am for you, little dove?"

"Yes." She nods, her eyes dragging down my body until they

lock with the tent in my sweatpants. Slowly I draw them down my thighs, my cock so hard it slaps against my stomach the moment it's freed.

Wynter's strokes of her clit speed up as my hand wraps around my aching cock, precum pooling at the tip.

The moment feels impossibly intimate seeing as not one part of me is touching her. The electricity whirling around the room makes it almost impossible for either of us to breathe.

"Use your other hand and fuck yourself with your fingers," I order, tightening my grip around my cock. My hand and I are pretty well acquainted, but it's never felt this fucking good.

Wynter's eyes widen, but a moment later, she's obeying me by sliding a finger into her drenched sheath.

"More," I growl.

She squeezes a second finger in beside the first, and despite how wet she is, she winces slightly at the burn of the stretch. She hasn't been fucked since we were together eight years ago, I've made sure of that, made sure I would always be the only person to ever slide into the paradise between her thighs. Before I can slide into her sweet pussy, I'm going to need to put in some work to make sure I don't hurt her, because the moment I sink back into the heaven between her legs, I'm never going to want to leave.

"That's my good girl," I murmur as I watch her work her fingers to bring herself closer to the edge.

"It's too much after I just came," she whines, but she doesn't stop moving, not even for a moment.

"You better get used to coming more than once, dove, because the moment I get my hands back on you, I'm going to make sure you come so many times and so hard, that you won't remember your own fucking name," I growl.

Her mouth drops open, her plump lips forming the perfect O and I barely hold myself back from sinking between the perfect pillows. But I won't touch her. Not yet. There's plenty of time for me to fuck her mouth in the future, and I can be patient.

I tear my eyes from her mouth and drag them down her naked body, all smooth lines and perfection, until I lock on where her hands are moving at the apex of her thighs. I could watch this all day, listen to the gentle moans of ecstasy. Her pleasure is my favorite drug.

"Oh god," she whispers like a prayer, the sound of her wetness filling the room. She's so fucking turned on she's dripping, her sweet honey gushing around her fingers as she works herself.

I barely catch myself when I reach to touch her. Everything about Wynter Saint James is tempting, and she doesn't even know it. One of my biggest regrets is that she doesn't see herself the way the rest of the world does, that I took away a part of her when I left. The selfish bastard in me rejoices in the idea no other man has had Wynter the way I have, that by breaking her the way I did, she couldn't trust anyone in the time I was away, but she'll never feel like that again. She'll always know her worth, she'll know exactly how I see her, because she is everything.

"Not God, dove." I chuckle.

"You haven't touched me. You can't take credit for any of

this," Wynter breathes.

"Are you trying to tempt me, little dove?"

She shakes her head against the pillow, her blonde locks spread around her like a halo. She looks downright angelic, and part of me wants to take my beautiful angel and make her fall to the depths of hell right alongside me.

"I think you are, dove. I think you're a siren trying to tempt me into the ocean." I lean over her, careful to keep our bodies from brushing against one another. "I think you want me to take over because you know how well I can play your body."

Wynter's eyes dilate as a moan slips from her lips. She's so fucking turned on she's all I can hear and smell, her sweetness begging to be enjoyed. "No," she says quietly.

"Liar." I smirk. "I don't need to touch you for you to be dripping for me, Wynter. All you need are my words and you'll soak through the sheets. Now tell me, little dove, has anyone else ever had this effect on you? Have you ever rubbed your sweet pussy for anyone else and felt this wet and needy?" I know the answer. I haven't allowed her to get close enough to anyone for that to be the case.

Wynter pulls her bottom lip between her teeth as she considers her answer. If she's smart, she won't lie to me, not about something like this. In the end, she shakes her head. "No. It's only ever been you," she whispers, closing her eyes to break the moment.

"Open your eyes," I growl. "I want you to look at me when we come together."

Ice blue looks back at me and I groan as I squeeze my cock

harder, I'm so fucking close to the edge I'm barely holding on, but we're coming together whether she likes it or not.

"Are you ready to come, dove?"

"Yes." Wynter nods, her movements beneath me becoming shaky and less precise with each second that passes.

"I want to hear my name on those pretty lips as you come, little dove." I lean down until our faces are so close we're breathing the same air. It would be so easy to crash my lips down on hers right now, to taste her as she comes, but I don't. Being this close to her is enough. For now. "Come for me, Wynter," I demand through clenched teeth as my balls tighten and the base of my spine tingles with the need for my release.

She doesn't disappoint as her entire body tightens, both hands freezing for a moment as the pleasure takes over. Her entire body shakes under mine, and a moment later, my cum is covering her milky skin in thick ropes.

Wynter's breaths come in hard and fast, her chest rising so high her nipples brush against my chest hair, only adding to her own pleasure. Her orgasm goes on and on, her fingers moving in tandem to tear every last bit of ecstasy from her body.

She sags into the mattress, exhaustion overwhelming her the moment the pleasure ends, and I can't help but smile. A few hours ago, she felt she could lean on me while she was vulnerable, and now she knows her body is just as much mine as it always has been.

"Always such a good girl for me, dove," I murmur. "Let's get you cleaned up and you can get some sleep."

She nods against the pillow, her eyes drifting closed the moment I climb from the bed and head into the attached bathroom for a cloth. By the time I return, she's relaxed into the bed, her breathing back to a gentle rise and fall.

A smile tugs at my lips as I take long strides to where she lies in the bed. "Wynter," I whisper, brushing long strands of gold from her face.

She groans, her nose scrunching in distaste as my thumb strokes her cheek gently. Being able to touch her again, to feel her skin beneath mine after so long, it's all I can do not to climb into the bed beside her and never leave. She's fucking addictive, and just the sight of her has my cock stirring again.

"Come on, dove. I'll clean you up and tuck you in."

Her eyes flutter open and look up at me. For the first time since I walked back into her life, she looks at me with something other than contempt in her gaze. I see the broken girl I left behind and the trust she's put in me tonight, a trust I can't break.

Not again.

"Open your legs for me, little dove." I kneel beside her on the bed, and she complies immediately, watching with bated breath as I move to touch her. I shouldn't. I know I shouldn't. But I crave the closeness the same way she does. I need it. "Good girl."

I start by wiping her cum from her thighs, and then as gently as I can manage, wipe her heat. She flinches under my touch, her pussy too sensitive after the two orgasms she's given herself in the last half an hour, but she doesn't pull away. Once I'm sure she'll be comfortable enough to sleep, I wipe my seed from where it landed against her stomach and mound. A part of me wants to leave it there so every man that dares look at her knows she's mine and mine alone, but I have to tamp down my caveman tendencies, even if only for now.

Once I'm satisfied I've wiped our combined releases off her soft skin, I throw the cloth onto the bedside table and bring the sheets up around her naked body. "You did so good, little dove," I praise.

Wynter preens under my words of encouragement as she barely keeps her eyes open. I've missed seeing her like this, so open and happy, but if I have it my way, this is how she'll be all the time from here on out.

"Are you leaving?" she asks quietly.

The words almost break my resolve to leave the room because there's nothing in this world I would rather do than slip in between the sheets beside her and sleep with my cock nestled between her ass cheeks.

"Like I said, dove. I'm not going to touch you until we've cleared the air between us, and if I were to get into bed with you, I would have my hands all over your body." I flash a smile that has a blush covering her cheeks. "But make no mistake, Wynter. The moment we've talked, the moment the air is clear between us, we will never spend a night apart." I lean down until my face is only an inch above hers, so close her scent calls to me. "Get some sleep," I whisper and press a gentle kiss to her forehead.

As I turn to leave the room, I don't miss the way Wynter presses her eyes closed to ward off the tears that rise to the surface. She doesn't trust me. She doesn't believe I'll be here in the morning, but there's nowhere I would rather be than right here with her.

By the time I open the door and chance one more look over my shoulder, her eyes are closed, the sheet wrapped around her tight, and the smallest smile sits on her lips. There's nothing I wouldn't do for this woman, except leave. I'll never do that again.

DEAD OF WYNTER

Thirteen

Wynter

Every night since my parents died has been longer than the last. Some nights I lay awake, staring at the ceiling as I think about all the things that need to be done or all the ways we could take down Russo for what he's done to our family. Other nights I can't stop thinking about their last moments on earth and how scared they must have been as their car careened down a cliff. And then there are the nights I think about the years I still have to live without them. My wedding without my father to give me away, my children without their grandparents. Those are the nights I break and no matter how hard I try, the tears won't stop.

But not last night. Last night I slept soundly for ten straight hours. I didn't wake up with nightmares of Angelo Russo hurting my family, I didn't dream of my parents being torn from my life. Instead, I had a dreamless sleep thanks to the earth-shattering orgasm Everett gave me without ever touching me.

Even as I woke, his scent still lingered within the room, on the sheets, and even on my skin despite us never coming into contact with one another.

By the time I get through my morning routine and trudge down the stairs, the sun has been up for hours and voices carry from the kitchen. I'm usually the first out of bed in the morning, my dreams plaguing me until I can't stand it anymore, but it's nice to be the last one up for once.

"Good morning," I chime.

Snow looks up from where she's sitting at the table, a spoonful of cereal pausing at her lips. "What the fuck is wrong with you?"

Rayne scoffs. "Why don't you say what you really think, Snow?"

"I just mean she's usually grumpy in the morning. It was weird enough that we didn't find her half a coffee pot deep when the rest of us got up, but this is just plain wrong."

Emerson shakes her head from where she stands at the stove, frying what smells like bacon. "Don't listen to them, Wynter. I'm glad you slept in. You needed it after how emotional yesterday was."

"This is why she's my favorite sister." I wink at Snow before crossing to the coffee pot. I may have slept through the night, but I still need coffee to function, I'm not an animal.

Storm and Everett are missing, probably in the office strategizing. That's where they spend most of their time. Everett on his laptop tracking every Russo movement, and Storm on the phone trying to get a lead. It's not ideal, but it's working. The sooner we get a lead, the sooner we can get the fuck out of this house before one of us kills someone.

A knock at the door startles me even though realistically it shouldn't. No one gets past security without express permission, so I carefully place my coffee on the counter and head to the door, only barely sparing a thought for the sweatpants and sweater I threw on before coming downstairs. Security around here has seen all of us in worse, it's too late to start being modest now.

I swing the door open and find one of the front gate security guards on the doorstep holding a box. "Miss Saint James, this was just delivered for you." Carl extends his arms, the small, unmarked package crossing the threshold of the door.

"Oh, thank you for bringing it up. I could have come down to grab it during my run though." I smile and take the box from him.

Carl has worked for my family for as long as I can remember and is one of the nicest men I've ever known. If I had to hazard a guess, I would say he's in his late sixties, married with a bunch of grandbabies he dotes on. When I'm here, I often stop by the security booth just to catch up on all the family gossip.

"Mr. Saint James said he didn't want any of you ladies that close to the gate."

I sigh. "Of course he did. Well, thank you again. And please call me Wynter."

He cracks a smile. "Of course, Wynter." By the next time we speak, he will be calling me Miss Saint James again. It doesn't matter how many times I ask, he always reverts back to the formality that has always made me uncomfortable.

I close the door and lean against it for a moment, staring at the box in my arms. The fact it's unmarked apart from my name scrawled across the top is a little disconcerting.

"Who was at the door?" Everett's voice startles me.

I can't for the life of me work out why I'm so jumpy today, perhaps sleep is so foreign to my body that it's had the opposite effect on me to everyone else.

"Carl. Something was delivered for me," I tell him, unable to meet his eyes after what we shared last night.

Everett takes long strides until he's just a few feet away, but it's the box that he's focused on with his brow furrowed. "Give me the box," he says in a low voice.

"What? Why?"

"Just do as you're told for once, Wynter," he snaps.

I look down and understanding dawns on me. There could be anything in this thing. Literally anything. A bomb. A body part. Anthrax. I hold the box out to him carefully, my hands suddenly shaking with fear. We've always lived our lives with a certain level of danger, but I forget that it's amplified now we're at war.

Everett takes the box from me and takes off down the hallway toward the office Storm is using, and I can't help but trail after him. If someone has threatened me, I want to know about it. He places it down on the old mahogany desk in front of Storm.

"Why the fuck would your security bring an unmarked package to the front door while we're at war?" he roars. "It could be a fucking bomb and it could have blown up the second Wynter got her hands on it."

I flinch at the anger in his voice more so than his words. I've never seen him with such barely controlled rage.

Storm stares at the box for a few moments, as if deciding what may be in it. The likelihood of it being a bomb is very low. The war we're in with the Russos will be slow like a chess game and bombing your enemy in their home is the opposite of controlled.

"Wynter, get out," Everett growls, not even bothering to look up at where I'm standing in the doorway.

"Excuse me?"

"I said get out." The softness he showed last night is all but gone now, leaving behind the cold, hard man I've only ever heard about. He's never spoken to me like this, never been so abrupt with me, and I can't help but think maybe he's changed his mind, maybe last night was a mistake to him.

"No."

His deep blue eyes shoot up to meet mine, fire brewing in the pools. "Come again?"

"I said no. That box is addressed to me. I want to know what's in it."

Everett stalks across the room before placing both hands on my hips, pushing me until I'm backed against the wall in the hallway, his body pressing into me roughly. "I swear to God, Wynter, if you don't stay out of this room while we make sure this isn't going to kill you, I'm going to tie you to your fucking bed where nothing and no one can hurt you."

"Everett," I whisper, my voice wavering with a mixture of fear and arousal building deep within me.

"Don't argue with me about this. If there is one thing that I will not bend on, it's your safety. Now go anywhere in this house except for this room or I swear to God you won't like the consequences."

I drag my bottom lip between my teeth as I consider my options. Rationally I know I should just leave the room, but I'm just as involved as they are. I should at least know what's in the box. But he has a point. Whatever is in the box could be designed to hurt me, and if that were the case, shouldn't I run in the opposite direction?

"I want to know what's in the box."

The sound Everett makes can't even be described as human. It's deep and loud and rough, and it kind of terrifies the hell out of me. "Do. As. You're. Told."

I stare into his eyes for long moments, considering my options. "Fuck you."

I shove his hands away from my body and start down the hallway. As much as I want to know what's in the box, it's probably nothing I need to see after burying my parents yesterday.

Plus, I need to get the fuck out of this house before I go insane.

DEAD OF WYNTER

Fourteen

Everett

I slam the door to the office so hard the walls rattle from the force before taking long strides back to the desk. That woman is fucking infuriating. She was when she was a teenager, and I don't know why I'm surprised that she's even more so as an adult.

Doesn't she understand I'm just trying to keep her safe? Doesn't she get that we're at war and this very fucking suspicious box that was delivered with her name on it could very well be a trap? Dealing with her only reminds me why I stayed single all this time.

I should have moved on after I left. It would have been easier if I cut ties all together and moved on with my life rather than watching from afar, but I'm nothing if not a glutton for punishment. And I've never wanted anyone other than Wynter. I tried. I fucked so many women I lost count, and none of them ever matched up to my dove. They couldn't hold my interest, and even during sex, I found myself imagining the woman I love beneath me.

"So things are going well then?" Storm smirks.

I glare at him before doing the same to the box. "Shut up."

"You would never have been interested in her if she weren't the way she is, and she's always been like this. She's always thought she knows better. It comes with the territory, I guess. Growing up in the environment we did with two older brothers who were involved in the family business." He shrugs.

"I just got her back," I whisper. "I can't bear the idea of something happening to her, it makes me homicidal. When I saw her holding the box by the front door…" I trail off. God, the idea of what could have happened makes my heart beat so hard in my chest it hurts.

"I know. Believe me, man, I know. Every fucking day in the family is another day one of us could get taken out. The accident proves that." He shakes his head, staring at the leather chair his father used to sit in every night with a glass of scotch and read.

He always said it was his way of unwinding and letting the horrors of the day go. I didn't understand that until I was older, until after I took my first life.

I scrub both hands over my face. It's like there's a live wire under my skin burning me from the inside out. "What do you think is in this thing?" I ask.

"Honestly, I have no fucking clue. I'm guessing not a bomb. It would have blown up by now."

I nod. "I agree."

Storm picks up a letter opener from the desk and carefully

slides the blade through the tape until the flaps give way beneath it. We both take a breath as he opens the box with the end of the letter opener, careful not to touch it just in case it's laced in poison.

The things the box could contain are limitless. The family receives any number of threats per day, usually body parts or the like, but what I'm staring at laying in the middle of the box takes long moments for me to put the pieces together.

"What the fuck is that?" Storm asks.

"It's a dove," I whisper. This threat isn't for Wynter alone. No, this is for both of us, and it's not a stretch to assume it came from one of the Russos. If I had to guess, I would say Elijah, but it could have been any of them.

His eyes move from the dead bird in the bottom of the box to mine, and I know he's thinking the same thing I am. I chose to leave Wynter to keep her safe. My family is dangerous, they have no boundaries, and nothing is off limits to them, but we made a decision to allow me back in her life, and the moment I did, she was in danger again, maybe even more so than when I left.

"Don't even think about it," Storm says quickly.

"What?"

"Leaving. I see it in your eyes. You think she's safer if she's far away from you, and that may have been the case eight years ago, but not anymore. We're all in danger. Every person in this house has a target on their back, and if anything, Wynter is safer now because there is nothing you wouldn't do to protect her, including throw yourself in front of anything that could hurt her."

"They threatened her because of me," I say quietly. "This may be addressed to her, but it's a threat to me. If I stay with her, they're going to hurt her."

Storm groans. "They threatened her before you came back."

"They what?" I growl.

"When Angelo was trying to get to Emerson, he said that if he couldn't get to her, he was going after Wynter and Snow. It's why we went into lockdown."

"And you're only telling me this now?" I shout. I should have known he wouldn't put the whole family into lockdown unless more than one of us was in danger, but fuck, he should have told me.

"At the time, we thought it might be an empty threat because of where it came from."

"Those passports…"

He nods. "Yeah. I took a lot of what he said with a grain of salt, however, I'm never willing to gamble with my family's lives, and I knew if he took one of them in place of Emerson that she would be beside herself and hand herself over."

"Which would turn Rayne into a complete psycho."

Storm nods. "Exactly. And we get threats every fucking day. I can't count the number of death threats I get, so it wasn't worth worrying you over. I was hoping the day you pulled your head out of your ass and came back wouldn't be under such dire circumstances, but not even I could have planned for the accident." He sinks into the chair behind the desk and sighs. "Dad would know what to do if he were here. He'd be able to give us a rock to look under, but I feel like we're just going around and around in circles."

"Have you been sleeping?" I ask.

"No. Not since the accident." He sighs and looks back into the box at the dead dove. The symbol of my love for Wynter lays mutilated in the bottom, and neither of us can keep our eyes off it for long. "How would they know you call her dove? You've always called her that, but I don't feel like it's common knowledge. The two of you never even went public, so there's no way anyone could know."

I shake my head. "I don't know. I've only ever called her that in this house, and even when I've spoken to my uncles, I never speak about her with them. I never wanted them to know how much she meant to me." That was the worst part of having to leave her, because I had no idea how my family even knew I loved her.

"Do you think we have a rat?" Storm asks.

"I don't think we should rule it out." I shrug. We've always bred loyalty. The Saint James family treats their men with respect. They are paid in accordance with what they do, and traditionally we've never had an issue.

"Have a look into everyone that comes and goes in this house that isn't a member of this family. I want to know every person they've spoken to in the last six months right down to their mailman."

I nod. "I'll get on it now."

"And Everett?"

"Yeah?"

"Don't leave her again. She won't survive it."

Those words ring through my head as I leave the room in search of my laptop, because the reality is, neither will I.

FIFTEEN

WYNTER

The moment I'm out the front gates, I know this is a bad idea. Trying to convince security to let me leave at all was a task, but after agreeing to personal security they relented. I made up some bullshit about a friend of mine needing help, and when they called Storm to get his approval, I almost gave myself away with the sigh of relief I let out when he didn't pick up the phone.

But luckily Carl missed it and now I'm on my way into the city in the back of a bulletproof SUV. I have no idea what I'm going to do when I get there, or how long it will be before my brothers or Everett realize I'm gone and start blowing up my phone, but I also don't care. Being locked in that house without the right to leave, without the ability to walk to the goddamn front gate on my own is stifling, and any amount of time I can breathe is good enough for me.

Once we arrive at my apartment building I tell the driver I'm just running upstairs to get something for my friend. Another lie but why not add it to the rest?

"I should come with you, Miss Saint James. Your brother wants someone on you at all times," he tells me.

I nod. "I know, and I totally get it, but you're in a tow-away zone, if you get out of the car you might be towed." Another lie. The cops wouldn't dare take one of Storm's cars away, especially seeing as half of them work for us, but I'm taking advantage of the fact no one knows that. "I'll be really quick, and everyone thinks I'm still at the estate anyway." I flash him my most sincere smile.

He gives a short nod. "Okay, but if you're not back in five minutes, I'm coming in after you even if it means the car is towed."

"Of course." I smile before pushing the door open and walking as quickly and calmly as I can manage without alerting anyone to what I'm doing.

The moment I'm in the lobby I chance a look over my shoulder and breathe another sigh of relief when he's fiddling with the radio station rather than watching me. It's not until I reach the elevators that I look back again and when I find him still looking for a radio, I hit the down button. I'll have to go out through the garage, but at least I'll be able to get out without him noticing.

The moment I step into the elevator, I slouch against the wall. I'm being an idiot. What I'm doing is incredibly dangerous, especially seeing as I received what was very likely a threat to the house this morning, and every man in Russo's organization is looking for their next Saint James target.

Even knowing that, I don't go back. I hightail it out the back of the building and into a side street. At least I had the foresight to throw on some decent clothes and a bit of makeup before running away. Because that's what I did. I ran away like a petulant fucking child.

I lean against the wall of my building and drag in long, hasty breaths. What the fuck am I doing? I could get myself killed pulling a stunt like this.

I've never slipped my security before, that's Snow's thing. I've always stayed with them, I've always played by the rules of growing up in a crime family. What am I trying to gain by doing this other than potentially dying?

I shake my head at myself and pull my phone out to see if anyone has noticed I'm gone yet. Everett will probably be staying as far away as humanly possible after our altercation this morning. Storm and Rayne are too busy to know where any of us are, and Snow and Emerson will probably be doing their own thing. The only way I'm getting found out is when the driver comes looking for me and I'm not in my apartment.

I have no new messages and I realize part of me was hoping Everett may have messaged to apologize for the way he spoke to me.

With that, I head to the street adjacent to the one we parked on and hail the first cab I see. I might as well make the most of my freedom while it lasts.

Twenty minutes later, I'm paying my cab fare and walking into my favorite bar. It's the middle of the day so there aren't many people around which suits me just fine seeing as I'm not far from Russo territory.

Amber's has plenty of security though, and I'm as safe as I can be while being outside the estate without any of my own security. "Hey Chad." I grin as I take a seat at the bar. It's been too long since I've been here, and since I've had any time to myself. The time between our lockdowns was so short I only really had time to go to work and get a few things sorted there before we were at the estate planning funerals.

"Wynter! What are you doing here at this time of the day?" he asks. He's six foot five of muscle and the biggest teddy bear I've ever met. His hair is tied back in a neat ponytail and graying at the roots, and deep lines surround his green eyes. When I started coming here after college Chad was like a drink serving therapist. All the things that happened while I was away only seemed to add to my broken heart from Everett leaving.

"I need a drink. It's been a long few weeks." I half laugh. I wish I could tell him how true those words are, but I can't talk about family business with anyone, and maybe that's part of the problem.

"I was sorry to hear about your folks, kid." He frowns as he pours vodka into a glass followed by some lime and soda and pushes it across the counter. "Where's your security?"

I shrug, not wanting to tell him I slipped them just so I could have some privacy for a few hours.

"Those brothers of yours will kill me if something happens to you on my watch."

I huff out a laugh. "Nothing will happen to me here. This place is safe as houses."

"For most people, yes. For you, I'm not so sure."

I smile. "I'll be fine. Plus, I won't be here for too long. I just wanted to have a drink and sit for a bit."

"You can sit here as long as you want, kid. You know that." He smiles. "My son is around here somewhere, I'm sure he'd be happy to keep you company."

I laugh. Chad has been trying to set me up with his son from the first day I stepped into this place despite the fact he lives in Pittsburgh with a steady career I doubt he would leave to move to Chicago. "I'm glad he's visiting. I know you've missed him a lot recently." I take a long drink from my glass and let out a breath. I've never even met Jordan, and yet I shut down any possibility from the first time Chad mentioned him.

Classic Wynter.

"Hey Dad, where did you say you wanted the box of tequila?" a deep voice calls from the hallway behind the bar.

"Come out here for a minute, son."

A large figure appears in the doorway a moment later and I almost do a double take as my eyes roam the man's body. Jordan is tall just like his dad, the same piercing green eyes as the older man, and messy brown hair falls around his shoulders. Sharp, devastating cheek bones, and the most luscious beard I've ever seen in my life tops the solid wall of muscle standing in front of me.

Holy shit, Chad's son is a straight up hottie.

"I want you to meet someone." Chad grins, the familiar glint in his eyes. "This is Wynter Saint James." He motions to me.

Jordan's eyes drag over my body and a smile tugs at his lips. "Well how do you do, Wynter?" he drawls.

"It's nice to finally meet you, Jordan. Your dad is very proud of you."

I return his smile, because lord this man is something else. I've never been that interested in men that aren't the one who took my virginity. Every other man I've allowed to get close has only hurt me, and I've never felt strong enough to have my heart and body broken over and over again. But hey, you only live once and seeing as I have the world's biggest target on my back at the moment, might as well start living.

DEAD OF WYNTER

Sixteen
EVERETT

There's something almost soothing about pawing through the personal records of the people you think you can trust. I've looked under every single stone, pebble and everything in between and not one of the people that frequent the estate have a connection to anyone within the Russo organization. Which leaves us at square one.

How could they have known the nickname I call Wynter if someone hadn't told them?

I sigh and close the lid of the laptop, at least the task allowed me to calm down, and it would have given Wynter time to do the same. I stand from where I'm sitting on the lounge and head up the stairs in search for her, only to meet the eyes of a very panicked Storm as he rushes down the hallway.

"What's wrong?" I ask.

"Wynter's gone. She talked her way out of the estate and then slipped her security. I have no fucking idea where she is." I've never heard him sound so worried, even in the midst of chaos

Storm is calm, but at the idea of his sister being missing, he's panicking.

"What do you mean, she talked her way out?" I growl. "I explicitly told everyone working at the gate that she is not to leave this estate, or even go near the gate for that matter. Why the fuck would they let her out?"

"She told Carl I said it was okay, and then I missed a call from him while I was talking to Tommy." He drags his hands through his hair roughly. "Fuck," he shouts.

I'm back at my laptop a moment later, tapping into the trackers I have in her phone, handbag and every pair of shoes she owns. When I placed them there it was with the intention to only use them in moments such as these, but I'm guilty of checking them from time to time just to keep tabs on her.

"What are you doing?" Storm asks as he crosses the room to sit beside me.

"Tracking her."

"You put trackers on my sister?" He raises an eyebrow.

I nod. "Don't waste your breath, my foresight might save her life."

Storm shakes his head and huffs out a laugh. "If you were anyone else, I would kick your ass for stalking my sister."

I roll my eyes and focus on the map in front of me. "She's at Amber's."

"Is that one of her friends? I've never heard her talk about a Amber."

"No, it's a bar she goes to sometimes." I let out a breath. If she's there she's probably safe. I've been in there a few times to make sure it was safe for her, and the place has decent security and the owner seems to have taken a shine to Wynter from the first time they met.

"I'll grab my stuff and come with you." Storm stands and starts toward the stairs.

"It's fine. I'll go on my own." I barely stop myself from telling him he shouldn't come unless he wants to see me spank his sister so hard she won't sit for a week for pulling a stunt like this.

Storm laughs. "Lord help her."

Half an hour later, Steve is pulling up to the curb outside Amber's. This place has been around since the eighties and I understand why Wynter loves it so much. It's retro but in a classy way, the dark brick building fits seamlessly with the apartment buildings on this street, and the inside is warm and homely.

"I won't be long," I tell my driver. I didn't want to bring anyone along, but Storm insisted. It should only take a few moments to throw her over my shoulder and cart her back to the estate to tie her to the bed where she won't be able to escape again. I'm barely controlling the anger simmering under my skin. How could she be so fucking stupid. My entire family threatened her yesterday, at her parents' funeral who they murdered, and she thinks it's a great idea to gallivant around the city unprotected?

I push the doors open but the moment my eyes connect with Wynter I'm stopped in my tracks. She's sitting at a small table on the other side of the bar, her head thrown back laughing at something the guy she's with said. I've never seen her with him before, his thick beard and long hair don't ring any bells, but the way he reaches across the table to brush the hair out of her face makes me want to snap his arm in half. No one touches what belongs to me.

But instead I wait. I take a seat at the far end of the bar, order a drink and watch as my woman laughs and flirts with this nameless man. I haven't seen her smile like this since the night before I left.

She takes a sip of whatever she's drinking as the guy tells her a story animatedly, and when she laughs she almost spits her drink across the table. It's all I can do to drag my eyes away from Wynter and focus on the man who has captured her attention.

She hasn't shown much interest in men since I ran off the first few when she came home from college. It didn't take much, a few well-placed threats, and they were giving up the best thing to happen to them just the same as I did.

Nothing I've ever done was as contradictory as that. I couldn't have her so no one could. But the idea of another man with his hands on Wynter made me homicidal, and that was a mess I didn't want to bring down on the Saint James family.

The guy stands and quickly squeezes her shoulder as he disappears down the hallway behind the bar. It's my time to get her the fuck out of here. I throw a wad of cash on the bar to pay for our drinks and a tip for the scene I'm about to cause before crossing the bar and sitting in the seat the guy left vacant.

"Dove," I growl.

Wynter's eyes widen as she stares at me blankly. "How the fuck did you find me?"

"I put trackers on all your shit years ago," I tell her honestly. "Worked out pretty well for me today when your brother was losing his mind with fucking worry. How could you do this?" My words are harsh, but she needs to understand how angry we are. What she's done is stupid, irresponsible, and more than anything, selfish, and that's something I've never known Wynter to be.

Her face pales as she breaks eye contact in favor of staring at her drink. "I don't have to justify anything to you. And what the fuck do you mean you put trackers on me?"

"When I wasn't around to protect you, I needed to know you were safe." There's more to it than that, but she never needs to know how deep my obsession with her runs.

"You're insane."

"No, what's insane is you losing your security when we're in the middle of a war. You remember that Elijah threatened you yesterday, right? You haven't forgotten that the most psychotic person we've ever met might come after you?"

"What's your point?" She takes a long drink and I can't help but stare as she swallows. Fuck, even when I'm furious with her she's sexy as hell.

I sigh. "You have two options here, Wynter, and I suggest you think long and hard about which one you're going to take.

Option one, you walk your ass out of here and get in the car without any arguments, and I might not lock you in your room until the war is over. Or, option two and my personal favorite, you continue being a brat, I throw you over my shoulder, take you home and spank you so hard and for so long you can't sit for a week, before locking you up in an ivory tower where I know you're safe and nothing can hurt you." I shrug. "Your choice."

"You can't do that," she breathes, but there's something behind her eyes I can't place.

I place both hands on the table and stand until I'm towering over both the table and Wynter. "I most definitely can, Wynter, and after this stunt your brothers won't fight me on it."

Wynter leans back in her chair and stares at me for a few moments. "Fine." She sighs and finishes her drink before digging around in her purse.

"I've already paid," I tell her.

"Oh, I know. I'm leaving Jordan my number." She flashes me a smile as she scrawls something on a piece of paper.

Doesn't she know when you play with the devil you can expect to be burned?

I take a deep breath to stamp down the anger, even if it is only for a few seconds to get her out of here and then I throw her over my shoulder without a second thought and cart her toward the door, but only after I've picked the piece of paper up and shoved it in my pocket. There's no way another man is having my woman's number.

"Everett, put me down," Wynter squeals.

126

"No." I slap my hand down on her ass and she jolts immediately.

"Should I call your brothers, Wynter?" the bartender asks.

She sighs. "No, thank you Chad. Unfortunately, my brothers sent this asshole to collect me. Tell Jordan I really enjoyed speaking to him."

Before Chad can reply, we're out the door and I'm carefully placing her into the back of the car. I should have checked the street when I walked out, it's what I've been trained to do, but Wynter is distracting as hell. She makes everything else in my mind disappear until it's just her sitting in the center of my world.

"What the fuck? You said if I agreed I could walk myself out?" she hisses.

"That was before you tried to give another man your phone number." I move toward her until my face is only a breath from hers. "You. Are. Mine."

"No, I'm not." Wynter crosses her arms across her chest in a defensive gesture.

"Yes, you are, dove. You were mine the first time we met, and mine every day that we were best friends, and every time I stole a kiss, or you allowed me to touch you, you became a little more mine. But it was when you trusted me with your heart and your body that you should have known you would never belong to anyone else again, Wynter."

"You left me." Her voice wavers as her eyes turn glassy with tears. "You lost the right to be my anything when you left. And you can claim I've always been yours all you want, but that doesn't make it true, Everett."

"Oh, but it does, little dove. Now be a good girl and behave on the way home and maybe I'll go easy on you for your punishment." I smirk. That's not happening, but if it will make her sit still, it's worth the little white lie.

Dead of Wynter

SEVENTEEN

WYNTER

"Punishment?" I whisper as the blood rushes from my head. It's been a long time since I've heard that word directed at me, and fear rises through my body until it chokes me, reminding me of all the reasons I never let men get close to me.

"Yes, little dove. You were beyond careless today. Anything could have happened to you, and you need to be punished accordingly."

The familiar feeling of panic grasps my lungs until I can barely drag a breath in. I never wanted anyone to know about this part of my life, about the part of me they didn't know was broken, but with each second that passes I realize Everett is about to find out my dirty little secret and he'll never look at me the same way again.

"Wynter?" Everett's worried eyes focus on my face and I almost can't take it. Because I've been so mad at him for not telling me why he left, but I've been holding just as much back as he has. "Hey." He grasps my chin between his thumb and forefinger and forces my eyes up to meet his. "I'll never give you more than you can handle. You have to know I wouldn't really hurt you."

I try to shake my head to break our eye contact, but he won't allow it. I should know better than to even try, but I'll never learn. "Let me go," I whisper.

"Never."

That single word holds so much meaning and the power behind it is almost enough to tear me out of my panic. Almost.

"I keep telling you, Wynter. You're mine. Every single part of you belongs to me, just like every single part of me has always, and will always belong to you." His fingertips trail across my cheek, soothing my racing heart just enough for me to drag a breath into my lungs.

He watches me closely, his eyes surveying every move I make as he continues his gentle strokes of my cheek until I'm leaning into him. After all this time he still has the ability to read me like a book. He knows what I'm feeling almost as well as I do, and most of the time he knows what I'll do long before I even decide to do it.

It's only when the car comes to a stop at the front gates of the estate that he finally tears his eyes away from mine and I feel the loss immediately. He's holding me together as my body longs to fall apart.

"We're home," he says quietly.

The car pulls up the long driveway and stops outside the stairs leading to the front door. Before I can say a word, before I can move a muscle, Everett bundles me up in his arms and carries me through the house, not stopping to acknowledge any of my family and their questioning gazes. Storm looks partially amused as we pass him on the stairs, but behind the wall he builds to protect himself, he was scared. When I disappeared and he didn't know where I was, my big brother showed something he doesn't very often.

Fear.

The moment we reach my bedroom I know I'm in trouble. The soft, caring Everett from the car is gone, and he's replaced by a man I should be terrified of.

He places me in the middle of the room and stares down at me, his gaze burning into my skin. "Why did you run?" he asks.

I close my eyes for a moment and take a deep breath, relief flooding me that he doesn't ask why I panicked when he mentioned punishment. "I needed some space. I can't be locked in this estate all the time, and being close to you when you're hot and cold…" I shake my head. "I'm always waiting for you to leave again."

"Have you listened to anything I've said since I came back? What part of 'I'm not going anywhere' did you not understand?" he growls.

"The part where you've said that before," I snap. "You promised you would always be with me, you promised we would see the world together. And none of that meant shit to you when you left me without a word."

"I had to! I didn't leave because I wanted to, Wynter. I've

spent eight years watching you from afar, seeing you live your life, watching you thrive without me, and it's been the cruelest form of torture I can imagine."

"Then tell me why you left."

He takes a deep breath as if considering what the next words out of his mouth are going to be. "Not yet."

I scoff. "Of course. Okay, if you can't tell me that, what was in the box?"

"Nothing you need to worry about." He tears his eyes away from me and my stomach drops. This is what the rest of our lives will be like if I allow myself to fall at his feet. Him giving me half-truths and keeping secrets, and I deserve more than that.

I turn around and head toward the bathroom just to get away from him. I'm not stupid enough to think he'll allow me to step foot out of this room, but at least I can try to get myself together in the meantime.

"Where are you going?"

"Away from you. You keep telling me how things are going to be, you keep telling me that I'm yours, but if that were true you would tell me what the fuck is going on. I am just as much a part of this as you and my brothers. I'm the one that made the threat, so of course I expected retaliation, but you won't even do me the fucking courtesy of telling me what the fuck was in the box that was addressed to me," I yell. The fury I've held back since the night he walked back into my life with no explanation bursts out of me all at once until red hot tears roll down my cheeks. "And if you don't respect me enough to tell me what's going on, I'm going to respect myself enough to walk away before you break my heart again."

Strong hands grasp my hips from behind and spin me so quickly I almost lose my footing, but a moment later my back hits the bed and the air leaves my lungs. Everett pins me down with his body, the gentleness he showed last night in this position at complete odds with how he's handling me now. "You will not walk away from me, Wynter."

"But it's okay for you to walk away from me? Got it," I snap.

A deep rumble escapes from his throat as he stares down at me. Being pinned down by anyone else would have a sense of dread and terror rolling over me, but not Everett. Even as my mind and heart fight him with everything we've got, my body succumbs, knowing it's safe in his hands. "Have you listened to a word I've said since I walked back into this house, Wynter? Or are you only hearing what you want to hear?"

I glare at him but make no attempt to free myself from where he's trapped me beneath his body.

"I will tell you everything you need to know, but not right now. And as for the box, it doesn't matter what was inside, all that matters is that you're safe, and that's how you're going to stay, because if you ever pull a stunt like the one you did today, I will not hesitate to lock you up and throw away the goddamn key."

"Even if it makes me hate you?" I ask quietly.

"I'd rather you hate me while you're alive than love me while you're dead."

His profound words leave me without a rebuttal, something

that doesn't happen very often. I've been in meetings with some of the most powerful people in the world looking down on me, and I've always had a response for them, but not Everett. He renders me speechless more than I'll ever admit to anyone.

"Now, here's what's going to happen, and I promise you will not like the consequences if you fight me on this." He gives me a pointed stare. "You are going to strip for me, without complaint or argument, and then you are going to bend your pretty ass over the bed and accept your punishment like a good girl."

I stare up at him through wide eyes, but I can't find my voice to say no. I should. There are a million reasons I shouldn't allow him to do this to me, and the scars he'll find are only the beginning of them, but for some reason I can't help but nod. Something in his eyes tells me he needs this, and maybe I do too.

Dead of Wynter

EIGHTEEN
EVERETT

E ven as I watch Wynter strip for me, I know there's a reason she turned white as a ghost the first time I mentioned her punishment. Her hands are shaking, her entire body trembling as she pulls the knit sweater dress from her body, followed closely by the knee-high boots and stockings until she's in nothing but a black lace bra and matching panties that barely cover her pussy.

Her eyes meet mine and the fear behind the ice blue makes my stomach lurch. She's scared of me.

"Come here." I motion toward the edge of the bed where I'm perched and she comes to me immediately, not hesitating for even a second. The moment she's within arm's length, I tug her until she's perched on my lap. "You're afraid."

Wynter lets out a shaky breath before nodding once, her eyes looking anywhere but me.

"I would never do anything that would really hurt you, dove. I just want to make sure you think twice the next time you think about running away from your security in the middle of a war." I wrap my arms around her waist and hold her close to me. The way her body shivers under my touch worries me. Is there something she isn't telling me? "If this is too much for you and you can't handle it, I want you to tell me straight away, okay? It's meant to hurt but not so much so you can't stand it."

"I know," she whispers.

"What do you mean, you know?" I gently pull her face around to meet mine.

"This isn't my first punishment."

I stare at her for long moments as I try to wrap my head around those words. How can that be the case? I've tracked her for every moment of every day for the last eight years, there is no way she had someone punishing her and I didn't know about it. But the way her lip wobbles under my gaze, tells me she's telling the truth. "What aren't you telling me, Wynter?"

"You'll see." Her eyes drop from mine as she tries to climb from my lap, but I tighten my hold on her. "Everett, just let me show you," she whispers, her voice breaking under the weight of the words.

I hold on to her for another moment before finally allowing her to climb off my lap. For some reason the moment feels charged and as she slips her panties down her legs and reaches back to unclip her bra, I can't help but stare at her perfect body.

It's not until she bends over the edge of the bed that I see what she was talking about. White and silver lines cover the soft skin of her ass and the top of her thighs, unmistakable marks that must have been made with a belt. The air leaves my lungs as my legs shake beneath me so violently I almost lose them from beneath me.

"Wynter..." I can't find the words to ask the question I need to ask. I scramble to put the pieces together, to understand how this could have happened if I never had my eyes off her, but I come up short every time.

Her body shakes as a gentle sob racks through it. Her quiet cries mingle with the sound of my racing heart. I reach out to brush my fingers over the scars smattered across her backside but she flinches under my touch, something that's never happened before.

"You've been punished before," I say. It's not a question, more so repeating the words she spoke not too long ago.

"Yes." Wynter chokes on the word and I almost pull her back into my arms. Almost.

"When did this happen?"

"When I was at college."

"What were you being punished for?" I should be asking who did this, but the chances of her telling me seem so slim that I decide to make it one of the last questions I'm going to ask.

Wynter barely manages to keep her feet beneath her as another violent sob threatens to pull her over. "Does it matter?"

I take a deep breath to push down the thunder raging through my veins and move back to where I was perched on the edge of the bed before, quickly bundling Wynter in my arms until she's cradled against my chest. The anger trying to break through the surface is only magnified by how upset she is.

"Of course it matters, dove. Someone hurt you and I want to know why." I brush my fingers down her back gently, hoping it will soothe the onslaught of tears streaming down her cheeks.

"Stop," she whispers, pressing her hands into my chest in an attempt to get away. "Now you can see I'm used up goods, just let me go."

It's long moments before I process her words enough to understand the meaning behind them. Used up goods. Wynter is a lot of things, but she'll never be that. She could have fucked every guy in Chicago in the last eight years but she'd always be mine. "You are not used goods, Wynter. Why the fuck would you say that?" I growl. Barely controlled violent rage simmers under the surface, but I channel it all into making sure she's okay.

"Because that's what he said," Wynter sobs, burying her face into my chest as hot tears roll down her cheeks.

Seeing her cry has always been the hardest thing for me. When she was a teenager and broke her ankle right before a big ballet recital, I held her for hours as she sobbed, and every single moment was pure torture for me. A man like me doesn't usually have a heart, not one that hurts for other people, but mine beats for Wynter, it always has, and it always will.

I take a deep breath to steady my racing heart. "Who said that to you, Wynter?"

She shakes her head against my chest, but she doesn't respond and I don't know how to make her tell me what happened.

Because I need to know, there's no chance I'm letting her out of this room without some answers, and even then the chances are getting dicier by the second. This is the only place I can keep her safe, and if it's the difference between her being safe and hating me, or free and dying, I'm going to take the former every single time.

"Do your siblings know about this?" I ask once her choked sobs ease.

"Storm knows. He dealt with it," she whispers.

A fresh wave of anger rolls over me like a wave in the ocean. Why the fuck didn't he tell me? We had a deal when I left that I was to know anything and everything that happened in Wynter's life and being beaten by what I can only assume was a belt seems like something I should have fucking known about.

"I asked him not to tell you. It wasn't long after you left and I went to college, and I didn't think you would care, but in case you did and came back just to leave again... I couldn't handle it. So I asked him not to tell anyone, including Rayne and Snow."

The explanation does little to calm the vibrant red in my vision. It does nothing to help ease the tension so tight I'm almost certain my entire body is going to snap, and it doesn't even begin to remove my own self-loathing. She was hurt because I wasn't there. If I never left, she wouldn't have been in that position, because I never would have let that happen.

"Don't be angry at him. It was my own stupidity, and it's dealt with already."

Before I can think better of it, I'm flipping her onto her back and leaning over her, my fingers grasping her chin so she's forced to look at me. "Of course I'm angry, dove. I'm fucking livid that someone hurt you and I wasn't the one to kill them. I'm furious that my best friend didn't tell me someone hurt *my* woman. And I'm fucking devastated that someone else has marked you and therefore you think you're used goods." I force the words through gritted teeth, barely controlling my need to cover her body with my own marks.

Wynter's mouth drops open and I can't help but focus on her luscious lips quivering under my gaze. She looks perfect when she's underneath me, exactly where she belongs. "I wasn't yours then," she whispers.

"You have *always* been mine, Wynter. And you always will be." I rest my forehead on hers for a moment, taking the time to breathe her in. The intoxicating mixture of vanilla and sin fills my nose, and it takes all I have not to take her right here and now. But there are secrets we're both holding close to our chests, and until they're out in the open, I'll have to keep my hands to myself.

DEAD OF WYNTER

NINETEEN

WYNTER

S hame creeps up and grasps my throat like a vise. I never wanted anyone to see the marks he left, never wanted anyone to know about the part of my past I desperately wanted to keep hidden. That's the thing about living in the public eye, there are one of two ways things can go. One, you have all the power and influence at your disposal and can bury it when things like this happen. Or two, the press get ahold of it and your life implodes on itself.

Thankfully Storm took care of it long before anyone else could get wind of what happened, and then we never spoke of it again. I've never felt as ashamed as I did when I called Storm to help me, begging him through tears not to tell anyone what happened. The anger and disappointment in his eyes still haunts me.

The way Everett looks down at me isn't too far removed from that. He looks angry, angrier than I can ever remember seeing him. His jaw is tight, and the fire in his gaze burns into my bare flesh. I didn't think it through when I stripped completely, because now I'm vulnerable for more than one reason. His words hang between us long after he says them, their meaning not lost on me.

"That's not true," I finally say.

"Why? Because I left? Or because you slept with someone else and they hurt you? Or for some other reason you're concocting in that pretty little head of yours?"

Not for the first time since he carried me into the room, my mouth drops open. The things this man says sometimes astound me. "I never slept with anyone else," I admit quietly.

His eyes widen and a look of relief washes through the flames. "You didn't?"

I shake my head. "No, that's why..." I barely stop myself from telling him that's why Craig hurt me.

Everett closes his eyes and takes long, deep breaths. He's trying not to frighten me, trying to calm himself down enough that he won't accidentally hurt me while I'm vulnerable, but that's one thing he doesn't know about me. He doesn't know that I like the pain, I thrive off it. It's been a long time since I've allowed myself to want it though. After Craig I couldn't trust anyone to deliver what I needed without taking it too far. But the need for the burn always simmers just beneath the surface.

"That's why what, Wynter?" he asks quietly, the tension throughout his whole body vibrates through us both as he barely contains the anger.

"That's why he punished me." I wince at my own words. All getting into this story is going to achieve is Everett never letting me leave the damn house again, but I have a feeling he's not going to allow me to continue brushing him off.

He carefully places me down beside him and pushes up from the bed. He immediately starts pacing backward and forward across the room with his fingers tugging at the ends of his hair. The agony written across his features breaks my heart, and for the first time since he walked back into my life, I believe every word he's said. If Everett didn't care about me, and he left without caring what it did to me, he wouldn't look like he's about to drop to his knees in pain. The anger radiating from his every pore wouldn't be as pronounced if he didn't mean when he said I'm his and always have been.

Everett loves me. He's always loved me. And he didn't leave because I wasn't enough. Those are the thoughts running through my mind as I climb off the bed and take careful steps toward him, approaching him like I would a wild animal. Because that's what he is when he gets angry.

"Everett," I say gently, reaching to brush my fingers down his arm. With anyone else I would be ashamed of my body, ashamed of standing here naked, but with Everett I feel safe.

"Sit back down, Wynter," he growls, but I don't move a muscle. He needs me, and after all the times he's held me together when I was falling apart, it's my turn to do the same. "I need you to sit down because I'm fucking terrified I'm going to hurt you when I'm this angry."

"You won't," I say quietly as I take another step toward him, blocking his path when he moves to start pacing again.

"This is my fault." He squeezes his eyes shut. "I was meant to protect you. I thought I had."

"This is not your fault. It happened a long time ago when I was in a bad place, but you are not to blame."

"You wouldn't have been in a bad place if I didn't leave."

"That may be true, but we don't know that. We don't know that when I went off to college that the same thing wouldn't have happened."

"It wouldn't have happened because I could have protected you better," he roars.

"Protected me from my own security?" I raise my brows. The words slip through my lips so easily you wouldn't think I was hitting him was a bombshell, but I am. Telling him who left me broken and scarred seemed pointless only a few minutes ago, but the moment he started blaming himself was the moment I knew I needed to tell him the truth.

His eyes snap up to meet mine and the fire is back, except now it's burning hotter than I've ever seen it. "Your what?"

TWENTY
EVERETT

Surely I heard her wrong. That's the only thing that makes sense.

Because the idea that her security, the person Storm hired to take care of her while she was away from home, the person I personally interviewed before I left to make sure she would be safe in my absence, abused her to the point she's scarred.

Wynter takes a deep breath and lets it out slowly. The sight of her standing in the middle of the room naked is almost enough to settle my racing heart. Almost.

"Craig, my primary personal security while I was in Boston, took a liking to me."

She pulls her bottom lip between her teeth as she considers how to tell this story without me losing it, but there's no chance I'm not going to flip my lid when it comes to someone putting their hands on my woman. "After you left, I discovered the only way to stop the emotional pain I was in was to feel physical pain. It started small at first. Just snapping a hair band on my wrist was enough to pull me out of the dark place I found myself in. Then it escalated to a rubber band on the leg. I didn't think of it as self-harm, it was just a way I dealt with the pain in my heart.

"A friend of mine noticed and mentioned there was a club that might help me channel the pain in a more productive way."

"A BDSM club?" I ask carefully.

The girl I knew wouldn't have even known what BDSM stood for, but the woman staring back at me with apprehension in her eyes isn't the same person I fell in love with, and maybe that's a good thing. I'm not the same boy she remembers, the years I spent away from her hardened me, and maybe it's a good thing she's not the fragile version of herself she once was.

Wynter nods. "Yes. And it was good for a while. On my forms, I stated that I didn't want anything inherently sexual, because I wasn't ready to…" She lets out a heavy breath. "I wasn't ready for any other memories to compete with our first time. I wasn't ready to let go of it, and I thought if I slept with someone else, if I allowed them to touch me like that, that maybe it would taint our time together somehow." She pauses and shakes her head as if frustrated with herself. "The first few times I went, I managed to slip Craig so he wouldn't know where I was going and what I was doing and so he wouldn't tell Storm."

"So if you didn't go to the club to fuck, what did you go for?" I know the answer to the question even before I ask it, but I need to hear her say the words. I was always gentle with my dove, but that never came naturally to me. And the mere idea that she knows about the things I crave is almost enough to calm the thundering anger pulsing through me.

Wynter sighs. "This is so embarrassing," she mumbles. "It started off as spankings. The endorphins seemed to help distract me from my heartbreak and being able to slip into that happy place." She smiles sadly. "It was the only time I felt alive. After the first few times I went, one of the guys there encouraged me to try a few of the other things. The flogger, paddle, even the whip, and it was... I don't know how to explain it."

"Freeing?" I offer.

She nods. "It felt like coming home."

I reach for her for the first time since I climbed from the bed, pulling her toward the sofa under the window. I bundle her up in my lap and immediately I'm more calm. Just having her in my arms settles the beast fighting to break free. I have a feeling I'm going to need something to ground me through the end of this story, and she's the only thing that can. "Go on," I tell her quietly.

Wynter closes her eyes and leans into me, and I can tell she's struggling to find the words. "One night I didn't do as good a job as usual when losing Craig, and he followed me. When I got back to my dorm room he was there, and he started telling me I was a whore, and that I needed to be cleansed by God. He said that I was living in sin by going to that club, and that he needed to be the one to absolve me of those sins." She winces.

"I didn't know Craig was religious," I say as softly as I can manage. I ran the background check on him myself, and I remember everything about the people I assigned to her care. That definitely didn't come up.

She shrugs. "He started quoting Bible verses to me, and when I tried to run… he grabbed me and told me the only way to repent would be to lay with a man who was one with God." She blanches as the words leave her lips. "And when I said no and told him Storm and Rayne would kill him for even suggesting that, he laughed."

The question is on the tip of my tongue. She said she hadn't slept with anyone since we were together, but what she's getting at wouldn't be the same thing. What she told me before wouldn't be a lie. "Did he…" I can't get the words out. I can't ask the woman I've loved since before I knew what love was if the man I hired to protect her violated her.

Wynter shakes her head against my chest and lets out a shaky breath. "No, thank god. But he told me I needed to be punished under the eyes of God, that if I wouldn't lie with a godly man, then I would need to be punished by one. It all happened so quickly I didn't even have the chance to fight him off. One minute I'm walking into my dorm, and the next he had me tied down."

I tighten my arms around her, reminding my little dove she's safe, and reminding myself that nothing is ever going to happen to her again because I will never be far away. I thought I was protecting her all those years I spent away, but I should have realized there was nowhere safer for my girl than by side.

"I've never been so scared in my life, Ev. I've never felt more vulnerable or exposed."

She buries her face into my shirt, trying to find the strength to get through whatever is left of the story I'm not sure I'm strong enough to hear.

"I had had a particularly intense scene with someone at the club, and my ass was already on fire when he pulled my dress up. Normally I liked feeling it for a couple of days because I could lean a certain way and the pain would pull me from the dark places in my mind. But then he started calling me a whore, telling me I needed to repent for laying with a sinful man like those at the club. I tried to tell him it wasn't about sex but he'd made his mind up. And then he told me if I liked pain so much, he would deliver God's will with his belt."

An involuntary shudder rolls through her body.

"It was like nothing I'd done at the club. It was excruciating from the first strike, and every one of them after was harder than the last. I thought I was going to pass out from the pain, but I knew I had to stay awake, I couldn't leave myself even more vulnerable by losing consciousness because he could have done anything to me then."

Anger vibrates through every fiber of my being, and even holding Wynter isn't enough to calm the overwhelming fury. I should put her down so I don't inadvertently hurt her, don't hold her too tightly and mark her beautiful skin more than it's already been marked. But I can't bring myself to let her out of my arms. I need her close, I need to know she's okay.

"You don't have to keep going if you don't want to."

Part of me hopes she'll take the out I'm giving her, because I don't know how much more of this story I can handle, but she shakes her head once and takes a deep breath before continuing.

"It went on for so long I didn't understand how his arm wasn't sore. I could feel my own blood running down the backs of my legs, and I was questioning whether I wanted to survive or not. But then, by some miracle, my roommate walked in and heard me begging for him to stop, heard me sobbing and Craig sprouting bullshit scripture to make what he was doing to me okay. She knocked him out with a lamp and tied him up with the belt he used to beat me. She tried to help me but everything I did hurt. I couldn't stand, or sit, or lay. I couldn't get the cuts wet even though I knew they needed to be cleaned. I thought I liked pain until that day, and now the idea of a punishment brings me to the edge of a panic attack." Tears roll down her cheeks in hot streams as she tries to talk through her sobs. "I called Storm and told him what happened. I left out the part about the club and he flew out straight away and took care of Craig. My roommate was the one to deal with him, because I couldn't get dressed and it took hours for the doctor he called to clean the wounds.

"Storm hung around for a few days, sleeping on our couch and making sure everything was in order with the school seeing as I couldn't attend classes, and when I was finally ready to talk to him once I could put clothes on, I begged him never to tell you what happened. I didn't want you to come back because you felt obligated to, or because you had some bullshit sense of guilt. He didn't like lying to you, I could tell, but I thought it was for the best at the time. I was in such a bad place that I think if you came back just to leave again, I probably wouldn't have survived."

TWENTY-ONE

WYNTER

I hoped I would never have to tell that story again, that whoever I ended up with after all was said and done either wouldn't notice or wouldn't ask any questions. But that never would have been the case for Everett. The moment he walked back into my life I should have started preparing for the eventuality that I would have to tell him about the darkest day of my life.

Does that make it any easier now? Nope.

He holds me so tightly, and for so long, telling me silently that nothing will ever hurt me again, that he'll make sure of it.

His fingers brush along my bare back gently and it's the only thing keeping me together. The warmth gives me something to focus on other than the memories threatening to tear me apart. It's been a long time since I allowed myself to think about that night, and even though at times I've craved the pain, I've always tamped it down because I could never allow myself to be that vulnerable.

Except, when Everett talked about punishing me when we walked into the room, the fear didn't seem so bad, and if I'm really honest with myself, it was mixed with something else, something I haven't felt in a long time.

Longing.

Need.

Arousal.

It's been such a long time since I felt whole, since I had all the pieces of myself that make me, me, but maybe I can have it all now. Maybe I can have Everett, and I can have the pain, I can find that little place where everything around me is quiet and calm, but this time with a man who cares about me.

I didn't miss the way his eyes flared when I mentioned enjoying the pain punishment gave. He liked the idea, maybe even as much as I did.

"I should have been here," he says quietly. The room was so silent for so long the words almost startle me, but it's the pain behind them that breaks my heart. It's the reason I never wanted him to know. I thought if I could save at least one of us from the horrors of that night, maybe it would be enough.

I shake my head as I angle to look up at him. "Don't do that."

"Don't do what, Wynter? I left and you were hurt. And worse than that, I wasn't the one that killed the piece of shit," he growls.

I push against his chest and stumble across the room to the bed. My legs are still shaky beneath me, but I need to put some distance between us. The closer we are, the harder it is to think.

"Stop it. It doesn't matter now. It's in the past. And even if you never left, I still would have gone to Boston, and you wouldn't have. You would have stayed here. So I still would have had security, probably Craig, and I still would have got hurt."

"If I was here, you wouldn't have gone to that club in the first place."

He follows me across the room, his body vibrating with barely contained rage. Every muscle in his body is so tense I wonder idly whether it's possible for them to snap under such immense pressure. Everett doesn't stop until he's towering over me, his chest rising and falling so quickly his breath is coming out in rough pants.

"Do you know why, dove?"

I shake my head, trying to stand my ground. My own heart races, the heavy beats enough to make it hard to take a breath.

"Because I would have given you every fucking thing you needed."

"He still would have had the same opinion," I whisper. "I always would have discovered I liked aspects of BDSM, and while you may have given me what I needed, that still would have left Craig with the opinion I was a jezebel who needed to repent for my sins. I still would have been in a different city than you, I still would have had Craig as a guard. Everything still would have played out exactly the same way." I try to reason with him, but from the looks he's giving me it's not working.

163

"That's where you're wrong. Some of that may be true, but if I didn't leave, I would have been the one that killed him, and I would have dragged it out for days, making sure he felt every bit as helpless and terrified as he made you feel, and you wouldn't have been going through it alone. You wouldn't have been dealing with the pain I caused when I left on top of the trauma of what he did to you."

"You're impossible," I groan, finally tearing my eyes from his. I don't know how to make him see that it wasn't his fault.

Everett chuckles long and deep. "Dove, we both know I'm not the impossible one."

I glare at him for a moment before reaching for my robe laying across the bottom of the bed. I can't have this argument while stark naked, it gives him an unfair advantage.

"Don't you dare," he snaps and I hate the way my hand stops in its place. "I did not give you permission to get dressed."

"Last time I checked, I didn't need your permission to put clothes on."

"Well, now you do. After the bullshit you pulled today, you need my permission for just about everything."

"My brothers aren't going to allow you to keep me locked up and naked in here until the danger is gone," I hiss.

"I think you'd be surprised at what your brothers would allow me to do, little dove." He smirks.

"What the fuck does that mean?"

He shakes his head. "Maybe someday I'll tell you."

"How about today?"

"No. Today we're going to talk some more."

"While I'm naked?" I ask.

"Yep." He sits on the edge of the bed and pats his knee, but I don't move from where I'm standing, my arms crossed against my chest. "Don't you think you're in enough trouble?" He raises an eyebrow.

I huff out a frustrated breath before moving to perch on his lap. It's one thing to use him as a seat when I'm upset, it's an entirely different story to do so just because he says so.

"See, you do know how to be a good girl." He brushes the hair from my cheeks, his fingers lingering for a few moments before moving to draw gentle circles into my thigh, and the other wraps around my waist to hold me in place. "I want to ask you a few questions, and I want you to tell me the truth, okay?"

I nod hesitantly, there are so many things he could ask that I wouldn't want to answer, but at this point, I think I'm out of options.

"Did you ever go back to the club after Craig hurt you?"

"Yes," I answer quietly.

"Did you scene while you were there?"

I shake my head. "No."

"Tell me what happened."

I stare at him for a moment, trying to decide if I think I can get out of it or not, but by the way he's looking at me, I suspect he'll get the answers he wants regardless of how much I argue. "A few months after the incident, I was sick of being afraid of my own shadow, I was in a darker place than I had ever been before, and I wanted to take control of my own life. I thought I would be able to walk into the club and scene with one of the Doms I used to scene with and it wouldn't be an issue."

I don't miss the way Everett tenses at the mention of another man touching me, and he isn't going to like the rest of what I have to say any better.

"When I arrived I spoke to the Dungeon Master on duty and went over what had happened to me and he understood why I was there, so he found one of the softer Doms who I had scened with when I first started going. We sat down and had a drink and again, I rehashed everything I had been through in painful detail, each time the story only made me feel more sick to my stomach. He was happy to give it a go, just a gentle spanking to see if I could handle it."

"And could you?" Everett asks through gritted teeth.

I shake my head. "No. The moment I was bent over his lap and he was rubbing my ass I freaked out. I was absolutely beside myself, couldn't breathe through the panic, and the owner got so worried he called an ambulance." I laugh despite there being nothing funny about the most mortifying night of my life.

"Do you miss it?"

"The club? I mean, I guess. It was one of the only places I've ever been where I could just be myself. I didn't have to be a Saint James, or a businesswoman. I could just be me." I shrug.

"No, do you miss the spankings? Do you miss being punished?"

"I guess so." I shrug. "I haven't allowed myself to want it in such a long time that I barely remember how it feels. I miss the quiet though, the peace I felt when I reached that place. Especially now there's so much going on all the time, I have so much responsibility. It would be nice to just... be for a while."

It's a pipe dream, something I know can never happen again, not without being sent to the hospital with another panic attack.

"Let's try."

TWENTY-TWO
EVERETT

She didn't expect those words to come out of my mouth. And hell, I didn't really expect them either, but the fact she even knows what a flogger is, let alone liking one being used on her, has my cock so fucking hard against the zipper of my jeans it's painful.

I won't be able to tie her down and punish her right this second, but it's something she could build up to again. If that's what she wants. I won't force it on her, not after what Craig did, but it could help her. It would make her feel whole for the first time since that night.

The look of concern across her features is cute, the way her brows pull together and her nose crinkles slightly as if she thinks the words are the single most insane thing she's ever heard, and hey, they may be. I may have read the story wrong, but the way she spoke about the club and BDSM was like she was talking about an old friend she hasn't seen in years.

I bring my hand up to brush my thumb across her cheek in a

reassuring gesture. She knows I won't hurt her, if she didn't she would have flung herself halfway across the room the moment I suggested it, but she's curious.

"We won't do anything you're not ready for, dove. But you miss it."

Wynter nods slowly, as if she's afraid of her own answer. "I do."

"So let's try." I shrug.

She sighs and tries to push off my lap again. She keeps doing that when the conversation veers in a direction that makes her uncomfortable, but I'm not having any distance between us ever again. If this is something she needs, it's going to happen.

"Everett, I need some space," she says quietly.

"Too bad. No more space. No more secrets. No more distance."

"So you're going to tell me why you left then?" She quirks her brow in the most adorable sign of defiance.

I chuckle and shake my head slowly. "Nice try. But I will tell you everything you need to know once I'm sure you're coping with the loss of your parents. I don't want to be the reason you shut down." The truths I have to tell her are ugly and she's going to hate hearing them, she'll probably even disagree with the reason I left, but there's no going back now. I did what I did, and we both have to learn to live with that.

Wynter rolls her eyes. "Well I guess there are still some secrets then, huh?"

"Did you just roll your eyes at me, little dove?" I growl.

The corners of her lips pull up into a devious smile as she shrugs. "Maybe."

"See, dove." I lean in until my lips brush against the shell of her ear and an involuntary shiver runs through her entire body. "You're begging for a punishment," I whisper.

"No, I'm not."

I chuckle right before I sink my teeth into the sensitive flesh beneath her ear and relish in the little gasp of mingled pleasure and pain that tears from her throat. "Liar." I run my tongue along the ridges of the bite mark I've left in her skin before moving just below it and biting into her again. "See, you know what I think, little dove? I think you *love* the idea of me bending you over and punishing you for running away today. I think your head is telling you to say no, but your body is begging you to give in because you *crave* it."

"No," she breathes, the word barely audible to either of us over our racing hearts.

"All these lies are only going to add to your punishment, dove."

"I can't." She shakes her head as she moves her icy blue eyes to meet mine.

There's fear behind the pools I fell in love with, but it's mingled with a myriad of other emotions. Excitement. Nervousness. Arousal. They're all there swirling around relentlessly, overwhelming her. This is why she needs this. She needs for it all to go quiet for a while. She needs someone to take the decisions out of her hands, just for a little while so her mind can rest.

"Yes you can, dove. You know me, you trust me, whether you accept that or not. And you know I would rather die than cause any harm to you, don't you?"

She nods slowly.

"So why not give it a chance?"

"You say that like it's so damn easy."

"That's because it is. You want this, and I can give it to you in a safe environment. You'll have a safe word, I wouldn't restrain you, and I'll be able to tell if it gets to be too much for you. I know you, dove, and I'll know if you're struggling." I press a kiss to her temple, my arms tightening around her. Just having her back in my arms is like coming home. Being back with her is all I've thought about for the last eight years, even as I walked out the door that morning, I had to stop myself from turning my ass around and crawling back into the bed beside her very naked body.

Wynter tugs her bottom lip between her teeth, gnawing on it as she consider what I'm offering. That mind of hers has always been a problem, she's always overthinking every single possible outcome of her decisions. It's why she needs this so fucking badly, and if I'm honest with myself, I need it too.

Over the years, I've dabbled in BDSM. In the time before Wynter turned eighteen, when I was in love with my best friends little sister and trying to fight against what I'd known for as long as I'd known her, I found myself at clubs just like the one she mentioned during college. And then after I left, when I needed the world to stop, sometimes dishing out punishment to a sub was the only thing that could do it.

But doing it to Wynter is going to be a whole other story. It'll be more than just an outlet for all the pent-up tension between us, it'll be more than missing her and desperately trying to feel anything for someone else. It's more than all of that.

"You're thinking too much." I brush my thumb along her cheekbone as I hold her eyes on mine. "What have you got to lose?" When she starts nibbling at her bottom lip again I gently free the battered pillow of flesh and rub it carefully.

"If I let you do this, I'll lose everything when you leave again, and I don't know if I'm strong enough to survive that." She blinks back the tears pooling in her eyes.

"I'm not going anywhere, Wynter. I don't know what about those words you're not grasping, but you need to start accepting it, even if I have to tell you every hour on the hour for the rest of our goddamn lives. I'm never leaving you again. I couldn't even if I wanted to. I spent years fighting my instincts, fighting to leave you to your life to keep you safe. But I'm done with that. I'll keep you safe from anything that threatens to harm you, and I'll never let you go. You're mine, little dove. You have been since the first time our eyes locked, and you will be for the rest of our lives, even if it means locking you up."

The words sound so natural rolling off my tongue I almost miss how fucked up they sound. But I don't care. I couldn't give a shit about the fact I sound like a raving psycho, or that at some point I'm going to have to admit to stalking her for the last eight years and she'll almost definitely try to run again. All I care about is giving my woman exactly what she needs, and when she gives me a small nod and squeezes her eyes shut, I breathe a sigh of relief that she's going to let me.

TWENTY-THREE

WYNTER

Even as I nod, I know I'm fucking insane. That's the only explanation for agreeing to allow the man who broke me to punish me, despite my very logical fear of being punished since a crazy man belted me within an inch of my life.

And yet, I can't bring myself to change my mind, because he's right. I do need this. I need to feel in control of something, even if it's handing that control over to someone else for a little while.

"I don't know if I'll be able to," I whisper, not trusting my voice not to break under the pressure weighing over my entire body.

Everett smiles, his fingers moving down my face until he has my cheek cupped in his huge hand. "That's okay, dove. We're just going to see how we go. There's no pressure, you won't be in trouble if this isn't something you can handle. I can always find other fun ways to punish you when you break the rules." He winks.

"You don't think it's weird that I like this?" I ask quietly. I expected him to leave the minute I started talking about BDSM clubs and enjoying impact play, but if anything he seemed to perk up at the knowledge that I even knew what a whip was used for in the bedroom sense.

He chuckles as his hand moves down slightly until it rests at my throat, applying the slightest amount of pressure. "I'll let you in on a little secret, dove. I *love* that you're into this stuff, because there's nothing I want more than for you to submit for me."

My mouth drops open and I stare at him for long moments. Is he serious? I never went any further into the scene than impact play, what makes him think I can deal with everything else that comes with being a submissive?

"I can see that pretty little mind turning over, don't worry so much."

"Don't worry so much?" I snap. "I don't know the first thing about any of this, except for how to be punished, and even that I don't know if I can do anymore. Please enlighten me on how I'm not meant to worry."

He smiles and his eyes tell me all I need to know even before the words leave his mouth. "The whole point of this kind of dynamic, little dove, is to allow you to relinquish all your worries to me. Let's just try and see how we go. If you don't like it, or if you're scared, we'll stop and we don't ever have to bring it up again."

"But it's what you want," I point out.

"No, Wynter. You are what I want. Does the idea of dominating you turn me on? Hell fucking yes it does. But do I *need* it? No. All I need is you. If it meant I got to be with you every day for the rest of my life, I would burn the fucking world to the ground."

I squeeze my eyes shut to tamp down the rush of emotions that hit me all at once. Emotions I never thought I would feel again, ones I don't even know how to begin processing.

"We don't have to start this today. We can wait until the dust has settled and all the doubts you have about how serious I am are gone. But if this is something you need, then I am more than happy to give it to you."

If it weren't for his rock-hard cock pressing against my ass, his eyes would tell me exactly how turned on he is. The arousal clear as he stares down at me with an intensity I almost shy away from, the heat burning into me with the most delicious fervor.

I take deep steadying breaths before nodding. "I want to try. But I don't really know what I'm doing," I admit.

A devilish smile tugs at his lips and I squeeze my thighs together, he has no right being so fucking attractive. His eyes drop to where I'm trying to easy the ache pooling between my legs. "I'll teach you everything you need to know, little dove. Starting with this." His hand snakes down my body and pulls my legs apart. "Your body is mine to pleasure, mine to punish, and mine to torture with your own need. The only relief you will be given is the relief I give you."

Everett's fingers trail up the inside of my bare thigh, his touches so gentle I almost wouldn't feel them if I wasn't hyperaware of every single move he makes, and every touch

177

he gives me. "I can smell your sweet pussy, little dove. Is it weeping for me?" he asks in a low voice that almost has me clamping my legs together around his hand in the hope it will give me some relief. "Answer me, Wynter."

"Yes," I whisper, barely trusting my own voice.

"Good girl," he praises as his fingers move higher toward my wet heat. "Here's what we're going to do. We're going to move back over to the sofa and you're going to lie across my lap. Until we've trialed this a few times, you will be completely unrestrained unless you ask me to hold your hands. We'll start with just my hand, and if and when you're more comfortable, maybe we'll move on to other implements. How does that sound?"

"Okay." I nod.

The smile Everett gives me makes my insides clench with a combination of love and heat. I never stopped loving him, not for a minute. Not when he left. Not when I couldn't breathe without him. And not when he walked back into my life and destroyed all the progress I made. I've loved Everett for every second of every day, since before I knew what love meant, and I'll love him for every moment, of every day I spend on this earth, and maybe even then.

He lifts me carefully until my feet touch the plush carpet and his eyes roam over my bare skin. I wish he would let me put some clothes on, but when he looks at me like this, like he's never seen another woman like me, it takes away every bit of nervousness and self-consciousness that tries to rise to the surface.

Everett takes my hand in his much larger one and guides me

over to the sofa before sitting down and patting his knees. "Over you go."

I suck in a nervous breath and follow the command before I can back out. The moment I'm settled over his knee, his hand is moving gently across my ass, rubbing soothing circles into my bare flesh.

"You're trembling, little dove," he says quietly.

"I'm sorry," I whisper.

"You never need to be sorry with me, dove. Do these scars hurt at all? Any nerve damage that you know of?"

I shake my head, looking over my shoulder at him. "No pain, no nerve damage."

His lips quirk up in a smile. "Good. Now if you get overwhelmed, I want you to say 'red' for me and I'll stop straight away. I'm so proud of you just for agreeing to try, so even if we get one swat in and it's too much, I'm still going to count it as progress, okay?"

"Okay."

"I want you to keep your hands flat on the sofa cushion. I don't want them getting caught up in the action and you getting hurt."

I almost laugh. He's getting ready to spank me and he's worried about me getting hurt, but instead I nod once and turn back to bury my face into the sofa. Part of me is thrilled at the idea of getting this part of my identity back, but the other is mortified that Everett is staring at my naked, scarred ass right now, his palms trailing comforting circles around the damaged flesh.

"I need your words, dove. I'm sure you know communication is very important in these circumstances," he reprimands me.

"I'm sorry. Yes, I understand," I say quickly. I've been around enough Doms to know something like this can earn you extra punishment, and I'm already questioning my ability to handle what's owing to me.

"Good girl."

The first strike is more gentle than I would have expected, but obviously Everett is testing my endurance, and for that, I'm grateful. Where I expect to feel panicked, I feel calm.

"Okay?" he asks as he rubs the sting into my skin.

"Yes."

Another strike comes down on the other cheek and makes me jump but doesn't bring the memories I expect to the surface.

Three more come in rapid succession, taking my breath away in the most delightful way. The sting begins to settle in, and every time his palm makes contact with a place he's hit before I jump.

"How are you doing, little dove?" Everett asks, his hands moving over the burning skin, massaging the heat deeper.

"Good," I whisper, looking over my shoulder to see his satisfied smile.

"Not scared or anything?"

"No, I'm okay," I assure him. I'm relaxing more and more

with every swat he lands, and each one leads me closer to that place I long to be, the one I've missed since Craig took it away from me all those years ago.

"I'm so proud of you, dove," he praises quietly. "Are you ready for the rest?"

"I'm ready." I nod, handing my body to him and trusting him not to break me.

Four rapid fire smacks hit the backs of my thighs and make me cry out, the heat settling between my legs is almost as painful as my tender ass, the need to come so strong I can barely breathe through it. The fire burning on my ass hurts in the most delicious way, and it takes me long moments to realize the wetness on my cheeks is my own tears soaking the cushion under my face.

Another six hit hard and fast, and a moment later I'm bundled up in Everett's arms and he's wrapping a soft blanket around my shivering body. I'm not particularly cold, but the endorphins are firing almost to the point of dizziness, and my body is reacting to the overwhelming feeling of being whole.

My mind drifts to a place that feels both familiar and foreign, a place I haven't been in such a long time it feels like a lifetime. Everett whispers quiet praises, his face buried in my neck as he brings me down slowly and carefully from a high I forgot was so addictive.

The warmth of Everett's embrace serves as the perfect blissful state I've craved for so long despite myself. After Craig hurt me, I didn't think I'd ever be able to find myself in this place again, but of course it's Everett who brings me home.

We sit for long minutes, Everett holding me with such tender care it only makes the tears falling against my cheeks come faster, my ass throbbing from the brutal spanking he gave me, but the way he has me positioned has all weight off the burning flesh.

I move my head until I'm looking up at him, finally able to think through the clouds in my head.

Everett smiles down at me, his thumb brushing the tears from my cheeks. "There's my girl," he says quietly. "How are doing, dove?"

"Good," I whisper.

"You did so good, Wynter. I'm very proud of you for facing your fears." His eyes are full of pride and something I shouldn't allow myself to hope for.

Love.

Twenty-Four

Everett

Once I've settled Wynter into her bed and made sure she's asleep, there's something I need to take care of. I barely managed to keep my anger under wraps in front of her, but I don't give a shit how much she begged him not to tell me. Storm should have told me she was hurt.

I'm still trying to wrap my head around how it could even happen, but it must have been in the months I couldn't get into the dorm rooms to put cameras and trackers on everything, and she didn't take a lot of the things I planted bugs on before she left.

Vaguely I recall a couple of weeks a few months into college that she didn't leave her room at all, but I assumed she had the flu and no one ever thought to correct me. I didn't even think much of Craig's disappearance. Security isn't always long term because they're normally running from their own lives, and at some point they want to go back.

I burst into Storm's office without knocking and startle both him and Rayne who are huddled around a laptop on the desk. "Why the fuck didn't you tell me what happened to Wynter when she started college?" I growl, all the tenderness I showed her just a few minutes ago is long gone and nothing but anger remains for the men sitting before me.

"What happened to Wynter when she started college?" Rayne asks, his eyes turning to his brother and a look of confusing falling across his features.

Storm sighs and closes the laptop. "I had hoped it would take you longer to find the evidence," he admits.

"What evidence? Can someone tell me what the fuck is going on and what happened to my baby sister? Who the fuck do I need to kill?"

"No one, I took care of it," Storm tells him.

"Took care of what?" Rayne snaps.

"I had a right to know. We had a deal." I slam my fist into the door, the wood shaking violently from the force.

"Had a right to know what? I swear to God one of you motherfuckers better tell me what the fuck is going on before I lose it." Rayne's own anger is palpable. I assumed they both knew, that Rayne would have been the one to handle it, but clearly I was wrong. That should give me reason to pause, that if Storm hadn't told their brother what happened, maybe it was reasonable to not have told me, but I'm way past rational right now. Rational went out the window the moment the door of Wynter's room clicked shut behind me.

I stare at Storm for long moments, my head tilted as I wait for him to tell his brother all about what he hid from us. He sighs and leans back in his chair. "When Wynter was in college, someone...hurt her." He chooses his words carefully, but if he thinks he's getting away with being vague, he has another thing coming.

"Violated her," I correct and Rayne's head whips around so quick I swear I hear his neck crack from the pressure.

"What the fuck is he talking about?" Rayne snaps at his brother.

"This isn't exactly something we want to know about as her brothers," Storm says, his eyes locked on mine.

"Yeah well, if you'd called me like you should have, I would have taken care of it. I would have taken care of her," I reply, my arms crossed over my chest.

"You'd just left her!" Storm roars, slamming both hands down on the desk in front of him. "We all agreed it was what was best, but you don't know how broken she was without you, Everett. You don't have a fucking clue. I couldn't risk calling you just so you could leave again. She wouldn't have survived, especially after what Craig did."

"Craig, as in her security? And what do you mean, violated her?" Rayne growls. He's nearing the edge of his tether and if Storm doesn't start giving us answers soon, he's probably going to tear this office apart. The violent streak in him has calmed since Emerson walked into his life, but that doesn't mean the thought of his family hurt won't set him off like fireworks on the Fourth of July.

Storm sighs. "Yes. Wynter's security when she first moved to Boston hurt her. He..." He sucks in an unsteady breath as he prepares himself for the words to leave his mouth. "He tied her down and hit her with his belt repeatedly."

"What the fuck?" Rayne roars as he stands from his seat so quickly the chair flings back and hits the ground in a heavy bang. "Why the fuck would he do that? And why the fuck didn't you tell me?"

"She asked me not to tell anyone, but you two by name. She didn't want both brothers to know what he'd done to her, and she didn't want Everett coming back because he felt guilty that she was hurt."

"How bad was it?" Rayne asks through gritted teeth.

Storm takes another deep breath and looks longingly at the whiskey across the room. "Bad. The doctor took hours cleaning the wounds. I tried to get her to go to the hospital, but she wouldn't. She couldn't. She wouldn't even let me in for days." He drops his head into his hands in a sign of defeat. In all the years I've known him, I've only seen him look like this twice. The first was the night I told him about what I'd done, and why I had to leave. And the other was a week ago as we tried to work out where to start looking for his parents' murder.

EIGHT YEARS AGO

All I've done for the last hour is stare at the note in my hand. The writing only seems to hold my attention more as time passes, the way the handwritten note is scrawled messily across the page, the threat in the words clear and precise. It doesn't take a genius to work out the intent behind them, or even who sent it.

My family have always been a bunch of psychotic assholes which is why I never wanted anything to do with them. When I was young, my mother shielded me from the worst of it. My father's affairs, the abuse, both physical and verbal, and all the things I saw that no child should have to, including watching as my father killed my mother in front of my eyes.

It was strange how differently the Saint James family ran the same operation my father had. They bred loyalty and respect, where my father ruled with nothing but fear. The night I heard him order a hit on a woman and child for the misgivings of one man was the night I knew I didn't want to be anything like him.

As terrible as my father was, he's nothing compared to the other side of the family. The Russos are another breed of awful. They've always been the scum of this city, but since my father died they've only escalated. By marrying my mother off to my father, they thought they guaranteed themselves the key to the city, but they didn't anticipate the takeover.

I managed to keep my friendship with the Saint James family a secret for a long time. When I slipped out for the night here and there they didn't seem to notice, or care for that matter. I lived with Uncle Angelo, the unattached, bachelor of the family, but also the cold, ruthless leader. He wasn't home enough to give a shit about the parentless nephew he never wanted.

And when they found out, I moved out the same day. The Saint James's welcomed me with open arms, and I've been here ever since, with the exception of college.

But as I stare down at the note in my hand, I know deep down this is the last night I can spend in this house. I'm putting Wynter in danger just by being here, and I can't risk her. I *won't.*

Wynter is everything good in the world. She's beauty, and light, and happiness all rolled into the most stunning package I've ever seen in my life. She is my life.

We've spent the last few years skirting around one another, but since she turned eighteen a few weeks ago tensions have been high. The subtle kisses and touches aren't so innocent anymore. They're filled with passion and need for all the years we've had to wait for our time. And now that it's here, I have to leave. Talk about cruel fate.

By the time I force myself to leave the refuge of my bedroom and head up the hallway to Storm's room, my hands are shaking and I'm barely able to hold on to the note. It's burning my hands with the threat scrawled across it, and the longer I hold it, the deeper the dread seems to bury itself until it seeps from my pores like a virus.

The moment the door swings open and I'm face to face with my best friend he knows something is wrong, he knows me well enough to know the catatonic state I find myself in is a very bad sign, and the moment he eyes the note in my hand he pushes past me and knocks on the door across the hall.

"Rayne, we've got a problem."

TWENTY-FIVE
WYNTER

"I don't like this," Everett says for the eighth time since he walked into the kitchen this morning.

"You don't have to. This is the best way for us to travel," Storm tells him.

I feel like I'm stuck in a never-ending time loop that I can't escape from no matter how many times we go around and around.

"I mean, I don't like that the girls are leaving the house. It's risky," Everett huffs.

"And I've told you that the lawyer has requested all of our presence for the reading of the will, and they said they can't come to the house to do it, so we all have to go to the city," Storm explains… again.

It has to be Groundhog Day, that's the only explanation for this constant loop.

"I still don't like it," Everett grumbles.

I wrap my hands around the mug in front of me and bring my lips to the rim, inhaling the sweet caffeine. I was going to wait until we got to the city to get one of the fancy coffees I like, but when Everett almost had a coronary at the idea of making a pit stop along the way I quickly made myself a cup and sat my ass down at the table with Snow and Emerson as we watched the never-ending pissing match.

"You don't have to like it, but it's happening." Storm shrugs. They've been cold toward one another since everyone woke up this morning, and if I had to hazard a guess I would say they had words last night about the secrets I forced my brother to keep. Everett was never going to let it go, I don't know why I wasted my breath in the first place. "And we're doing it the safest way we know how."

"Like we're the goddamn royal family." Rayne rolls his eyes. "I'm with Everett on this one, I'm not comfortable sending Emerson in a car on her own."

Storm sighs and scrubs his hands down his face. "She's not on her own, she's with three security guards."

Rayne pins our brother with one of the scariest looks I've ever seen cross his face. "Yes, I've seen how that's played out before and our security basically handed my woman straight over to the enemy. Excuse me if I don't want to repeat that experience," he growls.

"This is the only option we have. It's too risky all going together, they could take out every last Saint James if they played their cards right, and I'm not willing to risk that."

"But we'll let them take their pick of the litter of who to take out?" Everett asks, his brows raised.

"Of course not. Like I explained this morning, we made the decision on the day at the very last minute so there's less chance of a coordinated hit. We're each taking one car with three security, and we will all drive in different directions to meet at the same place. I'm not understanding what your problem with this is."

"My problem is exactly what you just said, your plan only gives us less chance of a coordinated hit. Do you know what would give zero chance? Not going. Staying here in the estate where there's more security than the White House and no chance of any hits." Everett shrugs like it's the easiest thing in the world. Watching these three bicker only reminds me of when we were kids fighting over a toy, except now the three of them are big and scary and much meaner than they were then. "You'll understand one day what it feels like to have your heart living outside your body as a living, breathing human, but until then you're not going to understand how Rayne and I feel."

My heart seizes at his words and I quickly look down at my mug again. Those words could mean anything, but from the way his eyes burn into the side of my face I know they're directed at me. When I woke up this morning after sleeping for so long, and so deeply I wondered if I'd dropped dead for at least some of the night, Everett was nowhere to be seen and there was no sign of him having slept beside me. He's obviously staying true to not touching me until he's told me everything, as frustrating as that may be.

Storm looks from Rayne to Everett and back again. "I'm

sorry, but this has to happen today. We've already put it off longer than we should have and the board are getting antsy. We know what the will says, but they don't and if we don't establish our claim on the shares of Frost Industries, there will be takeover attempts, and Dad would turn over in his grave if we allowed that to happen."

"I don't understand why Emerson and I can't travel together, and Everett and Wynter. Then you and Snow can go separately."

"Because Emerson and Everett are part of this family, and as such have just as much of a claim on Frost Industries as the rest of us. If all biological Saint James siblings go down, there are things in place for the surviving members of the family to take over."

"There are?" Emerson asks with wide eyes, looking at Rayne for confirmation but he just shrugs.

"Of course there are. Until we all start popping out babies, we need a plan b for the eventuality that Russo is going to take us all out." Snow shrugs like it's the most natural thing in the world.

I glare at her for a moment before swiping her cup and bringing it to my nose, cringing at the smell of whiskey. "It's a bit early for this." I pass the mug back.

"Yeah, well, it's not every day you get to find out what percentage of your family's business your parents thought you were worthy of," Snow fires back.

"Can we go back a few steps to where we discussed the plan b…" Emerson looks equally sick and horrified at the thought of taking over the company, and I don't blame her. Even I have moments when I think about something happening to Storm and me being saddled with both sides of Frost Industries. The boardroom I can deal with, but if this shit with the Russos has taught me anything, it's that the sinister side of our business dealings are way above my head.

"You don't need to worry about it, sweet girl because it's not going to happen." He glares at Storm for bringing it up in the first place. The idea that myself and all my siblings could be taken out of the picture makes my heart ache but having people that our legacy can be passed on to makes me feel a little better.

"I want to know," Emerson snaps, she's freaking out, even if she is good at hiding it.

Storm sighs. "In an ideal world, if it's only us that are out of the picture, you would take Wynter's position, Everett would take mine, and Tommy would take Rayne's. There are other contingency plans, but that's best-case scenario."

"Best-case scenario?" she yells, the panic in her voice clear. "How is that best-case scenario?"

Rayne sweeps her into his arms and holds her tightly against his body, pressing a gentle kiss to the top of her head. "Shh. It's not going to happen, so it doesn't matter." He shoots a glare over her head at Storm. "Why don't we go finish getting ready?" It's not a question and he immediately steers her out of the kitchen before anyone can say anything else to freak her out.

"What did I do?" Storm asks, watching as they leave.

Everett shakes his head and a short chuckle falls from his lips.

"You'll get it one day, bro. We should do the same." He turns to me and I stare at him for a moment.

"Why would we get ready together?" I raise an eyebrow and take another sip of my coffee.

"Because I said so. Let's go." Everett motions for the door and I roll my eyes as I stand and carry my mug to the dishwasher. By the time I meet him in the doorway there's a small smirk playing on his lips. "Already itching for another punishment, little dove?" He whispers so quietly I barely hear him.

I shrug. "Maybe."

DEAD OF WYNTER

TWENTY-SIX

EVERETT

From the moment we leave the house my palms are sweating. I knew at some stage we were going to have to have to leave the estate. Our lives can't stay on hold until we're able to take the Russo family down, but that doesn't make it any easier to know Wynter is out of the safety the estate gives us. Storm wouldn't allow me to travel with her either, which only adds to my anxiety.

The lawyer's office is modern, too much so for my liking, with clean lines and clinical white at every turn, but the eightieth floor at least allows for incredible views of the city that almost make up for the rest of the office.

We sit around a conference table with the lawyer at the end as he tells us about how the Saint James assets are being distributed. It seems like something that should be morbid, but every person in this room has sat in on big board meetings in some capacity, and we all channel that to distract us from how close to home this really hits.

"Storm will have the controlling interest in the shares, followed by Wynter, then Snow, and then Rayne," he explains.

The latter chuckles. "Even they knew I'd be terrible holding the reins. Pun very much intended."

The lawyer stares at him for a moment, as if he can't understand how he could be making a joke in the wake of their parents death, but Rayne ignores him and grabs Emerson's hand on top of the table before the reading of the will continues. "There are some assets that will be distributed between the six of you."

"The six of us?" Emerson asks, her eyes wide as they meet mine across the table. She didn't know them long enough to know that the Saint James's adopt people the moment they meet them. They did it with me, and they did it with her the night they met her at the gala.

"Yes, Mrs. Saint James." He gives her a tight smile, barely looking up from the strew of papers laid out in front of him.

"The late Mrs. Saint James has divided her jewelry up between the three women and has some set aside for the future Mrs. Storm Saint James," he explains and earns a scoff from the man himself.

"Even in death, she's holding on to pipe dreams of me getting married." There's no humor in his voice, only affection for the woman who raised him.

"They also wrote you all a letter which my assistant will pass around to you now." He motions to the older woman who looks just as uncomfortable being here as the rest of us.

We each thank her as she hands us an envelope and I stare

down at mine for long moments, emotion bubbling in my chest as I stare down at my name scrawled across it. The familiar handwriting makes my heart ache for the only parents I ever really knew. They took me in when I had nowhere to go. They gave me food when my father refused to give my mother money for groceries and I was starving. And they showed me what a family is meant to look like.

I tear my eyes away from my own letter and look around the table as each one of my family members is looking down just the way I had been a few moments ago. This makes it feel real. The funeral was one thing, but even that we turned into a mission to deliver a threat to Angelo. This is divvying up their personal belongings between us like they were nothing more than money to us. It has me biting back nausea as I reach for the untouched glass of water sitting in front of me and downing it in several long drinks.

"The estate will transfer into Storm's name effective immediately, however there is a clause in the contract that states if any of your siblings, including Mrs. Saint James and Mr. Masters, and any future generations, need a refuge, the estate is to be open to them at all times." The lawyer continues through list after list of assets, and as each item is distributed to the people sitting around the table, the more heavily it weighs down on me.

"Now, the final thing on the list is the funds in their bank accounts. As I'm sure you can appreciate, your parents knew none of you are hurting for money, and as such they decided unanimously the last time I saw them that the money sitting in their account will be donated to the Chicago Center for Youth."

Emerson's hand seals over her mouth as a muffled sob claws up her throat as the lawyer continues. "As you can imagine, that is quite the sum and I will have final figures by the end of the day now that the interest from last month has carried over. I understand you're the best person to speak to about how to make this donation, Mrs. Saint James."

She nods quickly as she leans into Rayne but doesn't say anything. She's overwhelmed by the generosity just like she was the night of the gala, back when she was just a person I did recon on for Rayne. But as I watched through the security feed I hacked into to get a glimpse of Wynter, I knew she was different, that she would be the first person to join the family since I did so many years ago.

"Very good, well in that case, I think that's all that we need to discuss. I've had a copy of the distribution made for each of you for your records, and there will be some paperwork I need each of you to sign, but I understand this is a very hard time for you all and don't want to keep you from your time of grief. If there's anything I can do for any of your through this difficult time, please let me know and I will be happy to do anything I can."

We say our goodbyes and walk together to the elevators, none of us saying anything as we clutch the papers to our bodies. Before I can think better of it, I pull Wynter against me, needing to feel her close even if she pulls away a moment later. But to my surprise, she doesn't. She nestles into my side and the moment makes my heart clench with relief. She's not pulling away from me anymore. Last night did exactly as I hoped it would, it made her see I'm not going anywhere again, and finally she believes I won't leave her like I had to in the past.

"Same plan on the way home?" Rayne asks, his arm wrapped tightly around Emerson's shoulders.

Storm nods. "We're all going back to the same cars. I considered switching them out, but that would look suspicious and we risked the new cars being tampered with, at least these ones Everett scanned before we left... twice."

The smirk on his lips brings a smile to my own lips. Okay, so maybe I went a little over the top, but having Wynter out of the estate is making me antsy with every second that ticks by.

By the time we make it to the parking garage below the building the girls have wiped the tears from their eyes and the masks they've worn every time we've been out in public appears back on their faces. I hold Wynter for a moment longer than I should before letting her go as I cross to the car I arrived in. Storm was smart not to switch out the cars, I guess he's learning, but I don't trust anyone outside the six of us.

I'm just climbing into the back seat of the SUV when I hear a sound that makes my heart shatter into a million pieces.

"Everett!" Wynter screams in terror, and I'm moving long before I've even processed the sound.

TWENTY-SEVEN
WYNTER

Considering we just divided our parents' worldly possessions among ourselves, we're all in a pretty good mood as we make our way to our respective cars. I didn't say anything this morning when Everett and Storm were talking about it but knowing that everyone I care about is out in the open right now has wave after wave of nausea rolling over me.

I had hoped once we got here that it would settle, but the longer we've been exposed, the more anxious I'm feeling. The Russo family is ruthless, and Elijah Russo is the worst of them. He doesn't get involved in a lot of the politics within the city, but he's a stone-cold psycho, and he's set his sights on us. On me.

Security stand around each of the cars and the moment Everett moves away from me I feel the loss immediately. I don't know when, or how, it happened, but he's quickly become my security blanket again, the only thing that can make me feel safe as we weather the storm the Russos are bringing down on us.

The door is opened for me and I thank the guard quietly as I take my seat, and the moment I do I hear a click as my weight settles. My stomach drops through the floor as tears spring to my eyes, horror washing through my entire body.

I've seen enough movies and read enough books to know what that sound is, and somehow the Russos have delivered their next move before we could even think of our own, before we could wade through our grief and come up with the best way to bring them down once and for all.

Before the meaning of that click can process, I call for Everett, needing him with me, needing him to tell me everything is going to be okay when we both know that's the complete opposite of the truth.

Thomas, one of the security guards, looks at me with panic in his hazel eyes. If I remember correctly from when he's guarded me in the past, he was in the marines before he signed on with my family, so he knows exactly what that sound was and his face reflects exactly what I'm feeling.

"What's wrong?" Everett bounds toward us and I put both hands up.

"Stop," I shout. "You can't touch me, you have to stay a few feet away."

"What? Why? What's going on?"

The rest of my family gathers behind him flicking from me to Thomas and back again.

"You all need to leave. It might be a trap."

"What might be a trap? What the fuck is going on?" Everett

yells and I take deep breaths so I don't move suddenly.

"When I sat down, I heard and felt a click beneath my seat. Thomas heard it too," I tell them calmly. "There's a pressure bomb under me, and if I move, if my weight shifts, we're all going up in flames." The calm that settles over me is eerie. Surely I should be panicking.

Everett's face drains of all color as his eyes flick from my face to the seat I'm sitting on and back again, but he doesn't say anything, he just stares, and I don't entirely blame him. Behind him the rest of my family stands with the same look of horror on their faces, the fear in Snow's eyes, the anger in Storm's, the rage in Rayne's, and the terror in Emerson's.

"Go," I whisper.

"No way." Storm shakes his head as he takes a few steps forward until he's standing next to Everett. "Who do we know that can diffuse a bomb?"

He shakes his head, as if clearing the fog and turns to my brother for a moment. "It depends what kind of bomb it is. I need to get close enough to check if it has a timer, and then if it's military grade or homemade."

"What difference will that make?" Rayne asks as he steps forward as well. Every moment they stay is another moment my heart is lodged in my throat, and I can barely breathe around it.

"If it's homemade, we're in trouble because we don't know how stable the explosive is, and they may have built it to be difficult to diffuse," Everett explains.

"Like the one you designed a couple of years ago?" Storm

wonders aloud.

Everett nods. "Exactly. I designed that to make whoever was diffusing it second guess themselves. But we face another set of issues if it's military grade because that means the number of people we can call on is limited without raising questions of our own involvement in illegal weapons and it will be very touchy. If Wynter moves even slightly it could go off because that's what they're designed for."

"Fuck," Storm roars as he starts pacing back and forth.

"You need to go. All of you. They could wipe out every Saint James and every succession plan we have and our whole company would be left in the hands of Tommy. Could you imagine?" I hear the hysterics in my own voice, even as the calm settles over my perfectly still body.

"I don't fucking care, Wynter," Everett snaps. "Do you think anyone in this fucking parking garage gives a fuck about succession plans right now when you're sitting on a goddamn bomb?"

"I care," I growl. "I will not be the reason our entire family goes down before we can even make a move."

Storm looks behind him and takes an unsteady breath before turning to Rayne. "I want you to take Snow and Emerson home. Go in one car, sweep the whole thing before any of you think about getting in. When you get back to the estate I want you all to go to the panic room and wait there until you hear from us."

"I'm not leaving you here," Rayne argues.

"Yes, you are. Wynter is right. Everett and I will stay with her and get this sorted, but until then I need you to take our sister and your wife and get them to safety. I don't trust anyone right now because somehow this was planted with all of these fuckers standing here. Drive yourself, use the emergency failsafe system in the house to lock down every door and window, and go to the panic room." Listening to Storm's quiet instruction gives me something to focus on as the gravity of my situation finally settles over me.

I'm going to die.

The startling reality should have dread seeping into my veins, but instead I can't take my eyes off Everett. He probably doesn't realize how much he affects me. How even though I'm sitting on a bomb, I feel safe because he's near.

There are so many things I haven't had a chance to say, so many things I wish we had time for, but our time is being cut short. All those years we wasted, all time we spent apart, none of it matters anymore, not as I look death in the face.

All that matters is the stolen moments we have left.

Rayne hesitantly takes Emerson and Snow toward the car closest to the exit, but it's clear none of them want to leave me. Storm made the right call. We don't know who we can trust anymore, and it's becoming more and more clear we have a rat somewhere in our organization.

"Ev?" I whisper.

His eyes shoot up to mine before he takes a few careful steps toward me. "What is it, dove?" he asks gently.

I close my eyes to tamp down the tears that rise to the surface. Fuck. I didn't think saying goodbye would be so hard, but I guess it's not often you get the chance. Usually your life is torn from you and there's no opportunity to say the things that would remain unsaid. "I think you and Storm should go and evacuate the building in case this goes up, and then you should go home and bunker down with the others."

"No fucking way, Wynter," he snaps.

I squeeze my eyes shut. "I don't want you to die because of me," I whisper.

"Don't you get it, Wynter. If you die, my life isn't worth living," he hisses.

"So we should let Russo blow all three of us up?"

"No, because you're not getting blown up, I'm going to figure out how to get you out of here, and then you're never leaving the fucking estate again."

I huff out a small laugh, trying to stop my body from shaking. "I'm surprised you were able to stay away for so many years with the level of caveman you've got going on."

"It's only because he always had eyes on you. If not for that, he wouldn't have lasted the first year." Storm chuckles as he pulls his phone out of his pocket.

I stare at Everett for a moment before he too cracks a smile. "He's right, you know. It never felt like I was away because I could always see what you were up to. Sometimes when you were on the phone, I would imagine you were talking to me, it was one of the ways I could stay sane during that time."

I shake my head and hold the giggle that threatens in. "I should be really creeped out right now."

"But you're not?" Everett quirks a brow.

"No, I'm not." Because the idea that he was never far makes some of the tension in my gut ease. Maybe he's right. Maybe this isn't it for me. If there's anyone that can get me out of this, it's him, and I have a feeling he'll stop at nothing to be able to take me home when this is all over.

Twenty-Eight

Everett

E very second Wynter sits on that bomb is a second and a half too long.

In the time it's taken me to get close enough to the car and get my phone under the seat with extreme precision I normally only use when building something, Storm has called everyone in his contacts and assembled a bomb squad any military would be jealous of. But the fact that I have to put my woman's life into a stranger's hands is unacceptable to me. If I thought I could learn how to diffuse a bomb in the next ten minutes, I would be doing it right this moment, but that's not practical, and it would likely end even worse for Wynter than whatever these guys do.

But at least if they blow her up, I'll be standing right next to her. That's something, right? "It's handmade," one of them confirms.

"But whoever made it seems to know what they're doing, which means it's stable," another tells us.

"As stable as a fucking explosive can be, I guess," Storm mutters. Out of the three of us, he's the one taking it the hardest. He's going over and over in his head all the moments that led us to this one, but he's not going to find an error. The only mistake we made was leaving the house, and if we had brought only one car, we would all be sitting where Wynter is right now.

"We're going to diffuse it now. One of us will climb in the other side and hold the device steady while another will carefully diffuse it. Once the pressure point is disabled we're going to get Wynter out and then remove the device so it can be detonated in a safe location."

It all sounds fine, and if it wasn't my entire life sitting on top of the bomb, I would think it's a great plan, but because it's Wynter sitting there looking so calm I'm wondering if I might have to take her to the hospital on the way home, I can't think straight to know if this is the best move.

I look to Storm who is staring at me and I realize we're both hoping the other will have the answer, but it's him who sighs and nods. "Do it."

Wynter flinches at the command and I don't even realize I'm moving until I'm standing beside the car with a gentle hand on her shoulder. I need her to know she's not alone. I tried my best to convince Storm to leave, to tell him that the rest of the family needs him if things go pear-shaped, but he didn't even entertain the idea of leaving us.

"Ev," she whispers, the nickname only she uses rolling off her tongue quietly as she turns her head to look at me. The fear in her eyes is almost my undoing, but there's a quiet strength behind them. Everyone underestimates the women in this

216

family, but if we make it out of this, the Russo family better believe it will be Wynter coming after them.

"Yeah, dove?"

"I'm sorry I was so harsh when you came back. I don't know why you left, but I know you had to have had a reason. I'm sorry I didn't see that until now." Her eyes press closed as a few stray tears draw dark paths down her cheeks.

"You better not be trying to say goodbye to me right now, Wynter, because you're not going anywhere other than home," I growl.

"Everett, I need you to listen to me," she snaps. "You know me. You know I need to prepare for every eventuality, and I can't die without you knowing that I forgive you. I forgive you for leaving, and for breaking my heart, and for storming back into my life like you own it. I'm sorry that something kept us apart for eight years and you had to watch me live my life from afar. I'm sorry I begged Storm not to tell you what Craig did to me. I'm sorry I ever doubted how you felt about me."

More tears trail down her cheeks and I ache to reach out and brush them away, but even that could be enough to set off the device, and I'm not willing to risk it.

"Dove," I say quietly, my heart breaking more and more with each tear that rolls down her cheeks.

She's right, I do know her, and in her mind there's every possibility she won't survive this. It's not entirely unreasonable seeing as she's perched on top of a bomb, but I can't let her go on.

"You're not going to die. You and I are going to live to be one hundred and then we're going to die in each other's arms."

Because that's the only way that's acceptable. I can't leave her unprotected, and I can't live without her. That's why I'm standing here right now, that's why even when she begged me to go I couldn't.

"You don't know that." She sighs, tearing her eyes from mine only for long enough to look at the men currently poking around under her seat. "I love you, Everett. I loved you when we were just kids and had no concept of what those three words meant. I loved you when you kissed me on my eighteenth birthday and then disappeared into the night. And I loved you even when my heart could barely beat it was so broken."

Her words make my heart stop as I process them. I've only ever heard those words from her lips once, and it was when I took her virginity, one final selfish act before I left without a trace. All these years I thought that would be the only time she would say it, that even when I inevitably came back and tried to explain why our time apart was necessary, that she would always resent me for leaving her. "I love you too, dove," I whisper, barely able to breathe through the emotions crashing through my body like a wrecking ball.

Wynter gives me a broken smile as the two men start talking around us. They need to be perfectly still and be able to communicate flawlessly for this to work, and us finally sorting our shit out isn't going to help that. I look up at Storm who is pacing backward and forward a few feet away. There have been few times in my life that I've seen the man look so worried, but most of them have been concern for his family.

There's a reason he's here and not with the rest of them in the bunker at the estate. He's the true leader of this family, and there's nothing he won't do for them, including be blown up by the bomb they're sitting above.

"You guys should go," Wynter whispers so quietly I barely hear her.

"No," I growl under my breath. Soon enough she's going to understand that I'm not going anywhere. She's stuck with me and there's nothing she could ever do to change that.

"We're just getting ready to diffuse now," one of the guys tells us and Wynter squeezes her eyes shut as quiet sobs claw their way out of her throat. I tear my eyes away from her only long enough to see Storm has stopped pacing and is staring at us with barely contained horror.

There are long moments of silence where the only sound is the men removing cords, or at least that's what I assume they're doing. I've dabbled with bombs before, but only in a controlled environment when creating the weapons of tomorrow, not under a high-pressure situation where we could all very well die in the next thirty seconds.

Wynter and I stare at one another and I swear neither of us breathes, too scared to make a move just in case it's what sets this thing off. I hold my breath for so long I'm not sure my lungs will hold air again, and then the most wonderful words I've ever heard come out of the technician's mouth.

"All clear, get her out of here."

TWENTY-NINE

WYNTER

I hear the words, but I can't move. The thoughts raging through my mind feel like they're taking over. What if these guys work for Russo? They seemed to know so much about the device, maybe they were the ones that planted it in the first place.

"Dove," Everett says quietly as his hands cup my cheeks.

"I can't." I shake my head, petrified to move a muscle despite them saying it's safe.

"Yes you can, little dove." The man moves from under my seat and Everett is there in a second, his thumbs moving carefully across my cheeks wiping the tears away as they fall. "Do you trust me?"

I nod quickly, because despite everything, despite all the pain he caused when he broke my heart, I trust him more than anyone else in the world.

"Okay, here's what we're going to do. I'm going to lift you out of that seat real slow and then as soon as you're clear, we're going to get out of here and go home. How does that sound?"

No one would ever expect Everett to be so gentle. Most would expect him to be rough and rowdy considering the size of him, and the muscles that protrude even through his suit. But the way he looks at me, takes care of me, it's like I'm the most precious piece of china in the whole world, and he's holding me in his hands, promising not to let me break.

"Okay." The word leaves my mouth before I have time to think it through, but for some reason when he looks at me like this, I lose all ability to deny him anything. He could take me anywhere, do anything, and I would let him.

Everett smiles softly as he leans in and presses a kiss to my forehead. His lips hover against my skin for a few moments as he breathes me in, reminding himself I'm still here and that I'm going to be okay. And then a moment later he's carefully sliding one arm under my knees, and the other behind my back.

"Ready?"

"Yes."

I press my head into his shoulder and before I have a chance to rethink my answer he's swung me out of my seat and turned his body so his is between me and the car. My mouth drops open and I hold on to him so tight my arms ache, because he just put himself between me and a bomb that could blow at any minute. A second later he's running across the carpark so quickly I wonder how it's possible considering his size and my extra body weight.

"Has this car been checked?" Everett barks at someone.

"Yes, I checked it myself," Storm says as he steps toward us. I don't open my eyes but I can feel him standing close as the silence drags out for what feels like forever. "Are you okay, Wynter?"

"Of course she's not okay," Everett snaps. "She was just sitting on a bomb, unable to move for two fucking hours. You find me someone that would be okay after that."

"I'm okay," I whisper, but I keep my eyes pressed closed and my hold on him tight. I'm alive and that's all that matters. Their attempts to take us out have failed today, but if we're already at bombs, I'll hate to see what it will be when they inevitably escalate.

"Let's get you home, little dove." Everett holds me so tight the pressure borders pain, but I need it. I need the pain to remind me I'm alive, and that's exactly what I'm going to need when we get home.

Everett holds me the whole drive back to the estate. He has the seatbelt wrapped around both of us, and his hold never eases as he whispers words to me that I can't process. I've never felt so overwhelmed with emotion like I am right now. Fear, and relief, and a heart bursting with love. It's all hitting me in one big tidal wave of feelings, and I don't know how to wade my way back to the shore.

Storm speaks into his phone quietly, trying to put the pieces of how this could have happened together. It shouldn't have been possible, and that's the point. The cameras in the garage were disabled before we arrived in case the Russos were tracking us that way, but that also means we have no evidence of who could have planted the bomb, or how they got past the security. The only thing that makes any sense is that it was someone who works for us, and that's a big problem.

The moment the car stops in front of the house, the door flings open and Snow and Emerson come bounding down the steps, both throwing themselves onto Everett and I before we can even get out of the car.

Tears stream down their faces while Rayne follows behind them, his eyes looking just as broken as the rest of ours. Today was a near miss, too close for comfort, and we're all feeling it.

"Thank god you're okay," Snow sobs into my chest. Everett was only able to turn us in the seat before the cavalry arrived, but there's nothing in his hold on me that indicates he's frustrated with the situation.

"I'm okay," I whisper as I reach for Emerson's hand and squeeze it. It feels like she's been a part of this family just as long as the rest of us, and I can only imagine the hell these two women have been giving Rayne since we made them leave the parking garage.

"I was so scared." Snow pulls her head back to look me over. "Are you hurt?"

I shake my head. "No, not hurt." Not physically at least. I think the fear I've felt today will live with me for a while, but I'm not in any pain if that's what she means.

"Let's get you inside, little dove," Everett whispers into the crook of my neck.

I nod. I've been shivering since the moment he pulled me from the car, my entire body trembling uncontrollably, but I'm not cold. Not really. It's the adrenaline violently forcing its way from my body.

Everett carefully lifts us both from the SUV and caries me up the front steps and into the house. The moment the front door closes behind Storm the sound of the automatic lock system sounds throughout the house. I'm glad Mom and Dad decided to have that installed, otherwise we'd all be back at Rayne's penthouse, and as lovely as that place is, it's not big enough for the six of us not to kill each other.

I burrow into Everett's chest, breathing him in with each step he takes. The scent of sandalwood and vanilla fills my nose and I can't help but do it again and again. He uses the same aftershave he did when he was younger, and it calms me almost as much as his arms around me.

"Take her up to her room," Storm says from somewhere behind us. "Then I need you and Rayne in my office."

"No," Everett replies simply. "I'm not leaving her like this, so you and Rayne can deal with this shit, and I'll take care of Wynter."

"The girls can look out for her," Storm argues and I hold on tight as Everett stops abruptly and turns around, his entire body tense as he stares at my brother.

"I know you don't get it, but Rayne does. I cannot leave her when I almost lost her today. We'll be fucking lucky if I can let her out of my sight in the next goddamn year let alone the next day," he growls.

"He's right, Storm. If it was Emerson in that car there's no way I'd be leaving her even for a minute."

"Don't you fucking get it?" Storm shouts and I immediately cower into the hard chest I'm leaning on. "We're all sitting here while they're plotting how to take us down. We need to get ahead of them. Wynter was right earlier. He could have taken the whole goddamn family out and we wouldn't have seen it coming. There's a rat somewhere in our organization, and if we don't work out who it is, we may not be here in a year for you to allow my sister out of your fucking sight."

Everett's body is vibrating with anger, but his hold on me remains firm and strong. "No Storm, you're the one that doesn't fucking get it. Just you fucking wait until you meet the woman that destroys you, and you wait for the moment they're in danger. Then we can discuss this." He turns away from my brother and starts toward the stairs without another word.

It's not until he carefully places me down on the bed that I really see just how angry he is. His face is red, and his jaw is so tight I'm worried he's going to snap something.

"Maybe you should go strategize," I whisper. "I'll be alright."

His head snaps around to face me and the fire in his eyes almost burns me on the spot. "Not you too! I couldn't give a shit about getting back at them right now. All I care about is making sure you're okay."

"I am okay, Everett. I promise. Not a scratch on me. But today could have ended very differently. We need a plan," I try to reason with him, but I should know there's no reasoning with the men in this family.

Dead of Wynter

THIRTY

EVERETT

The rage rushing through my blood only seems to deepen with each moment that passes. The more I think about what happened today, the more I consider what could have happened, the more I want to throw Wynter over my shoulder and take her away from this place. Away from the war. Away from my family. Away from danger.

And if I thought she wouldn't kill me for doing it, we'd already be on a plane halfway to the other side of the world right now, but she won't leave her family, and she won't leave Frost Industries.

I prowl across the room like a lion chasing my prey, but Wynter doesn't move a muscle. She watches me curiously, each step I take carefully considered until I'm looming over her. She follows my gaze, her head reclined all the way as she holds my eyes. Anyone else on this earth would have flinched away by now, they would have seen a predator coming at them and cowered. But not my little dove.

"Keep pushing me, Wynter. I promise you won't like the consequences," I force through clenched teeth.

Her eyebrow quirks up and the corners of her lips tip up in a mischievous smile. "Won't I?" she challenges.

If it was any other day, if she hadn't just sat over the top of a highly explosive device for two hours as she told me she loved me because she thought she was going to die, I'd probably crack a smile at her sass, but the darkness calls my name. It beckons me, and any second now I'm going to snap. "You're playing a dangerous game, little dove," I growl as I bring my face closer to hers until our breaths mingle. "You're not ready for the level of punishment I need to give you right now, so here's what we're going to do. You're going to get undressed and have a bath, a shower, I don't give a fuck. You are going to wash away any evidence of what happened today, and then you're going to come back and I'm going to hold you until I feel like I can breathe without needing you in my arms. Okay?"

Wynter shakes her head. "What if I want the punishment?" she whispers.

"Little dove," I warn.

"You need it, Ev. I can see it in you. You need this, and you gave me what I needed last night, I want to give you what you need."

"I don't want to scare you, Wynter," I say quietly. "Yesterday, the idea of punishment almost made you have a panic attack. You are not ready for what I need to do to you right now." The words come out low and rough, my desire and darkness mixing.

"Try me." Wynter shrugs but never tears her eyes from mine. She's staring the devil in the eye and she doesn't even fucking know it.

I growl and push myself away from the bed. The longer I spend with her on the bed, the more tempted I am to strip her bare and feast of her sweet body. But I swore I wouldn't touch her until she knows the truth, and until she understands how dangerous being with me truly is.

It wouldn't be fair for me to take her before she can make a decision about the monster she loves. Not that it will make any difference, but at least she'll know who I am going in.

"I can handle it, Everett."

"No, you can't. Not yet." I shake my head and resume pacing up and down the length of the room. At least if I keep moving it distracts me enough that I'm not tempted to go against everything I'm trying to do and use her body the way I crave.

Wynter groans before hanging her legs off the edge of the bed.

"Don't you dare get off that bed, Wynter," I snap.

She rolls her eyes at me, and I immediately want to take her over my knee again. She's pushing me, seeing how far she has to go before I'll give in, but I meant what I said when I told her she couldn't handle what I need right now. "A couple of things. One, you told me to shower or have a bath, neither of which I can do from bed. And two, you just told me you're not going to punish me, so what are you going to do if I move?" she challenges, her eyebrows raised in defiance.

Fuck. I forgot how much Wynter lives for the fight. She will push and push and push, until she gets exactly what she wants,

231

and if that's not one of the most equally infuriating and sexy things about her, I don't know what is.

"I swear to God, dove, if you get off that bed right now I'm going to tie you to it for the next week and bring you to the edge so many fucking times you won't even know your name by the time I finally take pity on you and allow you to come."

I stalk toward her again, unable to hold myself on the other side of the room as I should, and I don't stop until we're so close our noses brush as I bend over her. "But then, after days of denial, after you begging me so many times to allow you the release you crave, then I'll give it to you, over and over and over again, until you're begging me to stop."

Her breath hitches, but she doesn't look away, not even for a second. She's holding her own against the big bad wolf, and it's only making my cock harder.

"Is that what you want, little dove?" I ask, my hands moving until they're pressing into her thighs. "Do you want me to torture you with your own pleasure?"

Wynter shakes her head and a smirk tugs at my lips because I know I've won, but then she speaks. "If that's what you need to let go of all the anger you're holding inside, then do it. But if you need to punish me, if you need me to submit to you and accept your punishment, then that's what I'll do." Her words are even, as if she's said them a million times before.

It's long moments before I can think of anything to say. She has always been the only person who could render me speechless, and I'm almost happy to say that's still the case.

"Not today," I say quietly. "Not while I'm this wound up. I'm afraid I won't be able to stop once I start, and I don't want to scare you away from it when you just got it back."

She nods once. "Okay, not today. But if we're not going to do that, then I think we should go strategize. I'm assuming whatever was in that box yesterday wasn't a bomb, and it wasn't big enough to be anything else all that dangerous, so Angelo has escalated a lot in a very short amount of time, and I think we need to start thinking about how we're going to play this."

"How *we're* going to play it, huh?" I raise my brow. I'm not sure when she started thinking this was a group effort that involved her, but there's no way on earth I'm going to put her in harm's way.

"Yes, how we're going to play it. You guys can't use me when it's convenient and then leave me on the sidelines for everything else. I'm a part of this. That's pretty fucking obvious considering the package yesterday and then my car being the one targeted."

"It's too dangerous."

"So was sitting on top of a bomb today, but I did that," she snaps.

"I didn't put you in that situation. If I had had it my way, you wouldn't have left the damn house today," I growl.

Wynter glares at me, all the ice in her eyes directed at me with barely contained fury. "Can I go shower now?"

This goddamn woman is going to be the fucking death of me.

THIRTY-ONE

WYNTER

I expected Everett to say no to me helping plan our next move. Of course I did, because he's infuriating, overprotective, and just about the most pig-headed person I've ever met, only beaten by Storm. The thing is, he doesn't have a say in the matter, and that's all I can think about the whole way through my shower as he hovers by the door.

Every few seconds his shadow moves past the open door, which would have been closed if he hadn't have barked orders at me that he wanted me in his sights at all times. If he wasn't being such a dick, I would almost think it's cute. But he is, so I don't.

I take a long time washing my hair, shaving my legs, washing away the day from hell. The longer Everett has to stew about what I said, the closer his resolve will be to snapping. He may know me like the back of his hand, but he forgets that I know him just as well. I may not know what he's been doing for the last eight years, or what he does to make him think he's such a dangerous predator, but I know his soul.

When I finally shut the water off and wrap myself in a towel, I think about putting my robe on, but then I decide against it. If he wants to play a game, he better be ready to lose. I soak up some of the water from my hair before discarding the second towel and making my way back into my bedroom without sparing him so much as a look.

The towel I've wrapped around myself barely covers my ass, and so much as leaning forward will expose it to him, so naturally that's the first thing I do as I approach my drawers. I'm not looking for anything in particular, in fact, I have no intention of getting dressed any time soon, but just knowing he's staring at me, and that it's torturing him is enough to have me opening every drawer and coming out empty-handed each time.

"What the fuck are you doing?" Everett finally asks when I move to my bedside table and open the drawer there. The contents are limited to my Kindle, a vibrator, and some lip balm, so I close it before answering.

"I'm sorry?"

"What. Are. You. Doing?" He takes heavy steps toward me, prowling across the room like a man on a mission.

"Oh, I'm looking for something." I shrug, moving both hands to the knot in the front of my towel.

I turn away from him and back to the drawer, because I've never had a very good poker face and the moment he figures out I'm taunting him is the moment he's going to snap... why did I turn away again? Don't I want him to snap? To take me even though he shouldn't.

"What are you looking for?" he asks.

I stop what I'm doing and think for a minute. Fuck. I should have actually had something I was looking for in the eventuality that he would ask. "My vibrator," I tell him noncommittally. I'm quite literally poking the bear and hoping like hell he's going to bite.

There's nothing but silence for so long I almost look over my shoulder to make sure he's still there, but then I feel him. His heat only a breath away from my bare back, the anger vibrating from his body only making the fire between my thighs rage hotter. I bend forward again and open the drawer and pull out the small pink bullet vibe I take whenever I spend a night away from home in case the mood strikes me. Luckily when I stayed here the weekend before my parents died, I left in a hurry and completely forgot to pack it. It's been the last thing on my mind since I've been here, but right now I can't think of anything else.

"What do you think you're doing with that, little dove?" he growls, the question so low and deep it almost makes me drop it. His breath whispers across my back and an involuntary shiver makes its way across my skin.

"Thought I might do a little self-care." I smirk to myself, barely able to keep a straight face. I want to get a reaction out of him, I want him to snap and take me the way he wants to, the way he's denying himself.

A steel bar of a forearm wraps around my waist and tugs me back to him until I collide with solid muscle. His body is hot and hard against my back, and the towel I'm wearing does nothing to protect me from the burn.

"You're playing with fire, little dove."

I close my eyes for a moment to steady myself, his touch sends me to the edge of my consciousness until I'm teetering on the precipice like a tightrope. Every rational thought disappears, and all that's left is Everett.

"I don't know what you mean."

Before I can take another breath, he's turned me to face the bed and pushed me face first into the plush mattress. His weight follows closely, and all I can feel is his heat and hardness against my back.

"You know exactly what I mean, Wynter," he drawls right before his teeth clamp down on my shoulder.

I hiss out a breath, the pleasure and pain mingling together and making it hard to conjure a response. With anyone else I would be able to think clearly even as they play my body, but not him. Everett has always been able to render me speechless, even when we were still kids and had no idea of the attraction growing between us.

"The other night I told you your orgasms belong to me. You don't get any pleasure, unless I say so, and I know for a fact I made myself very fucking clear." Another bite right next to the last once, except this one stings more and for a moment I wonder if he's broken the skin. His tongue laps at the sore spot, his lips brushing over the battered flesh sensitive from his assault. "So I'm certain you weren't intending to get yourself off right in front of me, were you, little dove?"

Goose bumps make their way across every bare piece of skin and I barely withhold the moan teetering at the edge of my throat. Fuck. When he talks like this I want him to take me, I want him to do every dirty, fucked-up thing he wants to my body, and I'll lie here and take every bit of it. But that doesn't detract from the fact he thinks I'm too fragile to include in things that certainly involve me. That's the problem with men in families like mine, they always see women as weak. We're the lesser species, and that's just the way it's always been. There are positives to their reasoning. They think we're so precious that putting us in danger is for the detriment of the family itself. We're the ones that hold everything together, we're the ones they come home to at night and forget about whatever horrors the day held.

But that's not how it is anymore. Or at least it shouldn't be. I'm just as capable of running both sides of this family as Storm is. I've trained for it, and while I haven't been *as* involved in the darker sides of our family's legacy, I have studied it. I know every detail about every man that works for us, right down to the runners on the corners. I know the ins and outs of every single facet of Frost Industries, and that's what they seem to forget.

"That's exactly what I was intending to do," I say as steadily as I can manage.

The confession is a lie, but I'm hoping he won't know without being able to see my face. It's always been easier to lie to him without having to look him in the eye when I do it. That's how I avoided telling him about Steve Dobbins who tried to touch me junior year. Everett was in college at the time, but we spoke every day, just the way best friends do. If my brothers didn't find out and tell him I would have been free and clear on that one. I wiggle beneath him, testing just how much room I have to move, and I'm not disappointed when I find he has me pinned completely.

"I mean, you did basically just tell me that you're not going to punish me because I can't handle it, so really, what possible consequences could there be for a little self-care?" I smile to myself. It's been too long since I could push him like this. Before it was innocent, I just liked to see the possessive, protective streak flash through his eyes, but now it's more. I want him to unleash the monster he holds at bay.

DEAD OF WYNTER

THIRTY-TWO
EVERETT

I almost can't tell if she's serious or if she's trying to push me off the very steep cliff I'm standing on the edge of. Without being able to see her tells, I almost miss the one she doesn't know about, the way I've always been able to tell she's lying to me.

Every time my little dove tells a lie, she tenses. It's the slightest of movements, and if you weren't as utterly obsessed with her as I am you would never catch it, even if you were holding her, but I see it.

A chuckle claws up the back of my throat, and as much as I want to stamp it down, I don't. The smile that pulls at my lips to accompany the laugh feels out of place after what we've been through today, but she's safe, she's in my arms, if I can't be happy about that, what on earth can I smile about?

"What are you laughing about? It's true," she lies again.

I press a gentle kiss to the skin at the nape of her neck. The longer I go thinking I'm not going to touch her until she knows the truth, the harder it is to stop myself from doing such simple things like this.

"You trying to get your own way by pissing me off. It's cute."

Now I'm the one trying to get a reaction. I've called her that so many times over the years, and every single time she puffs up like a fucked off kitten, and every time it makes me hard as a fucking rock.

"I am not cute," she snaps.

"What would you call it, dove?" I place another kiss to her shoulder blade, and then several along the angry teeth marks I've left behind. Wynter's creamy skin looks impossibly beautiful with my marks, and I can't wait to cover her with so many, so often, that she'll grow used to them being there just like the birthmark on her thigh.

She wriggles beneath me, seeing if she can get free, but she's not going anywhere. I love having her trapped under my body, love the feeling of her warmth against me, the feel of her perky ass pressed against my impossibly hard cock. It would be so easy to slide right into her pussy like this. Unzip my pants, bring the towel up a few inches, and then sink into her so fucking deep she doesn't know where she ends and I begin.

Maybe I've been going about this the wrong way. Maybe I should have come at it from a different angle and made her think everything that's about to happen between us is her idea, but I don't have the patience for that. I need her on my own time, I can't afford to wait for her to make the right decisions.

I wasted eight years, and I'm not about to waste one more second with my little dove.

I lean more of my weight into her back, pressing my cock harder into her ass as I grind slightly. It's not a part of the plan but fuck the plan. Who cares if she knows why I left, as long as she recognizes it had to have been for a good reason. Maybe I'll never have to tell her.

It's a nice thought, one I've contemplated more than a few times since I walked back into her life, but after the package that was delivered yesterday and the bomb today, all the pieces will start to fall together, and her self-preservation will take over.

When the choice is her life, or me, can I really bank on her choosing the latter?

"What were you trying to achieve with this little performance, dove?" I breathe.

"I don't know what you're talking about," Wynter whispers. "I was almost blown up by our enemies today, I think I deserve an orgasm or two."

"If that's what you wanted, little dove, you should have just asked." I smile against her neck right before wrapping my hand around the front of her throat. "Why don't you ask me for what you need, Wynter?"

I hold her with the slightest of pressure. Not enough that she can't breathe or speak, but enough that her body squirms beneath mine, just the way I like it. All those years ago when I took her virtue and left in the middle of the night, I only gave her a taste of what I like. Even back then I enjoyed the finer things in life, like the submission of a beautiful woman.

"I don't want anything from you."

I smirk and tighten my hold on her throat ever so slightly. "Liar. Try again."

"Everett," she warns and there's the slightest hint of fear in her voice.

You wouldn't hear it if you weren't obsessed with every move she makes. You'd miss it, maybe even mistake it for something else altogether. The subtle rise in the way she says my name, the little breath she lets out to steady her composure. I've seen her do it a thousand times. I know every single one of Wynter's emotions, every one of her little quirks. The way her nose scrunches when she tries not to smile. The way her lips turn up slightly when she's trying to hold back laughter. I've spent so many years studying her that I can recite every single one.

When she doesn't continue, I snake a hand under her body and move to prove my suspicions correct. She's soaking wet.

Seeing her pussy the other night as she brought herself to orgasm was one thing but running my fingers through her wetness is something entirely different. If I thought I would be able to stop before, if I thought I would pull away and keep my word, there's no physical way I can do that now.

"Is all this for me, little dove?" I whisper, nipping at her earlobe and relishing in the way her body tightens under mine. Fuck, I could do this all day. Tease her, bite her, mark her. Over and over again until all that's left is the writhing, soaking wet, mess of the woman I love. "Ask for what you want, Wynter."

She lets out a stuttered breath and buries her face into the bedding, muffling the moan trying to escape. Part of me doesn't want her to answer. Part of me wants to drag this out for as long as I can, just to make the moment last forever. It's the same way I felt the night I allowed myself something I never should have taken. But then she takes a deep breath, I know she's going to reply.

"I want you to stop holding back. I'm not going to break. I'm not the fragile little flower you and my brothers think I am. I sat at that table with you as you told them I was stronger than they gave me credit for, now I need you to believe your own words."

I consider her for a moment. She's not entirely wrong. I did say all those things, but it's a completely different situation to put the woman I love in danger. Because the idea of living even a moment on this earth without her has a fist wrapping around my lungs and holding on so tight I can barely drag in a breath. None of what she has said matters. I'm not putting her in immediate danger. Not today. Not tomorrow. Not ever.

Wynter is the most precious thing in my life and if she thinks I'm going to put her in harm's way, she's going to be sorely disappointed.

THIRTY-THREE

WYNTER

He's quiet for so long I think he's considering what I've said. I didn't intend on pushing him about this anymore today because I understand why he's acting like a possessive caveman right now. But somewhere along the way I started to walk the line between the two things I want.

To submit to Everett and him not treat me like a fractured doll.

And for the men in my family to recognize that I'm just as useful in this war as they are.

The two coincide more than you would think, both talking more of their underestimation than anything else, but it runs deeper than that. It's like the two parts of me colliding. The boss I show the world, and the person I haven't allowed myself to be since Craig hurt me.

And then after a few more moments of silence, I start to wonder if he's going to reply at all. His body weight is still heavy on my back, grounding me after the day we've had, but he's not rocking his hips into my ass anymore.

A moment later he flips me over and pushes me up the bed before climbing over me, settling his weight on me again. For a moment I wonder if he knows I need it, if he realizes that the small gesture is keeping me here with him, instead of allowing my mind to wander to all the possibilities of how today could have ended.

Everett's fingers brush across my cheek in a tender gesture I almost don't recognize. Not that he has ever been anything but gentle with me, but this seems like more, like he's staring into the depths of my soul and seeing himself. "You are everything to me, Wynter. You think the reason I want to clip your wings is because I'm controlling like your brothers, or old fashioned like every other organization like this one, but the truth is that I can't fathom living a day on this earth if you're not walking it to. Even when we were apart, I always knew you were okay. Hurt, but okay. But the idea that that may not be the case one day, that we could send you in like a sacrificial lamb and you may not walk out on the other side of it, that fucking kills me." He presses his eyes closed for a moment, emotions swirling around in the deep blue and threatening to spill over. "I just want you safe. Today was…" He takes a deep breath to settle the anger flicking across his features. "It was too close, dove, too fucking close."

I snake my hand up his body until his face is cupped in my palm. The warmth of his cheek leans into my hand and a part of me I thought long dead flickers to life. The flame only Everett can stoke lights for the first time in eight years, and it's like my heart has a reason to beat, and my lungs have a reason to breathe. "Nothing is going to happen to me. Do you know why?"

He shakes his head slightly, his face still resting in my palm, and something that doesn't belong in a man like Everett creeps into his eyes. Vulnerability. It's a weakness for men like him, something he can't afford to have, but the way he looks down at me, like I'm the finest piece of china left on this earth, and I'm about the shatter.

"Because you won't let it." I smile. "It doesn't matter if I'm involved in this takedown, or if you keep me locked here in this ivory tower until all the danger is gone. You'll keep me safe, and that's why I'm not afraid."

"And whose going to keep you safe from me, little dove? The same blood runs in my veins. They're going to keep coming for you until they're dead and buried, but what if I turn out like them? Or like my father? What then?"

I shake my head. "That won't happen. Just because they're your blood, doesn't make them your family. You grew up with us. With Storm and Rayne as brothers. With Mom and Dad as parents. And you and I were connected from that first moment. Do you remember?" I close my eyes as I reminisce on the moment my life changed. The moment I met the boy who made me believe in all the fairy tales I was told as a little girl. "Storm always used to talk about you, you know? And mom used to talk about what a nice boy you were, but that day... it feels like a dream even now."

I don't know why I'm allowing myself to walk down this path, because it's a dangerous one. Everett's childhood was anything but happy, except for the times he was with us. The nights he would show up on the doorstep at midnight, his bike in one hand, and his other clutching broken ribs from where his uncle had become frustrated with him. I was too young to understand what was going on, even if parts of me did. I'd seen plenty of blood by that age. Men being traipsed through our house at ungodly hours of the night and never leaving the basement. But there was something different about tending to Everett's wounds. Something intimate even.

"I remember," he croaks. "I thought you were an angel. I still do." His fingers brush through the blonde locks fanned out around my head.

"You're nothing like them, Everett."

"How do you know?"

"Because none of them are capable of love."

His eyes flash with emotion as he stares down at me, the moment turning into long stretches of silence as he processes the words I've said. He knows I'm right, but whether he's going to admit that or not may be an entirely different story. There's a fire in his eyes I've seen before, a determination that seems almost as familiar as the man himself.

He catches me off guard when his lips come down on mine in a passionate kiss, his tongue demanding entry the moment they lock and I'm powerless to deny him. I always have been. Because the reality is, even if Everett left me a thousand times, I'd take back a thousand and one times. The kiss is full of everything we've left unsaid over the last eight years. The emotions we felt the night he left, the ones we felt when we were apart, and the ones we've felt since he walked back into my life and reminded me what it feels like to be alive.

Everett's body rocks into mine, our hips align and I can feel him exactly where I need him. The fabric of his pants, and the barely there towel does nothing to shield me from the

252

heat. "This wasn't the plan," he groans between kisses, his movements only growing more impatient.

"Who gives a fuck about the plan," I moan as his lips trail across my cheek and down my neck, nipping and sucking as he travels across my skin.

"I was meant to tell you everything."

"I don't care about any of that, Everett. Nothing you could tell me would change how I feel, and it certainly wouldn't change how fucking badly I need you."

Before he can respond, I capture his lips again, and this kiss catches us both off guard. Everett pours every emotion, everything he's kept from me, everything we've been through, the pain of every moment we spent apart into the kiss, and I let him. He needs this just the same way I do, and I allow his to claim me in a way I haven't let anyone close to since he left. I can't help but wonder if somewhere in the back of my mind I always knew he would come back for me.

I reach up to wrap my arms around his neck and pull him closer, but he quickly gathers both hands into one of his and holds them above my head.

After everything Craig put me through, I never thought I'd be able to handle being restrained in any way, but the way Everett pins me to the mattress feels like coming home.

Being with him has always allowed me to be who I truly am, but this moment feels different. It's like all the broken pieces are clicking back together, and for the first time in as long as I can remember, my mind is quiet. I got a taste of this last night, but for some reason after almost being blown up, everything is amplified.

"Tell me what you need, dove," Everett whispers as he trails hard kisses along my jaw and down my neck, tearing moans from the throat.

"You," I pant. "I need you."

Everett rears back for a moment to look down at me, and when our eyes clash he searches mine for something. "I won't be able to take it easy, Wynter. This won't be anything like our first time." He's trying to scare me off, trying to convince me to wait without saying the words, but I need this. I need him.

"I don't care."

Dead of Wynter

THIRTY-FOUR

EVERETT

The words slip from her pretty red lips so easily it's almost like she's not signing a deal with the devil. Every moment I've ever spent with Wynter has been a moment I've held back, never wanting to frighten her with the monster I hide. But as fury rages through my body I can't hide that part of me anymore.

The devil begs to be unleashed, begs to see the light of day after so many years of hiding from the woman we both love, and if Wynter wants to meet him, who am I to say no?

"Okay, little dove, let's play your way." I drag my fingers down until they wrap around the front of her throat, ever so slightly restricting her breathing. "But there are rules."

She nods under my grip, her eyes dilated with the rush of endorphins spreading through her body. Everyone outside this room, the entire world, would think she's an innocent wallflower, but maybe I always knew she would be like this. That the darkest parts of me, would call to her.

"When I speak to you, I expect an answer. I need to know that you're okay, and I might miss your head nodding or shaking, so I need words, okay?"

"Yes," she whispers. There's the prettiest blush climbing up her chest, over her neck and up to her cheeks. It's almost the same color as her ass was last night when I spanked her and my palm inches to do it again.

"Good girl. We're going to run on a traffic light system, do you know what that means?" I ask. If she's been to a BDSM club, there's a good chance they used this with her. It's the easiest for a sub to remember when they're teetering on the edge of subspace, and that's exactly where I'm taking her tonight. She needs it, and I do too. I need her to give me her submission, and know I'll take care of it just like I will her.

"Yes." She nods. "Green means I'm okay, orange I need to slow down and talk, and red is stop."

I smile. Fuck, I'm lucky none of those Doms at that club claimed her, because she's just about as perfect as subs come. Obedient. A little bratty. And a whole lot of sexy. "Very good. Now, you are not to come until I explicitly tell you that you can. Do you understand?"

Wynter's eyes widen for a moment, her bottom lip disappearing between her teeth. This is the part of the scene she wouldn't have had much exposure to. She may have seen it as she walked past scenes at the club. If my girl was only there for punishments she probably wouldn't have experienced edge play before, but it's my personal favorite. Watching my sub writhe and beg and plead for her release only for me to take it away is one of my favorite things to do, and I have a feeling watching her in that situation is going to be my new favorite sight.

"Yes, I understand," she breathes. Every breath I feel under my palm, and it's a heady feeling to control something as basic as breathing.

"If you come without permission, dove, you will not be coming for the next week. I will bring you to the edge so many times, and so often, that you will forget your own goddamn name."

Her eyes dilate further and my cock stiffens at the sight. She loves it. The idea of me controlling her like this is driving her wild, and I almost can't restrain myself.

"Now, you know I will never do anything that would hurt you, but considering what has happened in your past, before I do anything we haven't done before, I'm going to let you know what I'm doing. I will not blindfold you, however I am going to tie you up. If at any time it gets too much and you're too overwhelmed with not being able to move, I want you to call out orange and we'll talk through what's going on, okay?"

"Okay, Ev," she says quietly.

"Good girl, Wynter." I smile down at her and take my time trailing my eyes down her body.

She's still mostly covered by the towel, but the silky skin peeking out is tempting me like the apple tempted Eve.

"Are there any hard limits I should know about? Anything you absolutely do not want me to do to you?"

"Belts. I can't." She shakes her head and her heart rate speeds up under my fingers.

"No belts," I assure her. It's not my implement of choice anyway, I've seen too many subs walk away with lasting scars so similar to the ones Wynter has because the Dom was slightly too heavy handed. In the right setting, with the right people they can be fun, and maybe one day I'll want to help her get past her fear, but for right now it's not necessary for either of us. "Do you remember how to present yourself, dove?"

Wynter nods. "I think so."

"Good. I need to go get some things from my room, I want you naked and in position when I get back," I tell her, but I can't bring myself to move. Her warmth below me feels so right it seems impossible to move, but when she wriggles beneath me I tear my body from hers.

Once there's some space between us my brain starts to function again. It's always been like this. Wynter has always clouded my vision, but that seems especially true now. Now I know what life is like without her in it.

If I were a good man, I would leave this room and not return until the thundering in my blood has calmed down. But I'm not a good man, and the only thing that can bring me down is Wynter.

"Are you sure you want to do this?" I ask even though I'm not sure how I'll stop if she changes her mind.

Wynter sits up, her tousled blonde hair falling around her face and down her chest. Her hand reaches for me and I can't help but take it, tangling our fingers together. "I need this just the same way you do," she whispers, as if the words are more than either of us can handle, and hell, they just may well be.

I squeeze her hand before breaking the contact between us and leaving the room quickly. The longer I linger, the more likely I am to fuck her without all the foreplay we both crave. I've only been back to my apartment once since the accident and I packed a lot more than clothes in the hope Wynter and I might find ourselves here.

A selection of my favorite toys have been stuffed into the bottom of my wardrobe and barely thought about since.

Once I close my bedroom door behind me, I make a beeline to the hiding place, looking for a few key items. I imagine this is how teenage boys feel when they have porn stashed in their bedroom in places their parents would never look, squirreling it around in the fear their mom will find it. I never had that experience. By the time I was old enough for porn my uncle was trying to have hookers take my virginity so I could become a man.

There are an endless number of implements I want to use on Wynter, and that I will at some stage, but I don't have that kind of patience right now.

I throw a few things in a bag and hope like hell I don't run into anyone in the hallway. Luckily I make it back to Wynter's room without being caught red-handed with a bag of sex toys and close the door quietly behind me. Nothing could prepare me for the sight waiting for me.

Wynter kneels beside the bed, her knees spread apart, giving me a peek at her sweet pussy, her head is bowed, and eyes cast down submissively, and her hands rest on her thighs, palms open and facing up.

I've never seen anything so fucking beautiful in my life.

"Very good, dove," I praise as I set the bag down on the bed and run my fingers through her impossibly soft hair.

Wynter forces herself to keep her eyes down, but that's the one thing I don't want. At clubs, and generally, in the lifestyle, subs are taught not to meet a Dom's eye unless explicitly instructed to do so, but that's not me, at least it's not when Wynter is involved.

"I want your eyes on me and what I'm doing to you at all times," I tell her and it only takes a second for her eyes to meet mine, a small smile on her lips. "You're very obedient like this considering you're usually so bratty."

"I am not bratty," she quips and then snaps her mouth shut.

I chuckle and squat down in front of her, my fingers grasping her chin between them. "Case and point, little dove. Anymore outbursts like that and I'll be adding to the punishment you're owed."

DEAD OF WYNTER

THIRTY-FIVE
WYNTER

My eyes widen at the words. Everett seemed so against punishing me today after what happened, he said I couldn't handle it, but he seems to have done a complete flip. If there's anything I need right now it's to be taken out of my head, to float in the bliss and know he won't let me fall.

The voice in the back of my head tells me to look at whatever he's put on the bed, but I know better than doing the opposite of what he's instructed me to do. I've spent enough time in the scene to know that will only make any punishment he has planned for me that much worse.

"Stand," Everett says evenly and I quickly do as he's told me.

It feels good to feed this part of me again after allowing it to remain dormant for so many years. It's not that I didn't want to submit in all those years, it's that I couldn't put one hundred percent trust into someone that they wouldn't hurt me like Craig did. Until now.

Everett knows me better than I know myself. It's always been this way, and I know he won't push me further than I can take, and if I safe word, he'll stop before the word even finishes rolling off my tongue. This is the only situation I would have felt safe, the only person I would have ever been able to do this with.

He smiles down at me, his fingers brushing along my cheek and down my neck. His eyes trail down the path his fingers move, and when they reach my breasts he lets out a low sound of appreciation. Both hands move to cup them, flicking the sensitive nubs and making me squeeze my legs together. "You are so beautiful, dove."

"Thank you," I reply quietly. The Doms I've played with in the past weren't big talkers, and I've never been with Everett like this, I don't want to upset him before we can really get started.

"You may talk freely, Wynter. Unless I tell you otherwise, I want to hear your words."

"Okay." I smile.

His eyes continue their perusal of my body, and I can't find it in me to feel shy. Usually having anyone look at me like this would be enough to make me want to cover up, but as I stand in front of Everett, feeling more vulnerable than I can ever remember feeling, confidence washes over me. The fire in his deep pools gives me everything I need to remain standing without the urge to cover myself. "As I mentioned, I would like to restrain you. Are you comfortable with that?" he asks, his eyes burning into mine before I can even respond.

He's looking for a lie. He thinks I might push myself further than I'm comfortable with in order to please him.

"I'd like to try," I tell him honestly. I don't know if I'm going to be able to handle it, especially if he's going to punish me while I'm tied down, but I like to think if there's anyone who can make it happen, it's Everett.

He nods once, a small smile playing at his lips. "Hands behind your back for me, little dove," he commands and I follow immediately. Even just following his orders feels freeing. It's been too long since I've been able to let go and just be. Since I've been able to rely on someone else for everything. And I like it. "You're being a very good girl, dove."

Something soft touches my wrists and binds them together. There's a moment of panic where my mind wanders to a place I haven't allowed it to go in a long time, but then Everett's back in front of me, his face soft.

"Okay?"

I nod, allowing myself to close my eyes for a moment to gather my composure, to remind myself I'm safe and no one is going to hurt me. When I open them again, Everett is staring at me intently, a flash of worry in his eyes. "I'm alright," I assure him.

He watches me for another moment before speaking. "I've bound your wrists with a silk scarf. It's not tight and if you tug you'll be able to release the knot. If you get too overwhelmed I want you to say your safe word and tug at the scarf to break free, okay?"

It's on the tip of my tongue to thank him for doing this for me, but he can see it in my eyes how thankful I am for him giving this part of myself back. So instead I say, "Yes, I can do that."

Everett smiles down at me before cupping my cheek in one of his big hands. "I'm proud of you, dove. Even if we get three minutes in and you safe word, I'm still going to be so fucking proud of you."

I preen under his attention, under his soft words that hold so much meaning, and even though I'm nervous, I know I can do this, because Everett will hold me up even when I can't hold myself, just like he always has.

"I want you to bend over the arm of the lounge over there, and then we're going to start slow."

He doesn't check in this time, and I'm kind glad for it. Every time he does it gives me an opportunity to back out, and even though the intensity of the anxiety coursing through my body makes me question myself, I don't want to stop.

I do as he asks, taking slow, measured steps across the room, acutely aware of my bound wrists and clumsiness, but I make it and do as he asks, carefully folding my body over the arm and repositioning until the cushioning is in a comfortable place.

The sound of a drawer opening piques my interest, but I don't lift my head from the softness beneath my cheek. If he wants me to know what he's doing, he'll tell me. Heavy footsteps grow closer and a bag drops behind me. Anticipation builds low in my belly, mixing with something else entirely. Heat. Every move Everett makes is like a lightning rod to my core.

"I'm going to give you twenty, but I want to trial some other things apart from my hand. I'll give you two with each and then check in before continuing. What are your safe words?"

"Green for okay, orange to pause and talk, red for stop," I rattle them off like I've done it a million times when in reality, I've only ever used the system once in the past.

"Good girl," he praises. "Five with my hand to warm you up, then we'll move on."

His palm rubs across my bare ass and a shiver of need rushes across my skin and takes my breath away. He doesn't make me wait long before his hand lifts and then comes down in a brutal slap that makes my hips shove forward into the arm of the chair. Another three come in hard and fast before he lands the last one and massages the burn in. I'm already panting and he's barely even started.

"How are you doing, Wynter?" Everett asks as he kneads the stinging flesh of my ass, massaging until the burn runs so deep it feels like it's at the bone.

"Green," I moan. The combination of startling pain and heat rush together to my core, setting my entire body on fire.

Everett makes a pleased noise in the back of his throat and I hear him rustle around in the bag he set beside me, but I stay where I am, face pressed into the cushion, fighting my inquisitive nature. His warmth returns behind me and I hold my breath for the feel of something on my already sensitive ass, but nothing comes. For long moments my breath is hitched, waiting, and waiting, and waiting. But he just stands there.

I open my mouth to ask what he's doing when I hear it. Buzzing. Familiar buzzing. Where do I know that sound from… I almost get all the way through asking myself the question when an assault of vibrations hits my clit and I lurch forward in surprise.

"Ev," I groan.

"You wanted to give yourself... how did you phrase it again, dove? Self-care." The words are darker than I'm used to hearing from Everett, and that only makes my pussy clench around the emptiness. The vibrations increase and I let out a hiss, every inch of my skin is alight with electricity, and every bit of pleasure he pushes upon me is felt throughout every cell. "This is what you wanted, isn't it?"

"Yes," I whisper through the climax climbing at the edge of my consciousness. Everett and I haven't been together enough for him to be able to play my body like this, and yet he is. He's sure of every move he makes, of the pressure he uses on my clit, on the gentle caress of my bare back as he drives me higher and higher, and the exact moment I reach the precipice of my release. That last one I know for a fact he knows because one second I'm riding the edge, ready to tumble over the edge, and the next there's nothing. "What the fuck?" I snap.

Everett chuckles. "Bad girls don't get to come, Wynter. Bad girls get edged until their legs shake with the need for release, until they're begging and promising every dirty deed under the sun just to be allowed to come."

My mouth drops open at the words and for a moment, the slightest of seconds, I think about saying my safe word. But it wouldn't be right because I'm not overwhelmed or unable to handle what he's doing to me, I'm just frustrated, which is exactly how he wants me.

DEAD OF WYNTER

THIRTY-SIX

EVERETT

I almost chuckle at her silence. I'm not sure why she's surprised, I told her this would happen if she disobeyed me, and that's what she's been doing from the moment we stepped foot back in this house.

Wynter will learn she's not in control, but only because I'm going to teach her. My little dove isn't going to know what hit her when I start training her to be exactly what I need, and this is just the beginning.

I press the small vibrator back to her clit and smirk as her body jolts again. She's so sensitive considering I've barely touched her and I find myself idly hoping this is how it always is between us. That she'll always crave me just the same way I crave her.

"Everett," she whines, her body barely able to remain still, but she's doing so well. For someone who has been out of the lifestyle for such a long time, she remembers a lot. Part of me is ropable that she ever allowed someone to touch her, that she would walk into a BDSM club unprotected, but then the rational, although small, part of my mind remembers that she was safer there than she was with her own security, and then there's barely contained rage boiling in my blood again for an entirely different reason.

"Are you close, dove?"

"Yes."

"Do you want to come?"

"So badly," she cries out.

I smile, watching as her body trembles from the pleasure I'm giving her, but the moment she stiffens is the moment I pull my hand away and throw the vibrator down beside her.

Wynter glares at me over her shoulder, the anger crossing her features only makes me want to chuckle more. She's so fucking cute.

"What's wrong, little dove?" I ask, my hand twitching to slap her ass again, but it's time to move on, just not until she turns back toward the cushion.

"I need to come," she whines.

I shake my head, slowly moving around to where she's bent over and kneel beside her. My fingers brush across her cheek, tears of frustration run down her cheeks. Oh my little dove has no idea what I have in store for her, how many more times I'm going to hold her on the edge just to take her pleasure away. She'll think twice about disobeying me in the future, because this is the real punishment. Sure, her ass is going to hurt, but there's something so much more fun about orgasm denial. "Not yet, little dove. You'll come when I decide and not a moment sooner, and if you do without permission, this will be your reality for the next week." I shouldn't be getting this much enjoyment out of her pain, out of her frustration, but fuck me if my cock isn't so hard it could cut diamonds right now. "Now, we're going to move on to the crop. Does that sound okay?"

Wynter's breath catches and she closes her eyes for a moment as she gathers her composure. "Yes, that sounds okay," she whispers.

I brush my fingers through her hair and smile down at her. "I'm proud of you, little dove. You're being such a good girl for me."

She preens under my praise and leans into my touch. She's like putty in my hands and I can't wait to mold her into the perfect little dove.

I give her a quick kiss, not allowing myself to linger for more than a moment before taking my place behind her again. I'm both frustrated and grateful I haven't stripped yet. The longer I stare at my beautiful girl bent over for me, the harder it is to go through with this plan. It's been too long since I've been inside her, too many years have passed since I slid into her tight heat for the first time and took the one thing I would never be able to give back. Not that I would even if I could. Wynter's virginity is the best thing I ever stole.

I swat my own hand a couple of times to test the force. Despite this being a punishment, I have to go slow with Wynter or she's going to retreat into herself and never want to try anything like this again, and that's not something either of us wants.

The first strike makes her gasp, and I hold back the next for a moment giving her time to decide if she's okay or not while I stare at the beautiful pink mark the crop left behind.

"Green," she whispers, her hips moving ever so slightly as her body searches for relief.

"Let me know if that changes, little dove."

I smile to myself as I rub the other cheek, preparing it for the blow it's about to receive before I land the next three alternating from cheek to cheek. Wynter yelps as each one lands, but she remains perfectly still for me, barely jostling the whole time.

"One more," I tell her as I rub one globe and then the next, the heat radiating into my palm.

Her hands clutch at the silk wrapped around her wrists and I move slightly to get the angle I need before swatting her swollen pussy lightly. The shock of the blow still makes her cry out, but as I rub her sensitive nub with the end of the crop, it quickly turns into a low moan.

"Still green, Wynter?" I ask, applying a little more pressure to her clit.

"Yes," she moans.

"Your pussy is so wet for me, dove." I remove the crop from her pussy to bring it around so she can see her juices covering it.

She smiles sweetly up at me, her eyes dancing with lust and mischief as they dart between the crop and my own.

"It's almost like you're enjoying your punishment," I admonish. It's not almost like anything, Wynter is loving everything I'm giving her. As frustrated as she is, she's getting closer and closer to the place she craves and I can't wait to get her there. "Clean it," I order.

Her eyes widen for a moment but I don't give her time to think about her options before the crop touches her bottom lip, and a second later her sinfully pink tongue darts out and across the smooth leather.

I barely stifle the groan clawing up my throat at the sight as she tentatively laps at the instrument that was causing her pain just a few moments ago. All I can imagine is her tongue moving up and down my length before she takes me into her mouth, and I barely stop myself from unzipping my pants and making that part of her punishment.

"That's enough," I growl when I can't handle another moment. I throw the crop down on the other side of the sofa and kneel by her head again, my thumb brushing along her bottom lip. "Since you're being such a good girl, I'll give you a choice for what comes next. Paddle or flogger?"

Wynter's eyes flare with fear and arousal. There are parts of her that are struggling to remain in the here and now with me, but the more she leans into what her body is feeling, the more she enjoys everything I'm doing to her. "I don't—" Her words cut off as she closes her eyes and takes a few deep breaths. "I don't know if I can."

"Where are you at, dove?" I ask, ready to scoop her up and untie her at a moment's notice if she says it.

"Green. I'm just… nervous." For a woman who is normally

so sure of herself, this is a rare show of the vulnerability she hides from the world.

I brush her hair from her face, my fingers carefully trailing down her cheek. "I understand. You're doing so well and if you want to stop right now I'm not going to be upset, but if you want to keep going, you know I'll never do anything that would really hurt you."

She nods. "I know. I want to keep going."

"I'm proud of you, little dove. How about we try to flogger first? I know you mentioned you liked it at the club?"

"Okay," she whispers.

I smile warmly at her before pressing a kiss to her lips, not allowing myself to linger for more than a moment because I'm walking a fucking tightrope of lust right now and spending too much time kissing her will have all my other plans going out the window.

Once I've drawn the flogger from the bag, I place the ends on her bare back and carefully trail them down so she can feel the soft leather. She didn't need to tell me for me to know why this bothered her, it's almost too similar to a belt, but I would never use anything so harshly on her. No matter how upset I was, not even if she begged me, I couldn't do it, and deep down Wynter knows that.

DEAD OF WYNTER

THIRTY-SEVEN
WYNTER

The feel of the leather on my back has my heartbeat speeding up and the edge of panic seeping into my blissful state. The memories of that night dance just outside my field of vision, but it's Everett's soft touches that hold me here with him, that stop my mind from carrying me away to the night I wished for death.

"Ready, dove?" he asks gently as his fingers trail up the length of my spine in a soothing gesture.

"Yes," I whisper, pressing my face into the cushion. The worst thing I can do is tense, it will only enhance the pain, but I don't know how to feel anything other than tense right now.

It's only a moment before the leather hits my skin in a gentle blow. This isn't about punishment anymore, and if I'm really honest with myself I don't think it was to begin with. This has always been about giving me back something I lost. The sting comes a moment later, but it's almost comforting. The burn of my ass hurts, but not in the way it did as Craig hit me over and over again. The pain Everett inflicts is sensual and sexy, it has a place and a purpose.

"Green," I say before I've really thought it all the way through. But then again, the safe words aren't there for me to think over. They're there if something is too overwhelming, too painful, and I'm not there.

He praises me quietly before continuing, and each hit is equally freeing as it is painful. The burn rushes through my body, my nerve endings firing with electricity, but the tears running down my cheeks aren't those of agony, they're tears of freedom, of letting go of something that has held me down for so long I almost forgot what it was like to let go.

"Wynter?" The concern is evident in Everett's voice as the heavy leather hits the carpet and a moment later he's kneeling beside me.

Every single part of me wants to reassure him, wants to tell him that he's done everything I asked him to do and that I'm not crying because he hurt me, but the emotions washing over me are too overwhelming to force words through.

He curses as he reaches for the silk wrapped around my wrist but I manage to pull my arms away from him before he can touch them. "Dove, I'm just going to untie you, I'm not going to hurt you." His words are full of agony. He thinks I'm pulling away from him because I'm scared, but that's the furthest thing from the truth.

"I want to keep going," I choke, the words barely audible around my sobs.

"No." He shakes his head. "We've done enough. I don't want

to hurt or scare you."

I gulp in breaths of air because I don't want this to stop. I need to tell him the tears aren't bad, that I'm releasing years of sadness, years of fear I've never been able to work through on my own. "I'm not scared. I'm not hurt." The words are rushed and barely audible, but they're enough to make Everett's hands pull back so he can look at me.

"Wynter, you've had enough," he says softly, but there's a bite behind it, one that only seems to stroke the fire burning beneath the tears falling against my cheeks.

"Keep going," I rasp through tears. "Please keep going."

He stares at me for a moment, as if deciding whether or not he should do as I'm asking. "Do you want to take a break?"

I shake my head. "No, please, keep going." It's hard to speak through the sobs, hard to think through the deafening sound of my heart beating in my chest.

Everett brushes the tears from my cheeks, conflict etched into his handsome face. "Tell me where you're at, dove. And I swear to God if you lie to me you won't be coming for a month."

I choke on a laugh and lean into his soft touch. "Green," I tell him, and when doubt crosses the deep blue pools of his eyes I feel like I need to explain as best I can while in the state I am. "The tears aren't bad tears."

Another moment passes before understanding crosses his face and a small smile tugs at his lips. "Okay little dove. Five with the paddle and then you're done, okay?"

I nod. "Okay."

He only lingers for another second before returning to his place behind me. The cool wood of the paddle rubs across my burning flesh and almost feels comforting, but I know that will be short-lived. Everett exhales a long breath as the wood lifts from my skin, and then the most deliciously blinding pain comes down on my already stinging ass.

I let out a yelp, but there's no panic, no fear. It's just Everett and I, none of the memories I expect to flood my vision, and even though I'm crying, even though tears are saturating the cushion underneath my face, a smile tugs at my lips as I say the word he's waiting to hear.

"Green."

Everett delivers the last four hits of my punishment in rapid succession, and each blow feels more and more like my ass is about to light the entire room on fire, but when the last one lands, all I feel is at peace.

The ties at my wrist give way at the same time the heavy wood hits the carpet, and before I can take my next breath, Everett has me bundled in his lap on the sofa. His hands are everywhere, the back of my head as he holds me to him, my back as he strokes comforting circles into the bare flesh. His lips graze my throat, my cheek, my lips, never staying in one place for more than a moment before moving to the next.

"You did so good, little dove. I'm so proud of you," he whispers into my neck, and he's not the only one. If you told me a week ago I was going to do what we just did, I would have laughed in your face and then would have proceeded to panic at the very thought, but as I curl up in Everett's arms, the burning of my ass reminding me of what we've just done each time the wounded skin brushes along his pants, all I feel is pride.

I faced my fears, and I did it with Everett by my side every step of the way.

I don't know how much time passes, but he never lets up his hold on me, never stops whispering calm words of encouragement as he kisses and touches every inch of my naked body, and I lap up every moment of it. There was a long time where I thought I would never be in Everett's arms like this again, where I thought I would never see him again, but to be here now, it feels right.

THIRTY-EIGHT

EVERETT

P art of being in a dominant and submissive dynamic is about trust. Trust that your partner will let you know if things have gone too far, and trust that your partner won't ever give you more than you can handle.

The more time that passes since I bundled Wynter up only makes me wonder if something went wrong, whether our communication was crossed somewhere along the way. She told me to keep going, over and over she said she was okay, that she wanted to continue, but the tears falling against her soft cheeks tell a different story.

But then again, she's not tense either. Her body is calm and relaxed as I hold her. She never flinches when I run my fingers across her skin or pulls away from the kisses I pepper anywhere I can reach. In fact, she leans into it. Every bit of affection I shower her with, she laps up like a tired kitten, so I keep giving it to her until the tears finally start to slow.

"I love you," Wynter whispers into my neck and my heart

bursts. Every time those words leave her pretty plump lips it feels like a fireworks show in my chest, and I hope I never take them for granted. I hope when we're old and gray and in a nursing home that those words still ignite the same fire in my heart.

"I love you too, little dove," I tell her.

"Thank you."

"For what?"

"For giving me back a part of myself I thought was gone forever." Wynter moves to look up at me, her eyes swollen from the tears she's shed, but the ice blue is more vibrant than I've seen since coming back. It reminds me of how they used to be when we were younger, before all the darkness of the world tainted my dove.

"You deserve the whole word, Wynter, and I'll always give you everything you need," I promise. "How about we curl up in bed and watch a movie or something?"

Her eyebrows knit together as if the idea of cuddling and watching a movie with me is offensive. "I'm not ready to stop."

"You've had more than enough for one day, Wynter." I shake my head. After her reaction to her spanking there is no way we're going any further today. It would be remiss of me to dismiss the healing she's done today but going any further could very well fracture her further, and that's the last thing I want.

"Keep going," she pleads, her eyes round and full of lust.

I watch her for a while, not committing to continue, instead watching to see if there are any alarm bells ringing. It's been a while since I've been in this kind of situation. After I left, BDSM was the only thing I could lean on to get me out of my head about Wynter, but after a while it stopped having the desired effect, so I stopped practicing.

Her tears have dried, and she stares up at me with a mixture of anticipation and hope. I've always been very good at reading Wynter, better than anyone else in her family, but I don't want to risk this being the time I read her wrong. She's watching me too, her eyes tracking every move mine make across her face and body. She's alert, doesn't seem to be distressed, and there's not a hint of fear in her eyes. Wynter doesn't shy away from my attention despite how vulnerable she must feel right now, and perhaps that's what makes me think maybe she is okay to keep going.

"Are you sure?" I finally ask.

"I'm sure." A small smile touches her lips and I can't help but press my own onto the soft pillows. I spent too many years being unable to taste her, and I don't want to waste another moment. The kiss is slow, but so full of emotion we both feel in the depths of our souls. Our lips move together in perfect harmony, our tongues probing and savoring the taste of one another with every swipe. I never knew a kiss could mean so much but sitting here with Wynter in my lap makes me believe in all the things I always thought were a myth.

When I finally pull away, her cheeks are flushed and her lips swollen as she stares up at me through big round eyes. She looks like a perfect temptress and an innocent virgin all at once.

"Here's what we're going to do, dove. You're going to drink some water because you're going to get dehydrated from all the tears you've just shed and what I'm about to do to you."

Her eyes flare with excitement as she draws her bottom lip between her teeth. I take another moment to stare at her, reminding myself over and over again that she's okay and nothing is ever going to come close to hurting her again because I won't let it.

I rearrange Wynter in my arms and stand from the sofa, quickly moving across the room and carefully lowering her onto the bed. She winces as her raw ass brushes across the sheets, but part of the punishment is sitting on a hot ass, and I'm sure she knows that. I press a kiss to her forehead before quickly moving to the bathroom and filling the bottle of water she keeps there.

When I return, I'm almost blown away by how beautiful she looks sitting in the middle of the big bed, her body bare for my eyes to feast on. A delectable blush makes its way from her cheeks, down her neck and spreads across her chest under my gaze, but she doesn't move to cover herself and the predator in me smirks.

I take long strides across the room and climb onto the bed beside her, quickly lifting her back into my lap. After everything we went through today I can't stand not touching her, and it's something she's going to have to learn to live with, at least for the foreseeable future. I unscrew the bottle and hold it to her lips, swatting away her hands when she tries to take it from me.

"Drink," I command.

"I can hold the bottle, Everett." She almost rolls her eyes but quickly thinks better of it. She doesn't want to earn herself another spanking so soon after the one she just had.

"I know you *can*, but I'm holding it." I shrug. These moments after an intense scene have always been my favorite, but with Wynter it's amplified, like nothing I've ever experienced before and I want to lap up every moment of vulnerability she'll give me.

She lets out a little sigh before opening her mouth and allowing me to feed healthy sips of water through her pretty, plump lips. I can't help but stare at the soft pillows as she drinks, wrapping around the tip of the bottle so perfectly, imagining how she'll look with my cock between them. That's the one thing we never got to do before, and I have to rectify that sooner rather than later because I know the sight of my cock disappearing into her warm mouth is going to ruin me.

As much as the sadist in me loves punishing a naughty sub, it's always been the aftercare I enjoy most. The trust they put in you during an intense scene should be unparalleled, but when they put their vulnerability in your hands and trust you not be break them, that's something special, and fuck me if it's not the best feeling in the world to have Wynter trust me like this.

Today she's given me not only her body, but her fears, her trust, her heart, and I'll never break it again. There's nothing on this earth that can drag me away from her, not even Satan himself.

Once she's drained the bottle, I place it on the bedside table and brush the stray hairs from her face. "Are you sure you want to keep going?"

"I'm sure." Wynter smiles up at me with trust in her eyes.

For a moment I'm torn about whether to go on as originally planned or if I should deviate and skip what's left of her punishment, but there's something about the way she looks up at me that tells me she can handle anything I throw at her because she needs this just the same way I do.

"Okay, dove. I'll be keeping a close eye on you, but this next part can get just as overwhelming as a spanking, so if it's too much make sure you safe word." I've never given a sub so many opportunities to get out of a punishment, but then again Wynter has always been different, and she always will be.

Dead of Wynter

THIRTY-NINE

WYNTER

As Everett lays me down in the middle of the bed, his hungry eyes feasting on me as they survey every inch of my body, I can't help but think about the night we spent together all those years ago. The night he took my virginity.

For as long as I've known him, Everett has been what I can only describe as hard. His childhood was almost non-existent, he saw things he never should have seen from such a young age, and he lost both his parents way before he should have.

But with me, he's not that man. He never has been. With me, Everett is soft and nurturing, his eyes are always filled with warmth when he looks at me, and the way he touches me like I'm about the shatter in his hands, it's almost as addictive as the man himself.

That's how he is right now, except where I usually see confidence, I see doubt. He's not sure how to proceed after I broke in his arms. He doesn't think I can handle what he has planned, but that's the thing he doesn't understand, and I can't quite find the words to tell him.

I can handle anything Everett does to me, as long as he never leaves again.

"Ev," I whisper, watching as he discards his clothes in a pile on the floor. Every inch of his perfectly toned body that he uncovers is my own personal fantasy come to life. "I need you."

His eyes flare with heat that matches the one burning between my legs, some of the doubt disappearing to make way for lust. Everett prowls onto the bed like a lion stalking his prey, and if he looks at me like this, I'm quite happy to be his meal. "Is your pussy aching for me, dove?"

I tug my bottom lip between my teeth to mask the moan clawing up my throat. He knows how he affects me, but for him to know that just his words can illicit undeniable pleasure seems almost too much right now. "Yes," I admit.

A predatory smile crosses his face and I can't help but squeeze my legs together hoping for some relief. His eyes track my movement and he shakes his head slowly.

"None of that, Wynter." His hand slaps down on my thigh and makes me jolt despite it being lighter than all the ones that have landed tonight. "So needy," he admonishes, his fingers trailing up and down my thigh where a red handprint is forming, likely matching the marks on my ass. "But you know you still have some punishment left, don't you, Wynter?"

I nod my head once, unable to find the agreeance he's looking for through the lust clouding my vision.

Everett smirks. "If you're good for me, I'll let you come as many times as you want. In fact, I'll drag so many orgasms from your body you'll be begging me to stop. Are you going to be a good girl for me, Wynter?"

Heat washes over me at his words. After not dating much over the last eight years, no one has spoken to me like this, and the only dirty talk I've been subjected to has been what I've read in books, but all his words serve to do is make my core ache for him. "I'll be good," I whisper.

"I know you will, little dove."

Everett brushes his fingers up my thigh and over my stomach until they gently trace the swell of my breasts. The light touch is almost maddening in itself, but he knows that. He knows exactly what he's doing to me, and just how much it driving me wild. His fingers move across my overly sensitive skin and leave goose bumps in their path, while I struggle to remain still for him. A switch has flipped and now all I want in the world is to please him, to be good for him.

Giving my trust and submission to Everett is like handing over my worries, my insecurities, and my pain to someone else so that I can just be, and if that's not freeing in itself, I don't know what is.

When his hands move back down over my belly, there's a fresh determination in his gaze. If I didn't know Everett as well as I do, I would miss the barely contained need vibrating through his body. The way his shoulders tense the closer his fingers get to my core because while I need to restrain myself from coming, he needs to stop himself from throwing in the towel and fucking me like his body begs him to.

That's the thing about orgasm control that a lot of people

miss. While until recently I haven't tried my hand at it, I've read a lot of books about these types of dynamics, and it's always struck me as interesting that only the control of the submissive is ever commented on, when in fact it takes just as much, if not more, control for the dominant party to restrain themselves. Having someone else's pleasure in the palm of your hand as you stop yourself from taking your own is just as hard to control.

Everett's fingers brush across my mound and I barely contain the moan caught in my throat. He's not touching me where I need him, but every touch of his skin on mine is lighting its own wildfire, and when they finally dip between my legs, the moan dislodges. The slightest of touches across my clit almost has me coming off the bed, but I remain still, knowing it will only prolong things if I thrash about, and that's something I can't handle.

"Your sweet pussy is gushing for me, little dove," he comments, a small smile on his lips as he watches his own fingers with rapt attention.

A strangled groan escapes my throat at his dirty words, and I feel the wetness gathering between my thighs right before Everett grips my knees and pushes them apart. He quickly repositions himself until he's laying between them, his face just a few inches from where I need him. He looks up at me through hooded eyes, mischief and heat dance in the deep blue pools, and I can barely handle the sight in front of me.

The moment this tongue makes contact with the oversensitive skin of my inner thigh I almost come clear off the bed, and when his teeth sink into the same place I let out a scream I should be ashamed of. After all, my entire family is in this

298

house, but as his lips trail toward my heated sex, I can't spare them a thought.

"Everett, please," I beg. I can't take much more of his teasing, so I may as well result in pleading with him.

His eyes meet mine a moment before he lowers his lips to my waiting pussy, and the moment they close around my clit I let out a relieved moan. I have a long way to go, I have no illusions that he's going to make this easy on me, but even just having some stimulation is enough for now.

Everett groans as he laps at my wet pussy, his eyes locked on mine as he feasts on me like a starved man. The sight is so erotic it only has more wetness gathering there, but he doesn't seem to mind. "You taste so fucking good, Wynter. I could spend the rest of my life between these thighs and die the happiest man in the world."

"Oh god," I moan as his teeth nibble at the sensitive folds, the line between pleasure and pain becoming more and more blurred the more time that passes.

"Not God, little dove." He smirks and I can't help but shake my head against the pillow. Even in the throes of passion he makes me laugh.

His fingers probe my entrance, drawing gentle circles where I need him to fill me, teasing me until I'm panting beneath him and willing to sell him my fucking soul if it means he'll ease the ache he's created.

I shouldn't be surprised when he gives me what I need though, when his fingers breach my pussy and immediately home in on the place inside me that sets me off like a nuclear bomb.

The feeling is heaven and hell wrapped up in an excruciatingly pleasurable package.

Everett's head lifts to watch me as his fingers thrust in and out of my tightness, curling as they pass my G-spot.

"Is that good, little dove?"

"So good," I pant, my fingers gripping the sheets beneath me with all the strength I can manage.

"I'm glad you think so." He smirks, his hand pulling back only enough to add an extra finger before pushing back inside me.

I scream out, the fullness taking me off guard. I haven't had anything more than a vibrator inside me in eight years, and he's starting to push my comfort.

Everett sucks my clit into his mouth, and some of the ache is eased by the additional pleasure. Somehow he always knows what my body needs even when I don't.

"Ev," I groan. "I can't."

"Yes you can, little dove. I'm just getting you ready for my cock," he murmurs against my clit. The sounds his fingers make as they push in and out of me are obscene, and yet it only seems to bring me closer to my climax. "You're taking it so beautifully, Wynter," he praises, and a moment later I'm right on the edge.

My head moves from side to side, the sensations overwhelming me until I can barely breathe, but I fight it. I fight my need for release, knowing that Everett will give me exactly what I need when he sees fit, and there's no sense trying to get there sooner than he'll allow.

FORTY
EVERETT

The way her pussy clamps down around my fingers only makes it harder to drag this out. As much as I want to deliver this part of her punishment, I don't think I'm going to be able to because I need her so fucking badly.

Wynter is so on edge she's panting, her chest rising and falling in harsh movements and she's gripping the sheets beneath her so hard the sound of threads cracking fills the room.

"Are you close, little dove?" I ask as I increase the speed of my fingers. Her pussy looks so beautiful stretched around my fingers and I can't wait to watch my cock sink into her tight heat.

"Yes, fuck…" she groans. "Fuck, Everett."

"Do you want me to fuck you now?"

She nods against the pillows. She's riding so high with both pleasure and frustration that she can't find the words to speak.

"Beg," I demand. If I can't dish out the last of her punishment because we're both so desperate we can barely breathe, I may as well make the most of it.

Wynter's eyes widen at my request and her body stills. It's only a moment, but fear flashes across her icy blue eyes and I almost abandon the whole plan. The words are on the tip of my tongue to tell her she doesn't have to, that I'll give it to her anyway, but then she opens her mouth.

"Please fuck me," she murmurs. "I need you to fuck me."

I groan at her words and take a deep breath to steady my racing heart. "Do you want my cock, little dove?"

"Yes. Please Everett." My name falls from her lips like a prayer and it's all the motivation I need. In what feels like the blink of an eye, I move to hover above her, my cock homing in on her pussy as soon as I'm in place.

I'm painfully aware of the fact she's going to be tight as hell, and that I have to be wary about hurting her even though I want to fuck her so hard all she can feel is my cock. "I'm going to try to take it slow, little dove," I tell her as I guide my cock up and down her soaking wet heat. Her pussy drips for me, calling for me to fuck her.

"I don't want slow," Wynter pants.

My eyes snap up to hers, searching for uncertainty but she just stares right back at me, her eyes telling me everything I need to know without her ever needing to open her pretty lips. Wynter needs this. She needs it hard, and dirty, and fast, just the same way I do. "Okay, little dove." I nod once before turning my attention to my cock sliding through her folds. Fuck, she's wet. So fucking ready for me. "I wasn't able to administer as much of your punishment as I would have liked," I admit and her eyes widen before I continue, notching my cock at her entrance but not entering her right away. "I wanted to hold you at the edge for as long as I could, wanted to draw out your pleasure for as long as I could restrain myself, but it turns out I couldn't do that for very long at all." I chuckle as I allow the first few inches of my cock to slide into her tightness.

We let out a collective moan, but it's not the sound itself that makes me pause. The only word I can think to describe it is rapture. We spent so many years apart, both thinking we would never have this again, but as I allow myself to push another inch into her, the significance of the moment settles over me.

"You will come when I do, and not a moment sooner, do you understand?" I'm holding myself perfectly still, my eyes flicking from her face to where we meet as my cock aches to sink into her all the way, to bottom out in the paradise between her legs.

"I understand." Wynter smiles, her eyes half lidded with the pleasure I've already given her as her pussy flutters around me, begging me to start fucking her like we both crave, but I'm already too on edge. Being here with her after spending so long on the sidelines of her life is surreal, and part of me is waiting to wake up from a dream. Because surely this isn't real. Surely Wynter isn't spread out below me waiting for me to fuck her.

Except, this is real life, and every moment that led us here seems almost irrelevant.

"Everett, please," she moans, wrapping her legs around my

back and trying to tug my hips forward.

I chuckle and shake my head. "Such a needy girl, aren't you, little dove?" I drop down until our faces are just a breath apart. So close her breath whispers across my face each time she exhales, but far enough apart that we're not touching. "But didn't I tell you I would give you everything you need? Don't you know I'll always give you whatever it is your body craves, just not on your schedule?"

Wynter draws her bottom lip between her teeth and nods. She looks so fucking beautiful spread out beneath me, her hair forming a halo on the pillow, her eyes watching every move I make, and her lips, fuck me her perfect pouty lips switch between being trapped between her teeth and dropping open in need.

Unable to keep myself still any longer, I slam my hips forward until I'm buried so deep in her sweet cunt she's all I can feel. Wynter screams as I bottom out inside her, the invasion bringing tears of pleasure to her eyes. Fuck, she's so beautiful when she cries for me.

"Oh fuck," Wynter whines, her hips lifting from the mattress, but I keep us planted where we are. I need a minute to get ahold of myself so I don't come the minute I start thrusting, no matter how tempting it is. There's something primal inside me that begs to fill her with my cum, to claim her in the most basic way, but I want to savor every single moment.

"Your pussy is clamping down on me so tight, little dove," I tell her.

"Please," she begs. "Fuck, Everett, please move, please fuck me."

I groan and close my eyes for a second to get control of the tingling at the base of my spine. I'm not going to last. It doesn't matter how badly I want to drag this out, I may not have a say in the matter the way things are going.

"You're so pretty when you beg, Wynter." I draw my hips back and surge forward again, and a predatory groan tears from my throat. The sound so foreign it's barely human. "Jesus fucking Christ," I growl through clenched teeth as I start a steady rhythm.

She's so tight and her pussy clamps down on me every time my cock brushes along her G-spot, so naturally I angle my hips to make sure I hit it every time.

Wynter brings her hands up to cup my face, and I find myself lost in the look in her eyes. Pure ecstasy and love linger in her gaze and it makes it all the more difficult to keep my thrusts measured and even.

She's close, it's obvious in the way her cunt flutters around me, her inner muscles dancing along my length, but I want to draw it out a little longer.

"Rub your clit for me, Wynter," I order. She's already on the edge of climax, but I want her fucking desperate.

Her small hand slips between us and immediately starts rubbing measured circles into the oversensitive bundle of nerves, causing her pussy to tighten around me even farther, almost dragging me off the cliff I'm barely balancing on.

"I can't," Wynter whimpers. "It's too much, I can't." Her head thrashes from side to side as tears pool in the corners of her eyes.

"Of course you can, little dove. Do you know why?"

She shakes her head, her hand still moving between us despite how overwhelmed with pleasure she is.

"Because I told you to."

Her eyes flare with a mixture of heat and defiance, but she wouldn't disobey me, not about this. Wynter may not have been in the scene for very long, but she knows exactly how important it is to follow orders.

"Isn't that right, little dove?" I coax.

There's a pause where I think maybe I have her pegged wrong, that maybe she won't jump whenever I tell her to, but then a strangled moan escapes her throat and she nods. "Yes."

"Good girl." I smile down at her. One of her palms still rests on my cheek and I can't help but lean into the warmth.

Being here with Wynter, being inside her after dreaming of this moment for so many years, it's almost like it's a fantasy, like any moment now I'm going to wake up and my cock will be in my hand, not in the woman I love.

A long whine claws its way from Wynter's lips, her eyes squeezing shut for the slightest of seconds as she tries to hold on to her control.

"That's it, dove, hold it for me. I know you want to come so badly, and you will, just wait a little longer."

Her eyes meet mine again and my strokes falter. The number of times I've been lost in her eyes in the years I've known her, even when I was living on the sidelines of her life, is countless, but the way she's looking at me right now, the love and trust in her gaze, it threatens to drag me over into the oblivion waiting for us both.

I'm not going to last much longer, it's been too many years since I've been buried inside my woman, and my cock knows exactly where it is. It's home.

"You feel so fucking good wrapped around me, Wynter. This pussy is a fucking national treasure," I groan, my rhythm speeding up slightly as I bring us both closer to the abyss.

"Fuck, Everett," she moans.

"Are you ready to come?"

"Yes, so fucking ready."

I chuckle. She's the only person who can make me laugh when I'm balls deep inside them, and I wouldn't have it any other way. "Good girl."

"Please," Wynter pants. "Please, I need to come."

A wicked smile tugs at my lips and I reposition myself slightly to bring one of my hands to her cheek, mirroring hers on mine. The moment is intimate, more so than anything I've experienced, and it's almost overwhelming. Having her in my arms, safe, finally mine again, it's too much.

The tingling in the base of my spine passes the point of no return, and it will only be a matter of seconds before I'm filling her with my cum. "Come for me, Wynter," I command.

She shatters beneath me, her entire body tightening, her pussy clamping down on me so hard I can barely move through the fluttering muscles, and then she's writhing beneath me, shaking from the force of the pleasure rolling through her.

"That's it, little dove. I want it all. Give me every last drop of your pleasure," I growl through clenched teeth. "I'm going to fill your cunt so often you're going to smell like my cum and no man is ever going to come near you because they'll know you're mine." I grunt the words as I lose all rhythm, rutting in and out of her, chasing my own bliss as she comes apart under me. The moment I fly over the edge white light flashes across my vision and my entire body stills for the briefest of moments before I start thrusting with wild abandon.

Hot ropes of cum fill her, and it snaps something inside me. The tether I've held on to for all these years, the one I've forced myself to hold since the day we met tears in half, and all I can think about is claiming her in every single way she'll let me, and maybe even then some.

I collapse above her, holding my weight just enough not to crush her while we both fight to catch our breaths, but I make no move to pull out because I'm not ready to leave her warmth. There are words I should say, things I need to admit, but instead I roll us both until she's sprawled across my chest, exactly where she's meant to be.

DEAD OF WYNTER

FORTY-ONE

WYNTER

I pace the length of Storm's office over and over again. I've been like this for the last half an hour, and every moment we spend in here is another moment I can't sit still. My heart beats hard and fast in my chest as I listen to the other end of the phone line as Rayne and Tommy lead a team of our men in a raid of Russo's warehouse. Everett is running point from behind the desk, his headset on as he guides the team with the use of security cameras and maps he shouldn't have access to.

The fact they're allowing me to be a part of this at all is a small miracle, so I'm trying not to alert my brother and whatever Everett is to me that I'm freaking out. While I've trained to take over the business in the event something terrible happens to my brother, I've never been a part of this side of things. There's a file saved on my computer with the instructions of what I would do and who I would contact to help me, but Storm never wanted me to see it unless absolutely necessary.

And apparently absolutely necessary translates to if I'm almost blown up and find myself the main target of the enemy.

Everett and my brothers came to blows over my involvement, but ultimately I had the final say, and now I'm here, I'm not totally sure I chose right, not that I'll ever admit that to them.

"Can you stop pacing? You're going to wear a hole in the carpet." Storm smirks from where he's perched on the other side of the desk.

I glare at him but don't stop my back and forth. The motion is keeping me from having a nervous breakdown because my brother is in the middle of enemy territory and his wife is none the wiser in the other room.

That used to be me. It's always been that we didn't know when something big was going down until afterward, and I'm starting to think I liked it that way. But I demanded to be a part of this, and so I have to stand by my choice.

"Seriously, Wyn, they're fine. And anyone dumb enough to go after Tommy when he's got a weapon will be dead in three seconds flat."

Everett chuckles from behind the desk, shaking his head at the two of us but he never draws his eyes away from the three monitors in front of him. I always suspected Everett still worked for Frost, but I never had any proof. There were programs that were built that had his signature on them, even if no one ever admitted it, weapons that had a flare I recognized, and there were always a lot of mysterious phone calls. In all fairness, that last one isn't totally unheard of anyway because of the line of work the men in my family are involved in, but I always suspected it.

"Just because Tommy is a raging lunatic doesn't make this any less stressful," I snap. I mean, he's not totally wrong because that guy is an actual sociopath, and he *loves* it when people start shooting at him, but that doesn't make me worry about them any less.

"You don't have to stay if you don't want to, dove," Everett says softly, his eyes finally dragging away from the screens for a brief second.

I shake my head. "I'm fine. I just need to keep moving."

He watches me closely for a moment and then nods once before turning his attention back to the screens. The idea of my involvement is growing on him, but he's not there yet, despite the fact this mission was mostly my idea.

The Russos would be expecting a personal attack like the ones they've administered on us. They have extra security, just like we do, and that means they have pulled people off their locations to make up for the loss when they took Emerson, and Tommy, being Tommy, got a little trigger happy. They've been going after our business interests for months, maybe even longer, and we haven't hit back, always chasing our tail with personal security. So I thought it would be best to go back to basics and hit them the same way they have been us.

It's not a full proof plan by any means, but it's going ahead so it must have some merit. The way my brothers stared at me as I delivered the plan was equally in horror and in awe. They want me as far from this as I can be, but I was right when I said I needed to know this side of the business if there's even the slightest chance I'm going to have to run it one day.

Sound on the other end of the line draws my attention to the desk and I stop pacing for the first time since the call started. My breath stills as I listen to the sound of gunfire, so much that my body flinches as every bullet is fired. I only drag my gaze away from the phone for long enough to look at Everett and Storm, but they both look equally relaxed, as if our family aren't currently being fired at.

The gunfire goes on for so long I worry I'm going to pass out because I keep forgetting to breathe. The sound fills the office, and the longer I stand here staring at the phone, the more I struggle to remain on my feet. My body begs me to crumple on the ground, to fall to my knees and pray for my brother and Tommy to be okay.

Considering he is a total lunatic, Tommy and I are quite close. He's been like a brother to me since we were teenagers when he came to work for us. I've never asked about his background, but I've seen the scars littering his pale skin that I can hazard a guess at the life he lived before he came to us. Over the years he's covered the scars with so many tattoos I don't think he has an inch of free skin left, but I try not to think about it too much.

The moment the line goes quiet I squeeze my eyes shut as my breath stutters in my chest. It's almost too quiet, and the thought that my brother isn't going to walk through the front door, the thought of consoling his wife and attending his funeral like we did our parents, it's enough to have nausea rolling over me.

For the first time since he sat down, Storm seems something other than relaxed, his jaw is tight as his eyes remain locked on the phone on the desk. Everett is in full work mode, his fingers flying across the keyboard in rapid motions with his brow furrowed.

I'm about to ask what the fuck is going on when a voice

fills the line and my lungs can finally drag in a breath. "Motherfuckers," Rayne roars.

"What's going on?" Storm asks, standing from his seat to round the desk.

"It's empty. The motherfuckers moved their shit," Rayne growls and I sink to my knees on the plush carpet. This is my fault. We've no doubt lost men today, and it's all because I thought we should hit them where it hurt, where the money was.

"How many men did we lose?" I ask from my place on the floor. I think about trying to stand, but my legs aren't capable of holding me right now.

Silence greets me on the other end of the phone, and I'm back to holding my breath as I await a response. "Tommy is doing the count now, but we've lost at least three men," Rayne tells me solemnly.

I close my eyes to hold back the tears. They're dead because of me, because of my choices. None of them would have been in that building if it weren't for me.

"And on their side?" Storm asks.

"At first glance about twenty, but we haven't done the count."

Everett blows out a breath and leans back in his chair. "That's a big hit for them, especially after we took out so many of their men at the club."

"Any idea what level the guys are?" Storm pipes up.

"That's the thing, these guys seem to be hired help, they're not their usual guys, so they must be keeping them close to the family."

"It was a trap?" The words filling the room sound like mine, but I don't remember saying, or even thinking, the words.

"It looks that way. They definitely knew we were coming. The team we took out are professionals," Tommy tells us.

My belly clenches painfully and the need to vomit gurgles in the pit of my stomach.

"More proof we have a rat," Storm muses. "Get home as soon as you can. We need to decide on our next move. Clean up should be there any minute."

"You got it," Rayne fires back.

"You need me too, boss?" Tommy asks.

"Just the two of you. We need to clean house and I don't know who we can trust right now."

"Got it."

The line goes dead and I allow my body to sink farther into the carpet as I bring my knees to my chest. Is this how Storm feels every time one of his decisions ends someone's life? The overarching sense of dread and guilt mingling together catches me off guard and I can barely breathe through the cocktail of toxic emotions.

"Fuck!" Storm roars, a loud crash fills the office but I don't bother opening my eyes. If smashing shit is how he deals with emotions, who am I to argue?

Movement beside me startles my shaking body, and a moment

later I'm being scooped up and held against a hard chest.

"It's okay, little dove," Everett whispers into my hair as he lowers us into the soft leather couch.

"What about any of this is okay? There are men who won't return to their families tonight because of a call I made." My voice breaks as I say the words aloud for the first time.

Another crash on the other side of the room causes me to flinch and burrow my face into Everett's chest. "Storm, will you stop that?" he growls.

"Wynter wanted to be a part of this. She wanted to prove she could run things if something happens to me, so that's what we're doing," Storm shouts.

Everett's arms tighten around me protectively and I sink into the feeling. "Don't you remember the first time your call resulted in someone dying?" he snaps. "Because I fucking do. You went on a three-day bender and Rayne and I had to fly to fucking Vegas to bail your ass out of jail. I think Wynter's reaction is more than justified."

"Of course you do," Storm mutters as he leaves the room, slamming the door so hard behind him the walls shake with the force.

Maybe I'm not cut out for this. Maybe they were right to keep this part of our business away from us for all these years.

I allow myself to bask in the comfort Everett offers, to breathe in his warmth and settle against his hard body. He always seems to know what I need. He always knows how to make everything better even as the world crumbles around us.

The door swings open and this time I do open my eyes to find Storm in the doorway with a box in his hands and his face pale.

"What is that?" I ask quietly.

"It's addressed to you."

DEAD OF WYNTER

FORTY-TWO
EVERETT

The moment my eyes make contract with the box a sinking feeling settles in the pit of my stomach. It's not that the box looks particularly suspicious or that it's marked in a way that anyone else would find it worrying, but whatever is in that box is going to hurt my little dove, and that's not acceptable.

Despite allowing her to be a part of the decision making and takedown of the Russo family, I've avoided telling Wynter what was in the first package that was delivered here for her.

The moment she pushes against me to stand, I know I have to come clean, that despite all my good intentions of protecting her, she needs to know the full extent of the threat.

"Did you check it?" I ask as Wynter clambers from my lap.

Storm shakes his head, eyes glued to the package as he places it on the desk in front of the monitors I was using. "It's not a bomb. They swept it at the gate."

Wynter crosses the room toward the desk but I quickly tug

her back into me. If there's something in the package that can hurt her, I'm going to be standing between her and it. "Everett," she hisses. "You are not kicking me out this time, I'm officially just as involved and complicit as you two so you're not keeping me in the dark."

"Stand behind me," I growl and to my surprise, she listens to me.

"What was in the first one?" she asks.

"A dead dove," Storm answers.

Wynter's body stills behind me, her breathing stuttering for the briefest of moments. "How do they…" She trails off, asking the same question we asked ourselves when it arrived.

"The rat," Storm and I answer at once.

Understanding crosses her features and her body visibly shivers.

"You don't call me that in front of anyone."

"I know. We think it has to be someone close, but we can't pinpoint who, and even after I checked everyone's backgrounds, they all came up squeaky clean," I tell her.

"And we've triple checked everyone who knew we were going to see the lawyer?" she asks.

"No one has so much as a friend six times removed of any of Russo's people," Storm says.

Wynter closes her eyes and takes deep breaths, each one sounding more steady than the last. When the ice blue reappears, any fear from before is long gone, and she's back to being the fierce queen I know her to be.

"Open it."

Storm sucks in a breath as he cuts the tape holding the box closed. We both peer over into the box while Wynter remains behind me where I put her.

"Motherfucker," Storm roars, his hand sweeping the monitors from the desk in one swift movement. The contents isn't a bomb, but I almost wish it was. It would likely cause Wynter less pain and end this war before it can really begin.

"Do I want to look?" she asks, her fists holding on to the back of my shirt in a vice grip.

"Probably not," I admit. I should throw her over my shoulder and cart her out of here so she never has to see the contents of the box, but I don't want her to resent me for keeping things from her, even if I'm only trying to shield her.

Wynter moves slowly until she's staring down into the box. The color drains from her cheeks and her hands fly to cover her mouth as her eyes flit from item to item.

It's not any one thing in the box that is most horrifying, because all of it is equally so. Every single thing is more twisted than the last, just for different reasons, and separately most people wouldn't think twice about any of them.

I place my hand on the small of Wynter's back to remind her I'm here as I look up to meet Storm's gaze. The fire and fury swirling around in the gray is darker than any I've ever seen. We've had threats to the women in the family before, Emerson was kidnapped for god's sake, but no one has ever gone after one of them like this, so personally. It's like they've pulled all the worst moments of her life and threw them in a box.

Another dead dove.

A newspaper with her on the front claiming her to be the 'Queen of Chicago' and a broken crown beside it to represent her fall.

A doll with blonde hair and ice-blue eyes lying face down with red pen marks all over its ass and thighs.

And a note with bold writing clear enough to read without ever having to touch it.

BETTER LUCK NEXT TIME, YOUR HIGHNESS.

Wynter's eyes shoot up to meet Storm's and the two of them stare at one another for a moment. "How the fuck could they know about this?" She pulls the doll from the box and shoves it toward him. "How the fuck does anyone know about this?" she shouts. "You're the only fucking person on this earth that knew up until a few days ago. There were no photos taken, I never told another soul, so who the fuck did you tell?"

Storm's face is ashen, the color completely drained as he stares at the doll meant to represent the day she was violated. I'm curious about who knew as well, because Rayne and I were never told, and the fact that someone else knew makes me ropable. "There were photos," he murmurs and Wynter stills beneath my hands, her eyes widening as she waits for her brother to continue. "I had the doctor take a few on a disposable camera just in case we ever needed it."

"In what universe would we need it?" Wynter cries. "Are you fucking kidding me right now, Storm? I was fucking violated by a man you hired to protect me, and *you* thought it was pertinent that we have evidence that that happened to me?"

"I thought if there were any lasting impacts from your wounds a doctor might need to know what happened to you," he admits.

"But that's not why you've kept them all these years," I say. I don't know how I know, maybe it's the way he's avoiding eye contact, or the way his head is hung in shame, but I consider this man my brother, and I always know when he's lying.

"No, it's not." He shakes his head and collapses into the chair behind the desk.

"How could you?" Wynter whispers, her body crumpling into mine.

"This is the part of the business you don't understand, Wyn, it's why I never wanted you or Snow involved."

"Because you have to keep dirt on your own fucking family." Wynter's yelling now and there's no amount of comfort I can give to ease this hurt.

"That's not what this was." Storm's eyes flare as they finally meet ours again. "I killed a man who has ties to some serious fucking fire power, men that we wouldn't want to meet in our goddamn nightmares, and I killed him for what he did to you. I will never feel sorry for what I did, no matter the amount of heat this family gets for my actions, someone hurt my baby sister and he deserved a much worse death than even I could give him, but in the event that some of that family came looking, I thought it may help to have evidence of *why* I killed him. People like that understand loyalty, and if showing them the fucked-up things he did to you meant they didn't come after us. It was a precaution," he explains.

Wynter's body shakes violently, but without being able to see her face I can't tell if it's fury or pain causing the shivers. I wrap my arms around her and hold her against my chest, making sure she won't fall if her legs buckle beneath her. "It's been eight years, Storm. I think the statute of limitations is well and truly over."

Storm is still being evasive. His eyes dart around the room, sweat drips from his temple, and the man who always has his shit together looks moments away from crumpling.

"What aren't you telling us?" I ask.

He sighs, his head leaning on his hands on the desk. "There was a... breach a couple of months ago."

"A breach?" I ask incredulously.

"Yes. The photos were in my office at Frost Industries because I thought no one would be dumb enough to break into a building for a company that literally designs half the world's security systems."

"Why the fuck didn't I know about this?" I growl.

"Because I didn't want you to," Storm snaps. "You forget who runs the show, brother."

My body stills as blinding red crosses my vision. Anger pumps through my veins, and the only thing holding me back is the woman I love in my arms. Her softness soothes me just the same as it always has, ever since the first time she patched me up after my uncle hurt me.

FOURTEEN YEARS AGO

Red clouds my vision, but not because I'm angry. Blood drips into my eyes as I stagger up the drive of the Saint James estate. It's a miracle I made it here at all considering one of my eyes is so swollen I can't see out of it, and the other stings from my own blood.

But this is the only place I'm safe. The family I wish I was born to. The one who are the enemies of my own but still give me everything I need without me having to ask.

I drop my bike in the driveway and clamber up the stairs, tripping several times on the way up before knocking on the door. While I wait, I lean against the frame, finally allowing the pain to break through the walls I built until I could get to safety.

The Russos don't believe in weakness. They don't believe that a man should feel pain, and therefore any sign of agony would only lead to being beaten even more.

Today's injuries are courtesy of training, or at least that's what Uncle Angelo called it. Sometimes when he's bored, he'll pit my cousin and me against one another. Elijah is a few months younger than me, but he is a little taller and a whole lot stockier than I am.

The aim is the same as survival of the fittest, but what that really translates to is enjoying his nephews beating the life out of one another until one of us taps out.

Except, tapping out isn't the end of it. God, I wish it was. I've watched some professional boxing over the years and I know the concept, but that's not how he plays it. When you tap out, you're giving up, and Russos never give up. Despite the fact I don't share a last name with the piece of shit, I still fall in that category.

This is the first time I've fled to the refuge the Saint James family offer me, but when I ran it was the only place I could think about coming. It's the only place I'm truly safe from my uncles.

A mess of blonde flashes across my vision and when I look up, I'm met with ice blue filled with horror.

"Oh my god, Everett, what happened to you?" Wynter shoots forward to help me into the house.

Everything in this house is nice, too nice even. It's kind of funny that this was my father's house, even if we never stayed here. I never even came here. My mother preferred to be closer to the city, I guess being isolated here with the devil himself wasn't that appealing for her.

The first time Uncle Angelo found out I knew the Saint James family he tried to fill my head with lies. Of course I know Ron killed my dad and took over his operation, but the reasoning my uncles gave me is so farfetched I can't believe they thought I would believe them.

I don't answer the angel I've become obsessed with, instead letting her help me inside and hoping I don't drip blood all over the expensive furniture. When she tries to steer me into the lounge room I immediately halt.

"Not in here," I say.

Wynter watches me for a moment, as if trying to find

something within my beaten gaze before nodding. "Okay, let's go into the bathroom."

I let out a sigh of relief. Although I trust the Saint James family, I already owe them so much, and I know in the line of work we're in that's never a good thing and seeing as I owe the Russo family for taking me in after my father was killed, I already owe entirely too much.

Wynter tries to support as much of my weight as she can, but she's so tiny she's barely holding any of it. I won't tell her that though because it would make her sad, and I never want to see her anything but happy. Her smile has quickly become my favorite thing in the world, and sometimes when I hang out with Rayne and Storm, it's mainly in the hope that I'll see her.

We've grown closer over the last year and even though she's a few years younger than I am, she's one of my best friends, but it would still be weird for me to come over just to see her.

She helps me perch on the toilet lid and busies herself looking through the cupboard for the first aid kit. "Are you going to tell me what happened?" she asks.

"No," I reply. Wynter is too pure to be tainted for the shit my family does, especially what they force Elijah and I to do to one another.

Her eyes dart up to meet mine before nodding. "Okay, we don't have to talk about it if you don't want to." She pulls the kit out and places it on top of the vanity. "But if you ever do need to talk about anything, I'm here for you." The small smile playing on her lips is both comforting and concerning. Doesn't she know I could never taint her with my darkness.

"Thank you, dove." The nickname I've been calling her in my head for the last year slips from my lips, but I don't try to take it back.

She watches me for a moment, unsure she heard me correctly, but she doesn't question it. Instead she opens the kit and starts cleaning my wounds. With anyone else, I would try to hide my pain, but not Wynter. She won't judge me for flinching when antiseptic seeps into open wounds, or laugh if I swear from the pain, because she's not like that.

Wynter is the kindest, gentlest person I've ever known, and being around her settles the wounded parts of me that have always felt like gaping sores.

FORTY-THREE
WYNTER

E verett's body still vibrates with anger twenty minutes after the words leave Storm's mouth and I dragged him away to cool down. We can't be at each other's throats. That's what they want. They want to divide us because we're easier to take down one at a time than we are all at once. I don't need to be involved in the darker sides of Frost to know that, it's a basic business maneuver, one I've used myself a time or two.

I'm sitting on Everett's lap on the lounge across the room from where Storm still has his head in his hands. The evidence of his earlier outburst is still scattered across the room, but I can't move right now, not while Everett is holding on by a thread. I keep thinking if I hold him a little tighter, if I kiss him a few more times, maybe it will settle the barely contained rage beating through his body, but it doesn't.

"Can I ask you something?" I whisper.

"Anything," he replies immediately.

"Why do you call me dove? I've never asked, but I've always

been curious." I've ached to ask this question for fourteen years, ever since the first time he called me it and my heart burst from the nickname the boy I had a crush on gave me.

A small smile tugs at his lips and some of the tension he's holding fades away beneath me. "When I was a kid, my mother and I used to go to this park in the afternoons after school to avoid my dad. He was only ever home for a few hours, and we tried to stay out of the apartment for as long as we could. And every day we saw this family of doves. They were so peaceful to watch, and even though there was a playground there, I used to find myself sitting beside my mom watching them. You bring me that same peace, and the same happiness I felt when I was a kid watching the doves with my mom." He smiles sadly and my heart bursts with love for the man holding me.

I blink back tears of joy as I gather his face in my hands and lean down to capture his lips with mine. This kiss is slow and gentle, but full of emotion. For the first time since he's been back I'm not hurried in my movements, just needing to feel his lips on mine, his tongue dancing with my own, as we say all the words through the movement.

Footsteps in the hallway make us part, but I rest my forehead on his, not ready for the moment to be broken. There's so much I need to say to Everett, but I'm not sure I have the words, and I think he feels the same. He's still avoiding telling me why he left, and I'm starting to think I may not want to know.

The door opens and Rayne and Tommy trudge in. They're still in their tactical gear, black combat boots and a mixture of blood and dirt covering their faces, but I don't flinch. Somehow this isn't the most disturbing thing I've seen tonight. "Make sure you shower before you go see Emerson," I say. She isn't as fragile as he thinks she is, but she worries about him. Every time he walks out the front door she's worried, and him coming home covered in the blood of our enemies probably isn't going to do much to ease that concern.

His eyes meet mine briefly before looking to Everett, and then Storm. "What the fuck happened?"

"Another package was delivered," Storm mutters from behind the desk, finally looking up at the rest of us.

Tommy moves straight to the other side of the room and perches on the arm of one of the seats, and a moment later he's got his knife out dragging it across his forearm. I remember the first time I watched him do this with horror, but after a while it was almost mesmerizing. He never presses hard enough to draw blood, or at least not when he's been around me, but just enough for a bite of pain.

Rayne's eyes widen and his eyes dart to the box still open on the desk. I'm not really sure what we do with this kind of thing, and honestly, I don't think I want to know. As involved as I want to be, I still think there are things I'm better off not knowing. "What's in it?"

Everett's body stills beneath me again, the calm I had managed to push on him gone in an instant, but it's Storm who answers. "My mistakes."

I sigh and climb off Everett to cross the room to where Storm is sitting. "You need to snap out of this self-pitying bullshit. You made a mistake, but we're your family, we're not going to hold it against you forever."

"I might," Everett mumbles and I roll my eyes.

"Do I want to look?" Rayne asks.

"They know about what Craig did to me," I tell him.

"Craig, as in your old security?" Tommy questions, his first words since he walked into the room.

I let out a long breath. "Without rehashing the worst day of my life, Craig hurt me pretty badly, and the Russos have photos of my injuries."

"Photos? Who the fuck took photos of your injuries?" Rayne's eyes meet mine with a blaze of fury behind them, and rather than responding I look at Storm, waiting for him to explain himself, but he doesn't.

"You had photos taken of our sister's beaten ass?" Rayne growls.

"As collateral if Craig's family ever came knocking."

"What the fuck happened with Craig?" Tommy growls and I let my head drop back as I take deep breaths to calm my racing heart. I never thought I would have to tell anyone what happened, and in the space of a week I've told more people than I have in the eight years since it happened.

"Just look in the box," I mumble as I collapse into one of the chairs across the desk from Storm. If we're going to talk about what our next steps are, I want to be front and center. They're coming after me, and I deserve to be a part of the planning.

I stare at the ceiling while I wait for the two of them to check what's in the box, and when both of them make an inhuman sound, I know they've seen the doll. Everything else in the box is disturbing, but it's not a creepy doll that looks like me complete with the marks that still haunt my nightmares.

"What the fuck is this?" Tommy roars and my eyes immediately flit to him, a look of rage I've never seen on the already terrifying man.

Rayne takes the doll from him and he looks to me, pain and regret clear on his face. "You don't want to know," he mumbles to Tommy.

"Okay, enough about the package. They're coming after me because I was the one that made the threat at the funeral, which at least means we know who they're going to keep coming for. My question is, what are we going to do next? We obviously have a rat. There's no other explanation for how anyone knows Everett's nickname for me, or how they knew to clear out the warehouse. So who knew we were going to do this tonight?" I ask.

"Everyone in our ranks," Rayne replies. "We wanted everyone on high alert for such a big operation. We needed to make sure if there was a possibility we were all taken out, that we weren't leaving any businesses or our people as sitting ducks."

I sigh. "Okay, new question. Everett, can you have a look at cameras in the area, maybe the highways that lead to and from the warehouse to see if we can figure out when they moved it?"

Everett finally joins the rest of us around the desk, picking up the monitors Storm threw across the room and by some miracle they turn on. When he notices my surprise, he smirks and a short, dark chuckle fills the room. "After the fourth set

I had to replace I built heavy duty monitors so they could withstand Storm's tantrums."

I shake my head and lean back in my chair, something tells me it's going to be a long fucking night and there's entirely too much testosterone in this room for my liking.

FORTY-FOUR
EVERETT

The way Wynter takes charge of the situation has my dick so hard I'm surprised no one has noticed the tent in my pants. She's been barking orders at each of us for hours as she uses her own laptop to watch security footage at Frost Industries around the time of the breach.

Storm is on the phone doing damage control from the mission, calling families to let them know their husbands, sons and fathers aren't coming home tonight. As much as I'm pissed as hell at him, I don't envy him for having to do that job.

Tommy is on the phone on the other side of the room coordinating security teams to mitigate the risk of the rat being able to do anything without someone noticing. He's switching up the usual pairs, trying to make it impossible for them to make moves against us without their new partner tipping us off, but even that could fail.

And Rayne is pawing through files on all of Russo's men that we're aware of. If we can't find the rat through our own people's background checks, maybe there's something in theirs we can use to link. After all, it's not impossible to have things removed from the record, but were they smart enough to remove the evidence on the other side?

I've watched so many hours of traffic camera footage that I'm ready to throw the monitors across the room the same way Storm had earlier. Watching shit like this is the most monotonous task I ever have to do, except when I used to watch Wynter for hours at a time. That I could do all day.

A truck catches my eye on the interstate on the way out of the city. There's nothing about it that seems particularly suspicious. Apart from the four black SUVs surrounding it. One in front, one behind, and one on each side. I change views to the next camera, the truck still traveling the same route. "Where are you taking it?" I murmur to myself.

"Have you got something?" Wynter perks up, her eyes brightening for the first time in hours.

"I think so." I switch to another camera at the next exit, and then the next, until finally they exit at a turn I had almost completely forgotten about, one I've driven so many times I almost can't count, never willingly. "Fuck," I groan.

"What?" Storm crosses behind the desk, looking at the screens until his eyes settle on what I'm looking at. "Is that…"

"Yep."

"Can someone tell me what the fuck is going on?" Wynter demands.

"We know where he's taken the stuff from the warehouse," I tell her.

"And?"

"There's this farm on the outskirts of the city, it was my father's property, he left it to me in his will, but Angelo took it over because he was my custodian and I never wanted it anyway. It has... bad memories."

The words don't seem like enough to describe all the times I was forced to kill people there, for them to be fed to the pigs like some old mafia movie. It was part of our training to take their place when the time came. Elijah loved it. The blood. The hunt. The kill. He thrived on it. Hell, he still does. But killing for the sake of killing never sat well with me.

Wynter's eyes track my movements, a hint of knowing behind the ice of her irises. There were days at a time when she wouldn't hear from me when we were younger, and every time I came back I was more withdrawn. She was always the only person who could bring me back, who could distract me from the guilt. Don't get me wrong, I've killed my fair share of men for Frost, but never for no reason, and never against my will.

"Is there enough space out there?" Rayne asks.

He and Storm know of the farm, I told them one night during a drunken bender when I left Wynter and we went to set the place on fire. Except, when we got there I couldn't do it. Something about it felt meaningful to the man I had become, a man free of my family and their influence. Now I wish I watched the fucking place go up in flames.

"We haven't been up there in a few years to scope the place out. There's more than enough space, but only a few small buildings," I say, quickly bringing up a satellite feed.

If they had the foresight to build on the land, that could mean they've had this plan in motion for years, which means we are more than a little behind the eight ball. My eyes scan the screen as I locate the farm, and when I find what I'm looking for I can't help the roar that climbs up my throat.

"Motherfuckers."

"They've built on it?" Rayne asks.

Storm is over my shoulder looking at exactly what I am, and his own intake of breath tells me when he sees what I'm seeing. "Oh yeah. Looks like a goddamn army base. Security, bunkers, the whole nine yards."

"Which explains why they've been quiet on the streets. They're getting ready for something big," Rayne muses.

"They're getting ready to take us out," Wynter whispers.

"Okay, so at least we know where their shit is, but I don't know how much luck we're going to have hitting it, especially with a rat in the mix to tip them off," Storm says as he starts pacing. It must be a Saint James trait to think better as you walk around a room aimlessly.

"We need to hit one of the cousins," Tommy suggests. "They're coming after Wynter, so it's time we go after them. They've had the upper hand the whole time because you've been mourning your parents, and before that we were just trying to get on our feet after Emerson was taken. It's time we get ahead of the game and start taking down key players."

Storm nods and takes another look at the screen. "We need to figure out who we can trust, or we need to hire in some help who won't betray us."

"I know some guys." Tommy pulls his phone out and starts tapping away. "I can probably have them here by tomorrow, they're based in New York, but they're not loyal to any one family."

"Which means they could double cross us just the same as anyone else," Rayne groans.

"Nah, not these guys. They always get the job done, guaranteed. And Russo doesn't have any allies in New York, at least we do." Tommy shrugs as if that's comforting to any of us. The fact that we have to rely on people outside the family, that we've never met doesn't sit right with me, but I don't know what other choice we have right now.

"Call them," Storm says and then turns to me. "Let's go to bed. It's four in the morning and we've done everything we can for tonight. Tommy, if you can have your guys here as soon as possible, we can't wait long to retaliate because even though you killed every motherfucker in that warehouse tonight, them not returning from the mission will tell them we hit them."

Wynter says a quiet goodnight to everyone and is the first to leave, closing the door gently behind her. She held her own tonight, even when everything was falling apart and she had the most vulnerable time in her life exposed, she held her chin high and got on with it.

"We underestimated Wynter," Storm admits.

I smirk. "Told you."

He glares at me. "You shut the fuck up. I just mean that she handled everything, she got straight into research without having to take a minute, she called shots like she was fucking born to do this."

"She was." I smile. "The two of you are cut from the same cloth, except she doesn't destroy shit when things go south."

"I swear to God," Storm growls.

"That's enough, you two," Rayne snaps. "I think we were too hasty in not teaching her this side of the business."

"Dad would be rolling over in his fucking grave if he knew we had his little girl working on this shit," Storm retorts.

"No, he'd be proud as hell that his daughter is a strong woman who can bring men to their fucking knees." Rayne looks to me, a smirk playing on his lips. "I guess I won't have to beat your ass if you break her heart again, she'll do it for me."

"There will be no heart breaking. The minute this shit is over, there's a ring going on her finger."

"Aren't you meant to ask our permission or some shit?" Storm asks.

"Your dad gave it to me, it was in my letter." I chuckle as I stroll out of the room. Wynter may be able to make men fall to their knees, but my little dove is about to fall to hers for me.

DEAD OF WYNTER

FORTY-FIVE

WYNTER

The moment I leave the office there's a weight on my chest I can barely breathe through. I had no other choice but to hold my own in there, to prove the men in my life wrong when they said I couldn't handle it. Except now that I'm alone, the emotions I've been stamping down all day are rushing toward me and threatening to take me down.

I'm not so naive to think we've never been in this kind of danger before, because that's almost certainly not true, but this feels different. The energy in the office was a mixture of fear and anger, and both reared their ugly heads more than a few times in the hours we spent in there.

Snow and Emerson are long asleep, probably for the best. If my sister knew what was going on she would be panicking, and Emerson already worries about Rayne so much, I would never want to add to that.

The moment I reach my room I strip out of the stale clothes I've worn all day and head for the shower. I turn the water on as hot as it will go, and the moment I step into the stream, the heat burns away the filth of the day. I may not have physically got my hands dirty, but I'm the reason men aren't returning to their families tonight. When I look down at the water draining, I almost expect to see red, almost expect there to be blood washing away, but it's only clear water on the shower floor.

I stand under the stream for so long I think the water may run cold soon, but it never does. Hot water beats down on me and I allow the sting of it to draw me back to the moment, to stop my mind from wandering into the far corners of itself I never want to return to. Tonight will go into the box of things I prefer not to think about, the one I hold only for the worst days of my life.

By the time I drag myself from the burning water, my skin is red and sensitive, and I don't feel any more settled than I did going in. I towel off slowly, taking my time because the idea of getting into bed and closing my eyes makes my heart speed up with panic. All that awaits me are nightmares I'm not ready to deal with.

I wander into the bedroom and startle when I see Everett standing by the window, his back toward me. It shouldn't surprise me that he's here, we haven't spent a night apart since the bomb scare, but there's something about his demeanor that has heat pooling in my core.

"On your knees, little dove," he commands and I drop without thought, doing as he says immediately. Perhaps that should annoy me, that my body listens to him even before my mind can process what he's asked of me, but it doesn't. "Good girl," he praises as he finally turns toward me. He's still fully dressed in slacks and a white button-up shirt with the sleeves rolled up over his impressive forearms. His eyes sweep over my bare skin and he frowns as he moves toward me. "Wynter, do you want to explain why you're as red as a fucking lobster right now?"

I open my mouth to reply, but before I can, he's tipped my chin up to look at him, fury behind the deep blue. "I-I had a hot shower. I felt dirty," I tell him truthfully. I don't know if it's the answer he wants, and the idea of disappointing him makes me draw my bottom lip between my teeth.

"And you thought it was acceptable that you harm yourself in the process? That you harm what belongs to me?" He raises his voice, but I don't flinch away. Everett would rather cut off his own hands than hurt me, and that thought gives me comfort.

"I-I didn't," I stammer.

Everett tugs me to my feet and holds my arm in a punishing grip as he drags me across the room to the full-length mirror. "Does this look like it's not hurt?" he growls, pointing to the red splotches across my chest.

I stare at our reflection in the mirror, completely distracted by the people staring back at me. Wet blonde hair sticks to my naked chest and arms, my pale skin marked with red while Everett looms over me, his eyes darkening with anger as he stares at my chest. He's still fully dressed, and the power extruding off him is intoxicating. His jaw is set in a hard line, ticking every now and then with barely contained anger.

"Answer me, Wynter," he snaps.

"It doesn't hurt," I whisper, tearing my eyes away from the

god of a man to look at my own body. The red does look angry, but my skin is numb, depleted of any feeling, almost as if my heart feeling so heavy takes away any physical pain.

"You talked back to me tonight. I think you need to be punished."

A shrill of excitement courses through my body. I shouldn't relish in the thought of him marking me, but fuck I do. The reminders he leaves on my skin at night distract me from my realities during the day, and I need that. I need that distraction.

He must notice the way my legs press together because he shakes his head slowly. "You're not coming tonight, dove. Tonight we're going to make better use of that smart mouth of yours."

I barely contain the moan that claws up my throat, and as badly as I want to come, I want to please him more. I want to give him the kind of pleasure he gives me every time he touches me.

"Do you like the sound of that, Wynter? Do you want my cock in your pretty mouth?" The words are quiet, but the menace behind them only serves to make my heart beat faster with excitement.

"Yes," I admit.

"Back on your knees," he demands and I fall to my knees as gracefully as I can manage. Despite years in the public eye, I haven't quite mastered the art of grace. "Legs apart, I want your pussy so fucking desperate for relief it's not going to get."

Everett has been demanding before, but this is something

else altogether. I almost want to say it's harsh, but the way he looks at me, like I'm his entire world, I know that's not the right word.

I do as he asks, pushing my thighs apart and the moment the cool air hits my already wet pussy is like an electric shock. I hope he's joking when he says I'm not going to be allowed to come, because if that's the case I'm going to be a dripping mess.

"Always so responsive to me, little dove," Everett muses as he circles my kneeling frame like a lion circling its prey.

It's not the first time I've compared him to a beast who could be the end of me, and I'm sure it won't be the last. The man is pure power, his mind, his body, and his soul scream it, and who am I to argue?

"I'm not going to fuck your sweet pussy tonight," he tells me and I hold back the whine trying to escape. "Don't look at me like that. If you wanted to come all over my cock, you should have thought twice about talking back."

I open my mouth to snap back but think better of it. I don't want to prolong my denial. I've never been especially good at delayed self-gratification, and although Everett has made me wait for a little while before I'm allowed to release, I have a feeling he's not fucking around on this.

He smirks. "Good choice, little dove."

His hands move to his belt and I watch with rapt attention as the leather moves through the loops. The sight should probably make it hard to breathe after Craig, but for some reason Everett doing it only makes me want to rub my thighs together that much more.

"Are you okay for me to tie your hands with this?" he asks, holding his belt up in one hand.

My heart skips a beat as I wait for the panic to come, but it never does. If anything, it only adds to the excitement. "Yes," I whisper.

A small smile pulls at his lips. He's treading carefully around what he thinks may be my triggers, but if I'm really honest with myself, I don't know if they apply to him. I trust him with everything I am, with my heart, my body, and every other part of me. He would never knowingly harm me, not in a way that is irreversible. Of course we both get off on my pain, but he'd never hurt me in a way that would break me.

All Everett has ever done is build me back up, and every move he's making only proves that.

DEAD OF WYNTER

FORTY-SIX

EVERETT

Pride blooms in my chest when she stares at the belt in my hand with heat instead of fear is, because if anyone else were holding it, she would be panicking. I know Wynter better than she knows herself, and I would put every dollar I have on that, but for some reason, she trusts me implicitly.

I won't break that trust, not ever again. She doesn't realize that yet, but she will. Soon she'll see there is nowhere on this earth safer for her than kneeling at my feet.

Slowly, I kneel down behind her, taking a moment to breathe her in. The vanilla of her body wash wafts over me and I almost snap, almost put her on her hands and knees and fuck her right here, but I claw onto the last of my own restraint. Not tonight.

Tonight my little dove will give me everything I ask of her and will be left needy and desperate at the end. I bet she'll beg so prettily for more. The thought makes my cock harden further in my slacks. I've been hard since the moment she stepped out of the bathroom, but even more so after she fell to her knees for me, the sight alone made it hard to stop myself from blowing in my pants like a horny teenager.

It's never been like this before, not with any other woman, and not even with Wynter when we slept together the first time. We were both nervous I guess, and desperate for one another after so many years of forcing our desires down. But this is pure and dirty and unhurried. It's us.

Carefully, I wrap the belt around her wrists, looping it until it's secure and I'm sure she can't break out. She's putting a lot of trust in me right now, and that isn't lost on me. She's giving me not only her submission, but her fears. Not only will she have her mouth full meaning she may not be able to safe word, she has now given up mobility of her arms.

"Are you okay, dove?" I ask quietly, moving around until I'm squatting in front of her.

Wynter's lip quivers slightly, but she's not afraid. There isn't an ounce of fear in her eyes. "Yes, I'm okay."

"Good girl." I smile, brushing my fingers down her cheek until my hand wraps around the front of her throat, the slightest amount of pressure there to make sure she's paying attention to me. "I'm going to fuck your mouth, dove, and you're going to take everything I give you, aren't you?"

"Yes," she moans, her legs practically vibrating with the need to close.

"You are not to speak unless spoken to, or unless you need to safe word, do you understand?"

"Yes," she replies quickly.

I smile down at her before pressing a gentle kiss to her parted lips. She's so fucking beautiful right now and it takes everything in me to back away from her even for a moment. Slowly, I begin unbuttoning my shirt. Each button that slides through its hole has her undivided attention as she waits patiently for me to undress. I consider just pulling my dick out while fully dressed, the idea has a lot of merit, but I want to be naked for this.

I slip the shirt off my shoulders and Wynter's hungry eyes rake over the exposed flesh, flitting from one arm to the other and then settling on my wide chest. "Do you like what you see, little dove? You look like you're ready to eat me for breakfast."

"I love what I see," she says reverently and a smile tugs at my lips.

I continue to undress, unbuttoning my slacks and pushing them down my thick thighs, uncovering my very hard cock. I don't make a habit out of free balling it, but now that Wynter is back in my life I like to have as little barrier between me and her sweet pussy as I can manage.

Wynter draws her bottom lip between her teeth as she stares at my cock hungrily.

"Do you want my cock?"

"Yes." She nods, her eyes never moving from what she wants.

"Beg."

She looks up at me, the smallest amount of surprise playing in her gaze before her eyes settle on mine. "Please fuck my mouth. I want to taste you." Where I expect to hear uncertainty in her voice, all I hear is confidence and it only makes my cock harder.

I squeeze the base, trying to calm the fuck down as I step toward her. I'm so amped up I can barely see through the haze of lust clouding my vision. "Open," I command and her mouth pops open for me in the most delectable O. She's so fucking perfect it hurts. "Eyes on me always."

Wynter nods but doesn't respond, instead choosing to keep her mouth open for me.

"Good girl," I praise, closing the distance between us and wiping the precum leaking from my cock along her lips.

Her sinfully pink tongue darts out and wipes the sticky mess away, a satisfied groan filling the room.

I move one hand to the top of her head to keep her steady while the other one stays wrapped around the base of my cock to help guide myself into her hot mouth. The moment her lips wrap around me, I swear I've died and gone to heaven. Her sweet tongue draws circles around the head the moment it slips into her mouth.

"Fuck, Wynter," I moan.

I've had a lot of blow jobs over the years, but nothing compares to the feeling of her mouth sliding down my length in slow, measured strokes while she looks up at me with all the trust in the world.

"You look so beautiful with a mouthful of my cock." I gently run my fingers through her hair, guiding her back and forth as her rhythm starts to pick up. God, if she keeps this up, I'm going to be blowing down her throat any second now.

Wynter moans around me sending vibrations through my oversensitive cock and dragging another groan from my throat. I'm trying to allow her to have a little bit of control, but the urge to take over and fuck her throat is almost too much for me to tamp down. But not yet. She wanted to taste me and I'm going to let her do just that.

She sucks like a woman possessed, her legs spread below her but her hips still rocking as if there's relief to be had. But we both know there isn't, not unless I allow it, and that's not going to happen. I've threatened withholding her orgasms over and over again, and the only way she's going to learn is by me following through. Plus, I get a sick kind of satisfaction by having her wet and needy for me.

I pull my cock from her mouth and run the tip along her lips, dragging the combination of precum and saliva along the pouty pillow.

"This fucking mouth," I murmur. "Trust me?"

"Yes," Wynter answers immediately.

I smile down at her, taking in the sight of her on her knees for me, her legs spread, eyes gazing up, her full lips parted. She's a goddess. "I'll never give you more than you can handle," I remind her right before I shove my cock back into her warm mouth and don't stop until I've surged forward and my cock nudges the back of her throat. I pull back slightly, enough for her to drag in a breath and then I'm thrusting my hips forward again. My grip on her hair tightens as I push my hips back and forth, each time feeding her more of my cock.

Wynter gags around me as I try to push past the reflex and into her throat. "Let me in, dove," I whisper as my fingers brush through her hair comfortingly. "Breathe through your nose, and let me in."

Her body relaxes under my touch and I wait a few seconds before trying again. She gags again, but this time I slip right past and into her tight throat.

"Fuck." My head drops back as I start thrusting at a steady pace, making sure she has enough time to pull in a breath before surging back in.

It's not long before the tingling in my lower back and balls is overwhelming and I know I'll have no other option but to come down her throat.

"Are you going to take my cum like a good girl, dove?" I grind out, barely able to put words together to form a sentence past the blinding pleasure my girl is giving me.

She nods as best she can with her mouth full of my cock and I lose all rhythm, pumping in and out of her with wild abandon. Wynter's eyes are on me, full of tears and love. It's a weird combination to be obsessed with, but it's what pulls me over into an orgasm so powerful I don't know how I remain standing. My fingers tighten in her hair as if it can keep me on my feet as my release takes hold and thick ropes of cum coat her mouth.

Wynter sucks hungrily, taking every drop I give her and it only drags the feeling on and on until we're both panting from exhaustion. When I slip my cock from between her lips, they're the most delectable shade of red and somehow my dick responds to the sight. She's irresistible, a siren calling me from the deep.

Without a word, I bend over and scoop her into my arms before crossing the room, tugging back the comforter and slipping her between the sheets. Her eyes track me as I move around the other side of the bed and climb in beside her, immediately pulling her back into my arms.

"You were such a good girl for me, little dove," I whisper into her neck, pressing gentle kisses into the soft flesh.

"Good enough for an orgasm?" she asks.

I chuckle and pull her in closer. "Not tonight."

She huffs out a sigh and I don't miss the way she rubs her thighs together. I don't need to touch her to know her desperate pussy is wet, but she won't be getting any relief tonight.

"Should have thought twice about talking back." I shrug into the pillows. "Now stop pouting and go to sleep, or I'll extend your orgasm ban."

"Good night," Wynter chimes and I can't help but laugh. We're finally where we were meant to be, even if it is in the midst of chaos.

FORTY-SEVEN

WYNTER

At first I don't know what wakes me up. There are peaks of the sun through the crack in the curtains, but it's not enough to pull me out of my deep slumber. I don't need to pee, which is usually what wakes me up, and the room and house are completely quiet.

Ever so slowly, realization washes over me and pleasure floods my core.

"Good morning, little dove," Everett whispers into the crook of my neck as his fingers gently stroke my core.

"Good morning indeed," I moan, pushing my hips back until my ass makes contact with his impressive length.

"I thought seeing as you were such a good girl for me last night that you deserved a reward, how does that sound?" he murmurs.

"Really fucking good," I gasp as his fingers brush along my clit and send electric currents of pleasure through my entire body.

He chuckles. "Your pussy is so wet for me, even in your sleep. Always ready for me to take you."

"Please," I whimper. His movements are too light, not enough for me to get anywhere near the release I so desperately crave.

"You'll get everything you need soon, dove. Be patient."

I almost tell him he can be patient after being denied a release all night, but I hold it back to avoid more teasing.

"I dreamed about your tight little pussy last night," he tells me, the roughness of his sleepy voice causing my body to quiver with need. "I dreamed about fucking you just like this. Sliding into your wetness and fucking you long and slow, dragging out every moment of pleasure for the both of us."

I whimper, both loving and hating the idea of my release being drawn out longer than it has already, but when I feel the blunt tip of his cock at my entrance, I don't hesitate to push my ass back into him. "I need you," I whisper into the quiet room.

Everett presses a kiss to my shoulder blade as his cock penetrates me, stretching me almost to the point of pain, but it's the most wonderful kind, the kind that makes my heart feel just as full as my pussy.

"You're so tight, little dove."

He pushes forward until he's buried inside me to the hilt and stalls there. I want to beg him to move because the longer he remains still inside me, the more the ache turns into a burning need.

"Who does your pussy belong to, Wynter?" he growls in my ear, nipping at my earlobe before kissing the same spot.

"You. It belongs to you," I pant.

"Damn right it does. And who do you belong to? Who holds your body? Who holds your heart?"

"You. All of me is yours," I admit, and for the first time the truth of those words washes over me like a warm wave of emotion. I'm his. I've always been his. When I was a teenager experimenting because I couldn't get my brother's best friend out of my mind. When I went to BDSM clubs seeking something to make it all go away. All those years I spent with an Everett sized void in my heart. I've been his since before I even knew what that meant.

Everett groans at my words and finally starts moving. His hips make contact with my ass with each slow thrust, and his cock hits the spot inside of me that makes my toes curl. "You're all mine, little dove. And I'm all yours. Always."

The combination of his words and the feeling of him taking me so gently brings tears to my eyes, but they're not sad tears, they're not freeing tears from a punishment. No, they're happy tears. They're the kind of tears that fall against your cheeks when you realize your soulmate is holding you in their arms like you're the most precious thing they've ever held, and I allow the tears to fall. For once I don't try to stuff my emotions into a little box where I don't have to deal with them, because these ones I want to deal with. I want to feel everything with Everett. The love. The pleasure. The pain. Because all of it is worth it to be here with him.

Everett's fingers weave around me until they're drawing

gentle circles into my oversensitive clit in the same rhythm as his hips thrust into me. His other arm wraps underneath me and holds me still for him to do as he pleases to my body. "You can come as many times as you want this morning, Wynter. You've been such a good girl, and you deserve a reward."

I moan my relief, thanking any god who will listen that I won't have to hold my impending orgasm until he's ready to allow me to fall over the edge. "Thank you," I whisper.

"Your pussy is clamping down on my cock," he tells me as his fingers press down more firmly on my clit, bringing me right to the edge of oblivion.

One, two, three more thrusts and I'm falling. White flashes in my vision as I tumble into an orgasm that holds my entire body prisoner, taking away all ability to move and control the sounds I'm making, and I hand myself over, allowing every last ounce of pleasure to seep into my pores.

Somewhere in my consciousness, I can hear Everett speaking to me in gentle tones, words that don't register in my bliss-filled state, but ones that mean everything.

"Fuck, dove, you've drenched my cock," he groans, his hips moving a little faster now as he starts to chase his own release. "That was so fucking sexy, Wynter. Feeling you come, your entire body shaking with the force. I want to feel it again. You're going to come again." His fingers start rubbing the sensitive nub at the crest of my pussy harder.

"I can't," I pant. I've had orgasms back to back before, in fact, I almost always do, but that orgasm ruined me, and I don't think I can handle another one like it.

"Yeah, baby, you can," he grunts, pulling my hips back into him farther and the new angle has his cock hitting my G-spot almost savagely. His movements aren't rough, far from it, but the overwhelming sensations border on painful, and yet, little by little, the familiar tightening in my core starts to return.

"Oh god," I cry out.

"That's it, little dove. I want you to scream for me," Everett grinds out, his cock pulsing inside me. He's waiting for me.

"Everett, it's too much," I sob tears I hadn't realized were tracking down my cheeks.

"It's never too much between us, Wynter. Come on baby, come for me, come all over my cock."

And somehow I do. The orgasm hits me almost out of nowhere, and slams into me so hard it takes my breath right out of my lungs, tearing a scream from my throat. Every muscle in my body tightens at once, the blinding pleasure radiates through me until it's all I can think about.

"Goddamnit, fuck," Everett groans right before his cocks starts pulsating inside me and thick ropes of cum fill me. The room is filled with a primal roar, and even as my orgasm begins to recede, the overwhelming feeling in my chest is there in its wake.

We lay in silence, his cock still lodged inside of me, holding his cum in my pussy as we catch our breath. The sound of our joint panting is all I can hear as my mind begins to come back to itself.

"Can I ask you something?" I whisper, the gravity of the question I'm about to ask is too much, too loud on its own even before the words fall from my lips. The perfect moment we have shared is about to shatter, and I almost tell him not to worry about it before he can answer me, but I need to know. I can't spend another day allowing myself to fall for the man whose body is still inside me without knowing.

"Anything," Everett murmurs, his strong arms pulling me back until our bodies are pressed together without an ounce of space between us.

"Why did you leave?"

DEAD OF WYNTER

FORTY-EIGHT

EVERETT

H er question shouldn't catch me off guard, but it does. In all fairness, I am still buried inside her after some of the most intense sex I've ever had, so talking about the day I tore both our hearts out seems like it may ruin the moment, but I've avoided it for too long. I should have told her the moment she opened the door the night her parents died, but I've put it off time and time again, and it's time I come clean.

I sigh and gently pull my softening cock from her tight pussy, groaning when I feel my cum leak around me. The primal caveman living within me aches to push my seed back inside her, but it's not the time to listen to that part of me. I sit up in the bed and pull her up as well until she's straddling my thighs with no chance to run from me. I don't think she will, but I'm not willing to chance it.

Wynter's eyes are wide as she stares at me. The position we're in gives me a great view of her naked body, but it's not the time, and for once, my dick understands that.

"When I was in college, I wrote a program that could be used as a weapon. When I built it, I didn't really think about the potential of it falling into the wrong hands, it was just something to pass the time, and I thought it could be the next big piece of technology for Frost. Your dad had already planned to hire me the moment I was out of college, and I wanted to have something ready to release to hit the ground running.

"When it was finished, it was a fucking masterpiece. It was going to change the way we look at security systems for computers, phones, tablets, you name it." I sigh. "But then my family got wind of it. I don't even know how they knew because I hadn't had anything to do with them since before I turned eighteen, and yet one day Angelo and Paul showed up at my apartment with an ultimatum. Hand over the program, or they were going to take you."

Wynter gasps, her eyes flashing with fear and understanding, but I can't stop now, I have to tell her everything before I lose my nerve. Of course, I could leave it at that. There's no more explanation needed, but there's more to the story she should know. I never want any secrets between us, not even this.

"I remember them leaving and trying to work out how they even knew how I felt about you, because we were still skirting around our feelings, so how could they know?" I shake my head. "But even then everyone knew how obsessed I was with you, and it put you in danger. At first I thought I could call their bluff, but then notes started to arrive. Threats against you, vivid descriptions of what they would do to you if I didn't do as they asked. I called a meeting here at the estate with your parents and Storm and Rayne after I got a particularly vulgar note, with photos of you attached. It was time for us to come up with a plan together. But there was no plan. I only had one option, and that was to leave you. We knew that if you knew why I was going that you would try to stop me, and as awful as this sounds, we needed it to be convincing. So when I left and you fell apart, word spread very quickly about how I didn't give a fuck about you, and that's what we needed to happen."

The words leave a sick feeling in their path, saying all of this out loud after so many years feels like reliving my worst nightmare, but I guess it kind of is. The day I skipped town and left Wynter laying in this bed on her own, with no explanation, it was the worst day of my life but it was a necessary evil, one that I had to live with.

"What was the program?" she asks, her voice barely above a whisper.

I suck in a breath. "To put it simply, the program could hack any network in the world in a matter of minutes. The reason I designed it that way was so I could reverse engineer a protection software that not even this program could crack, but it didn't occur to me at the time just how dangerous being able to hack anything on earth is. Banks, military forces, the CIA at your fingertips in a matter of moments. Looking back at it, I was so stupid, how did it never occur to me? But I was young." I shrug like that makes any of it okay, like putting the love of my life in danger over and over again could ever be okay.

Wynter closes her eyes but tears still leak through her lashes. Her breath comes in faster as she desperately clings on to control of her emotions, but it's only a few seconds before a sob cracks through her chest and she buries her head in my bare chest.

"I thought you didn't love me like I loved you. I thought I was a dumb kid who thought my brothers best friend loved me. I spent the last eight years believing I wasn't worthy of your love," she rasps between an onslaught of tears. "I thought I imagined everything between us."

I grasp her shoulders in my hands and draw her back until we're staring into each other's eyes. Her face is stained with tears, but she's never looked more beautiful than she does right now. "You didn't imagine anything. I loved you from the moment I met you. I loved you before I understood what love was. I've loved you every single moment of every single day since you first walked into my life, and leaving you was the single hardest thing I have ever had to do."

She squeezes her eyes shut as she chokes on her sobs, years of repressed emotions rising to the surface all at once. I move my hands to her face until her cheeks are cradled in them. "I never want you to doubt my feelings for you, little dove. You are worth everything, worth so much more than I will ever be able to give you, but I will spend every moment of the rest of our lives proving how much you mean to me and trying to make up for all the years we lost because of my stupid mistakes."

This time when she burrows into my chest I don't stop her, instead I wrap my arms around her back and pull her as close as I can, trying with all I am to hold her together as she falls apart in my arms.

Wynter sobs into my chest, her tears soaking the bare skin beneath her face, and I hold her through it as she lets go of all the shit I put her through. I hate myself for leaving the way I did, loathe my very fucking existence, but what I did was for her. It was to save her a fate I wouldn't wish on my worst nightmare, because I've been a part of that family, I've been held against my will when I so desperately wanted to escape, and I would never allow her to go through that hell.

E IGHT YEARS AGO

I stand at her bedroom door for so long I lose track of time, and the longer I stand here, the harder it is to wrap my head around what I'm about to do. I'm leaving in the morning, transferring colleges and moving across the country to get as far away from her as I can, and I hate myself for it because it's going to hurt her.

Wynter should never feel pain, or sadness, or regret. All I want for her is life, and that's why I have to go, because the other option is too heinous to even think.

I've stood here a hundred times before but I've never felt so dejected staring at the white door as I do now. I raise my hand to knock, it's time and I can't put it off anymore. Every day I stay here is another day she's in danger, and I can't have that.

The door swings open and Wynter's shining eyes meet mine. Her hair is pulled in a messy knot on the top of her head, and a loose tracksuit hangs from her body shapelessly, but she looks so fucking beautiful it hurts. Wynter is a timeless beauty, it doesn't matter what she wears or if she has a dab of makeup on her face, she's the most radiant woman I've ever seen.

It's been hell keeping my hands off her for the last two years. One day she was the best friend I loved without realizing what that meant, and the next she was a woman. The change should have seemed gradual, but to me it was immediate, and I've been fighting a losing battle ever since.

"Hey." Wynter beams at me, pulling her headphones from her ears. "I didn't know you were coming over tonight."

I smile, not because there's anything happy about right now, but because these are the last moments we will ever spend together where she doesn't hate me. This is the last time she looks at me like I'm everything. Hell, these are the last moments she'll look at me at all.

"Hey, dove." The nickname falls from my lips so naturally, just like it has since the first time I said it out loud.

She pushes the door open for me to come in before walking back toward her bed where textbooks are spread out. "Sorry for the mess, I'm just getting ahead in some of my course readings," she explains.

"You don't start college for another month." I chuckle.

Normally when there is a threat within the family, we just put extra security on that person for the foreseeable future and it's not a problem, but Wynter going out of state for college complicates things, and it means we have no other option than to make it look like I never loved her in the first place.

"I know, but I want to make sure I'm prepared. And I want to be able to go out and party, and have fun, and not have to worry about the three thousand pages of textbook I should be reading." She shrugs and starts to gather the books up, placing them on her bedside table.

"Partying, huh?" I raise a brow.

"College experiences and all that." She winks and it snaps something inside me. The tether I've been walking on since the day we met, the one that has kept me at a safe distance, only stealing a kiss on her eighteenth birthday because I couldn't go another day without knowing what she tasted like.

One moment I'm standing by the door, and the next I'm hovering above her on the bed, barely containing my need to consume her. She lets out a surprised gasp, but doesn't pull away, only stares up at me with wide eyes.

For long moments we stare at one another, and then at once our lips clash and my tongue demands entry immediately. If I'm never going to see her again, I need to have her just once. I need to allow us both to feel what it's like to come together like thunder and lightning.

Wynter lets out a startled noise, but doesn't pull away, in fact, her arms wrap around my neck and pull me closer, holding me to her as I tell her how I feel with nothing but a kiss. The moment is everything I've dreamed of and more, and even though it makes me a selfish bastard, even though taking everything I'm about to take from her will only end up hurting her more once I'm gone, I'm going to do it anyway. I need to know what she feels like before I go.

Her hands move down my back until they're pushing my T-shirt up my back and I break our kiss for long enough to whip it over my head and discard it across the room. Wynter's eyes roam hungrily over my bare chest and an animalistic growl claws up my throat a moment before our lips fuse together again.

Nothing has ever felt as right as her body beneath mine, her hands moving across my skin as she gives me everything, and that's why I should stop. I should tear myself from her and leave right now, but I'm not going to do that, and maybe that makes me an asshole, but I can't go without us both knowing what it means for us to be together like this.

"Everett," Wynter moans and the sound of my name on her lips is so intoxicating I can't get enough.

"Say it again."

"Everett, please."

"Please what, little dove?"

"I need you," she whispers.

The words hang between us as I stare into her eyes looking for doubt. I know she's a virgin because I've been fending off boys from her since she was sixteen, and although she used to get mad about me crashing her dates, now I think she does it just to see me get mad. That's something I've been trying not to think about since we decided I would leave. At some point Wynter is going to meet a man and get married and have a bunch of kids. Some guy is going to have the life I've been dreaming of for the last four years, and I'm going to have to watch from the sidelines. It's what I deserve, but that doesn't make it an easier pill to swallow.

"What do you need, Wynter? I need to hear the words."

A deep blush covers her cheeks and I dip my head to kiss the pop of color. I could get drunk from this, just from being close to her and her innocence. "I want to... I want you to..." She can't get the words out and I'm not patient enough to wait.

"Do you want me to take your virginity, baby?" I drawl.

"Yes," she whispers.

We stare at one another for a few seconds, the gravity of her admission hanging between us before we start tearing at each other's clothes. Her sweater is torn over her head revealing the silkiest skin I've ever seen in my life. The lace bra she's wearing shows a peek at her rosy nipples and I moan at the sight.

Her hands work at the belt of my jeans as she tries to free my cock as quickly as possible. My own hands work into the front of her sweatpants and I moan as my fingers brush against her wet panties. "Is this all for me, little dove?" I ask.

She nods as she starts working on the button of my jeans. I've never seen her like this. Wynter is always so controlled, so prim and proper, but right now, she can't strip me fast enough. I like this side of her, the side she keeps hidden from the world but shows me without hesitation.

When Wynter is stripped down to nothing but a pair of small black panties, I allow my eyes to feast on her bare skin. There's a part of me that wants to mark her milky skin so badly, but I can't. It's bad enough I'm taking something I can never give back, I can't also force her to stare at bruises on her skin for the next week. There has to be a line.

"Fuck Wynter, you're so fucking beautiful," I rasp.

Her arms twitch with the need to cover herself, but they never move. She's being raw and open with me, and I wish I could show her the same courtesy.

I shuck my pants and shoes quickly, the loud thud my boots make as they hit the ground only makes her giggle, but the moment I'm naked, I'm on her again, kissing and licking every inch of her sweet skin, savoring the flavor I will only taste this once.

"Tell me, little dove, why haven't you lost your virginity to some boy at school?" I taunt.

Wynter's breath hitches and her head falls back into the pillow, giving me all the access I need to her throat. "Because you always scared them away," she moans.

"Teenagers have been sneaking around for centuries, try again." I lick a path from her collarbone all the way up her neck and then repeat the process on the other side.

"I... I..." Her hips rise to meet mine, her slick pussy brushing along my cock and tearing a moan from both of us. "Because I saved it for you," she admits.

"Fuck," I groan. "I want to take this slow, but I don't think I can."

"I don't want you to. I need you," she whispers. "I need you to fuck me."

How am I ever meant to leave her when she's saying shit like that? I force the thought from my mind and focus on the task at hand. My hand snakes down between us and carefully parts her folds. "Has anyone ever touched this pussy, Wynter?"

"No, just me."

"And who do you think about when you touch yourself?" I ask as I circle her clit carefully. As selfish as I am, I'm not going to take her virginity without warming her up first. I'm not a complete monster.

"I think about you." Her hips lift from the mattress, begging for more, and I'm happy to oblige. I slide my fingers down to her entrance before entering her with one finger, eliciting an erotic moan from her throat.

"Is that so? What am I doing in these thoughts?"

"This. You're touching me, fucking me, claiming me."

The pressure in my balls feels like they're about to explode just from the sound of those words falling from her pouty lips, but I take deep breaths to calm myself. At this rate, I'm going to blow the moment I slide into her.

"Fuck, Wynter."

I withdraw my finger from her tight heat and press a second in beside it, her pussy stretching around them so beautifully. Part of me wants to draw back onto my haunches and watch them disappear inside her, but I can't miss a moment of her eyes, or even her sharp intakes of breath each time my fingers brush against the place inside her threatening to detonate her.

Wynter's arms wrap around my neck and she tugs me down until our lips crash together and a strangled moan tears from her throat as I increase the pressure on her G-spot. I need her to come so I can get inside her, and I've never been known for my patience.

I feel the moment she reaches the edge and hold her there for just a moment, just long enough to say, "I want you to scream for me, dove."

And scream she does. Her body shakes beneath me, and her eyes close as she's overwhelmed by the pleasure I've given her. Her tight cunt grips my fingers and the mere thought of sliding my cock into her has my balls tingling with the intense need to come.

The moment Wynter's body stops shaking from the intensity of her release, I slide my cock into position, notching it at her entrance and groaning at the feel of her wetness on the head of my cock. "Are you sure?" I ask.

"I've never been more sure of anything in my life."

Hours later, I have Wynter bundled up in front of me, the sweet scent of her shampoo clouding my vision with each breath I take. Over the years, I've had my fair share of sex, but what we just did was so much more than that. It was two forces coming together, two people who have longed after one another for so many years, finally allowing themselves a moment of weakness.

I couldn't bring myself to leave while she was awake, couldn't bring myself to see her heart break in front of my eyes. I hold her for another moment, committing the moment to memory, because that's all it will ever be. I will never hold her in my arms again or breathe in her scent. I'll never kiss her, or touch her, or tell her how much I love her. So this is all I have.

When I finally tear myself from the bed, I spend another few minutes staring at her sleeping form, the angel laid out in front of me, and then I dress quietly before fleeing from the house like the coward I am.

I never deserved Wynter Saint James, but after what I just did, there's a special place in hell for me.

Dead of Wynter

FORTY-NINE
WYNTER

I t takes a lot to intimidate me. I grew up in a mafia family, my brothers are both scary motherfuckers, I stood up to our enemy at my parents' funeral without so much as flinching, and I have a friend who genuinely enjoys torturing people. But somehow Tommy isn't the scariest person standing in the room right now.

I'm starting to think that maybe I should have waited with Snow and Emerson while this conversation took place, more so for self-preservation than anything else, but now looking at the four men who are taking up most of the space in the room, I'm not sure I can hack this.

Storm and I are sitting behind his desk and having the huge wooden structure between me and them is oddly comforting. Everett has his laptop on his lap to my left, and Tommy and Rayne lurk on either side of us in case someone makes a wrong move.

The other men, the blindingly good looking, scary as hell men, stand in front of us with varying degrees of interest written across their faces.

Tommy steps forward with a strained smile etched across his lips. The only time I've really seen him happy is when he's been kicking the shit out of someone, so I'm not particularly surprised by the discomfort on his face.

"I'll do a quick round of introductions and then we can get started." He points to the first man who if I had to hazard a guess I would think is the leader.

He's dressed impeccably in an expensive charcoal suit and his copper hair is styled to perfection, but it's his eyes that caught me the moment he stepped foot in the room. One blue, one green, but both as mesmerizing as the other. He's older than the others, probably falling within his mid-forties, not that that makes him any less attractive.

"This is Crew, he is much like the Storm of the operation, however, does tend to be a bit more... hands on." He gestures to the next man towering over the others.

He must be six foot seven easily and built with muscle on muscle. His button-up shirt is unbuttoned at the top and sleeves rolled up to reveal tattoos across scarred skin. His dark hair is clipped short on the sides and slightly longer on the top and if I didn't know better I would think he has a military background. His eyes look like he would rather be anywhere than here, cold, dark and disinterested.

"This is Kaos."

"Looks like you could deliver some chaos, brother." Rayne cracks a smile and the other two men follow suit, but not either of the ones who have already been introduced.

"You've got that right." The blonde man with messy hair and deep green eyes chuckles, patting the big man on his back. He's dressed almost as well as Crew, but without a jacket, his shirt open enough to get a peek at an impressively toned chest.

"This is Bishop." Tommy gestures, and then moves to the last man, the one I'm most intrigued by.

If I weren't completely obsessed with Everett, I could definitely see myself lusting after all four of these guys, but there's something in the last one's eyes that piques my interest. His wild eyes are as blue as the ocean, and his hair chocolate brown. He wears a pair of tight black skinny jeans and a hoody, much more casual than the other three, and every bit of skin visible is covered in tattoos, including a few on his face. This man looks like he eats girls like me for breakfast.

"And this is Kovu."

I pray for any woman that gets into bed with any of these men, because Jesus.

"Thank you for coming all this way, gentlemen," Storm says kindly. "Why don't we take a seat so we can get to business?"

Crew and Bishop step forward to take a seat but the other two remain standing, their eyes flitting around the room just the same way Rayne's do when we're in an unfamiliar place. "We're very interested to know why we were beckoned to Chicago by the great Storm Saint James," Crew's words sound sincere, but they're anything but.

"Do you always do business with your women around?" Kaos looks at me dismissively before his eyes track back to my brother.

Storm leans back in his chair and looks over at me for just a moment. "My sister, Wynter, is learning the ropes of the family business to take over if something were to happen to me," he explains and my head whips around to look at him. Should we be openly telling people that? "And she also happens to be the one the Russos have set their sights on."

"Ah, so that's what this is about, protecting your pretty little sister," Kaos taunts.

Bishop hits the man standing behind him and rolls his eyes. "What loudmouth over here is trying to say is that we don't do vendetta killings. That's not our jam."

"It's not a vendetta killing," I say. "We do not want to take out the Russo family because they're picking on me. I'm a big girl and I can take a lot more than a few death threats, a car bomb, and a bunch of creepy things in a box. We want them dead because they've stolen from us time and time again. They kidnapped one of our own. And they killed our parents."

The men collectively stare at me for a moment as if they're not sure what to do with a woman putting them in their place, but I'm not done with them yet.

"Up until recently, our families had a truce, or so we thought. The Russos broke the truce. They've been actively making moves against us for months, including stealing several shipments of cargo, and trafficking human beings on our turf. Now, if you're going to waste our time, you can leave." I stand as if ready to escort them out. It's a bluff, a good one, but a bluff regardless.

Bishop bursts into laughter and at first I think he's laughing at me, and by the feel of Everett tensing beside me, I don't think I'm the only one. "Jesus, I like her." He points at me. "Putting you fuckers in your place."

I stare at him for a moment before smiling and plopping back down into my seat. If there's anyone I can't afford to look weak in front of, it's the men in this room.

O nce The Legion leaves, we're all on edge. I'm not sure whether it was the topic of conversation that has gotten to us, or if there's more to it, but my skin is crawling with discomfort. Their fee is substantial, but then again, we are hiring contract killers to take down a criminal organization, so it was bound to attract a hefty price tag.

We sit in silence for long minutes as we consider the gravity of what we're about to do. We're going to war, and in a way we haven't ever done in the past. We are the bigger organization, we have more firepower and with The Legion on our side, I think we're going to get through fairly unscathed, but even the possibility of someone I love being hurt is making my palms sweat and chest tighten.

"Those guys were dicks," Rayne says from where he's collapsed into the lounge.

I scoff. "You've got that right. And I thought you lot were assholes."

"Careful, dove," Everett growls beside me and it makes me giggle. It seems like a strange time to laugh, but what's that old saying, *if you don't laugh, you'll cry?*

"What are we going to tell the girls?" Storm asks.

"Nothing. Snow isn't in a good place right now, and Emerson is still dealing with everything that happened before the wedding. They're better off in the dark on this one," I tell them.

One by one, four pairs of eyes fall on me, surprise filling each of their distinct eyes. "You want to hide the fact we're about to take out our enemy?" Tommy asks.

"Not completely. We should tell them that there are plans in motion, but I don't think either of them could deal with the risk we're going up against here. Every time Rayne leaves the house, Emerson is panicked the whole time he's away. Snow is barely holding on by a thread. You know she snuck out the other night to go drinking?" I shake my head. Everett was less than impressed when he got the call and had to go get her when he was in the middle of getting his dick sucked. "She's about as close to off the rails as she's ever been, and this could really tip her over the edge."

"I agree. It's the way it's always been done for a reason, and while I acknowledge we are making certain allowances in the new generation, I don't think either of them should be burdened with this stress," Storm says.

A giddy excitement replaces the bubbling fear. Tomorrow is the day we take out our enemy and finally end their torment on our family.

FIFTY

EVERETT

The morning comes with ominous light. The estate is covered in a thick layer of fog, as if an omen for what is to come. It didn't matter what I did through the night, I couldn't sleep. I thought the rough session Wynter and I had would have knocked me out, but as she drifted to sleep in my arms, I was wide awake. Even after waking her up twice to try to exert some of the excess energy vibrating through my body, my eyes couldn't close and my body couldn't relax.

There is so much left to do, and each hour drifting by reminds me of that. The wheels are in motion, but to ensure we make it out the other side without unnecessary complications, there are things that need to be done that I would rather not do. Things we can't tell Wynter about, no matter how involved she is.

It's early when I slip out of the bed, leaving her sleeping alone. It's not lost on me that this isn't the first time I've snuck out in the early hours of the morning with the possibility of not returning, but there's so much more between us now. When I left last time, there was love, more than I knew how to deal with, but it wasn't like this. It didn't feel like my next breath depended on her being safe and healthy and mine.

The office door is open as I walk in, still pulling my shirt over my head, and Storm and Rayne look just about as good as I feel. Tired. Resigned. A little hopeless.

"Surprised it took you so long," Rayne mutters, his eyes closed and head dropped back against the lounge.

"I don't like her waking up without me," I admit. It's too fresh, and with everything going on, I wouldn't blame her for assuming the worst, even if there's nothing on God's green earth that could tear me away from her willingly.

Storm nods, the skin under his eyes stained with dark circles as he reaches for the cup of what I can only assume is coffee. "We have to go to the farm," he says the words we've all been thinking since last night. "And you need to call your uncle."

"Yep," Rayne groans.

"And we can't tell Wynter why," I add.

"Double yep." Storm sighs.

"It's not the first rescue mission we've been on." I shrug.

"No, but it's the first we've had to infiltrate something so big," Rayne points out.

I collapse into the seat beside him and scrub my hands over my face. "Rayne should go. He has the best knowledge aside from me of the way the farm is laid out, even if they've changed the whole fucking thing since the last time he was there."

"Tommy will come with me. He'll be better in the field than he would stuck here. Storm will stay here with the girls. We can't have them unprotected," Rayne says.

"I'm not sitting this one out, bro. I know I hang on the sidelines a lot for a lot of reasons, but this is too important." Storm stands, crossing the room to where we're sitting and taking a seat in the chair opposite us.

"Don't argue with me on this one, Storm. You make most of the calls, but you don't make these ones. It's safer for the girls if you're here with them, and it will be comforting for Snow if it's you. If she's really as fragile as Wynter was saying, it's best we don't push it. This is what Tommy and I are trained for, and Everett has other places he needs to be."

Storm grumbles something under his breath and then nods. "Fine. But I don't like being the only one sitting out."

"You're not the only one. Wynter won't like not being involved either." Rayne chuckles.

"Thank god she's not going. Could you imagine this one if she was in any imminent danger?" Storm gestures to me, his laugh filling the room.

I glare at him. "I can't wait for you to meet your woman and understand what we go through," I grumble.

"It'll never happen. There ain't no taming me." He winks. The day that man falls hard and fast for a woman will be the day Storm Saint James falls to his knees, and I can't fucking wait.

399

FIFTY-ONE

WYNTER

The bed beside me is cold when I wake, and my heart skips a beat as I remember the morning I realized Everett was gone. It's been a frequent feature in my nightmares over the last eight years, and I can't help but wonder if I'll always have this reaction when he's not in bed in the morning.

I sit up and look around, my body relaxing when I notice his shoes by the door and last night's clothes thrown hastily beside the hamper. Maybe he's just gone to get some coffee.

My stomach growls angrily, and I try to remember the last time I ate. Was it yesterday? Or maybe dinner the night before? Deciding I definitely need to rectify my overwhelming hunger, I reach for my phone and pad out into the kitchen. We're still on complete lockdown, so there's no one in or out of this house who isn't blood, or Everett and Tommy. We don't trust anyone, and honestly, I can't see that changing anytime soon. We're no closer to finding the rat than we were when we realized we had one, and we've exhausted all of our options apart from waiting for them to make a move in front of the wrong person.

Another rumble vibrates through my stomach, forcing me to put one foot in front of the other and open the fridge to survey what we have. Despite each of us being well off in our own right, I've never been the biggest fan of having staff. We never had nannies, and when we moved here to the estate, we did have a cleaner and a gardener due to the size of the place, mom always cooked all of our meals and did all the shopping on her own.

I stare at the contents of the fridge and sigh. The milk is out of date, there's one rasher of suspicious-looking bacon haphazardly wrapped in cling wrap, and one egg. Have we been to the store since the funeral?

"Wynter," Tommy says from behind me, an amused smirk playing on his lips.

"We have no food," I tell him.

"I know, I came down a little while ago fucking famished and had that exact look on my face when I saw the contents of that fridge." He chuckles.

"Can you run me over to the store and I can pick some things up? I'd go on my own, but you know, rival criminal organization wants me dead and all that." I half laugh despite it being far from funny. Every time I make light of the situation, I think Everett's head is going to explode, but I'm hoping Tommy will be able to see the funny side.

His head drops back and he barks out a laugh. "I see the dilemma." He nods. "Get dressed, we'll leave in ten."

I quickly scurry back down the hallway and throw on the first clothes I find. Normally I put a lot of effort into my appearance because any time I don't, I end up in the gossip columns with a drug habit, a breakup, or an eating disorder. You name it, I've had it as far as they're concerned. But today, I just don't have it in me.

I'm surprised I could sleep last night considering what the day will bring. Death and destruction, two things we've had entirely too much of recently. And yet I slept soundly because Everett held me through the night. His strong arms holding me together when I should be falling apart.

It's still early and the rest of the house is quiet apart from muffled voices in the office. I think about interrupting them to see if there's anything they need, I even get as far as raising my hand to knock, until I hear the words they're saying.

"We can't tell Wynter," Storm says.

"I know. We've been over this every which way, and her knowing only puts her in more danger than she's already in." Everett sighs.

Part of me wants to burst into the room and demand to know what they're talking about, but the other part is hurt. I've proven myself over and over again. Every time they've expected me to fall apart, I've risen, and yet they're still keeping shit from me. It would probably hurt if I wasn't so fucking used to being kept in the dark.

Anger radiates through my body as I make my way toward the front of the house where Tommy is waiting for me. There's a good chance he doesn't know what they're talking about in there either, so there's no point asking, and even if he knew, he probably wouldn't tell me.

"You ready?" Tommy asks from the doorway. His tattooed arms are covered with a long sleeve Henley, the black ink only visible on his neck and hands, but that doesn't stop him from looking intimidating as hell.

"Absolutely." I force a smile to my lips.

Tommy's Aston Martin sits idle at the bottom of the steps. He must have moved it while he waited for me to get ready, and the moment I lower myself into the sports car, the engine roars to life and we're speeding away from the estate.

My phone vibrates in my hand and my eyebrows pull together as I read over the text a few times. The message from Clara, my assistant, doesn't sit right with me. There's something about the words she's chosen that has alarm bells ringing in the back of my mind.

Hey Wyn, any chance you can pop into the office asap this morning, I need your signature on a few things.

The request would be perfectly reasonable if I hadn't been signing documents electronically on my tablet for the last few years. I can't remember the last time I signed an actual piece of paper, and there's nothing in the office that would need my immediate attention. I've purposely been scaling back on work since Mom and Dad died to allow myself time to heal.

"We need to go to the office," I say.

"Why?" Tommy looks over at me, his eyebrows furrowed with an edge of annoyance.

"I think something's wrong."

He stares at me for another moment, but something about my

eyes must tell him I'm not overreacting and he takes the turn onto the highway without another question. He's always had more faith in me than the other guys have.

"Call Everett to tell him where we're going. I don't feel like dying for taking his woman somewhere without telling him," Tommy says as he weaves in and out of traffic with practiced ease. Driving with him should be terrifying because every time I peer over at the speed we're going faster than the last, but the rush is almost comforting, and the sooner we get to the office and make sure Clara is okay, the better.

I unlock my phone and my thumb hovers over Everett's name. They're keeping secrets from me, and the defiant streak my brothers love to point out surges to life. Before I've consciously decided what I'm doing, I'm typing out a fake message and not hitting send, all the while keeping Tommy in the corner of my eye to make sure he doesn't catch on.

They can't be mad when we get back, I did as I was told and took one of the big strong men to protect me, so what harm can it do them not to know where I am for a little while.

FIFTY-TWO

EVERETT

I hate this.

I hate keeping shit from Wynter after I promised I would never keep another secret from her again, and even though it would put her in more danger, and hurt her more, to know what we'll be doing tonight while she sits at home, I still hate every single second of making the plan without her.

Wynter has been incredible these last few days. Whenever we're out of ideas, she has one. Whenever we feel dejected, she's the ray of hope we need. And to leave her out this time around just feels wrong. She's going to fucking lose it when she finds out, and I have no doubt in my mind that she'll target that anger at me. But it's worth it if she's safe and won't ever have to know what the darkest sides of Russo's business look like. She doesn't need that, and I won't show her unnecessarily.

As much as Wynter wants to be involved and she has held her own every step of the way, there are things about what we do that would break her, things that would make her see us in a different light, and that's not something I'm willing to risk.

Storm blows out a long breath and rests his head on the backrest of his chair. We're all tired, but this is weighing on him differently than the rest of us. Now his dad is gone, there's no one to go to for advice, no one to speak from experience, and although he hasn't said it aloud, he's feeling a little lost right now. The whole family is relying on him, and I don't envy the guy for that. "What time are you moving out?"

"Probably early afternoon to give us a chance to do some recon, but we won't hit until the sun goes down. I was thinking maybe if we hit at the same time The Legion hits the club as extra cover. They'll call for backup and leave the farm slightly less protected," Rayne explains. We've been over a hundred different versions of the night, but this is the one that makes the most sense, even if it does mean leaving things to chance.

"Sounds like a plan," Storm says. "I want you to take some of the guys with you, but I don't want them to know where you're going or what you're doing until you're there. Take the van so they don't get tipped off and take the signal blocker so they can't get a warning out if they're the rat."

Rayne and I nod, but neither of us says anything. The air in the office is thick with anxious anticipation, and all I can think about is curling back around Wynter and holding her for a few more hours.

I tap my phone and the screen bursts to life. A message from Tommy among the work emails I've been ignoring catches my attention.

Taking Wynter to the store for food. Be back soon.

"Motherfucker," I hiss, panic settling over me.

"What is it?" Rayne asks, sitting upright in his seat for the first time since I walked in hours ago.

"Tommy took Wynter out of the house," I tell them as I type a reply calling him every name under the sun and ordering him to bring my woman back immediately. The rational part of my mind is desperately trying to tell me I'm overreacting and that if there's anyone who can take care of Wynter, it's Tommy, but the possessive caveman in me is forcing his way to the front.

"Tommy would die before he let anything happen to Wynter," Storm reminds me.

"I know that," I snap, my body on fire with the need to protect her and know she's safe.

Before I'm even conscious of what I'm doing, I've crossed to my laptop and I'm activating the tracker on her phone. I have the app on my phone, but at least on the laptop, I can hack into cameras to check where she is and that she's safe.

"What time did they leave?" Rayne asks.

"Almost an hour ago."

"The store isn't far away, surely they'll be back soon," Storm attempts to reassure me.

The map loads and I stare at the screen for long moments as I process what I'm seeing. "I'm sure they would if they were at the store," I grind the words out as fury radiates through my entire body.

"Where are they?" Storm asks.

"Frost Industries." The moment the words fall from my lips, I'm jumping into action. Something isn't right. Tommy wouldn't take her so far away from the estate without telling us first, which means the trip wasn't planned, and if it wasn't planned, there has to be a reason for it.

Five minutes later, Storm and I are sprinting out the front door, leaving Rayne behind to make sure Emerson and Snow are safe, but all I can think about is getting to my woman as quickly as possible.

FIFTY-THREE

WYNTER

D read washes over me the moment we step into the
elevator. There's something wrong, and while I can't
quite put my finger on what it is, it has the hairs on the back of
my neck standing on end.

I glance over at Tommy beside me and notice the tick in his
jaw and the way his hands clench into fists. He feels it too, the
ominous atmosphere that threatens to suffocate us.

If I'd known we were coming into the office, I would have put
a little effort in, at the very least I would have thrown some
makeup on, but I can't seem to find it in me to care that I'm
wearing activewear with my hair tied on the top of my head,
and not a lick of makeup in sight.

When my parents died, Storm and I gave blanket approval
for our staff to work from home in order to give them their
own time to grieve. Our parents were very involved in the
company, even after retirement. Mom used to bring cakes
in for everyone, and Dad used to run around at the company

picnics with the kids like he was one of them, and their loss was a big shock for not only our family but for the people who work for us as well. I've never been more grateful for that idea than I am as I step out of the elevator and there are only a few people milling around.

"Wait here, I want to do a sweep," Tommy orders and I nod. There's no sense arguing with these men when they go into protect mode, so why would I waste my breath?

It feels like an eternity since I was here last, but in reality, it's only been a couple of weeks. So much has happened I almost can't reconcile the person I was the last time I stepped off the elevator and the person I am today.

As weird as it sounds, I'm stronger now. I've always been able to hold my own, always been a strong, independent woman, but now I know just how far that strength extends.

I reach into my back pocket and pull out my vibrating phone. It's the third time Everett has called me in the last fifteen minutes, and I have a feeling he knows exactly where I am. Perhaps I should feel guilty for not telling him where we were going and making him find out on his own, but if he wants to keep secrets, two can play at that game.

My thumb hovers over the answer button, but there's no doubt in my mind that he can hack into the cameras in the building to check on me, and I don't want to talk to him right now.

Footsteps draw my attention from my phone, and when my eyes land on Clara, I almost smile. The terror in her deep brown eyes wipes any happiness from my face. Her dark brown hair is curled around her face, but I don't miss the bruise forming on her cheek.

414

"Clara, are you okay?" I rush toward her.

"There are some men in your office waiting for you with the guy you arrived with," she chokes out before leaning forward to whisper, "They have guns."

My eyes widen and I struggle to keep my face neutral, not wanting anyone to see the panic ravaging my body. "What were your instructions?" I ask.

"To come get you from the lobby and return with you."

"Okay, I'm going to walk in front of you, and you're going to remain behind me at all times, okay?"

She nods, tears gathering in the corners of her eyes.

I reach for her hand and squeeze it. "It's going to be okay. I promise they won't hurt you anymore."

"They have your friend," she tells me.

I crack a smile. "Good luck to them. The moment Tommy is free, I want you to move behind him and he'll keep you safe."

"Okay." Her voice is small and full of fear, but she understands, and that's all that matters right now. Getting her to safety is my only priority.

The moment I step into my office, there are eyes on me, and my skin crawls under their observation. The three senior members of the Russo family sit on what is usually my side of the desk. Their leering gazes glide down my body leaving filth in their path, but my face remains disinterested.

"You're in my seat," I sneer as I glance at the corner of the room where a huge man is holding Tommy. His eyes are murderous as they flick between Clara and me.

"My apologies, Wynter." Angelo chuckles but makes no attempt to rectify the situation.

"It's Miss Saint James to you," I snap. I shouldn't be poking the bear, not when he could kill me where I stand before I could even blink, but I can't help myself. I want every member of the Russo family to know I'm not afraid of them, even if it's a lie.

"She's fiery," Paul comments.

"Our nephew has good taste," Tony adds, and my stomach revolts. Everett is nothing like his family, but every time I'm reminded of the blood running through his veins, memories of all the wounds I've tended to on his skin flash across my vision.

"Take a seat." Angelo gestures toward the chair in front of the desk, but it's not a question. If I don't sit, he's going to make me, and I'd like to avoid any of these men getting their grubby paws anywhere near me.

I lower myself into the chair and glance over my shoulder at Clara by the door. Her body shakes violently, and I long to wrap my arms around her and provide her the comfort she so clearly needs.

Tommy's eyes are on her too, a keen interest I've never seen in them. "I'd like you to allow my assistant to leave," I say, turning to face three sets of cold eyes.

"It's cute you think you're running anything here, bitch." Paul glowers across the desk.

I roll my eyes and immediately reprimand myself. Do I have a goddamn death wish?

"Apologies. You are in my office, in the building my family owns, on our turf, but excuse me for thinking I have a say in what happens here."

The snark in my tone isn't intentional, but I've been underestimated my whole life, and the men sitting across the desk from me think I'm weak. They think they can scare me by turning the tables on me in my own office, but they don't realize how strong I truly am. I'm not going to bow down to whatever they think they have over me, because they're in my territory and a queen protects what belongs to her. "I think it would be best for Clara to leave as she has no involvement in the sides of our business that correlate with yours," I explain truthfully. She may know some of what we do behind closed doors, but I've tried to keep her as far away from it as I could. She's too sweet for the likes of our darkness.

Angelo considers me for a moment, and I take the time to do the same. My eyes remain locked with his cold ones, my face remaining impassive and almost bored. The show I put on for them is part of the fun, and the longer I can draw this out, the more chance I have of Everett showing up to help. He nods once. "The girl may go."

I look over my shoulder at Clara, who is still standing in the same place, eyes wide and unsure whether his approval is some kind of trap. "Go," I whisper, and a moment later, she's running out the door. I turn back to Angelo and force a polite smile to my lips. "Thank you."

"I'm quite a reasonable man, Wynter," he says, and I barely hold back the snort of laughter.

I nod. "It is quite reasonable to kidnap and torture one of our women."

A booming laugh fills the room, and my eyes dart to Tony, who has both hands on his stomach and his face turns red from his chuckles. "Fuck. I see why Everett likes the girl. So full of fire."

Angelo smirks, his eyes never moving from me. "Yes, I'm starting to think maybe I took the wrong woman. You are, after all, unattached. I know my nephew hasn't married you or knocked you up yet. And how much fun it would be to break your will," he muses.

For a moment I consider lying and telling them I'm pregnant, just to prevent them from trying, but even if that were the case, the baby would still have their blood running through its veins and would still be considered an heir even if I would never allow any child of mine to be a part of the heinous things the Russo family is known for.

"What can I do for you, gentlemen?"

"We just wanted to have a chat."

DEAD OF WYNTER

FIFTY-FOUR

EVERETT

"Did your nanna teach you how to drive?" I growl at Storm.

He glances over at me with panic in his eyes. "Shut the fuck up and get into the goddamn security feed."

As stupid as my uncles are at times, they have really stepped up their game recently. In addition to breaking into Frost Industries, they have also managed to take down our security system, which means I have no fucking idea what's happening inside that building right now and the longer I spend without eyes on Wynter, the more dread fills me.

"Don't you have fucking cameras on every inch of her life? Why not her office?" Storm snaps.

"Because there were already cameras in there that I had access to. There was never any reason for additional surveillance anywhere in the building."

"We're changing that. I want a backup system installed that

no one knows about."

"Already way ahead of you."

I've spent the last twenty minutes since we got in the car trying to break through whatever block they've put in place, but whoever did it is good. Just not better than me. I look up as we enter the city, high-rise buildings surrounding us. Storm weaves through traffic, honking at anyone who gets in his way. I've seen him rattled more times in the last few weeks than I have in the entire fifteen years I've known him, and it doesn't suit him. Storm is always calm, he always has been. Every exam we did in school, I spent the whole night studying and making myself sick at the idea of failing. My only option was college, because the other option was to follow in my uncle's footsteps, which is a fate worse than death. But not Storm. He would spend a couple of hours reading over his notes and then go about his life until he walked into the classroom. When he took over Frost Industries, it wasn't planned. Ron had a heart attack a few years back, scared everyone half to death, and as soon as he was well enough, he signed it all over to Storm, saying his life was too short and he wanted to enjoy what was left of it. But Storm was anything but rattled. He took to running a company like a duck to water, and he's been doing it ever since without blinking an eye.

Except the man yelling at pedestrians crossing the street is anything by calm. He's manic, and he's afraid, and he's so far removed from the man I've been best friends with for half my life that I almost don't recognize him. For once, I'm the calm one. I'm the one thinking everything through and plotting every single scenario because that's my only option. The alternative is the love of my life being hurt, or worse, and that's not something I'm willing to entertain.

My fingers fly across the keyboard, breaking every line of code individually. Whoever they have on their side is far from a novice. They're experienced, but I built these systems with the idea of being hacked in mind, and I planned a hundred different ways in. The first ones I tried were the easiest, and they were blocked, but now I'm carefully weaving my way through the invisible maze, carefully setting off alarms in places I'm not in to draw their attention from what I'm really up to.

Under normal circumstances, I would enjoy playing a game of cat and mouse with another hacker, but all I can think about is getting to Wynter as quickly as possible.

"Do you think it's a coincidence they pulled this shit the same day our hit is meant to happen?" Storm asks, his fingers tapping on the steering wheel impatiently.

"I actually think it might be. There's no way they could know what we have planned for today. No one in the house knows apart from the people in the room."

"It could have been The Legion."

I shake my head. "It's not. I've been monitoring their movements and phones since they left our house."

His head whips around to face me. "Are you fucking kidding me, Everett? Are you trying to get all of us, including my baby sister killed?"

I shrug. "I trust Tommy's recommendations, but guys like that have a reputation that I don't like to put all my hope in."

Storm mutters under his breath before slamming his hand down on the horn again. We've been at a standstill for too

423

long, and if I were a more suspicious man, which I am, I would think there's a diversion in place to keep us away from the building for as long as possible.

"Fuck yes," I murmur as I finally get control of the systems, quickly pulling the fire door closed behind me to ensure the other hacker can't get back in.

"Are you in?"

"Yep." I quickly start searching through the camera views until I find the one I'm looking for. I've spent enough time watching this particular camera that I know it hits every inch of the office apart from the far corner, it's why I suggested that office for Wynter when she first started working for Frost Industries after college, not that I would ever admit that to Storm.

"Is she okay?"

I stare at the screen for a few moments, trying to decide if I should tell him what I'm seeing or not. All three of my uncles sit on the side of the desk Wynter is normally at and let me tell you the view is not as good. My girl sits in the seat across from them, only the back of her head in visible on the grainy black and white feed. Yeah, we need to upgrade this shit as soon as possible. The system I put in place only piggybacked from the cameras that were there to begin with, so they certainly aren't state-of-the-art by any stretch of the imagination. Two figures step forward, just the top of their heads appearing in the frame, but it's enough to know a man is holding Tommy in the corner with a gun pressed to his temple. My heart rate triples at the idea of Wynter being unprotected.

"Everett?" The fear in his voice drags my eyes from the screen to meet his.

"We need to get through this traffic right fucking now."

FIFTY-FIVE

WYNTER

I fold my hands in my lap, trying to appear as unaffected by my current situation as I can. I don't have the same experience with masking my feelings that Storm and Rayne have developed over the years, but I can't allow the Russos to know they've scared me.

Angelo surveys me, as if waiting for me to crack under the pressure of his gaze, but it's not going to happen. I will never allow myself to be fragile in front of them, even if it means falling apart the moment I'm out of their eye line. "I understand you and my nephew have formed something of a relationship," he finally says.

I shrug. It kills me to undermine what Everett and I have, but I realize the kind of danger I'm in as a result of our relationship, especially from the men who are sitting across the desk at me. All three of them seem calm, considering they're in enemy territory without enough backup. "We've had some fun," I tell him nonchalantly.

Angelo chuckles, his head shaking from side to side. "I think you'd call it more than that from what I've been hearing. By the sounds of it, the two of you are inseparable." He doesn't give me any time to reply before he goes on. "There's no sense lying to me, Wynter. I have eyes and ears everywhere, but I'm sure you've realized that by now."

I take a deep breath and let out a bored sigh. "Are we getting to the point soon?"

"Of course, dear." Angelo shuffles some papers across my desk I hadn't noticed until now, and I focus on what I think may be photos. I don't want to hazard a guess at what he's going to show me, because there's every chance my stomach isn't going to be able to handle it. I can handle death, and blood, and drugs. All of that is a necessary evil in our business. What I can't handle is the shit the Russos deal in. The darkest sides of Chicago I wish didn't exist, the sides that will be abolished the moment we take over their operations.

"Isn't it funny how we have been one step ahead of you every step of the way? We knew how to grab Emerson. We knew where your parents would be and when. We knew the nickname my nephew so affectionately uses for you, and that awful thing that happened to you in college. And we knew the precise night and time you would be coming for the warehouse."

"We are well aware you have a rat within our operation, and we've already figured out who it is," I lie. There's no reason he needs to know that we've been in complete lockdown for the last few days, or that we sent all our men on different operations and hired an entire new team to guard the house just in case. None of that seems pertinent right now, so I'm going to keep it to myself.

"Have you though, Wynter?" he asks, a wicked smirk tugging at his too-thin lips. "Only someone close to you would know all of that. Someone who the entire family trusts implicitly."

My eyes drop to a photo he's placed in front of me. Everett is sitting in a booth at the club with his uncles, a half-dressed woman sitting in his lap and her almost dead gaze perfectly captured in the image. His hand is wrapped around her waist, holding her tightly as he laughs at something one of his uncles says. No.

"I'm sure you're thinking, this can't be what it looks like," Paul says.

"That's what they always say." Tony chuckles. "Women always have too much faith in the men in their lives. Always believe they would never lie or cheat. But what you don't realize is the only way to get ahead in the world is to lie and cheat."

I open my mouth to speak, but nothing comes out. Instead I pull the image closer and check the date stamp. A few days before the wedding, after Emerson was taken. What the hell was he doing with his uncles after what they did to our family?

"Let me talk you through what's happening here, shall I?" Angelo's voice is smug, and I don't need to look up at his face to know it mirrors it. "That's your boyfriend with one of our whores on his lap. She's a real good one too. Knows just how to suck a cock."

I take a deep breath to settle the nausea bubbling in my belly. Every word out of his mouth sounds like a lie, but I can't argue with this photo, can I?

"Do you remember when we bought her?" Tony laughs, his head falling back against the headrest. "Her husband swore black and blue she was the lousiest lay to ever walk the earth, but there's nothing a few good beatings can't fix."

"You get real good at following orders when your life depends on it," Paul agrees.

"Everett got a real good taste of Missy that night. We usually sell them on after we buy them, but there's something about this bitch's mouth I just can't let go of," Angelo tells me. I'm pretty sure they're just trying to make me squirm, and it's working. Every word out of their mouths is more vile than the last, and the carefully constructed mask I've mastered over the years is barely holding on.

"She doesn't want to believe us." Paul half laughs.

Angelo nods and passes another photo across the desk, this one with what looks like a hundred women, all looking terrified. They're huddled together, the clothes they're wearing almost non-existent, and right in the middle of them is Everett. His eyes are watching the women, some so young I'm sure they're not legal, and this time my stomach can't handle it.

I dive for the wastebasket beside the desk, the almost non-existent contents of my stomach expelling from my body. Heave after heave until I know there's nothing left, but my belly still rolls with the need to throw up. I've slept with Everett. I've let him touch me, let him dominate me, let him cum inside me. I could have any number of fucking diseases, and I never would have been the wiser were it not for this little chat.

"He's lying, Wynter," Tommy says immediately before groaning, and by the time I turn around to look at him, his body is hunched over, his arms wrapped around his stomach.

"The proof is in the pudding, as they say." Angelo shrugs as his eyes lift to the doorway. "But you can ask him for yourself, I'm sure my dear nephew would be more than happy to tell you all the truth of his involvement with the family."

I look up and meet Everett's deep blue gaze. I may have been able to rationalize and lie to myself, but it's the look in his eyes that tells me everything I need to know. He lied to me, to my whole family for that matter. He was an accomplice to my parents' murder, people who treated him like their own son just the same way they did Storm and Rayne.

He was involved in Emerson's kidnapping and the car bomb that could have killed me.

There's no sense trying to lie to myself about what I already know. Everett is the rat, and the reason we couldn't figure out who it was is because he was one of the few people we never would have suspected.

I force myself to my feet and return to the seat I was sitting in a few moments ago, my hands placed neatly in my lap and my eyes staring at the ruthless men sitting across from me. "Is there anything else I can do to help you, gentleman? If not, I would really appreciate if you left. I have some work I need to get done."

Angelo watches me for a moment, his eyes burning into my vulnerable flesh before moving to look at the doorway. I can't bring myself to follow his gaze, not after what I've seen.

If I ever have to look Everett Masters in the eye again, it will be too soon.

DEAD OF WYNTER

FIFTY-SIX
EVERETT

There are many things I regret in my life.

Not protecting my mother from my father as a child.

Not being strong enough to run away after all the times the men in my family hurt me.

Leaving Wynter without saying goodbye.

Each regret hurts more than the last, but this one, this is the worst. Every single bone in my body screams at me to move toward her, it screams to tell her the truth. But the moment my eyes clash with Storm's, I know I can't. Not until this is over.

He knows the truth. He knows I would never be a part of the vile things they've accused me of, not in any way that really counts at least. But those photos are damning, and I have a feeling that even when I can tell Wynter the truth, she's not going to believe a word I say. A picture is worth a thousand words after all.

One by one, my uncles stand from behind Wynter's desk and walk toward the door where I'm frozen in place. Every step they take away from her allows me to breathe a little easier, but when Angelo stops to whisper something in her ear and her body visibly stills, it's only Storm's hand that stops me from lurching forward and tearing him away from her.

"She's okay," he whispers.

I take a deep breath and let it out slowly to calm my racing heart. If only we got here sooner, maybe we could have controlled what she saw, maybe we could have stopped them from filling her head with lies. Maybe we could have stopped her from hating me.

Angelo straightens and joins his brothers before making their way toward us, smug smiles on each of their faces. Paul and Tony file out of the room, the man holding Tommy following after them and leaving us alone with Angelo. "Now she knows the truth, dear nephew, perhaps now you will accept my generous offer. Isn't she the reason you always turned it down after all?"

My eyes lock with the back of Wynter's head, her body trembling as she tries to appear unaffected. Part of me wants to praise her for being so strong, for being the woman, no, the queen, I always knew she was, but that's not the plan.

What my uncles don't realize is that they've just given us the in we needed. We had a hundred alternative plans, but none of them are as good as the opportunity that has just presented itself.

I nod and take one more look at my beautiful girl barely holding it together and silently promise I'll make it all better once this is over, but until then I'm going to have to live with the fact she hates me.

"Shall we go?" he asks.

"Let's get out of here," I say, my voice sounding more even than I feel. Every ounce of my body is off balance.

My eyes lock with Storm's and he gives me a small nod to tell me he'll take care of her until I can get back to her. It should make me feel better, but it doesn't. Every moment Wynter hates me is worse than the last, even if it is for the best right now.

There's every possibility I'm being driven into a trap, but I've kept close enough to the family for them to extend me a certain amount of trust. Will they tell me all their plans for the Saint James family? Absolutely not. But will they let things slip about their operations with me around? It's how we've freed as many women as we have. By now they probably should have worked it out, but every time a shipment of women arrives in the harbor, I'm with them, and I've been with them from the moment I found out about it.

They were probably suspicious, but even when they frisked me and scanned me for bugs, they found nothing because there was nothing to find. Well, nothing they *could* find. The tracker embedded into my neck is so deep and protected any detector they would have access to scanned right over it. And the app I designed a couple of years ago allows Storm to listen to every conversation I have without me lifting a finger. The perfect combination to allow Rayne and Tommy to free as many trafficked women as we can before they can be sold to men who will be worse than even their darkest nightmares.

Chicago is full of men who take. They take from their families, from the city, from the people who trust them. And when they get the chance to have a pretty young girl who has no option but to obey them, there's no end to what they'll take from her. Which is why we do what we do. And why I'm allowing Wynter to hate me right now.

Unlike every other time, I knew this shipment was coming in well in advance. It's been planned because it's the biggest they've ever brought into the country. A thousand women will be delivered to the farm tonight. Women who have been sold or taken from their lives, women who are scared and broken. If my uncles have their way, they will be beaten until they submit, and then they'll be sold to men so cold not even I can fathom what could happen to them.

My knowing about this shipment puts our whole operation in jeopardy. If Rayne and Tommy show up and save them at the farm, there's no way they won't know it was me who set it up, and that's what makes tonight such a delicate situation. We need to have The Legion in just the right place, at just the right time, that they never know the girls were even taken because they're six feet under by the time tomorrow comes.

"That woman of yours." Tony blows out a whistle. "She's quite the spitfire. I bet she's fun in bed."

I swallow the growl climbing up my throat. The men surrounding me are vile and despicable in every sense of the word, and any of them even thinking about Wynter like that makes me want to kill every single one of them. But that's not the plan.

"That mouth needs to be put to better use though," Tony adds, but I don't look over at him sitting beside me in the back seat. I can't. If I look at him now, I'll fucking kill him for scaring my woman.

"Once this is all over, he can keep her if he likes, but I think we might want to bite off a piece too, see what all the fuss is about." Angelo smiles back at me and red blinds me. Over my dead fucking body, would any of these assholes be touching my woman. They got as close as they're ever going to get to my sweet dove today, and any closer, I would have ended it all right there in that office. "What do you think, Everett? Do you think you can share your girl with us?"

"She's mine," I grind out, my eyes moving to the window to distract myself from the rage bubbling inside me like hot lava threatening to erupt.

Angelo chuckles. "We'll see about that."

FIFTY-SEVEN
WYNTER

"How does it feel to know you've fucked a true Russo?"

Angelo's words replay in my mind over and over like the broken cassette player in my dad's old Cadillac. When he said them, I was still too shocked to react, to think of a reply, but now all I feel is blinding rage. It's like something deep inside me has snapped, and all the pain and anger I've held in a tiny box for all these years, has escaped. It's overwhelming, but at the same time, it's kind of freeing. My therapist used to tell me it's unhealthy to hold emotions in, but as we pull into the driveway of the estate I've never felt more powerful.

No one has said a word since we left the office. Storm and Tommy are in the front while Clara and I are bundled into the back seat. She hasn't stopped shaking since we found her under her desk after they left, and I wish I could give her more than I am right now. She didn't deserve to be dragged into this. My sweet, innocent personal assistant who never asked questions, who never called in sick and always knew what I needed before I did. Part of me wishes I had never hired her. We clicked that first day, and I told her she had the job on the spot, but she's too pure to work so closely with a Saint James. The darkness was always bound to bleed eventually.

"Wynter?" Storm says, and I finally drag my eyes away from the window. His brow is pulled together, the worry in his gaze clear as day. "Let's get inside so we can talk."

I nod, taking Tommy's outstretched hand to help me climb from the back of the sports car. The moment my feet are on the driveway, he's helping Clara's shaking body out. She hasn't looked at Tommy or Storm since we found her, fear oozing from her pores. I should reassure her that they're nothing like the men who hurt her, but the reality is that they are. And so am I.

Snow, Emerson, and Rayne stand at the top of the steps, their faces all filled with just as much worry as Storm's. I glance over my shoulder to find Clara bundled up in Tommy's arms before making my way up the stairs.

"Are you okay?" Snow asks.

"No," I whisper. I've never been further from okay. I'm not even on the same fucking planet as okay right now. The man I love. The man I've loved since before I understood the gravity of the emotion, has been lying to me the entire time I've known him. All the times I looked after him, all the times I held him after his uncles beat him, all the times our family helped him, it was all a lie. Everything was a lie.

"There's more to it than you think," Rayne tells me.

"I doubt that."

"Let's go into my office and talk," Storm suggests as he trails behind me.

"No, thank you." I shake my head. "You were right. I'm not strong enough to be a part of this side of the business. You guys take it from here."

Before he can reply, I'm up the stairs and closing my bedroom door behind me. I lean against the hardwood for a moment, needing it to hold me steady on my shaking legs, but when I look up and around the room, all the air leaves my lungs. Every inch of this room reminds me of Everett. Every single surface smells like him, every single corner has memories of him. If I close my eyes, I can feel him here with me, even when I know he's far away from here.

I slide down the door, my legs no longer able to hold my weight, and the moment my knees hit the ground, a painful sob claws its way from my throat and all the tears I never cried fall against my cheeks. Everything I ever loved was a lie, and it's that thought that plagues me until I can't keep my eyes open any longer, and my body drifts to the ground, succumbing to the unconsciousness it craves.

FIFTY-EIGHT
EVERETT

I t's been a long time since I've been to the farm, but it doesn't feel like long enough as I climb out of the black SUV and follow after my uncles toward the main house. This is the first time women are being delivered straight here, usually they arrive on ships at the docks, and that's where the handover occurs, but not this time.

Every security guard we passed, I committed them to memory. Every locked door is cataloged, and every turn we make as we wind through the house is memorized. We can't afford for any of this to go wrong.

The plan, although changed, is a perfectly timed, perfectly plotted series of events, and if even one thing goes wrong, I could end up dead and my uncles will have a chance at seizing control of Chicago like they've always wanted.

"Where's Elijah?" I ask. He's the wildcard in all this. He's loyal to his father and uncles to a certain point, but he's always looked after number one. Himself. If shit goes sideways, he'll either pull a gun on me, or he'll get the fuck out of dodge to save his own ass. That's why he was so good at Uncle Angelo's favorite game. It's why I ended up beaten and bloody more often than not. Elijah's survival instincts are stronger than anyone I've ever met.

"He's out on an errand," Paul answers, pushing the door open to the room I remember as being Angelo's office. I spent a lot of time in here when I was young, more time than I should have. This room is where I saw my first dead body, where I took my first life, where my uncle tried to force me to lose my virginity. That's the worst memory I have of this room. A girl, no older than sixteen, her scared eyes as she silently pleaded with me not to do it. I was too young to fully understand why she was there, or even who she was, but even then, I knew it was wrong. I begged Angelo not to force this girl on me, telling him I wasn't ready. That just earned me a beating. But the girl was taken away. I wish I could have protected her, I wish I could have taken her away from this hell and set her free the way I did myself when the Saint James family took me in.

I nod and take a seat on the old leather lounge that has been here for at least my whole life, longer if I had to guess. The things the old piece of furniture has seen over the years would give even the strongest man nightmares for the rest of their lives.

"So, Everett. Tell us what they have planned," Paul says as he takes the seat across from me while Angelo moves behind the large wooden desk, his hands clasped in his lap as he waits for the story I'm about to spin. Tony flops into the seat beside me and all three of them turn their attention to me.

I've rehearsed this lie so many times it should be ingrained in my memory, I should have been saying it in my sleep, but now I'm sitting here with the coldest men in the city, it takes me a moment to get it straight in my mind. "They're planning on hitting a bunch of your properties tonight," I lie. "They aren't going to attack Aces because they don't think you would be stupid enough to hide out there after taking Emerson and how easily they were able to infiltrate the building and area."

Angelo chuckles. "Looks like we're heading to the club tonight, gentlemen. I want our men at all our locations ready to take those fuckers out. It's time this ends once and for all."

Even though we're setting a trap for my uncles, the idea they think they could take my real family out makes my heart stop in my chest.

"What about the women?" Paul asks.

Always the women. He stopped being able to get legit pussy a long time ago, because if there's one thing he never quite grasped, it's that women talk, and if you beat them within an inch of their life when they don't suck your cock right, the next woman probably isn't going to be interested.

"When they are captured, I want them brought here. No one is to touch them until I've had the chance to survey them. I believe I will still take Emerson, Everett will likely lay claim to Wynter, although I meant what I said about wanting a piece of her, and Snow—" He shrugs. "She's anyone's game."

"She might make a good wife for Elijah. It would be better if he and Everett can start having heirs sooner rather than later, and she might be our best chance at getting him a good woman given his... tastes," Tony suggests.

447

My stomach rolls as they speak about the women I consider family in such a vile manner. With such little regard for the fact they are human and should have their own choices, their own free will. Am I hypocrite because I helped Rayne hold Emerson against her will in the beginning? Does that make me a monster just like the blood running through my veins? No. Because Rayne never would have hurt her, he would have done anything to protect her, he did *everything* to protect her. And even before she admitted it to herself, underneath all her fight, she wanted to be there.

"We'll see if he likes her when he gets back from retrieving them," Angelo agrees.

"Retrieving them?" The words fall from my lips before I have the chance to stop them. Tommy and Rayne would have already left to head here. The Legion should already be scoping out the club. And we've left Storm and the girls as sitting ducks.

Angelo smirks, a look so deadly and disgusting my own stomach flips with disgust. "Like I said, dear nephew, this all ends tonight."

FIFTY-NINE
WYNTER

onsciousness returns slowly, and at first, I can't work out what it is that has woken me. It could have been any number of things, from the uncomfortable floor I'm lying on, to the ache in my neck and shoulders from the position I fell asleep in, to the pain shooting through my scalp from crying myself to sleep. But as I lay here, eyes still closed, fighting the reality that comes with being awake, I know it's none of those things that woke me.

A loud bang outside forces me to sit up and my eyes to spring open. I look around the dark room frantically just in time to hear another series of bangs.

Gunshots.

I push myself up and tug the door open, sprinting up the hallway until I almost run straight into Snow. "Panic room, now!" I shout. The noise is getting closer and I have to get my sisters to safety.

"Emerson." Snow's voice shakes, her eyes as wide as saucers.

"I'm going to get her now. Watch on the camera and open the door when we get there," I tell her but by the time the last few words leave my mouth, I'm running as fast as I can toward the other wing of the house. When we started staying here, we decided to give Rayne and Emerson a room in our parents' wing, to give them privacy, but I'm now regretting that decision.

My eyes cast over the banister just in time to see the front door explode. The force of the blast knocks me into the wall, the sound causing my ears to ring painfully, but I don't stop running. I run as fast as my legs will carry me, thanking every god that my parents had the foresight to have multiple entrances to the panic room because there's no way we're getting back the way I've come.

Shouts fill the house and I keep running. Footsteps on the stairs behind me make my heart jump into my throat and my chest constrict painfully. I have to get to Emerson. Rayne won't survive without her. She's the air he breathes, the beat of his heart, his entire world. I can't let him lose her.

There's a niggling thought trying to break through my focused mind. This is Everett. He did this. He's been playing us this whole time. For years we trusted him with our secrets, and now he's using them to tear us apart.

I don't allow the thought to drag me under though. I can fall apart once my sisters are safe and not a moment sooner.

I burst into the bedroom Emerson shares with my brother and look from one side of the dark room to the other. "Emerson?" I whisper. I don't know why I'm bothering. The men that have infiltrated our home know we're here, but I don't want to tip them off as to where we are until I can get her to safety.

452

"Wynter?" Her head pops up from the other side of the room and I allow a sigh of relief to slip from my lips.

"We need to go right now," I say in a rush, glancing over my shoulder to make sure no one has followed me. If they're smart, and if Everett is the one calling the shots on this operation, they would have gone to the other wing first looking for Snow and me. Anyone who knows anything about my sister-in-law knows she'll go to the end of the earth to help the people she loves, and if they were to capture Snow and I, she'd come right out to save us, even if Rayne would lose his fucking mind.

When I'm sure they haven't ventured to this side of the house yet, I usher her out of the room and into the bedroom my parents used to have. Their combined scent hits me the moment I open the door and I stop dead in the doorway. All I see as I look around the room is them, their smiles, their laughs, they happiness. The emotions beg to be set free, but I don't have time to feel right now. If I want to live, and I want my sisters to live, I need to put everything back into that little box and hide it as far away as I possibly can until we're safe.

"This way." I step toward the wardrobe but stop in my tracks again when I hear voices coming up the way we've just come. "Quickly!" I whisper and throw the door open, quietly closing it behind us.

I pull the chest of drawers forward and reveal the door to the panic room, praying Snow is watching all the cameras and not just the door she went through. The quiet hum of the sliding door allows me to let out a breath, relief filling me. We're safe. We can ride out the attack in the bunker and deal with whatever is left once this is all over.

"Where are these bitches?" a voice on the other side of the door asks.

"Are you sure they're here?" another man asks.

"Get in right now," I whisper shout at Emerson. There's not enough time for us both to get in and pull the drawers back. Even though the panic room is virtually impenetrable, Everett does have the override code and I'm not willing to risk all of our lives on him not using it. At least if the drawers cover the door, it will give us enough time to close it again before anyone could get in.

"What about you?" Her green eyes flash with fear and I long to take it away, but she knows what it's like to be a prisoner of these men. Men so ruthless she still has nightmares about the time she spent with them.

"I'll be fine. You and Snow stay in there no matter what. No matter what you see on the cameras, no matter what you hear. You stay put, okay?"

For a moment Emerson looks like she's going to argue, but when Snow's head pops out and holds her hand out for her, she relents and drops to her knees, crawling through the door quickly.

"Be careful," Snow whispers.

I press my eyes closed to ward off the tears pooling in them as I listen to the door slide shut. I should have gone in with them. Surely Everett isn't so involved in this that he would put me at risk. Surely some of what he said he felt was real. But it's too late now, the voices are growing closer, and I quickly slide the drawers back into place and duck down behind them.

I have to have been in here for a reason and hiding seems like as good a reason as any.

The moment the lock clicks shut, I allow the breath I've been holding from the moment I heard the first gunshots out. At least they're safe. That's all that matters.

The relief is short-lived when the wardrobe door swings open and I curl up as small as I can behind the drawers, holding my breath to avoid making any noise. The sound of my own heartbeat feels too loud in the small space, and if I could stop it, even for a few moments, I would to keep myself safe.

"Why hello there, little thing," one of the men says, his voice velvet honey.

My eyes dart up and I'm faced with a sick smile looming above me, a gun aimed at my face. Perhaps the sight should scare me, it would most women, but for some reason the gun almost puts a barrier between us, at least for now. "Please," I whisper, my eyes wide and filled with tears. It's a tactic Rayne taught me when he was first teaching me how to protect myself. Lure them into a false sense of security that I'm not a threat, and then there's a better chance of escaping because they'll underestimate me.

"Sorry, sweetheart, gotta do our job." The taller man pushes past and pulls me to my feet.

"It's okay though, little doll. I'll take real good care of you once this is all said and done," the first man says and my skin immediately pebbles with a revolted shiver. His yellowing teeth are barely visible in the dim light, his crazed brown eyes enough to make me stumble over my own feet.

Okay, so maybe I don't need to pretend to be scared. Maybe I *am* scared.

"Shut the fuck up, Simon. Boss didn't pay us to creep the poor girl out," the tall man snaps. His large hand wraps around my bicep and he tugs me out of the bedroom and down the hallway. The thought of struggling crosses my mind, but what would be the sense in that? I'm not strong enough to take down both men, and not willing to risk it while they're both holding guns. The best thing I can do right now is play along until I can find an opportunity to strike.

"Where are the other two girls?" he asks.

"They're not here," I lie. "They both snuck out a couple of hours ago when my brother left."

"Snuck out?" He raises his eyebrows, scanning my face for the telltale signs of lying.

I nod. "Yeah. We've been cooped up in this house for weeks, and my sister Snow is a bit of a wild child," I explain.

"Why didn't you go with them then?" the other man asks from behind us.

"Cramps," I reply immediately.

They don't ask any questions after that, instead leading me down the stairs in silence. At least I've won one battle tonight. Now it's just time to win the war.

DEAD OF WYNTER

SIXTY

EVERETT

Every moment that passes that I'm not able to check my phone feels longer than the last. I need to check the cameras at the estate. I need to make sure the girls got into the panic room safely and turn off the override switch in the control panel. We only keep it on because Snow likes to lock herself in there and drink herself into oblivion on her particularly bad days, and now I regret not just letting her wallow in her own self-pity.

I didn't have to talk myself into being able to stay at the farm while the others went to hide out at the club because Angelo suggested I oversee the delivery. It's a test I won't pass and one they won't be around to see my fail.

The problem is they have an army of fucking men here with me and if I so much as think about pulling my phone out of my pocket, they're going to start asking questions. Every time I try to sneak out someone has a question for me, and I don't have any answers because this is not my ballpark. My area of expertise is computers. It's building shit and creating things that didn't exist before. Not human trafficking.

"Hey boss," a short, stubby man says. "How should we split the girls when they arrive?"

I stare at him for a moment, because how the fuck should I know how to separate women who have been torn from their lives and sold like livestock? But I have to have an answer. "This is my first shipment," I tell him honestly. "Do they come with papers? Names? Ages?"

He nods, his brows pulled together with confusion. He's wondering why my uncles would leave me in charge when I have no fucking clue what I'm doing, but I can't tell him they're testing me.

"Okay, good. I want them split by age." There. That wasn't so bad. I mean, if I can separate the fact these are human women I'm talking about, that is.

"You got it." He walks away quickly, and I lean back on the banister of the porch. Tommy and Rayne should be here soon, but I have no clue how I'm going to communicate with them with so many guys around. I have no idea how tonight is going to play out at all, and honestly, all I can think about is Wynter.

The hurt and disgust in her eyes when she believed every word my uncles fed her makes me feel sick to the stomach even thinking about it. But it's the imminent danger she's in right now because of me that has nausea rolling over me, and for the first time in years, there's nothing I can do to protect her. I can't follow her around on her date and threaten the guy in the bathrooms not to so much as touch her. I can't leak photos of the girls bullying her on the internet. And I sure as hell can't wrap her in cotton wool like I always wanted to.

"The trucks will be here soon," Dennis tells me. The man was one of my father's men who jumped ship when the Saint James family overthrew him and has nothing but hate for the people I consider family. The few times I've been around for conversations about them, he's made his distaste for them perfectly clear and it took everything I had not to pull my gun out and shoot him right between the fucking eyes. Wouldn't be the first time and certainly wouldn't be the last.

"Thanks." I give a tight smile and push away from the house, striding toward the three barns that have been built since the last time I was here. I declined a tour of the facilities earlier, deciding I don't have enough control of my anger right now to see the fucked-up stuff hiding behind those doors.

I briefly glance over my shoulder to make sure no one is watching me before quickly pulling my phone from my pocket and sending a text to Storm.

Elijah is coming for the girls. Get them in the panic room.

Once I've made sure that's sent, I open a group message with Rayne and Tommy and shoot them a text as well.

Shipment will arrive soon. Elijah has gone to the estate to get the girls.

I almost don't send the last part because Rayne might blow the whole mission at the idea Emerson in any danger, but I have to have faith he'll trust Storm to take care of her.

By the time I shove my phone back into my pocket, three black SUVs are coming down the driveway telling me the truck isn't far off. Thank fuck this is the last time I ever have to do this shit. I fucking hate pretending to be on this side, even if it does save innocent lives. The irony of that isn't lost on me. I work for one of the most infamous crime families in the country and I'm talking about saving lives, but we have a conscience when it comes to women and children. Something that isn't even in the vocabulary of the people of my bloodline. The Saint James family aren't monsters like the Russos are. They're good people involved in some shady shit.

The vibrating in my pocket almost makes me pull my phone back out, but it's too risky. Messaging them in the first place was a risk I had to take, but I can't do it again. As hard as it may be, I have to pray Storm got himself and the girls to safety the moment the first sign of an attack started.

Dead of Wynter

SIXTY-ONE

WYNTER

"**W**hat the fuck were you thinking?" Storm hisses the moment we're left alone, tied to the chairs from the dining room and positioned in the middle of the lounge room.

"I was thinking Rayne would fucking die without Emerson, and Snow is my baby sister. Of course I fucking locked them in the panic room and played dumb to these idiots," I growl, my eyes falling on the bleeding wound at his temple. The protective instinct calls to me to clean and dress the cut, but there's no way out of the coarse ropes around my wrists.

I shouldn't be surprised they brought the most abrasive rope they could find, and every time I try to wiggle my wrists through the knots, fresh cuts appear in my skin. But that hasn't stopped me. This is not how I go down. I'm going to kill Everett if it's the last thing I do. I'm going to look him point blank in the eye and shoot him so he knows exactly who ended his life. Anger has replaced some of the sadness, and at least I can use it to get me through the night. Because we will make it. We will get out of here. There's no other option.

"Everett's going to kill me when he finds out you're not in that fucking panic room. The whole reason he built it was to keep you safe in an emergency," he mutters.

"Don't say his name," I snap. It's easier to channel my rage when I don't associate him with the man I loved, the one who stole my heart and never gave it back.

Storm sighs. "He's playing them, Wyn. He's been playing them for years. He gets involved when we get wind of a trafficking shipment, we save the girls, and then he fucks off again until the next time."

My eyes snap up to meet his, looking for any sign of a lie. "What do you mean?"

Storm looks around to make sure the men haven't returned. So far, it's only the two guys who grabbed me, but I'm sure there are others around here looking for something they can use against us. "It started a few years ago. Angelo got it in his head that dear old nephew was going to come back to the family, and so he invited Everett to the club to discuss potentially reconnecting. They needed him for something computer related, if I recall, and we started making plans. Those photos you saw in your office, they are of him, but whatever Angelo told you was probably fabricated. The man wouldn't know the truth if it hit him in the fucking face."

I stare at my brother for long moments. No one has ever pulled the wool over his eyes, never been able to fool him. The man has been three steps ahead in every challenge we've ever faced up until now. But what if he can't see what's right in front of him? What if this was Everett's plan all along and now it's coming to fruition Storm can't see it for what it is?

"I know when I'm being played, Wynter, and Everett has never played me or anyone in this family. Everything he's ever done has been to keep you safe. Those first few months after he left, I honestly thought he was going to die. He got into fights, drank himself stupid, and took so many drugs I'm surprised he still has any brain cells. I know you're hurt. I know he hurt you and now you're jumping to any conclusion that makes him the bad guy. But he's not the villain here."

I open my mouth to reply but quickly snap it shut when I hear voices in the hallway. It's the two men from earlier but there's another two voices that are almost too familiar. One belongs to the most ruthless man of the Russo family, and the other is someone much closer.

Charles?

Storm and I look at each other at the same time, his eyes filled with the same shock I'm feeling. Our head of security is in on this? He's the rat?

The two bodies fill the room and I can't help but allow my mouth to drop open at the sight of them together. Out of all the people I suspected to be the rat, Charles was never one of them, I don't think I so much as considered him. He came to work for us shortly after I returned from college and he's never been anything other than sweet. His kind green eyes are dark now, danger lurking behind them as he looks at me with disgust, but I can't think of a single thing I could have done to make him so angry.

"The surprise when someone they trusted betrays them is always my favorite," Elijah muses.

467

"Charles, you don't have to do this," Storm says calmly. There's a reason he's the one running the company. He has Dad's calm demeanor while Rayne, Snow, and I have our mother's fire.

"Oh, but I do." Charles tears his glare from me and repositions it on my brother. "You did kill my brother after all, so I think it's only fair I kill someone you love. Poetic justice and all that."

Elijah sighs and flops down onto the lounge dramatically. I've met him a few times over the years and each time I have no idea what to think of him. "Everett isn't going to be happy."

"I don't really give a fuck about him. We had a deal, Russo," Charles growls, the bite in his voice causes me to flinch.

"We did," he agrees.

"If we could find one of the other bitches I would reconsider." His eyes turn back to me as if I'm the one with all the answers, but I keep my mouth shut. I'd rather die a thousand deaths than give up my sisters.

"Not Snow," Elijah snaps, his forest green eyes darkening.

The three of us all turn our attention on him, but it's short-lived. Charles returns his attention to me, the coldness in his eyes a direct contrast to the warmth I've come to expect. "I suppose it is poetic justice that it be you who dies, seeing as you are the reason my brother was murdered."

My brow furrows in confusion and I jerk my head to the side to look at Storm who seems equally confused until understanding dawns on us at the same time. "Craig," I whisper.

"Ding, ding, ding," Charles chimes. "You couldn't keep your fucking legs together and so my brother died because of you."

"That's not what happened," I tell him.

"Oh, I know exactly what happened, you little harlot. You were going to that sinful club, sneaking away in the dark of night to hide your shame. My brother only wanted to cleanse you. He was giving you a chance at redemption."

The blood rushes from my face, sweat gathering at my temples as I struggle not to fall into the memories of the night I wished for death. It's only now as I stare at Charles, that I see the resemblance to his brother. Perhaps I didn't see it before because he was always so nice, his face always kind, his movements non-threatening, but as he looks down on me with revulsion in his eyes, the similarities are all I see.

A strangled sob tears from my throat and I can't do anything to stop it. His words are so close to the ones Craig uttered to me as he beat me until I was bloody and broken that I almost can't differentiate this moment from that one. "You don't understand. I didn't go there for sex. I swear I didn't."

"Wynter," Storm warns calmly, and he doesn't need to say anything for me to understand the unspoken words. Falling apart allows him to win. And explaining myself to a madman is pointless. He's made his mind up about how this is going to go, and nothing is going to make him deviate from that path.

"It doesn't really matter what you went there for anyway." Charles drops his hands to his belt, and I squeeze my eyes shut. No. Not again. I'll beg for death before I allow him to hurt me the same way his brother did. "Stepping foot in a place like that is a sin in the Lord's eyes, and now you'll pay

469

for your family's transgressions with your blood."

Sixty-Two
Everett

Three trucks pull into the driveway one after the other, dust floating through the air and making the moment even more ominous than it already was. My stomach flips painfully at what I'm about to see. Even though we've done this a few times, it never gets any easier seeing the darker parts of humanity.

We have Doc and a few other trusted physicians on standby to tend to any injuries, but it's not the physical wounds that will need healing. These women have been torn from their lives and sold like they're little more than an object. The impacts of that will live with them for the rest of their lives.

The other men start pulling out their weapons, aiming them toward the trucks like the helpless people inside will be any match for them even without a gun, but it gives me the opportunity to do the same. My trigger finger has been itching since the moment I left Frost Industries, and I've never been more ready to end lives as I am right now. Every single one of these fuckers deserves a painful death for their involvement.

I understand needing to put food on the table, but there has to be a limit to what you're willing to do, and in my opinion that limit should lay somewhere well before selling other human beings for profit.

Something settles in me the moment the heavy gun is in my hand, the cool metal in my palm, and I can breathe just a little easier knowing I get to start killing people soon. I just have to hope Tommy and Rayne are close. After I sent the message, I was a little worried they would turn back around and defend the estate, but even if I have to do it myself all these motherfuckers are going to die tonight.

The trucks stop, one after the other and I hold my breath. The first time I did this, I wasn't prepared for the stench. These people have likely been living in their own filth for weeks, and combine that with small spaces, you have one hell of a smell on your hands.

Just as men step toward the back of the truck, their hands raised to pull the back doors open, loud gunshots ring through the air.

Thank fuck for that.

I duck down with everyone else, not ready to give myself away just yet. I'm in the thick of Russo's men. Even a whiff of my involvement and one of them may get the drop on me.

"Fuck. It's Saint James men," someone shouts.

"Take cover," another man yells. I almost tell him he can hide all he wants, but he's going to die like the scum he is tonight but decide to keep my mouth shut.

"Stay with the cargo," I order.

The moment I have eyes on Rayne, his eyes filled with barely controlled rage, holding the biggest fucking gun I've ever designed, I allow myself to stand and cross to where he's standing. For the first few steps, I keep my gun drawn to keep up the show I'm putting on, but as soon as I'm sure they have my back I lower it and shove it in the back of my jeans.

Tommy appears a moment later, a semi-automatic pointing toward the group of men on the ground. "I feel a bit like a bank robber, boys." He smirks. "Look at all these bitches cowering in the dirt."

I chuckle. "Now, now, Tommy, no need to rub salt in the wounds."

"But that's my favorite thing to do!"

"Can you two shut the fuck up? I want to get back to the estate and make sure my woman is okay," Rayne snaps.

"Fine." Tommy sighs and lowers his weapon, stepping toward the truck and wrenching the door open.

No matter how prepared I am for it, the stench never ceases to almost knock me on my ass. Scared faces hide behind the woman in the front, all of which seem dejected. Who knows what they've been through to get here. The last shipment we intercepted there were some girls who were just too far gone. They'd been through too much to recover and took their own lives. I understood it, but I fucking hated that there were people who did this shit in the first place.

"Call the house," I tell Rayne. It's the only way he and I are going to be able to focus on the task at hand.

He steps away from us, his hand sliding into his pocket and

retrieving his phone. My hand itches to do the same, but I have to keep an eye on these fuckers until we can exterminate them.

"It's okay," Tommy says softly. He's not the least threatening of us, but there are things in his past that make him the best person to deal with the initial contact. "We're not going to hurt you," he promises. "The men who planned to hurt you are all on the ground out here, and we're going to get you to safety where we can get you all seen by a doctor, okay?"

A few quiet voices fill the silent night and it's like music to my ears because this is the last fucking time we have to do this. After tonight, there will be no human trafficking in this city, and we'll never have to see the ugliness of trading humans for cash again.

Movement out of the corner of my eyes catches my attention and I quickly draw my gun, aiming it at Dennis, whose cold eyes are murderous. His own gun is gripped tightly in both hands and aimed at me. "I knew you would double cross your family. Told them a hundred times you couldn't be trusted, that you weren't with the Saint James scum just for information. But they never listened to me."

I laugh. "That's because you're a whining, driveling little shit who my uncles despise. But you're too loyal to let go of, and you've been with them too long to risk anything you know getting out."

"That's not true," he snaps, his finger tightening over the trigger.

"Isn't it?" I tilt my head to the side. I shouldn't be provoking the man, but I can't help myself. I've hated him my entire life, and now getting to fuck with him is just that little bit of extra fun I need right now. "Because even today, they told me not to let you unload the girls. Said you hurt a few the last time and they couldn't be sold."

His eyes widen. The only way I would know that is if it were true, which it is. This motherfucker is going to the grave knowing the family he gave his entire life to didn't respect or appreciate him.

"Everett," Rayne shouts, and I immediately turn my head to see his panicked gaze. "Emerson and Snow are in the panic room, but Elijah has Storm and Wynter."

Those are the last words I hear before gun shots ring out and an excruciating pain radiates through my gut. By the time I turn back to David, his smug smile is firmly in place. I grunt at the pain, but my weapon remains aimed at him, right in the middle of his fucking forehead. "Tell the devil I said hi." I smirk as I pull the trigger. The vibration bursts through my arm, but a gunshot isn't going to stop me from getting to my woman.

"Tommy, you stay here and coordinate the men. They're just waiting on the call. Have the trucks taken to the warehouse. I'll have doctors there, but Doc will be with us," Rayne says, his eyes locked on the blood seeping through my shirt.

"Can I kill these fuckers?" Tommy asks.

"Abso-fucking-lutely."

SIXTY-THREE

WYNTER

"You know, I told him to kill you," Charles says. "I told him you were better off wiped from the earth for your repulsive interests. I even suggested setting that vile club on fire with you in it, would have solved all our issues, but no, he wanted to cleanse you." He shakes his head.

I blink back the tears pooling in my eyes. I don't know how much longer I can hold it together, not when something so personal is being thrown about like it's the fucking weather, but I swallow down the sob threatening just below the surface. I have to be strong. He wants me to fall apart.

I can't bring myself to look at Storm, not while we're talking about this. I couldn't even talk about it when it happened. The explanation I gave all those years ago was vague at best, just the way I wanted to keep it. I didn't want my brother to know I ever stepped foot in a BDSM club, but now all the cards are out on the table.

"And where do the Russos come into all of this?" Storm asks, and I meet his eye appreciatively. The longer he keeps him talking, the better chance I have of breaking free of these ropes. I'm not sure what I'm going to do if I do manage to wriggle free, but that's a bridge I'll have to cross when I come to it.

"I reached out to them when I first started working for you, told them I was happy to give them inside tips. At first it was low-level shit, things they could have found out themselves with a little digging. But then I started climbing the ranks, and the tips started to get bigger."

The ropes slice deeper into my wrists as I tug at them. Droplets of blood slide down my fingers, but it doesn't stop me from twisting in every way I can to break free. Every time Charles touches his belt buckle, my stomach rolls at the idea of what he may be thinking, of what he could do to me.

"The day you made me head of security, I thought Angelo's head was going to explode he was so excited, but we held off making a move for a little longer, just long enough that I wouldn't be the first suspect. The first favor he called in was when he wanted to get his hands on that bitch your brother married. It wasn't hard to slip him the route they were going to take to the drop location, and no one suspected anything with all the other shit going on. Then it was your parents. I tipped them off when they left the wedding reception. And then everything else started falling into place. There came a time I knew it was inevitable you would figure out there was a rat in your ranks, but the longer I could keep you off my trail, the closer I would be to what I wanted."

"And what is it that you want?" I snap. The searing pain in my wrists combined with this asshole's monologue is starting to get on my nerves. I don't really give a shit about how we got here. It's like every villain in every movie feeling the need to explain their entire life, only for the hero to break free and best them in the end. I'm just waiting for that last bit to happen.

"To make you pay," he says simply. "The two of you here is actually the perfect situation for me. Storm is the one who murdered my brother in cold blood for doing the Lord's work, and you're the little harlot who tempted my brother, like Eve in the Garden, ever a temptation."

"Your brother beat me within an inch of my fucking life. I still have the scars of what he did to me," I hiss, angry tears gathering in my eyes. "God wouldn't want this. Have you even fucking read the Bible? Or do you just use it as a way to excuse your actions just like your brother did?"

Charles charges toward me, fury rampant in his eyes. His hand raises and a moment later, pain spreads across my face under the force of his punch. I shouldn't bait him, but I need to. Angry people make mistakes.

Elijah jumps up from the lounge and quickly pulls Charles away from me, his arms wrapped around the smaller man's chest as he tugs him a few feet back.

"What the fuck do you think you're doing?" Charles shouts. "We had a deal."

"And you'll have your end of that deal, but right now, Wynter is very useful, and until her use has been worn out, you are not to harm her," Elijah explains calmly, moving away from Charles.

"What is it exactly that I'm useful for?" I ask.

481

"You're the key to my cousin's cooperation. Once we're sure Everett is loyal, Charles here can do anything he pleases with you. But until then, we need the leverage."

My eyes dart to Storm who's already looking at me, an inkling of doubt appearing in the gray. He knows Everett will do anything to keep me safe, including betray the family.

"That wasn't the deal," Charles growls, charging toward Elijah despite the obvious height difference.

Elijah stares down at him with amusement dancing on his lips. "You need to remember your place, Charlie boy. You came to *us* needing help. And while all the information you've provided us has been very useful, you've officially run out of your usefulness. I'm willing to keep our deal, but not until I can ensure Everett is who he says he is."

I tug at the ropes again, breathing through the pain and biting back the cry stuck in my throat. This is our best chance. They're distracted, and if I can just get out of these ropes, there's a gun under the side table a few feet away. If I can get to the gun, I will not hesitate to shoot both these assholes square between the eyes like Rayne taught me and at the time, hoped I would never have to do.

The rope slips, and my eyes widen as the other pulls free, but I don't move immediately. I remain still as the two men in front of us face-off, waiting for my chance to make my move.

Storm's eyes drop behind me and he shakes his head ever so slightly, telling me not to make a move, but I have to end this. This has gone on for too long, and the more time that passes, the more chance Charles is going to get sick of waiting and at the very least, hurt me.

482

The sound of tires on the gravel of the driveway pulls all our attention and I take a deep breath. It's now or never. Gunshots fill the quiet night and Charles and Elijah both move to the window to see what the commotion is about.

Now, Storm mouths to me.

I drop to the ground silently and crawl behind Storm's chair, slipping the gun from its hiding place and standing the same way I have every time I've ever held a gun. The cool metal is heavy in my hands as I widen my stance, my legs shoulder width apart, my arms extended out in front of me as I take deep, steadying breaths. The first thing my brothers ever taught me about guns is that the worst thing you can do is shoot while panicked.

But I don't feel panic. My chest and heart are filled with nothing but peace.

Sixty-Four

Everett

Rayne takes another corner without slowing down and my body hits the side of the car harshly, knocking the wind from my lungs.

"Can you quit that?" I choke. The agony from the gunshot radiates from the wound itself throughout my abdomen and down my thighs. This is fortunately my first, and I hope to fuck it's my last because holy fucking shit does it hurt.

Rayne glares at me out of the corner of his eye and purposely does the same thing again at the next bend. "Get into the fucking security system and check on Storm and Wynter and leave the driving to me."

I sigh. I'm trying to hack into the cameras with the laptop Rayne keeps in his car, but they've shut the system down completely and it doesn't matter which way I try to sneak in, the only cameras I can get into are the safe room.

Snow holds Emerson as she shakes in her arms, her phone clutched to her chest, but the room is completely dark, the cameras that usually fill the wall behind them gray and fuzzy. It doesn't matter what I do, I can't get the cameras on, and I can't check if Wynter is okay. For all I know, they've already taken her and Storm, I just have to hope if that is the case, that they take them to the club because that's where they think they're safe.

"She's fine, Ev," Rayne says a moment before we take another bend, but this time I brace myself for the blow.

"You don't know that."

"Yes I do. I know my sister. There's no way she's going down without one hell of a fucking fight. She saved Emerson and Snow, got them both into the safe room and sacrificed herself. She's the strongest fucking woman I've ever met, and there's not a chance in hell she's going out like this." I've never heard Rayne talk about his sisters with so much pride, or sound so sure of their abilities.

"She fucking hates me, Rayne. You didn't see the way she looked at me at Frost today. I've never seen her look at someone with so much hatred and disgust as she did me today."

"She only had one side of the story."

"Does that really matter? I've lied to her over and over again. I've broken her heart, hurt her, and now she finds out I've been working with my uncles. I can't see how she's going to look past that." A wave of agony crashes down on me, and I hold the old blanket I have pressed to the wound closer, a hiss whistling through my teeth. I can succumb to the pain as soon as I'm sure my girl is safe, and not a moment sooner.

"How far away are we?" I ask, finally looking out the window. The roads are quiet for this time of night, the highway is usually bumper to bumper at this time, but maybe some god somewhere is looking down on us. Maybe they know how pure Wynter is, and that we're her only hope.

"A few minutes at most," he tells me, taking another turn but this time I brace myself for the pain. I need it.

The closer we get to the estate, the deeper the sinking feeling in my chest seems to get. What if she's not there? What if they've taken her?

Rayne skids into the driveway, the rear of the car spinning out as I grab a hold of the door to keep myself in place if we spin out of control, but he quickly pulls the car back in line and guns down the driveway.

"There's a gun under your seat. I think we're going to need it," Rayne says, nodding toward the gate where a line of Russo's men stand. I hate to think of how many people we've lost tonight, but it's nowhere near the number they're going to lose, including their fearless leaders. The longer we wait to hear how the hit went, the more nervous I'm getting. Tommy may trust The Legion but I sure as hell don't.

Bullets hit the car in loud dings, but I designed this car myself for Rayne knowing the shit he gets himself into. There won't be a dent no matter how many bullets they fire. He presses the button and both windows open as I quickly pull the gun from beneath me and aim it out the window. "You know you're going to have to get a dad car when you knock up Emerson."

"Fuck off," he growls, pulling the trigger with ease as he holds the car steady. This sure as hell isn't his first rodeo. Rayne lives for this shit.

The guards at the gate don't seem to be expecting us to start shooting so soon, their bodies hitting the ground long before we reach them, even with the considerable speed we're going.

"Uh, Rayne, no one's in the guard house to open the gate," I remind him when he gives no signs of slowing down.

"I know."

The gate speeds toward us and the moment the car makes contact with the wrought iron, my entire body absorbs the impact painfully. I may have reenforced the car to withstand a lot, but I don't expect the gate to buckle beneath the pressure of the Aston Martin.

Rayne doesn't miss a beat, his foot pressing down on the accelerator as we gun toward the house and our women. "We needed a new gate anyway." He shrugs.

Dead of Wynter

SIXTY-FIVE

WYNTER

"What do you have there, Wynter?" Elijah smirks. His eyes lock with the barrel of the gun, and where most men would be scared, his look almost amused.

"I think you should both leave," I say, ignoring his question altogether. I'm not going to dignify it with an answer, because he's only trying to get a rise out of me. He wants to throw me off balance, but that's not going to happen.

"I think we have the answer to where your cousin's loyalties lay," Charles tells him from his post by the window.

"As I suspected." Elijah shakes his head. "I've told my uncles so many times he can't be trusted, but what would I know? I'm the only one in the fucking family with any brains."

"Well, they'll be dead after tonight, so you won't have to deal with them for much longer." Storm smirks and I can't help but laugh. The poetic irony of the situation is too good not to get some joy from, even if it is short-lived.

Elijah's eyes flash with anger, his hand slipping into his pocket and retrieving his phone. He taps on the screen a couple of times before holding it to his ear.

I hold my breath as I listen for voices on the other end of the line. The commotion outside has died down to only tires on the gravel, and I can only assume Rayne and Everett will be here any moment, but I want to know if the Russos are dead.

"Fuck," he mutters as he dials another number and returns the phone to his ear. Each moment that passes, the rage etched into his features grows more prominent. He's realizing he could be alone in this, and that's the last thing you want to be in this business.

"Untie me and give me the gun," Storm whispers so softly I barely hear the words.

"No."

His eyes flare with annoyance, but I'm not backing down. I want to finish this. Craig hurt me all those years ago, and I never got my revenge. Storm killed him long before I had the chance to regather my strength and get the closure I needed. But now Charles is here, spewing the same shit his brother did, and it's my turn. For once, I don't want to be the weak little girl they've always believed me to be. I want to be the queen I was born to be.

The front door flings open, drawing everyone's attention to the doorway, giving me the opportunity to move around the back of Storm's chair and step closer to my target. I would have hit him from where I was, but I didn't want to take any chances. I've never actually shot a human being before and something tells me it's a little different from the paper outline at the shooting range, so I want my room for error to be minimal at most.

Elijah draws his gun and aims it at the doorway and my heart stops for just a moment. Any moment now, the man I love or my brother could be shot, and that's not something I'm willing to risk.

"Drop it," I say calmly.

"Or what, princess? You going to shoot me?" He's mocking me. He doesn't believe I'm strong enough to pull the trigger, but that's where he's fucking wrong.

I hold the gun steady and aim at his shoulder before squeezing the trigger as I breathe out. The power of the shot radiates up my arms, but I don't move from my position despite the searing agony in my wrists

"Fuck," Elijah shouts, his gun hitting the floor in a loud clatter. "You fucking bitch."

"I'd watch how you're speaking to me unless you want a matching pair," I growl, taking calculated steps toward where the gun is laying.

Footsteps in the hall pull my attention away from where I'm stepping for a moment, and I look up just in time to see Everett appear in the doorway. His own gun is drawn, blood soaking through his T-shirt. Rayne is a couple of steps behind him, not a scratch on him. I swear my brother never comes home wounded, probably for the best given how much Emerson worries about him.

I allow the breath I've been holding for what feels like hours to release and drop my attention back to the gun, but when my eyes lock with the spot it was a few moments ago, the floor is clear.

"Everyone drop your weapons or little miss bitch here is getting a bullet through the brain." Charles grabs me around the neck and panic threatens at the edge of my mind. My breath hitches in my throat, the relief I felt just a few moments ago is long gone.

Everett's face fills with rage, the fury in his eyes almost enough to knock me off kilter, but I stand strong. The gun in my own hand is still expended in front of me. I'm not ready to drop it yet. I'm not ready to give up the power it allows me.

"Charles?" Rayne's brows pull together as the cool metal touches my temple.

"I said put your weapons down," he shouts, causing me to flinch at the sound. I don't want to show any weakness, but if you can't be weak when you have a gun pointed at your head, when can you be?

My eyes meet Everett's, indecision dancing in the deep blue pools. I've stared into his eyes so many times since the day we met, and it only seems right that if these are the final moments of my life, that I spend them staring in the depths of the soul that brought me peace even in the wildest of storms.

I drop my gun first, making sure to drop it out of Elijah's reach. The heavy metals thuds on the rug as I drop my hands to my sides.

"You don't have to do this, Charles. You've worked for our family for years, whatever the Russos are paying you, we can pay you five times that much, ten even," Rayne offers.

"You think this is about money?" He spits, the droplets land on my bare shoulder and an involuntary shudder spreads across my skin. "This has never been about fucking money."

"What's it about then?" Rayne asks.

"This bitch is the reason my brother is dead, and you're all going to repent for your sins, including his death. Every last one of you deserves death, but none more than your precious queen." He hisses the word, the calm man who first captured us is long gone, leaving a crazed version so painfully similar to Craig it turns my stomach.

"He's Craig's brother," I whisper, filling in the blanks Charles is failing to fill.

"My brother wanted to save Wynter, he wanted to cleanse her of her sins, but instead he was murdered for his good deeds."

The anger in Everett's eyes only seems to glow brighter with each word said, but I hold them. It's the only thing keeping me grounded, the only thing keeping me from falling apart.

"He beat her," Rayne growls. "He deserved to die."

The gun moves from my temple and is held over my shoulder at my brother. "She deserved it," Charles yells. "This slut went to the den of evil. She sinned and sinned. What was my brother to do but cleanse her?"

Everett watches me closely, his gun lowered but ready to be used at a moment's notice. I take a deep breath before mouthing, *Shoot him.*

Time seems to drag as he stares at me, uncertainty filling his face. But if there's one person on this earth I trust not to kill me, it's the man I fell in love with. The one who was wise beyond his years when I met him, whose demons danced in his gaze, but who wanted to be better. The world is quiet despite the chaos around us, and he's all I can see, all I can hear, all I can breathe.

I see the moment he decides to do it. We're out of options, and this is the only one we have, our best chance at all of us walking out of this as unscathed as possible.

The moment the bullet leaves the barrel of Everett's gun, peace washes over me. Looking death in the face is a funny thing. There are two paths set out for me, one where I continue walking this earth with the people I love, and one where I don't. But it doesn't matter which way I go as long as they're okay.

The bullet tears through my side, agony piercing through every inch of my body despite the piece of metal causing the pain being so small. It takes the air from my lungs, making every breath harder than the last, and the moment the bullet exits my body, I drop to the ground.

Charles lets out a violent snarl when he realizes what's happening, but there are already three more shots being fired, and red stains the front of his white button-up shirt. "You fucking cunts," he shouts.

Rayne moves to restrain Elijah who lays motionless on the ground. I thought I only hit his shoulder, but maybe I did more damage than I thought.

I reach up and untie Storm, his hands slipping free from the rope easily. He scoops me up and carries me to the lounge, laying me down to inspect my wounds.

"You shot my sister," he yells at Everett.

"She told me to," he defends as he leans over the back of the lounge, his eyes dragging down my body, looking for any other injuries.

"If she told you to jump off a cliff, would you?"

"You know I would," Everett deadpans.

The sound of their bickering is the last thing I hear as I allow the emotions of the day to drag me under. The pain, the anguish, the anger, it all seeps into one and drags me into a peaceful state I've been longing for.

SIXTY-SIX

EVERETT

I don't know whether I did it intentionally, or if it was some kind of coincidence, but I shot Wynter in exactly the same place as I had been shot, and now we have matching scars. It's been a week since we both had bullets pulled from our bodies, but we're both healing well despite my insistence that Wynter not move a muscle so as not to slow the healing process.

She's a little sick of how overbearing I'm being but she needs to understand the guilt that ravages me every time I see the bandage wrapped around her torso. I did that. I shot her. I scarred her. And no matter what I do, I can't let it go.

Today is the first day I've allowed her to get dressed in something other than my shirts, and it's only because we're leaving the house, despite my insistence that we let the rest of the family take care of this particular task.

Wynter holds my hand tighter than normal in the quiet car, none of us have much to say about the outing, and our usually happy family all seem a little dimmer today. I guess it's not every day you speak terms with the enemy.

Despite my better judgment, we let Elijah go that night once we got confirmation his father and uncles were dead, along with most of their operation. Storm said it's bad for business not to have any competition, and it makes us a target, which I guess he's not totally wrong about. But still, allowing any member of my bloodline to live is against my nature.

When Elijah mentioned Aces being an ideal place to hold this meeting, I was a little surprised. After all, this is where his whole family died, but who am I to argue?

I help Wynter out of the back of the car and nod to Storm as he hops out of the car in front of us. He may not have been injured during one of the worst nights of our lives, but he's felt all of our pain.

My hand falls to the small of her back and I guide her through the front doors. I was surprised when Rayne told me Emerson had agreed to come here, but then again, I suppose now Angelo is no longer a threat, she's probably not as afraid. "You okay?" I ask.

Wynter looks up at me, a smile dancing on her red-stained lips. "Yes, Mom, I'm fine."

My eyes dart across her face, looking for any sign of doubt or hesitation, but there isn't any. She would have been well within her rights to be traumatized after everything she went through, but the only signs that she was ever hurt fade by the day. The bruise on her cheek is almost completely gone and is easily covered with a bit of makeup. Her wrists are still red and flaky, but Doc says as long as she takes care of the wounds, they shouldn't scar. And her bullet wound is healing even better than mine is. "Okay. If you need to leave, just say the word."

Wynter reaches up and brushes her thumb across my cheek, and I can't help but lean into her touch. "You worry too much. If I'm ever not okay, I'll tell you. But you have to let me be okay when I am."

I nod, breaking away from her touch as we near the stairs to the VIP area. "I'll try."

Wynter looks over her shoulder at Rayne and Emerson walking behind us and holds her hand out to her new sister, who takes it immediately, taking the support she's offered even though she's putting on a brave face.

The moment we step off the top step, I notice Elijah sitting in the place Angelo used to frequent. Every time I've ever stepped foot in this club, Angelo has been in that seat, and it's strange to see my cousin take his place. "Are you sure about this?" I ask Storm over my shoulder.

"Yes," he replies quickly.

My eyes move over the space, seeking any hidden guards. We agreed this was a friendly meeting, and as a sign of good faith, we left our own security outside, but that doesn't mean we're not prepared for an ambush.

"It's just us," Elijah tells us.

"Can never be too careful." Storm steps in front of the group and takes the lead to the booth, sliding in beside Elijah. I can see what he's doing even without him having to say it. He's putting his body between him and the rest of us, whether or not he's aware of the move may be another story.

Emerson's face drains of color as her eyes dart over the booth that holds some of the worst memories of her life. Rayne wraps his arm around her shoulder and presses a gentle kiss to her temple before guiding her to sit down as far away from the only Russo at the table as possible.

"Thank you for meeting me here," Elijah says.

"For what it's worth, I'm sorry it all went down the way it did." Storm smiles sympathetically.

"I'm not." Elijah shrugs. "My father and uncles were idiots. I'm glad they're gone."

The booth falls quiet and we all stare at him as we wait for a but. There has to be a but. Except, one doesn't come, instead he continues. "They were greedy. The only reason you ever deal in human beings is greed. I tried to explain to them that we could make more money without it, and save ourselves a whole load of drama, but what would I know?" He rolls his eyes.

"Wait." I lean forward, my elbows resting on my knees. "Let me get this straight, you wanted your whole family dead?"

"Not my whole family." He chuckles. "You're still here, aren't you? But yes, I'm glad they're gone. After Wynter shot me, I could have overpowered her, quite easily in fact, but I had a better chance of things playing out just like this if I didn't."

"And there I was thinking it was because I'm such a good shot," Wynter deadpans.

Elijah tips his head back, a laugh filling the booth before he looks around the circle, his eyes narrowing as they brush over Snow. She hasn't said a word since we got here, which doesn't surprise me seeing as Storm told her to keep her mouth shut unless spoken to. "I see why you like this one, Everett. She has such fire."

I growl, the noise primal and possessive just like my need for Wynter, but it only seems to make him laugh more. Storm shoots me a glare and I sit back in my seat, wrapping my arm around my woman and holding her against me.

"What is it that we can do for you, Elijah?" Storm asks.

"I'd like to take over my family's business, but without the competition. You take your territory, I'll take mine, and we'll mind our own business. I will agree to your terms around what I can and cannot deal in, and if someone were to ever challenge either of our power, the other would step in and stand beside that party."

"Like an alliance?" Storm's brow quirks up like he's not quite sure what to make of my cousin's proposal. That makes two of us.

"Exactly!" Elijah exclaims, his arms opening excitedly. "You probably think this is some kind of trap, but I've given this a lot of thought, even before the hit. I've been toying with the idea of taking the idiots out for a few years, and so I've been considering my options. Being a one-man operation isn't ideal. It leaves me open and vulnerable and without a succession plan. An alliance means that if something were to happen to me, my territory wouldn't default to whoever takes me out, it would default to you."

Storm sucks in a breath and his eyes meet mine. We've been friends for long enough we can almost communicate without words, but all he wants to know is if I think this is a trap, and honestly, I haven't quite worked that out for myself yet. If anyone were crafty enough to pull it off, it's definitely Elijah, but he seems almost excited by the prospect. I give a small nod, and Storm turns back to my cousin, taking him in for a moment before a small smile tugs at the corners of his lips. "Tentatively, we have a deal. I'd like to have another meeting, perhaps at Frost about what you're proposing to do to make money, but I think this arrangement could be mutually beneficial."

EPILOGUE
WYNTER

It's been a slow start to spring this year. The snow took a little longer to melt than last year, and the skies took a few extra weeks to clear. It's almost as if the earth knows the secret I've been keeping since the day Winter ended.

It's not that I haven't wanted to tell my family, it's just that with everything going on, being able to get back into the office and get stuck into work, I just haven't really had the time.

Strong arms wrap around my belly, and a gentle kiss is pressed into the top of my shoulder. "I missed you today," Everett whispers, placing another kiss on the sensitive spot of my neck he knows makes me desperate for him.

My own hands drop to where his are. Maybe he knows I've been keeping it from him. After all, his hands are right over it, protecting the baby he doesn't even know is growing inside me. I've been grappling with how I'm going to tell him since I found out a few weeks ago, but every time I planned anything, something would come up and one of us would be called away.

"I miss you every day," I tell him truthfully. After we rekindled our relationship, we spent days together locked in the estate, and while none of us have moved back to our apartments yet, we have moved on with our lives in every other way, almost like none of it ever happened.

Everett's arms move lower as he spins me, gripping the backs of my knees and lifting me until my legs are wrapped around his waist. "I guess we better use our time together effectively." He winks and a giggle lurches from my throat. It's been so easy between us the last couple of months, like there weren't eight years where he was the shadow I never knew I had.

The moment my back hits the plush mattress, Everett is over me, his body shielding me from the rest of the world. It's moments like these that remind me he'll always protect us. He'll always keep us safe and love us unconditionally. And we'll love him with every beat of our hearts.

"I need to tell you something," I whisper, my eyes fluttering to his heated gaze.

The corner of his mouth quirks up into a smile. "Oh yeah? I have something I wanted to talk to you about too." All too soon, his body rolls from mine and he sits up against the headboard before I can so much as sit up. I've been very lucky so far with the pregnancy, the only real symptom I've had is fatigue, and any day I don't spend with my head in a toilet bowl with morning sickness is a win for me.

"You go first," I offer. I haven't quite found the words yet. It's not that I think he'll be upset, because I actually believe he'll be the complete opposite, but maybe it's that the moment I tell him we're having a baby everything will change, and I'm not quite ready for the unknown just yet.

508

A blinding smile lights up his entire face and my heart melts. Ever since the first time this particular smile was directed at me when I was sixteen, it's been my very favorite sight. "I know you don't like surprises, which is why I thought we could discuss this first and then if you're happy with everything, then we can move forward with a plan."

I nod slowly, my brows pulling together with confusion. Is he about to tell me he knows? Is that the plan he wants to make? How we're going to care for a baby. But I don't want him to just know, I want to tell him and see the happiness in his eyes. I want to be the one to give him the gift he's always wanted. Before I'm conscious of what I'm doing, words are leaving my mouth at the same time they leave his.

"I'm pregnant," I say at the same time he says, "I think we should get married."

We stare at each other for long moments, both shocked by the other words. For a moment, I think maybe I was wrong about him wanting to have a baby. I just assumed after the time he told me we would have a bunch of kids by now if we hadn't spent eight years apart, but maybe I was wrong.

"I know it's a shock, and I wasn't sure how to tell you or if this is something you want. And I don't even really know how it happened. All I can think is that maybe the anti-biotics Doc had me on after I was shot messed with my birth control," the words fall from my mouth as they come to my mind, and I'm barely conscious of what I'm saying.

"Wynter," Everett says calmly, his body moving toward mine slowly so as not to spook me.

"If you don't want this, I can do it on my own. I've always

wanted to be a mom, and I know you'd be such a great dad, and you'd always keep us safe, but I understand if you need some time to decide if you want to be involved or not." Even as the words tumble out, they break my heart. I never envisioned being a single mother, and the thought of not having Everett by my side is almost too much for my fragile heart to handle, but I'll do what I need to do for my baby.

"Wynter, take a breath for me." Everett's arms wrap around me and pull me into his lap.

It's not until his arms close around me that I realize I was panicking at the edge of hyperventilating at the thought of going back to a life without him in it. "I'm sorry," I whisper, burying my head in his warm chest.

"Look at me," he orders and I obey immediately, the corners of his lips tugging up in a sly smile. "Good girl." His hands lift to my face and his finger gently drags down my cheek until he cups it in his warm hand. "I want you to listen to me, little dove. The words that just left your mouth are the best two words I've ever heard in my life." He presses a gentle kiss to my forehead. "You are going to be the best mother to our babies."

I sink into his arms, tears gathering at the corners of my eyes as I gaze up at the man I love with every beat of my heart. "I love you."

"I love you too, dove." He smiles. "When can we see her?"

"Her?"

"It's a girl," he tells me confidently.

"How do you know?"

"I just do." He shrugs. "Now, I know I said we would discuss getting married, but now it's not up for discussion. If you're having my baby, you're wearing my ring too."

"Okay," I agree.

"No, I mean it, Wynter. This is nonnegotiable. I want all three of us to have the same last name from the moment she's born."

"I know."

"Call Snow. We need to start organizing the wedding now. How far along are you? Are you okay if you're showing in your dress? Or would you prefer to have a courthouse wedding and then a big one after our little princess is born?"

A giggle rises from my throat as the tears I've been holding back slip from my eyes and down my cheeks. I've often thought moments with Everett were the best of my life, but at this moment right here, I can't imagine another time where I'll feel so completely and utterly happy.

Everett shakes his head at me and reaches into his jacket pocket for his phone. He holds it to his ear as we both listen to it ring out, but when it goes to voice mail, we both stare at it like the device has grown a head. Snow never leaves her phone, and she always answers it, no matter what.

He pulls it back and types in a different number. "Hey, can you ask Snow to call me when she's got a second?"

I try to listen for the reply, but the voice on the other end of the line is too quiet.

"What do you mean you can't find her?" he growls. "Your entire job is to watch her and make sure she's safe."

Another pause as they reply. My stomach sinks, and somehow I know there's something wrong.

"Find. Her. Now," he demands, ending the call and tossing the phone onto the mattress beside us. "Snow slipped her security again."

"I'm sure she's fine. She does this like once a week."

"She's been missing for hours and the tracker on her phone has been turned off."

The blood drains from my face and my heart beats painfully in my chest. "But you're the only person that can do that. There's no way Snow would be able to figure that out."

"I know."

DEAD OF WYNTER

Thank you for reading Dead of Wynter!

I hope you enjoyed Wynter and Everett's story as much as I loved writing it!

This series came to me a few years ago, and has lived rent free in my mind for a long time. Wynter is the reason this series exists, and this story is the first one that came to me. I loved them and their story from the moment they came to my mind, and telling it has been one of the highlights of my career so far.

Fall of Snow is available now on Amazon and will pick up right where Dead of Wynter left off.

If you enjoyed Dead of Wynter, it would mean the world to me if you left a review on Amazon and Goodreads.

You can follow me on Facebook and Instagram for updates on future releases and sneak peaks.

Keep reading for a look at Fall of Snow.

PROLOGUE

ELIJAH

My little Snowflake.

I've watched you for so many years, I feel as if I've always been a part of your life.

I've watched you cry when you're sad and smile when you're happy. I've watched you celebrate the good times and drown your sorrows in the bad. And each moment that I've followed you, is a little better I get to know you.

And soon, you'll be mine.

Your room is set up at my house, ready to cage the wildcat that hides under the surface. Most people wouldn't try to clip your wings, but I will. You need someone to take care of you, someone who knows you better than you know yourself to protect you from the world, even if that means protecting you from yourself.

The last few months have been hard on you, I understand that, but it doesn't give you the right to harm the body that belongs to me, even if you don't know it yet.

The moment you started down the road of self-destruction, I began moving things into place to ensure you wouldn't be your own demise.

I understand your heart is hurting, despite not having one myself, but I can no longer allow you the freedom you crave.

It is my hope that one day you'll understand why I did this, and you'll accept the life we are to have together.

You see, my little Snowflake, this plan has been in motion since the day we met when you were fifteen. Even then, you were the wild child of your family, as most youngest born are. There was something about you, something so completely entrancing that I found myself following you to see more. Like with most of my toys, I expected to grow bored, but if anything, the longer I spent following you, the more obsessed I became.

The feud between our families has certainly complicated things over the years, but now I'm running the show, I need a queen to stand by my side, and there is no one more fit for the job than you.

DEAD OF WYNTER

Made in the USA
Las Vegas, NV
24 October 2023

79618727R00308